ALSO BY JANE SOMERS

The Diary of a Good Neighbour

IF THE OLD COULD...

If the Old Could...

JANE SOMERS

Alfred A. Knopf   New York   1984

THIS IS A BORZOI BOOK
PUBLISHED BY ALFRED A. KNOPF. INC.

FIC

Library of Congress Cataloging in Publication Data

Somers, Jane   If the old could...
I. Title.
PR6069.042135   1984   823'.914   83-49027
ISBN 0-394-53757-2

Manufactured in the United States of America

FIRST AMERICAN EDITION

If the young knew…
If the old could…

French proverb

IF THE OLD COULD...

My heel caught as I stepped off the train. My right foot went into the gap. I fell. I was on all fours on the platform, among the people waiting to push on to the train. As I scrambled up, they were jostling all around me. I stood teetering, and saw a man stepping fast towards me, and was struck at once, even in that confused moment, by his command, his competence, his quickness. He caught me as I was going down again, and as a result of our joint attempts I found myself lying in his arms, one of my hands, the one clutching my handbag which I had held on to through it all, at the back of his neck. I began to laugh. A sad enough wail, but a laugh. His face, so close to mine, was attractive, intelligent. All that energetic incisiveness would have led me to expect a face much less—I am afraid there is only one word for it—sensitive than his. His smile was inquiring. I explained, 'I am a romantic novelist.' After the briefest pause he laughed, appreciatively, and then I was standing up beside him smoothing down my clothes, returning to myself.

We took each other in, liking what we saw, and showing it. And then I noticed, past his shoulder, that a girl stood watching us with a fierce closeness that dissolved the moment, for as my face changed he turned fast and, saying to me, 'Are you all right?', he went to her, took her arm and led her away. I was struck again, and painfully—though I need to understand and to study that pain—how his vigorous, almost careless, yes you *could* say debonair insouciance vanished, and even the set of his shoulders changed, as he took charge of the girl and was all responsibility.

I stood watching them go. Would he turn around? No. But the girl did. A suspicious and hostile face: his mistress?

Young girls fancy handsome elderly gents. In his fifties, I should say. Like me... I went slowly up and out, shaken more than I had thought, and by more than my fall. I was thinking, That was an unusual man, one that would stand out anywhere, in any crowd. You forget how mediocre most people are. Then, suddenly, one of the other kind. What did he think of me? Well, I knew, there was no mistaking that.

On the street, April showing itself in wild fast-fleeting cuds of white on bright blue, and a fitful sunlight. Oh, to be anywhere in northern Europe now that April is here. That was what I was thinking in Madrid only two days ago. I answer yes to more and more travelling for the mag. They say elderly women get itchy feet, travel all the time if they can. But I insist still that I am middle-aged. Oh, I do feel low. It is as well I didn't maintain a stiff upper lip and go to the office, but went home, rang them up, and said not today, tomorrow.

None of this would have happened were it not for Niece Jill's announcement yesterday. How many thousands of times have I got off the train at Tottenham Court Road? No, *don't* work it out. Have I ever fallen there—or anywhere else—before?

When I got back from Madrid yesterday the flat was not as usual as neat as a filing cabinet, but there were clothes everywhere, and Jill was in a state, all sighs and concerned looks. I knew. I was ready to weep and howl, and this it was that bouleversed me, for until it happened I would not have thought that hearing Jill was leaving would hurt me so.

'When and where to?' I asked.

'Oh, Jane, I might have known you'd get it at once.'

'I haven't asked *why*,' I said.

She said, 'I'm moving in with someone.'

'Male or female?'

'You know, Mark. The photographer.'

'Oh, Mark!'

At once, anxious: 'Don't you like him?'

'But, Jill, I've not done much more than approve his pictures. It hadn't occurred to me to think of him as a possible nephew.'

'I didn't say I was going to marry him.'

'What would your mother say?'

'It is what *you* say that I mind about,' said Jill softly, and I sat down with a bump and tried to be normal. She was near the window, watching me. The curtains were not drawn, and beyond her was a fast-moving sky full of white clouds lit by, presumably, the moon. There was a full moon in Madrid, so why not here? I thought again how very fond of her I had become. There she stood, slim, erect, for she holds herself very well these days, and very pretty. I might have guessed she was in love, so animated and alive is she. A credit to everyone concerned, Jill is.

I was thinking fast; and there was nothing to disturb, or to warn. Why should I be upset? What had happened? Everything was as it should be. Three years ago Jill had come to London town to seek her fortune, aided by her wicked worldly aunt who, with shameless nepotism, had got her a job in *Lilith*. There Jill had flourished, turning her hand to anything, mistress of all trades. She had been an amenable, sensible, kindly flatmate, handling her tricky aunt with tact. She had made friends, got a prophylactic dose of revolution-ary socialism, now over. She had found herself a young man and wanted to live with him. What could be more of a success story than that?

'Jill,' I said, 'I shall miss you most horribly.'

And began to cry. Jill, too. First, sniffs and deprecating little self-conscious smiles. Then slow painful tears. Then hot sobs, and we flung ourselves into each other's arms.

'Oh, Aunt Jane!' cried Jill.

'Oh, Jill!'

'And you didn't even want me here, to start with,' she accused.

'More fool me.'

We separated, with many a little pat and stroke, and stopped crying. She made us tea, and we drank it.

I saw there was more.

'Well?'

'Jane, you do realize that Kate will be on the doorstep as I move out?'

I thought about it, while she watched me, her great grey

eyes in lakes of glaucous paint over the edge of her cup. Kate has gone from bad to worse in the last three years. She did badly in her A-levels, refused to take them again as her parents wanted. She had asked me to get her a job in *Lilith,* and I had said she must see that there were limits to my introducing young female relatives into the mag. Sister Georgie, predictably, had rung up to say, Surely I could see my way to doing something? I said, 'As you know, I have your daughter Jill living with me. I would say that was something.' She said, 'Kate thinks it is very unfair, and I must say we do too.'

That had been last year. Since then Kate had been mooning around the house, deciding whether she would or would not study Spanish.

At last I said to Jill, 'I know I didn't want you here to start with, and as it turned out I enjoyed every minute. But Kate surely is a very different thing?'

There is nothing skimpy or dishonest in Jill. She did not say, 'Oh, it will be all right,' or, 'She's not so bad.' She said, 'Yes, she is a different thing. Altogether. I wonder if you really know how different?'

'Probably not. Though I have seen quite a few spoiled brats making the lives of my peer group miserable. You, my dear Jill, are the only young thing I have actually lived with.'

'Well, I would say that Kate is in a bit of a mess.'

'Do you know why? I mean, *really*?'

She thought. She sat there holding her cup on the arm of the big red linen chair, she in a white negligé, her—at the moment—red hair loose, eyes blank with memory. She was looking back into scenes of family life.

'Well, I don't know. Would you agree that people are *born*?'

'Yes, I would.'

'I would say that of us four Kate is going to turn out the mess.'

'Is that a life sentence?'

'I wouldn't be surprised.'

'Hard words.'

'Oh, you are thinking, *Sisters! They never got on.* . . . It's true, we never have. My idea of a bad time is one spent with Kate. It always was. But, the point is. . .'

'All right, I get the point.'

'As long as you really have, Jane. Because I wonder if you realize. . . it takes a strong person to stand up to you!'

I was sloppy enough to allow my sigh to be a bit theatrical: the start of a familiar joking game we have, Jill and I, where she says how I can't tolerate weakness and I'm tough as old boots, and I say that it is I who have to stand up to her. 'No, no, listen,' she was going on. 'Believe me, I am grateful—oh, no, not just for your letting me live here, though that is the best thing that ever happened, or for *Lilith*—I hope you won't think I'm ungrateful if I say that *now* I know I would have done well anywhere. But I learned *that* in *Lilith*. But it is *you* I'm grateful for. Because you never let anyone get away with anything. You have never let me . . . well, not everyone could take it.' A small 'humorous' smile, but only because the situation prescribed it, and her great sea eyes anxious on my face.

'Very well,' I said.

'Good.'

And soon she gave me a hug and went to bed.

I stayed on for a while, alone in this room, thinking that soon being alone would again be my condition. Oh, it was not that I minded. Aloneness has never frightened me, on the contrary. But I was going to miss, more than I want to admit to myself, the *youngness,* the freshness of Jill.

Who really is my younger self.

In the office I heard them calling her Chipov. So I thought, Why a Russian nickname, what is Russian about this brisk English girl? But no, it was 'Chip off'. A chip off this block. When Jill came to live here she was a tentative, watchful creature, all great eyes and apprehension, held together by her resolve that she would live here and benefit from her Aunt Jane. She tended to droop, to become listless. But she was herself, was Jill . . . Very soon, she became me, put on my characteristics, my mannerisms, my walk. Her voice is mine.

No, I did not see this at once; needed to hear the nickname first. Then I thought, Of course! And I started to observe myself in her, this mirror, on the whole flattered, thinking; Well, I am, rather *was* not so bad! But then, seeing something else, began trains of very different thoughts. . . A competent girl she is, every movement so right, her mind behind it. But controlled . . . over-controlled? Her quick grace, her flair— well, I never had that, or I don't think I had, or have. She seems to take command of a place as she walks into it, or expects to. Bossy, in short. Her voice is measured, usually humorous, or with an edge on it, signpointing absurdity or incongruity. It is the voice of one who has decided to give the impression that she sees the world as a comedy, on the whole an agreeable one. But this posture is an effort, a strain; she is by no means sure of the comedy. Every note and change and pitch of that voice is mine.

There is also, in Jill, a little hard streak of something— perhaps even an obtuseness?—that gives the impression of self-satisfaction. But is it? Does it not come from the effort it takes her to prove herself, self-absorption because of the difficulties of what she confronts, and which she is not going to admit to, even to herself.

Very interesting questions, this raises. First, and one that I have brooded about not a little: why did Jill not choose to model herself on those admirable citizens, her mother and father? If there were ever exemplars bound to be approved by every authority I can think of, then Sister Georgie and her husband Tom fit the bill best. If the textbooks are right, surely Jill would have 'internalized' one or the other or both long before she came to me? But no, it was Aunt Jane, of whose selfishness and shallowness she has been hearing all her childhood, on whom she chose to model herself.

Secondly, and I brood about this too: if that tentative uncertain girl *was* Jill, and what people see now a skilled adaptation, then with whom is Mark, her boyfriend, in love? For the rest of her life Jill will be a version of her Aunt Jane; and that is what people will mean when they think of her, speak of her.

Thirdly. On whom did I model myself? For I resemble neither of my parents, those worthy souls of whom I have to say, They had no style, no dash, no flair, no kind of distinction. No, probably when I was about Jill's age I admired someone in the old office, the pre-*Lilith* days, and admiring, became. And for thirty-odd years Janna James, then Janna Somers, has presented herself polished, finished, arranged, and this is what people see and know. But it is an artefact! I am even asking myself, When Sister Georgie complains of my superficiality and all the rest, perhaps she means that in my late adolescence I quite simply acquired a personality that seems to her false? Is there any point in asking her? As for her, *she* 'internalized' our mother, and that was that. Every gesture, tone of voice, habit. And very early.

And so Jill is off, having done everything right. I am sure she will continue to do things right; will not make a bad marriage, have a breakdown, become a whine in middle-age. I feel sure about her.

Yes, of course she will come and see me, I will see her in the office, we will be friends. It won't be the same.

Well, cut your losses, Janna. Cut your losses, Jane.

That's *that*.

What is the point of dreaming of wild April from the solid bourgeois pleasures of Madrid, and then seeing nothing of it? This morning I was up and out by seven, had breakfast in the little workmen's café, where they exchange pleasantries with me now, and walked slow, savouring, through the budding lanes of Hampstead down through Swiss Cottage and to the park. There I sauntered about, listening to the birds and wishing I knew cherry from apple blossom. Around me a pristine spring was dismissed by half an hour of hot summer, a big black summer cloud, a growl of thunder and a clap of warm rain, and spring came back, with innocent fickleness, for its blue and white was at once absorbed into a uniform grey, from which floated down a dozen large loose damp snowflakes to disappear on the unnaturally green grass. Autumn did not appear, and I walked out into the Marylebone Road and approved some rather good outfits in the windows of Monica, where I bought my white linen last summer. I was window-shopping, not for myself, but for Jill; and told myself to stop it. It was then nine. I had not wanted to be late, so I got on to the undergound at Baker Street and got out as usual at Tottenham Court Road, not catching my heel this time but with a pang for this man I would never see again. Walking slowly down to Soho Square, where I proposed to linger, not wanting to relinquish the joys of this delicious morning—for it was a spring morning again, and the spring flowers were massed in tiers at the street corner—I saw in front of me a man's back, and then, as he felt my eyes on him, his face, for he turned with his characteristic swift way and, seeing me, smiled as if this was nothing more than what he had expected, and said, 'Ah! So there you are! I hoped you might be somewhere about. Have you time for a coffee?' And we sat opposite each other at a table on the pavement, while people raced past to work.

He had his first breakfast, and I had my second, sticky nut cake and marvellous coffee.

We were both of us filled with a wicked, wild, racing delight, we could not stop smiling while we looked at each other with a frankness which, because it was so natural, was the best of it. He is weathered-handsome, tawny, with grey-blue eyes, not sea eyes like Jill's, but direct and shrewd. His hair is yellow, not silvered like mine, for I propose to keep my metallic locks, gold and silver. He is not tall, but taller than I am. A handsome man: what must he have been like when he was younger? And I was thinking how well we were matched, physically, and how well we would have been, younger. And he knew I was, and matched these thoughts with his own. Everything we said on no matter what subject seemed to be about us, and this amazing meeting of ours. It seemed impossible not to talk about ourselves, and yet by the time we parted I knew nothing about him except his name, Richard, and that he had just come back from abroad.

'What a marvellous time to come home,' he said. 'Not that it was an accident. I said to myself, No, I am not going to miss one more spring. And look how right I was!'

'Where have you been?'

'In America.'

'I was recently in New York. And I still wanted to come home.'

'Well, if I had been in New York—but no. There is only one country in the world to live in, and only one city. And here I am.'

The sky flung a handful of rain at us, with a *soupçon* of ice in it, then the sun came out hot, and we went on down to Soho Square hand in hand. We made, I know, a handsome couple: or at least, I knew, trained as I am to keep an exterior eye focused on how I look. As for him, he could scarcely have been unaware that people looked at us as we stood together in the middle of the square, spring on the trees and the white clouds racing.

We stood facing each other, quite ablaze with love.

He stammered a little as he asked, 'Will you have breakfast with me again? It can't be tomorrow—on Friday?' And as I smiled, 'I am taking the most appalling risk, not even knowing your name . . . where you live . . . no, don't tell me, just be here, same place, but an hour earlier?'

And so we parted.

I arrived in the office knowing that every gland in my body was shooting out magical substances and that my blood must be pure ichor. I had to go into my own room and shut the door and calm myself down with steady hard work.

I am working as hard as I have ever done. I still talk about retiring to live on my royalties, which I could do, and live very well; but when I did go on part-time, thinking to slide out that way, I came back again. The board asked me, and they were right. To lose both editors, Joyce and me, more or less at once: too much.

But when I do think about it, I have to be a bit uneasy. If *Lilith* would find it hard to do without me—fair enough, I've worked with, for, by, and from *Lilith* for—when I write down how long, it's a shock. Since the end of the last war. Decades. But suppose I can't do without *Lilith*? That's not so funny. Jill remarked, casually, not to be provocative, 'You're married to *Lilith*.' I didn't like that. Who really runs *Lilith*? Phyllis does, in tandem with Jill. These two clever young women are *Lilith*, and nothing happens anywhere in any department without their knowledge. They come to me for advice, but less often now. I travel to dress shows all over Europe, and do the public lunches: I am the public face of *Lilith*. These two girls, both of whom learned about clothes from me, will watch me as I prepare myself for a luncheon at the Savoy, or as I leave for Munich, and say, 'Janna, I loved that dress you had on last week!' Or, 'Jane, do you think that suit would be better with a cream shirt?' For I have been unable to recover my total dedication to how I look: I feel that keeping myself groomed and my clothes up to the mark amounts to a holding operation against an invisible enemy who is every day becoming stronger.

The formal structure is that poor Charlie is editor, with Phyllis as assistant and me as consultant, Jill as my helper. Oh, the amiable social Charlie, how fond we all are of him! Phyllis, who is after all married to him, and who manages him at home as pleasantly as she does in the office, genuinely seems to love him. But then, as Jill remarks, 'And so she'd better, if she's seven months pregnant.'

But so much time gets wasted while Phyllis makes sure that Charlie does this or that, or Charlie consults with Phyllis or Jill; people approach the editor, needing quick decisions, but cannot have them because first everything has to be discussed with Jill or Phyllis. A snap and a sparkle have gone out of *Lilith*. Never mind. It does well enough, making less money, but then so does everything now, and it is still a household word, bought by 'upmarket' women, mostly working. But we do wonder—perhaps it is bought as much by housebound women who want to be working? For, after all, cookbooks and fashion magazines are not bought to be used, but read, for pleasure: doors into fantasy worlds. . .

Lilith's formula is as it always has been—three quarters solid common sense, information, medical advice, the problems of being a consumer in a consumer economy; one quarter outrageous clothes and glamorous food which practically no one ever actually wears or eats.

I enjoy being in the office, and my travelling and my business lunches, but the thing is, it's all more of an effort.

The effort is in always having to be on show, presented, observed. At home I have been careful to be *there* for Jill; responsible, not a source of that dread infection (despised by me, and of course by worthy Sister Georgie whose life might be defined as a war against it) sloppiness, whether of behaviour or of anything else. *My* place, my refuge, the only spot on this wide earth where I can be myself, do not feel the presence of possibly critical eyes, is—my bed. Not even my room, for Jill has needed to be able to come in and out, so that she may be reassured her rights in me are not restricted. Oh, not too often, not annoyingly: but the fact is, it is not when I have shut my bedroom door that I have felt responsibility take its weight off me, but when I turn off the light. I lie in the dark and look at changing skies over rooftops and trees.

Jill moved out today. She stood with her cases and her bundles in the middle of the living room, waiting for the taxi, and looked at me appalled at the cruel choices that life imposes on us. Her young man is very nice. I approve of him.

I went to the little café at exactly the time of the tryst. He was not there. I sat at a corner table, pretending to be amused at myself, but my heart was a clench of apprehension. No one there but Gino, the handsome Italian behind the expresso machine, in a gorgeous black and white sweater which made him look, with his polished black head, like harlequin. The café is a cosy box lined with wood and trailing plants. Only the two of us. I refused to watch the door, then could not stop myself. I was wondering when in my life have I been in such a state over anyone? Never. My poor Freddie? Certainly not, and as a matter of principle! And, thinking of Freddie, which as a rule I try never to do, I realized I had been dreaming of him all last night; as if it were Freddie and not Richard with whom I was in love.

And I tried to exorcise him thus: I have been dreaming of my husband, badly treated by me when I was married to him,

not that I knew it until after he had died, nastily, of cancer.
And so what is the point of dreaming now that I loved him,
when I certainly did not then? It's sentimental rubbish!

And then, I realized I had used the words of Richard, 'in
love', and this touched off a typhoon of contradictory
emotions. First of all, I am afraid, pride: I, Janna Somers, in
love, and in this sudden inappropriate way, at first sight, with
someone whose name I still did not know. I, Janna, always in
command of my decisions. . . But all this was being put at
nothing, quite simply, by an outrageous delight, an energy
that made it hard even to sit still, and which was drawing the
young Italian's eyes to me though he did not know why. A
smart elderly? middle-aged? lady, ever so well groomed, that
was what he was seeing: and approving: the wearer of that
sweater would have to give me full marks for what I was
wearing. When Richard came in, or rather blundered in
because of panic, for he had imagined I would be outside at
the table on the pavement, his face cleared into a wonderful
smile, and he came fast to the corner where I was, and sat
down not looking what he was doing, but exactly as I was at
him: is it possible that this miraculous person actually exists,
I haven't imagined it all?

'It's raining,' I said.

'Is it?'

And we began to laugh, peal after peal, relief after tension.

'Gino,' said this man, Richard, 'coffee, cakes, cream—
everything!' And laughed.

'Certainly,' says Gino, all smiles and style and connivance
with our holiday mood, and in no time our little table was set
for a feast. Which, however, we were unable to touch.

This man, Richard, whoever he was, like a tarnished lion,
seemed all out of place in this domestic interior, too large.
And I felt, excessive, even dangerous to it. And yet I didn't
want to move, or to do anything, but sit there for ever, and
look at him. It wasn't only that he is handsome, and so forth;
no, it was that he seemed so familiar to me, this stranger,
kin—flesh of my flesh? Oh no, that's dangerous, that is!
Sitting here in my—for the first time in three years—empty
flat, writing, I think, Would I like to go to bed with him, and I

feel quite shocked. There is a *no* there, but why? I hold out my hands and look at them, so well kept and nice, with the rosy soft nails, and the rings. The hands of a matron, however.

We didn't say anything very much, sitting on either side of that table, leaning towards each other. We could not stop smiling, waves of energy flowed back and forth between us.

Then he said, 'Look, why don't we simply go for a long walk? In the rain?'

'I adore walking in the rain,' I said, and he: 'Of course you do! Well then!'

And, as he turned to signal to Gino, whose eyes had not left us for a second, I saw beyond him, on the pavement through the door, a girl standing, apparently lost, indecisive—the sombre dark girl he had been with when we first met. And some instinct made him turn too to see her, and with an exclamation he got up and was out of the café at once. I saw him take her by her two arms and bend over her, anger contained by tender expostulation. And then he moved her on out of sight. I felt as if the plug had been pulled out: dismay was now the air of the café; and Gino was *not* looking at me, but polishing glasses, holding them up to the light one after another, and squinting at them as if into a kaleidoscope.

I was there alone for perhaps fifteen minutes. I knew that he must be walking her well away from where I was. What I was examining in my mind's eye was the way, from the moment he had seen her, he had damped himself down; that cautious set of his shoulders, the responsibility.

When he came back, I saw a different man. This sober and responsible person sat down opposite me and looked at me, and was choosing words.

I said, 'It's your daughter, is it?'

'Yes, that's Kathleen.' Then he took both my hands, leaned forward and looked at me. 'Why don't we decide not to talk about any of it?' he said. Now what characterized him was a patience, a carefulness; there was irony but no criticism. I knew I was seeing the man as he was in his ordinary life, and wondered if I too dimmed down and diminished as soon as my claims and my boundaries imposed themselves?

'It is at this stage,' said he, smiling, but with a grimness in it, 'that I tell you, and then you tell me, all about ourselves. But why don't we decide not to?'

I said, 'Well, I know something pretty important about you already.'

'Yes, I know, I know. But let's try.'

'Very well.'

We went out, and I saw him look swiftly up the street and then down into Soho Square. A soft glistening rain. A tender veiled sky.

'I ought to be at work anyway,' I said.

'Tomorrow?' he said. 'Rain or shine?'

After work I went to bed at once. I have woken from a dream of Freddie. *Why*? A dream of loss and emptiness. Freddie was on the other side of a deep and dangerous river, full of black twisting water, and he stood there looking at me. I can't make out what it means, that look of his. If I'm not careful I am going to cry—and once I start, what sort of a flood will that be? Dare I go back to bed?

Well, I didn't. I sat by my window and looked up into the sky where a deep black had floating on it small white islets; I longed for the light to come. And here it is.

It is night again: and what a day it has been.

Just as I was leaving for the café, the bell rang. Before answering it I stood in the middle of the living room, now my own again, as orderly as if Jill had never been here. I was looking for something, anything of hers—a book, a scarf— but no. I had tears in my eyes when I answered the entryphone and heard Kate's voice. At once, anger! I said, 'Kate, it is eight in the morning, and I didn't know you were coming.' Sniff, snuffle, gulp. 'Oh, Aunt *Jane,* and I've been sitting on a bench in the street all night and it is so *cold.*'

I pressed the button. I waited, astounded, even alarmed at myself. I was a rage of emotion. Which I must not inflict on Kate. What I let in was a snuffling waif, an infant clown. Her hair is neglected punk, she wore baggy pink dungarees, soiled of course, and a T-shirt, orange. She was shivering violently, and gazing at me with hopeless eyes, china blue. Her grubby fingers plucked at her lips.

'I know it is no good my asking why you didn't even telephone first?'

'Oh Jane, but I was afraid you'd say no.' But she was stammering with cold.

She had let down a small (soiled) bundle near the door.

'Now you've made your effect, you could put a sweater on?'

She shook her head: helplessness.

'You haven't got a sweater? You have no clothes at all with you because you mean me to buy you a new outfit?'

She nodded, biting her nails, her face awash.

I got her one of my sweaters, and her listlessness vanished as she scrambled into it: I saw how she had been dreaming of getting warm.

'What time did you get into Paddington?'

'Eleven last night.'

'You were engaged perhaps in exciting metropolitan adventures?'

'I sat on a bench there, till the fuzz moved me on. They were horrid. And then I walked and walked till I got here. . .'

'My sister Georgie doesn't know you are here? She didn't give you money for the journey?'

'All my money was stolen. I was mugged.'

'The first thing you've got to do is ring your mother and tell her where you are.'

She drooped away to an armchair. Seeing her where so often Jill had been, contrasting the two of them, sent away my anger. Besides, I was realizing just what I had to contend with. Everything Jill does is characterized by competence: Kate bungles the setting down of a coffee cup.

I said, 'I have precisely fifteen minutes.' I rang Sister Georgie. Her voice, Home Counties homogenized.

'As I am sure you know,' I said, 'your daughter Kate is here. She arrived in London in the middle of the night, has already been robbed, has been wandering about by herself without so much as a cardigan. She simply arrived on my doorstep.'

'I suppose she was afraid to telephone,' said Georgie. 'She's afraid of you.'

'Then why did she come?' I said, and put down the telephone.

Seeing how much I wanted—but really!—to assault that girl physically, not from anger now but from sheer exasperation, I took my time in turning around to face her. She was not looking at me, but gazing dolefully out of the window.

Her hair, in yellow, pink and green tufts, stuck up, and she was gnawing her grubby little fingers.

'What does my sister Georgie make of your punkhood?' I inquired, but she did not answer or turn around.

'How about making yourself a cup of tea, getting yourself warm, having some breakfast?'

The blue doll's saucers of her eyes at once became visible, all hope.

'Tell me, can you really not get yourself some tea, at least?'

'I . . . I . . . I . . . was afraid to suggest it.'

'Well, I have suggested it.'

She did not move. I saw that her whole body was clenched in a steady deep shiver.

I went to the kitchen, switched on the kettle, cut some bread and butter, took it to her with some tea on a tray.

I was about to say, 'Never, not once, in the time your sister was here, did I have to wait on her.' But something stopped me. The something was, I am afraid, pity. I do not propose to be sorry for this Kate! I do not believe that it helps people to be sorry for them! The best you can do for anyone is to help them to independence. But *Kate*—the sight of this poor little tyke, wolfing down bread and butter, slopping down tea . . . shivering . . .

How was it possible she could turn herself out like that?—not care? Punk is *style*. I admire it, properly done. There's a girl at the corner, she's a pleasure, we exchange smiles as she even peacocks about a little for my benefit, miming a fashion model there on the pavement, often not only for me, but for her mates who are also punks, but not so elegant. She can look like a cat, little black ears carved out of her golden hair, black arms (gloves from a stall?), a suggestion of gallant tiger around the shoulders. Or a highwayman, black swinging cloak and a mask done in black paint from which gleam painted eyes, all enjoyment. It must take her hours: as long as I used to need when I still cared enough. Her style is intransigence, contained and formalized; poor Kate has taken some bottles of hair dye to the bathroom, stood on tiptoes before the mirror, probably sniffling, daubed paint on tufts of hair cut as she works, and then stood in the doorway waiting for her parents to say, 'Oh Kate, what have you done to yourself?'

'I've got to go,' I said.

'When will you come home?'

'I don't know.'

At this she looked at me differently. I am not saying that all that had happened had been a pose, an invention: she was too cold and miserable for that: but she had been for weeks, months, rehearsing claims and just demands: she had known what she was going to say to me and was determined to say it.

Her look was not at all that of one alarmed at being told she was to fend for herself: it was a thoughtful assessment.

I was interested that I was pleased to see she was capable of any kind of rational thought: simultaneously I noted panic in myself. I am not going to have my relationship (whatever it is) with Richard spoiled by this girl.

'How old are you, Kate?'

'Don't you know!' she sniffed.

'No. Eighteen?'

'Nineteen.'

'I'm not babying you, Kate! I'm off now. We'll talk when I've time. Here's some money. We need bread. I don't aspire to that healthy wholemeal your mother doubtless insists on, you can get in some decent French. Butter: I like Normandy. You'd better get some paté, eggs. If there's anything you want for yourself. . .' I added this last, forcing myself.

Before I left I stood at the door, examining her again, conscious that I had been in too much of a rush about everything.

I saw her hands trembling, around the cup.

'Kate,' I said, 'I'm not going to clear up after you, tidy up, be your nursemaid.'

She nodded, eyes down.

As I left the building I forgot Kate.

Everything in movement. Above raced, from west to east, plump white clouds on shallow healthy blue like Kate's eyes. As I passed the cherry at the corner, the wind lifted off a pink froth of blossom and dumped it with a flourish on the pavement. My hair was frisking around my face.

I was late, *late*: and as I ran into the little street and saw Soho Square a shrill spring green, Richard hastened towards me, took my arm, and said, 'Let's go.' I could not help glancing around for his daughter Kathleen, but he said, 'No, it's all right.' All the same he too looked around as we got into the taxi. He took my hands and held them to his face, and we sat dissolving in smiles.

'At this point, when people fall in love,' said he, 'it is customary to tell each other the story of their lives. Let's not make a present to each other of our pasts.'

'So you have already asked,' I said, or queried.

And he said, or stated, 'It signals the entrance into responsibility.'

'I have already seen that you have too much.'

'Then that's more than I want you to see.'

We went to St James's Park. It was just right for our mood. The grey waters, where we caught glimpses of the frivolous blue spring sky reflected, were crammed with fanciful ducks, in style rather like punks (when they get it right!) if you come to think of it. We stood hand in hand among the crocuses and daffodils and marvelled at the inventiveness of the world, while the spring exploded all around us.

How fresh and dazzling everything was; each flower or bird an amazement, a gift of love. And we realized our senses were at peak and a day like this might not come again, not ever, so rare it was; and how rare and hardly achieved our meeting. We walked about for hours, and felt life tingling in each other's hands, and if we looked at one another we could not stop smiling.

But somewhere else in me the thought kept popping up, to be suppressed: this has never happened to me. Not ever!

There was a point when we separated, he going off along one edge of the little lake, I on the other, and this parting was done with style, as if as a symbol or a foreshadowing, and because of the way this struck to the heart I was perhaps too ready to linger there watching him, only a few paces away but divided from me by water. It was my dream, Freddie standing on the other side of impassable water, and his long grave look. For a moment the intoxication of the day went, and I saw a man bereft of splendour, a middle-aged man, slightly stooped because of some invisible burden he carried, his tarnished locks adrift, a patient, quizzical face. I could see it all there, saw life, the way it drags down, pulls low, weighs, tugs, erodes; and I was trying to make myself see, there, where he was, himself as the young man; for there are times I don't know if it is this one I am seeing, my sudden companion who is battered and beaten like I am, or the young man I can see all the time more and more clearly: a light-stepping charmer, with a grave smile and blue eyes between fringes of sandy lashes.

And he too was staring at me.

I wanted to cry out; say, 'No, no—don't.' For if he was seeing the girl I was once, then that was even worse; for it was bad enough that Freddie should return to remember me, that cold girl, negotiating allowances of emotion, of sex—did I ever use the word love?—and who never, ever, had looked at him as if he might be the door to some wonder or astonishment.

That was a bad cold moment, as we stood separated by the muddy waters of the pond where the coloured ducks bobbed and dived, their orange feet scrabbling in the air as they forced themselves down, down, to puddle for weed at the bottom.

I felt so emptied and nothing, and he too; and we turned, but with an effort, dragging ourselves out of it, and met again at the corner of the lake, linking hands tentatively, as if what had brought us together to link them at the beginning might have gone for ever.

'You see,' he said, 'you see what lies in wait, if we are not careful.'

I, then—and my voice sounded to myself a stubborn, forlorn little statement: 'But perhaps we can't shut it all out.'

'Ah, I don't want to hear that from you. I mean, common sense.'

And I, dryly: 'I am famed for my common sense.'

And he: 'Yes, I daresay, but that's not what . . .'

And he quickly pulled me to him, and we stood, lightly enlaced. It is a strange thing, standing body to body with one's love, if the bodies are not young ones. The clothes we wore and which divided us seemed like statements, or reminders, of our real lives—not, as they were once, hardly to be distinguished from hot flesh. And, as I stood with Richard, there flashed into my mind a memory of me with Freddie, in some foreign place, Spain perhaps, one of our holidays, and me pulling off skirt, panties, to stand naked; while he stripped on the other side of a bed. I remembered and wondered, How was it that he did not take off my clothes, I his?—I was remembering the efficiency of the operation.

If I were with Richard, and *young*—I would wait for him to unbutton, slide sensuous stuffs off flesh, *take possession*. But Freddie was never allowed to possess me, perish the thought.

I felt Richard's rough cheek slide against mine, and he said, 'Do you have a photograph of yourself when you were a girl? Yes, I know that is crass, I should be able to imagine. Before you were married, or *serious*. Were you married? No, I don't want to know.'

'I was. I've been alone for—let's see. Yes, it must be five years, six. *Can* it be—really.' And dismayed, I stepped back out of the embrace.

'Let's go and have breakfast, lunch, something, a drink, we need it.'

We walked out of the park and found a little restaurant off St James's Street. The vividness of our senses had come back, and every mouthful seemed a miracle of tastes and savours. We ate—it didn't matter. A corner of bread with a bit of butter would have seemed a feast. We drank quite a bit of wine though, holding our hands around the glasses as if they warmed what we looked at, always each other for we could not take our eyes away.

And then we went through a showery glittery afternoon and walked and walked with no intention of ever stopping, until straight in front of me I saw a couple, a girl and boy. He had his back to a tree trunk, and held her in his arms, and her black Mediterranean hair sprawled all down her back and over his arms, and they were kissing.

Suddenly I was in a flood of tears, I who find myself in tears once a year with surprise and annoyance; but how many times have I wept in the last few days?

'Good God,' I heard myself say, as I stared at this young pair, lost to the world. 'What a fool I've been, what a fool I was.' When I came to myself I felt his comprehension of me, the moment, and was not able to return his look. For it was Freddie I was thinking of. If I could now separate them at all, Freddie, Richard. Richard put his arm around my shoulders and we walked past the lovers and towards a shop window where we saw ourselves. Some trick of the fading and changing lights in the glass made it easy to see myself, the pretty fresh girl with the crisp light hair and smiling eyes; I saw him beside me, the young man.

I don't know what he saw, or wanted to see.

We wandered on through the afternoon, stopping twice for coffee, and then it was early evening.

There was a withdrawal in him, and I was not surprised when he said, 'At six, I must leave you.'

Then: 'Tell me—on some other occasion, could I come to your place? You can't to mine.'

I said, 'This morning my niece Kate, my sister Georgina's second daughter—she has another daughter and two sons— arrived on my doorstep. It is her intention to live with me.'

'You have no children,' he stated.

'No.' Then I made myself say, 'It was not that I—that *we* decided not to but. . .'

'*I don't want to know* . . .' Then: 'I suppose we can't avoid plunging into each other's lives like dirty swimming pools, but let's put it off please for as long as we can.'

'My life,' I said, 'has been on the whole well ordered, often rechlorinated, the water changed.'

'That is what I am afraid of,' said he, and there was a pain behind the dryness that I, in my turn, was fighting not to have to know about.

But before we separated we walked along the Bayswater Road, and suddenly we saw a building being done up, with scaffolding up its side for four storeys, and on a platform on the fourth-floor scaffolding a little house, in scarlet, set there for the workmen to have tea in or to rest, and in the doorway sat a workman with a bucket in front of him in which must be a wisp of fire, for he held a sausage on a fork over the heat and waited with his knees apart for his meal to cook. And there was something so comical and pleasant in it that we laughed, holding on to each other, for the absurdity of the little red house so high up there and the sausage on the fork.

The strong exultation came back into us, and the burden fell off his back and he stood free and laughing, like me. Then we separated, with an assignation, but not for tomorrow. I do have to work some time, after all, even though I am a privileged elder stateswoman.

I went to the office anyway, to see if there was mail. Phyllis had gone, but Jill was there.

'I know about it,' said she. I thought she meant Richard, because of the vitality I could feel booming in me, but no, it was Kate of course.

She saw that I had had to tell myself she must mean Kate. She said, 'Has she been alone all day?'

'Presumably.'

'*Well!*'

'You are saying she can't be alone?'

'With all of us, the family, she hasn't had much practice at it.'

I seemed a long way from Kate, her problems, and I was not thinking of her as I sorted out my letters and looked at the diary for tomorrow.

Jill, who was at her desk which was piled with work, went on with it all for a few minutes, and then said, 'You should decide what to do about her. She's waiting for that. To call her bluff, if that's what you are going to do.' And then as I didn't answer, Jill cried out, 'Jane, you are sorry for her, aren't you?'

I said, 'I suppose so—if that's the point.'

'It is the point if it lets you in for more than you want.'

I said, vaguely, for I was thinking of Richard and if he had got home, what 'home' was, and what was the problem with Kathleen, 'I suppose after all it is just a question of having a sensible talk with her.'

Silence. When I looked up, Jill was smiling, as if to herself, but I was meant to notice it. 'It occurs to me, Aunt Jane, that in many ways you have had a very sheltered life.'

'You mean that Kate will be too much for me?'

'All right, don't say I didn't warn you.'

When I left she was still working. Enjoying it. I could see that pleasure of it in her: being able to do it, to do it well.

Pleasure: when I looked back at my life since I started working—before I was twenty—the strongest thing in it, in the way of pleasure, is how I felt when I proved to be so good at things. A consistent, years-long theme: me, working, *doing it*, doing it well. That has been my life's theme. And poor Freddie? The background to it.

And as I came home I was thinking of Freddie, though I try often enough not to. If he was the background to my life, was I to his? Probably. When he died and made a reckoning or account of his life, as I suppose one does, did he say to himself, My enjoyment was in my work? For he couldn't have said, Pleasure, that was Janna, that's what fun, pleasure, accomplishment has meant to me.

When I opened the door into the living room, I saw Kate asleep on the sofa, where she was when I left. The tray I had brought her was still by her, swept clean of every crumb. The sight brought home to me what Jill had said, and to collect myself I got through the usual small chores of homecoming, drawing curtains, switching on lights, getting myself a drink. In the middle of my cool and elegant room, lights so tastefully and efficiently disposed here and there, a vase, candy-striped cushions on the pale yellow chairs—amid all this, like a curtain going up on a play, the pathetic waif, her great clumping dirty shoes making marks on the grey linen sofa, the bundle still lying where she had dropped it near the door.

'Kate, wake up.'

She woke, stretching and yawning, but I still don't know if she had been awake all the time, listening to me move about.

'And now,' I said, 'we are going to talk. First of all, you will tell me what plans you have.'

Those pathetic, blinking baby-blue eyes! The slightly open, wet, pinkish mouth! The stubby childish hands plucking at her clothes.

'Kate, you are not going to work in *Lilith.*'

At this she flung herself about, heaved some desperate sighs, and ended by fixing me with a dramatic betrayed stare. I did not know, do not know, how much of all this was a prepared 'scene', for she must of course have known, for I have said so, that she will not work in *Lilith.* What I was convinced by was not the histrionics, but the limp defeatedness of her.

I was thinking, Suppose she was as clever and well presented and as 'together' as Jill was, would I introduce her into *Lilith*, nepotism or not? Actually, not; but I might ask one of the other magazines, in which of course I know so many people, to take her on.

I realized that the speech I had in my mind to make, was simply not on:

'Kate! You have not passed your A-levels. You have no intention of passing your A-levels. You are not fitted for anything at all—not even, as far as I can see, to do a little shopping when asked. First of all, your appearance. You will decide on what style is going to be yours, and I will go shopping with you. But whatever it is, it will be a lot of trouble. Life is a lot of trouble! Punk is a lot of trouble: so if that is what you want, then you must get up earlier in the morning, or set aside so many hours in the week. Think carefully about all this. Decide what you are going to study so as to. . .'

This speech, which could have been addressed to Jill with effect, even if she teased me for it, calling me pompous, headmistressy, disappeared into the limbo of unsaid things, and what I said was, 'Do you think a bath would help? Are you hungry?'

I ran the child's bath, lent her my best nightgown, in which she looks like a nine-year-old aspiring to grownuphood, cooked her an egg and some toast. All the while, I have to report—with distaste—attacked by tenderness for the poor little grub. What is the point of tenderness? I can't do anything for her. I made up the bed where Jill had slept, and put her into it.

I then telephoned Jill. Her young man Mark answered. His voice reminded me that Jill was the past: it set bounds and limits. But I had to say to Jill:

'This is the wicked and worldly but sheltered aunt. No—listen. I have a question, specific. Right? Very well. I find that, sitting in front of your sister Kate, any sensible remark or suggestion dies on my tongue. It is because, clearly, she is in some sort of breakdown or collapse or something of that kind. Right?'

'Jane, she has always been like that.'

'Very well, infantile. But. I was sitting there realizing that I literally could not say anything like that about Kate to Sister Georgie, your mother, either.'

'Ah,' said Jill, having got the point at once. 'Well no, you can't, can you?'

'I expect you to tell me why not?'

'Things are not easy at home.'

'It goes without saying that your adolescent siblings, the two boys, are making life hell for everybody, because it is expected of them—is that it?'

'Oh, not worse than anyone else's family. . . No, it is Kate, Kate herself. You see, my mother and father succeed at everything. That is their thing. What they turn their hands to, then in their hands it blossoms. Kate does not blossom.'

'Does your mother know this child is such a mess?'

'I think Daddy does, but I don't think my mother can face it. Because there is no cause for it, you see.'

'Yes, I do see. Very well, Jill. And thank you.'

'Any time. But if I were you, I'd send her home. She'll take you over, Jane.'

'Not if I don't let her.'

A week has gone. We are into May. The sun has been shining on trees covered with pink and white blossom, on tulips, and on acres of green grass where I have been walking with Richard. I took a week off from work; as always, I have quite a bit of leave owing to me. Instead of saying to him, But I have to work tomorrow, I say, Yes, where shall we meet? We have met in Regent's Park and in Green Park; in Hyde Park and on Hampstead Heath. When we meet at once springs up that reckless gaiety that characterizes *us*: we hurry towards each other, looking to see if *it* is still there, if, as we approach, we can feel the energy of delight that carries us through our long days together, our long and energetic days. Never have I walked so much! Richard laughs at me because I walk in my lovely smart shoes, over heath and heather, vale and hill. 'Why don't you get some walking shoes?' 'These *are* my walking shoes,' I say, holding out to him, as I stand on one leg, an elegant shoe that looks as if it is fit for no more than simpering around a drawing room. But I keep up with him, striding about and up and down. 'You are ridiculous,' he says, laughing, and his eyes take me all in and eat me up, for I know he likes my lovely clothes, though they aren't what they were in my dedicated days, and he notices, saying, 'That's a wonderful blouse,' and his hands on my arms are aware of the texture of the cloth there as well as of the warmth of the flesh under them.

I looked out old photographs. A discovery! I have very few of me. Or of Freddie. There are group photographs, *Lilith*, or of me in all my best clothes at some fashion do in Paris or somewhere. But photographs of *me*? A thought: I have spent thirty-odd years working in the fashion trade. For years of my life I cared so much about what I looked like that I was conscious if there was a strand or two less of thread on one button than on its neighbour; I am aware of the impression I make entering a room, or on colleagues, can assess what they think of what I wear by an inflection of the voice or a glance. My poor husband used to joke that he came second to what I wore. Yet not only have I seldom been photographed, but when I came on a photo of me at probably twenty-three or four, I was amazed. A really quite extraordinarily pretty girl. It was the freshness and vitality I had. This lovely thing is standing by a flowering bush, though I can't remember where, smiling quizzically at the camera. She wears a charming little flowered dress (I remember the dress!). Yet I never say to myself, as I know women of my age and old women do, 'How beautiful I was,' as I put out pictures of a younger self (the real one) on a shelf or table.

Finding this little picture gave me a bad moment or two. For I really had not made that effort, done that balancing act where you say, That's what I was, and this is what I am now. I assumed, vaguely enough, that I had not much changed.

I stood in front of my mirror, with the little photograph in my hand, and looked from one image to the other. If that girl had been asked to glance into the future, to see that woman there, what would she have said? I don't know. I can remember only that she was full of confidence and enjoyment. I saw in the looking-glass this rather good-looking woman, not badly made, solid rather than slim, with a face redeemed from ordinariness by the great grey eyes, and the pretty silvery chunks of hair that make people look: Is she grey, or is it a dye? That's compliment enough, I suppose, that they have to look. Taken feature by feature, putting one part of the body with another, shoulder, knee, neck, my smooth white forehead, you could say, Where's the difference? But the whole ensemble ... oh, that's a very different thing, and I have to face it; for the girl in the little photograph is so strong an assault on the senses, all dew and juices, that I can hardly believe I was unaware of it. And now, here is this solid woman with no light in her, no grace. It is all achieved, done for.

I saw something else as I stood there, looking from the photograph to *me*—it was me as I must seem to Kate. The unreachable accomplishment of it, this woman standing there so firm on the pile of her energetic and successful years. What a challenge, what a burden, the middle-aged, the elderly, are to the young. I never saw that before, or suspected it. I didn't want to think of Kate, at that moment, there; but I *was* thinking of her. Also of Kathleen, Richard's daughter.

As we were striding across the Heath on Saturday, hand in hand, laughing—for we laugh all the time, it seems—he stopped dead, pulled me up to him. Wandering away in front of us, there she was. I had a good look at her. A sleepwalker, that is the impression she makes first. The way she walks, or trails, her slow indecisions, for she stops, hesitates, goes on, might turn aside one way but then goes another. She's all stops and starts: a rather large dark girl, in her uniform of jeans and sweater.

But I was struck most of all by her watchfulness, her suspicion.

'Does she trail you all the time?'

'When she can.' The helplessness was back in him, and the burden was on his shoulders. He even seemed to stoop.

'What is she so afraid of?' I could not stop myself asking. Yet I most passionately approved his warning look at me: *I don't want this to end;* and yet I did ask.

'She is afraid I might vanish.'

'Because you have already?'

'*I* haven't. I have been careful not to.'

'Well, I see. Or I think I do.'

He said, 'Jane, Jane, let's *not*. Let's stave it off, do.' And he caught my hand and we began running across the rough grass. This was, I knew, to bring back the energetic wilderness of being together, and he teased me as we ran: '*Ridiculous*—shoes; *absurd*—Jane,' and we ran into the little road where the good coffee shop is that has the wonderful cakes, and we found a table in the corner and stayed there all afternoon, because the rain came down outside too hard for walking in.

Would I have believed I could spend three, four hours, simply sitting by a man, sometimes not talking, in contentment? We watched the people coming and going at the tables near us, and might exchange a smile or a look that summed up what we thought about them. We watched the little dramas and eavesdropped. Or we talked—what do we talk about, when so much cannot be said, or even approached? We make up stories about what we see; we tell each other about people we know. What this is, is a shared solitude. I spend so much of my time doing things by myself: walking, going to the cinema, sitting in cafés, talking to strangers, visiting galleries and museums, always by myself. And now there is someone else with me: and it is as easy and natural to be with him as to be with myself.

I asked him, though I knew, 'You spend a lot of time by yourself?'

'Oh, I don't mind, I like it,' he said quickly. And then: 'It's not that, I mind . . .' And the look at me: I have said more than I meant to. Don't take advantage of it.

I have also, this week, spent some time with Kate.

First of all, I bought her some clothes. The helpless passivity of the poor thing, always looking towards me to suggest, prompt and even decide. Jill on a similar jaunt only needed my chequebook.

Kate did not 'really' want to be a punk; 'did not mind' if she wore this or that. I took trouble, finding things that are well made, with some style, but as she puts them on, they dwindle into ineffectiveness. The pink and the green have gone from her hair, and she has an uneven crop, midbrown. I showed her how to use make-up, and said that with such eyes she could hardly go wrong. But she can and does.

I said to her that she must study something. I've sent out for pamphlets from schools, colleges, polytechnics.

I rang Sister Georgie and said, 'About this daughter of yours. Tell me, is there anything you have in mind for her to do?'

'Well, I don't know, you could have a talk with her, couldn't you?' This was so feeble, compared with ordinarily, that I was deflated. Where was my crisp and disapproving sister? Do I get good marks, perhaps, for having assisted her Jill towards this satisfactory condition of hers: job, London flat, young man? Half a good mark? At some point will I be judged as having atoned for my delinquencies? I have a feeling that this profit and loss account will never be balanced...

Kate rings her mother quite often. When I am there. I suspect not so often when I am not. Her voice is small, obedient; and on her face is the smile that goes with it, it is a biddable good-child's face, and she listens with little nods of agreement and consent.

I do not think Georgie has rung Kate. Certainly not while I have been there.

This afternoon, the last of my week in Elysium, we parted at a bus stop outside the Victoria and Albert. But as I stood in the queue and saw him walking away under the trees, up towards the park, I found myself in a panic that made me start shaking. I ran up after him, calling, Richard, Richard, and heard my voice weak and inadequate. He turned, smiling, but puzzled, because he could see my state. 'Do you realize,' I said, 'that if either of us failed to turn up at a rendezvous—well, we might never see each other again? I don't know your name, and I can't bear it,' I heard myself plead.

He put his arms around me and we stood resting side by side under a plane tree in full leaf. Late afternoon, a rich yellow light, and a bird was cheeping away about something or other overhead.

'My name is Richard Curtis. And yours is Jane Somers.'

'I never told you.'

'No, but you did mention your magazine and I rang up, got your name. I wasn't going to have you vanish.'

'I'm ridiculous,' I said, and left his embrace. 'The thing is . . .' I don't know why it was, but the future was casting long shadows, and I was thinking, This will soon have to end.

But why should it? I went back to the bus stop, and turned to wave: he was waiting for me to do it.

I can't bear that this will end, so I won't think about it.

I don't know when I have worked as hard as I have this last

fortnight. Three distinct and separate lives. First, the office. Because Phyllis has left to have her baby, Jill and I are doing her work. We sit opposite each other in the room where Joyce and I sat. Some of the old hands among the staff come in and say, 'It's like old times.' We make everything happen, and make sure that Charlie has plenty of business lunches. He's not bad at those, provided he is well briefed. He comes late and goes early, without apology. Phyllis's baby is an enterprise shared by the whole office. As he comes in, affable, smiling, he will say, 'The doctor says it might be earlier than we thought.' Or, 'Poor Phyllis slept very badly.' His secretary brings him tea with a little solicitous air and a connivatory smile. At this Jill and I exchange glances, as Joyce and I used to. Nothing disturbs our speed, efficiency, harmony, but Kate, who rings up several times a day. 'Jane, I can't find the sugar.' 'Can I borrow your silk petticoat, the one with the lace?' I swallow down distaste, for everything she wears is left with a sickly smell of sweat, no matter if she does bath every day, as I insist, and say, 'Yes, of course.' While Jill raises her pretty eyebrows and regards me, sighing at my folly.

I say, 'She tries on every stitch I have while I'm out anyway. I believe that is the only thing she ever does.'

Jill puts her chin in her hand, one, two, three, four pink nails emphatic against a pearly cheek, coral lips, that would be better set off by a pout, decisively set to match her mind, and she examines me with the frankest curiosity. 'What's got into you, Jane?'—and she really wants to know.

I don't want her to know, and I offer her symptoms rather than root, saying, 'What I can't stand is writing her off.'

'Who's writing her off? It's a question of her finding her level.' She says this with a little air of finality, like a housewife who says, Yes, now I've arranged everything: satisfaction in proper order. 'Don't you see?' she goes on. 'She's simply not *up* to what's been expected of her.' And, as my look indicates that I am willing, indeed need, to hear more, she says, 'She will get married, won't she? Someone of her own kind. Or become a nun, or something.'

'I've seldom heard anyone being disposed of so finally.'

'Well, Jane . . .'

Twice the telephone has rung, not Kate but Richard, and Jill has not watched me with frank curiosity, but busied herself, and even made a point of going out of the room.

I cannot prevent my voice changing—I am sure, my whole body—when Richard rings. I hear my voice lift into the gaiety of intimacy, and everything outside this magical unity, Me and Richard, goes away into a stupid darkness.

It takes time for me to come back to the ordinary world after these calls.

After the last, Jill left a good hour before asking, 'Jane, do you ever think of marrying again?'

She looked a little furtive, for she had not really wanted to ask, and for a moment I didn't like her, my lovely Jill. The word *marry* was like a whip, some deliberate hurt. I said, after a while, 'I have no plans at all to get married again.' And sat scarcely breathing; for to be married to Richard—well, I could not begin to conceive of such a happiness. And yet it was all nonsense, for everything that marriage has to be has been left out of our being together, even thinking about it. I was full of distress, and I had not expected it, and I went out of the room. When I came back, Jill was sitting, stricken, and her great sea eyes were swimming.

'I am *sorry*,' said she.

I sat down, I took the things to do up my smudged eyes from my bag, I began work on them, before saying, 'As you will have seen—I am well out of my depth.' I finished my eyes, put everything away, set my bag down tidily, and after all that said, 'Your frivolous Aunt Janna has had a depth charge set off in her, and she does not understand what is happening. And *no*, Jill, I do not want you to explain it to me.'

On the evenings I was not with Richard, coming back into my flat was an effort of my whole self: not because I don't know what I will find, but because I do. Kate flumps in the corner of the grey sofa, which is already her territory. It is a grubby island in my lovely room, covered with bits of clothing, odd bits of crockery such as an empty cup rolling there amid the detritus of assorted make-up, magazines. Kate does not read, but like a child looks at pictures. Usually she has plugged herself into a radio, and from between the wires that trail on either side of her head her face responds to the unheard (by me) din, and her eyes have the characteristic hypnotized look of these poor zombies. Her body might be moving rhythmically too.

I say, 'Kate, it makes people deaf, do you want that?'

She says, with the bright prattling eagerness which characterizes her manner with me, 'Oh, no, Jane, I'd hate it.'

'Then why don't you stop it? When I'm not here you could listen in the ordinary way.'

But she likes being plugged into her secret world, safe from outside impacts. And she is already a bit deaf. When she has unplugged herself, I have to shout for some minutes.

In Kate I am meeting an entirely new experience: someone who literally cannot hear what you say, quite apart from this intermittent real deafness. I have never before known anyone, I think, who, informed that to do something will make her deaf, would not decide to stop.

I go to the kitchen to see if she has in fact done the shopping I asked, not that I can't do it myself, but as a way of getting her active. She does go out, and she gets an approximation of what I've asked for, but it is never exactly what I've said, and I am even quite interested when I go into the kitchen: what will be there this time? A certain brand of coffee because the tin has an attractive pattern of gold and black; a red cabbage, because she was drawn to the colour; some tangerines, which she hasn't eaten, but she liked the sunny display on the pavement; five giant packets of potato crisps and some sticky buns.

I make supper for us out of what is in my cupboards and what she has brought, not wanting to discourage the child. But probably she doesn't connect the red mush on her plate which sets off the slim brown frankfurters with the silken magenta marvel she brought in from that wonderhouse, London.

What an effort it is to dim myself down, defuse myself, during the long evenings with Kate! I watch every word as it forms in my mind, I stumble about among words and phrases that won't 'upset' her; though it is not that, more choosing words that can arrange themselves into patterns that connect with her. I ask her what she's been doing during the day, as if it cannot possibly matter that she slept until twelve, tried on my clothes, trailed around a shop or two, and then sat jerking in the corner of my sofa to that violent music. I try to find out anything in the world that really interests her, but apart from Jill, about whose doings she is fanatically curious, there is nothing. She wants to be with Jill, to *be* her. She asks about Jill's flat, but I only glimpsed it briefly and cannot answer what she wants to know: is there room in it for her? If she knows Jill's escape from home three years ago was as much an escape from her as anything, she does not admit it. She asks what clothes I bought Jill, and I see her looking hopelessly at her own, already a collection of sad jumble. She wants to know about Jill's flatmate—which is what Jill calls him: 'Meet my flatmate,' says she, introducing her love, and I look on and want to say, Jill, Jill, *don't*—warning her against I know not what; and I really don't, sitting there examining her as I do the photograph of my youthful self, incredulous that she doesn't know what treasures she is—I think—locking up: hands off.

Then I talk to Kate about what she is going to study. She could, if she had the will, go to all kinds of classes and courses now, though it is drawing near to the end of the student year—a new arrangement of the calendar for me. But in the autumn she will go to the polytechnic and learn Spanish. I cannot think of anything easier. I talk of it, and she does because I do, as the entrance to some fabled existence (like Jill's) where everything will become possible: friends, accomplishments, independence.

In the meantime she proposes to droop around here. It seems as if the vitality that surges and jigs and flies about everywhere in the world is something she knows nothing about: she is not connected to it. There's a short circuit. An evening with Kate: I am exhausted. I even go to bed an hour earlier than usual, as early as eleven, to try and recover. I am appalled that this girl is here. I don't see how I can, as Jill says, tell her to leave. 'Well, tell her to go home, Jane!' I really would feel as if I were condemning her. But if she were not here, then Richard and I could . . . what? Come here for a meal? Lovemaking presents itself from time to time as an imperative, and then takes itself off again. How is it that two people who cannot meet without sending the temperature up all around them, nevertheless do not make love, nor, much, think of it?

It is that little picture of the young girl, what that means, that stops me? Stops *us*?

I have stood in front of my glass, naked. Oh, I certainly have been deluding myself. Not much changed, I've been thinking vaguely, adjusting over my ageing body the clever clothes I wear, with their textures and substances like skin, or flesh . . . When I do think—which I prevent myself doing—about making love with Richard, woe invades me, an emptiness, as if I were proposing to bring a ghost to a feast.

I dream about Freddie every night.

We make love all right. Strange, I have never had sexual dreams about Freddie. Sex we had; good sex, as the phrase goes, so what was there to dream about? I remember asking myself, when other people said they dreamed of sex. When he died I did not dream of sex, not as a feature of my dreamlife that I needed to take notice of: I had orgasms, I remember, in my sleep, but that was functional. Masturbation for me has always been practical rather than sensuous: I need it, I must relax, I get it over with, has been my attitude. It is because I have known what sex can be. But now when I go off to sleep I make wild and passionate love with Freddie, full of regret and longing. Crazy. We are crazy creatures, there's no gainsaying that.

Kate has asked, because of the evenings I have spent with Richard, 'Are you going to friends?' 'Have you been with friends?' I say, firmly, 'Yes, I am.' 'Yes, I was.'

'Are they nice?' she asks pathetically. Meaning, Would they like me? She even said sullenly once, 'Why can't I go? Are they famous?'

'Look, Kate, I have my friends, and you will have yours.'

As I said this, I experienced it, through her, as a rejection, a cruelty: like being told she was not going to be working in *Lilith*. Door after door closes in her face, and the glamorous world of real achievement is continually being withdrawn from her as she approaches it.

The poor bundle dwindled into the corner of my great sofa, and the tragic eyes of a mistreated child mourned at me.

When I see her to bed at nights—for if I did not she would sleep where she was, in a mess of crumbs, fragments of chocolate and potato crisps—I seem to see the ghosts of teddy bears and dolls. Should I buy one for her? Would that be another cruelty?

And then, my life with Richard. It really is another life, and I fly into it, my heels winged. Sometimes I arrive at our rendezvous with my hands full of flowers, somewhere to put my joy. Richard laughs when he sees them, straight into my eyes, so that my eyes dazzle with it, like too strong sunlight. He takes flower after flower, putting them in my hair, my belt, a buttonhole. I stand bedecked and people look, at first ready to be critical, but then getting the benefit of the spin-off from our enjoyment. Wherever we go, we pull others into our pleasure. Yesterday, we stood by a fountain in Trafalgar Square and one by one, like coins for luck, threw in freesias and late daffodils. We bought these off the pavement together, and the man said, 'The last of the daffs for this year,' and we bought bunch after bunch. When one of us stopped buying, the other bought another, until our arms were full. The flowers lay floating on the fountain, a drowned greeny-yellow on the light blue, and a couple of small girls pulled off their shoes and socks and paddled in to get them, shrieking and slipping while they threw the flowers to the edge of the fountain. 'Why do you want to throw them *away*, mister?' they yelled, paddling about to collect them; so we gave the small girls bunches of fresh ones from our mountain of flowers, and went on up St Martin's Lane, distributing daffodils to startled people who looked into our faces and then laughed. They probably thought we were actors from one of the theatres, creating a 'happening'.

We go into many pubs. We started by going into one to have a drink before the theatre, and Richard said he had forgotten about pubs, how marvellous they are. He said he misses them more than anything, abroad. He says there is nothing like them, anywhere else.

I have never been much of a pub-goer, and now I am wondering why? Well, for one thing, you need a companion, for a pub.

And how pleasant they are, London pubs. Every public place is like a theatre, but pubs most of all, because people coming in are so often regulars. Richard and I sit where we can, until we can get into our favourite place, which is a corner, so we can be out of the way and no one need notice us.

We drink Scotch, he with ice, and I without, and the two glasses stand close together and the light makes oily golden patterns in the liquid that repeat themselves on the table tops. What companionable and good-natured places they are, these pubs; how people do come and go, apparently without reason, but each caught tight into his or her little pattern, their trip into the pub a fragment of the pattern which is invisible to us. How various we all are, never a face repeated, the amazing mix and match: the doors swing in, a new face appears, you could never have foreseen its uniqueness.

And then we have our conversation. Well, if it is only one of our conversations, it certainly repeats most often:

Richard says, 'How is it they don't see what they've got, why do they all run it down so?' Changes it to, 'How is it *you* don't see . . .' Says, another time, 'I, we . . .' 'If we could only . . .'—see this or that, do that or this. It's nothing but woe, he says, on the television, in the newspapers, never a good word to say for—themselves, yourselves, ourselves.

I say, 'But things are bad.' I list unemployment and industries running down; and say how awful is the inefficiency, the muddle, so that you feel as if it is all running through your fingers, you can't grasp anything . . .

And he says that that is true of everywhere, it is because of everything being too big and unwieldy, that has nothing to do with Britain—us, you, them.

I tell him stories about *Lilith*, the grind and grit of making things work against what seems to me an amiable indifference to everything, a tacit agreement that it all doesn't matter.

He says that we—you—they, don't know what we have got. And what we have got is—people. He says there is a sanity and a sense, and a balance and a rightness; and we don't value it.

I say, 'I do value it.' And I tell him how I walk and walk around this city, and feed—which is how I feel it—on the people: the little scenes that stage themselves, the comedies, a spirit of surreal enjoyment that is always there, coming out in what a man says in the greengrocer's, or two girls on a bus.

He says, 'All the same, you are spoiled, all of you. You live here in this little oasis, surrounded by chaos and terror and by people who have to be afraid to say what they think.'

I say, 'It's time you came home to live.'

He says, 'I couldn't stand the way you are letting it all slide. Sometimes, when I'm away too long, I come back and it hits me, that there's something here, something special, but this time what is new is that you never stop running yourself down, and you let things go to pieces.'

He pulls a newspaper out and lays it on the table between us, and he has marked with heavy double lines: unemployment, the pound, strikes, Ireland, the state of our sewers, the crisis in the railways … And then, as I glance around the pub, at *them, you, us,* wondering if that man is without a job, or if that young couple over there have ever had one, if this apparent good humour, ease, confidence, is all a mask, he will say, 'How is it possible you don't see what you are doing?'

Today he said, 'Well, perhaps you deserve to lose it all. If you don't value a thing, you lose it.' Anger: a passionate and indeed violent regret. In Richard violence lies coiled, restrained.

But he was talking about us, him and me, just as much as about *them,* or *you*—he was skirting the edge of the personal that is forbidden us. And I was careful not to look at him, for I want him to believe that I am keeping the rules. *His* rules; for it is his rules that I am obeying. But is that true? Why have I been so reluctant to take out of my handbag, where it lies in an envelope that is getting soiled, the little photograph of me? Oh, I am as afraid as he is! Of the big issues—yes; but they are too much for me, as they are for us all; and very much afraid for Richard and me. So vulnerable are we, so easy would it be to blow what we have apart. A word could do it; a word or a look does often rip aside our enjoyment in each other, leaving us fumbling, so that we both scramble with words or a movement to cover it all over, talking about something else, making up nonsense as we do, for the pleasure of words, words, the game of them; or we get up from where we sit in a pub or on a pavement and we walk rapidly away from where the danger was.

It has been very hot. The spring trees, all pink and cream and white, are gone, and there is a full green instead. Summer. Yesterday I wore my yellow linen dress and sat with Richard on the pavement in the yellow sunlight, and he said, in the way he has of paying compliments, warm but with a regret in it that pays tribute to some ineluctability or other, the worm in the apple, 'Pretty Janna!'

I told him that to nearly everyone I am Janna, but not the family, and he said at once, 'Janna, of course you must be Janna, Jane is so solemn,' and he said the word heavy and dragging, Ja—a—a—ne, so that we both laughed at it. But I wasn't laughing altogether, because I could hear in that *Jane* the weight and the strictures of the family.

And that was the moment I was inspired, God help me, to take quickly from my bag the photograph, and give it to him. He did not know what it was as he took it, was uncomprehending, and then as he looked, his body tensed and he even sat up to put the picture down flat between the white china ashtray and the tall glasses of orange juice, and he stared down at that girl in her flowered dress for a long time. His breathing was shortened. I saw he was flushed. How I regretted giving it to him! How I suffered sitting there, my heart beating, knowing that something quite terrible had been done: by me, by me! I kept my eyes away, but could not prevent little anxious glances, and still he sat there, looking at me, thirty years lost and gone. Now he looked tired, even drained. And pale. Our gorgeous day, sunlight and hot blue

skies and people in summer clothes, all relaxed and smiling—
where was it? Or where were we? Not part of it any longer.
All kinds of thoughts presented themselves to me, to be
dismissed. Like: It's unfair. Like: He *asked* for a photograph
of me as a girl. Like: Is he blaming me for not looking, at
fifty, as I did at twenty? Like: *You're punishing me!*

He was in fact suffering, and badly.

He did not look at me: he would not. There was a
wildness, a bitterness there, and I felt that this was not to do
with me. Which made things worse; and I sat there scarcely
breathing, for breathing hurt, and what I wanted was to
move, fast, away from this scene, to almost anywhere at all.

And then he said, judiciously, giving me, or the situation,
its exact due, 'Congratulations!'

A little wind blew up the paper corners, red white and blue,
of the table cloth, and the photograph tilted up and would
have blown away. But he put his hand quickly over it, as if
over a butterfly, something he wanted to capture, and then he
looked at it again, with real pain on his face, and put it into
his breast pocket.

'Let's go,' he said, and hastily emptied money on to the
table for the drinks, much too much, and he walked off, with
me following him. We walked along the Old Brompton
Road, found ourselves in Cromwell Road, and did not notice
how the buildings were lowering themselves and becoming
shabbier until we found ourselves between Shepherd's Bush
and Hammersmith, in a maze of streets, the dense crammed
London people live in, not work in, and stroll and push
prams and shop for everything from Rice Crispies to yams
and flying fish and Mars Bars, and stand talking on
pavements saying, And then she said, and then he did . . .
And we still had not looked at each other. The hot sun came
down, the hot pavements hurt our feet, and we were
breathing fast because of how fast we had walked. We came
to a stop under a plane tree growing, it seemed, straight out
of the warm pavement, with under it two Pepsi-Cola cans, a
litter of ice-cream sticks, a bit of dirty newspaper, and a
child's blue ball with a jolly face painted on it in yellow. We
were looking into a minute front garden where a girl in an

orange bikini was directing a black snake at seven bright pink tulips growing out of a square foot of black earth. Glittering water encompassed the tulips; dark hair, iridescent in the sun, tossed about her shoulders, and on one hip she held a small, almost naked baby, browned by this week's heat. She saw us, playfully waved the hose so that the rays of water splashed about us, said, 'Hi!' and then, 'Have a good day,' in a strong Midwest accent, flung down the hose to lie in a coil, dribbling water, and lolled very white thighs indolently up her steps into her house: the door was standing open, to get a bit of air in.

And now he sighed, and still without looking at me, put his arm around my shoulders and we stood there gazing at the pink tulips, sparkling in the sun.

The heat continues. We all know that this week-old summer may at any minute vanish away for another year, and it is as if England breathes in sunlight as if each breath may be the last before blizzards strike. Everywhere bodies sprawl around on the grass of London's parks, acres of naked flesh; along the city streets go girls dressed for Hawaii or the Riviera, with naked shoulders that are flushed dangerously, white legs that seem to blush, and hair spread about to catch every luxurious ray. Jealous hoarders of every golden moment, we—Richard and I, together with the rest of the inhabitants of this chancy island—spend every second out of doors. Every second, that is, that we can; he with his still untold—to me—responsiblities, I with so much work in the office because of Phyllis's pregnancy. Nevertheless, I escape all the time and we sit in Soho Square among the pigeons and office workers and eat Jumbo Sweet and Sour Chinese Special Take Away Snacks, or pizza smelling of olive oil and real tomatoes, and then one or other of us says, 'But I have to go. . .' I cannot remember ever in my whole life feeling my heart go grey as it does when Richard says, 'My love, I have to leave you,' as it does when I have to say, 'Goodbye,' leaving him there alone on the bench.

＊   ＊   ＊

Our summer has vanished. Fitful rain, and everything soaked and green and lush. Richard said today, 'What was the reason you said you couldn't ask me to your place, I forget?' This was said hard and rough. And reluctant. Because of our nomadic, peripatetic life on pavements and in parks, in cafés, restaurants, theatres and pubs, always in public: our real life.

'I could ask my niece to go away for the weekend,' I said, after thought. At this he laughed; and so did I. It sounded so forlorn and ridiculous. But his eyes, resting on me, were critical. *Of me?* I am not sure.

Today, this scene. I had come in late, after supper with Richard. But I brought in take-away Chinese for Kate, because she never eats a proper meal unless I arrange it. She was, as usual, sitting in the corner of the sofa, plugged in and jigging her limbs about. She did not unplug herself as I put the food on plates and brought it in to her. She smelt sour, her face had that grimy look that some old people have when it has become too difficult to keep up maintenance.

She was going to eat, still plugged in, but I as it were waved to her from a farther shore and she hastily, but reluctantly, took the wires away from her ears. Then she fell on the food.

'Kate,' I said, 'I want you away from this flat this weekend.'

It was as if I had slapped her, and very hard. Her mouth, with food in it, fell open, and tears sprang from her eyes. Genuine tears. She was stammering with shock.

'But . . . but . . .'

'Kate . . .' I said, 'you must see that . . .' But she was incapable of seeing anything of the kind; it was as if I had said to a child of three: You must be out of your home this weekend. Incomprehension. Then frantic rejection.

'Why? Why?' she wailed. 'What have I done?'

'You haven't done anything, Kate! Surely it isn't odd that I should sometimes want my own home for the weekend?'

'Who are you having here?' she demanded. Now she was sullen and scarlet with anger. I was amazed. I was sitting there opposite her, trying to make sense of it all. Surely she didn't think . . . hadn't imagined . . . didn't believe . . .

'Well, I wouldn't be in the way,' she expostulated, indignant now; and the idiocy of it all made me lay down the law:

'Look, Kate. For this weekend. Saturday and Sunday. Surely you can go home for two days?'

She stared at me. I stared at her. What defeated me was the sheer lunatic impossibility of it all!

'How can I go home?' she wailed, turning it on, or so it sounded, so that I was even, for a moment, encouraged: I find that when she is play-acting in a rehearsed scene, is genuinely sullen, I am pleased. Anything that has an origin in energy, drive, self-assertion.

'I really cannot see why not,' I said. Then I saw her face change: excitement was there, a soft pleasure.

'I'll stay with Jill,' she announced. And far from having been insulted and injured, she was all expectation, and she sat there chatting away about Jill's flat and her boyfriend and how Jill and she had done this and that together at home.

I said to Jill today in the office, 'Would you mind having Kate for two days, this weekend?'

And now I saw that this was what she had really been afraid of all the time, for she was stricken, afraid—trapped. I saw her scrabble for a cigarette, saw her fingers shake. Where was my self-possessed and efficient Jill? An injured, threatened young thing, all pleading eyes and anxiety, sat there staring at me.

'There is something out of proportion, *ridiculous* about this whole thing,' I said. 'What am I asking? That you take your sister for two days—one night! She won't go home!'

'Jane! If you can't see—'

'She's bound to come to your flat some time. You can't forbid her to!'

'Once she's in, she'll never leave.'

'Jill, don't be so feeble. Where is Mark going to be then?'

'He certainly won't be there when Kate is.'

'Has he met her?'

'No, but I'll make sure he doesn't.'

'That's silly.'

A long silence. She sat hunched, puffing out smoke, rubbing her cigarette into the tray, then picking it up, looking at it abstractedly, throwing it down, lighting another, puffing away, until she was in a haze of blue smoke.

'You are not saying, I hope, that you are afraid you'll lose Mark because of Kate!'

She thought. 'No. Well, perhaps I am. Why should he put up with her?'

'Families,' I said, 'families.'

'Look at you and your sister. Jane and Georgina! You've always hated each other.'

'Nonsense,' I said briskly. But was struck: did I hate Sister Georgie? 'She may hate me,' I said.

'Obviously, you've hated each other's guts all your lives. You've both been reacting against each other, *off* each other, in everything.'

'Well, Jill, I don't want to spoil family mythology, but if Georgie has been obsessed with me, then I have not been with her. She may have spent her life talking about her awful sister, but I can assure you there have been years when I have scarcely thought of her at all.'

'Happy years,' said Jill.

'She hasn't been all that important to me.'

'Then why don't you simply send Kate *home*?' she demanded fiercely.

'I didn't send you home.'

She did take thought a little at that, looked conscious, made a little negative movement of her head, as if to say, I'm sorry. But she was too possessed by her fear.

'All my life I've been scared of one thing, that I would be landed with Kate for some reason. You say, *your sister*—but I didn't choose her.'

'Jill,' I said, 'for two days. That's all. I'll come and pick her up from your place on Sunday evening.'

'All this is because of that man. A weekend's love-in. Why don't you go to a sex hotel?'

I don't know how to write down what I felt at that. To say

I felt attacked . . . She might have hit me, thrown a sack of garbage at me . . . filth could have spewed from her mouth. I sat there, sick and dizzy.

'Oh God, Janna, Jane, I am sorry, I didn't mean it. Oh, how could I have? Oh, oh, what shall I do?' She was up, striding about the office, her hands clenched at her cheeks, staring at me, beating her clenched fists up and down in front of her as if hitting something in the air with them, invisible to me. Tears were shaking off her face and splattering about, she was ill with remorse and pain. And so was I.

'Oh, Jane,' she cried. 'Of course I'll have her. Of course. I'm sorry.'

And so, the weekend that caused so much emotion before it even started, is gone. Kate is in bed, after a bath and a good feed.

I am sitting in my bedroom which has until now seemed so comfortable and right for me, my setting, my home even; at odds with it. I look up out of my large window at the theatrical London sky, purple and mauve, hazy with reflected light, a sky that is never dark because of London lying there beneath it, throwing up its image to dazzle off cloud or dark. I have my diary here in front of me and I am writing in it, and it is as if there is no substance in me, I am empty, something has been taken away. But it is not sensible for me to feel like this . . .

I shall put off writing this until tomorrow.

Perhaps I'll have a bath. I hate bathing after Kate, it is as if her grime has got into the pores of the enamel, as if her stale odours are mingled with bath salts and the smells of warm dry towels. I shall get into bed and think of my love Richard with whom, it seems, I will never share a bed. A thousand swords lie between us.

On Saturday morning I wrestled Kate out of bed. Literally: she was curled up head to knees, her muscles clenched against me. By then I was feeling so awful about it all I nearly left her there, meaning to intercept Richard and say it was off. But if to go forward was clumsy, riding rough-shod over not only Kate and Jill, but me, too; then to retreat was absurd. I made her get up, did everything but actually put her clothes on her, put into her hands a cup of hot chocolate and a croissant, and then gave her money and a map of how to get to Jill's. Full of sullen and revengeful anger, she left, slowly. I saw her on the street staring up at my windows. My heart hurt me. And what of it? I am now expert in this world of the heart, that recalcitrant, obstinate, self-determining organ. For Kate my heart reacts with a dull grief, like hopelessness. Jill: a warm glow, probably a variety of selfishness, because of my part in helping her on. Richard? It is not a question of an organ situated in the middle of my chest: I think of him and I feel a smile on my face, and my feet begin to tap as if I want to dance.

I begin to see that dull pain which is what that sad bundle Kate demands of me as a symptom of inadequacy: mine.

I rang Jill to say that Kate was on her way. Mark answered. He sounded pleasant, but abstracted. They were laying the carpet in the bathroom, he said.

I then started on the business of tidying this flat. Mrs Brown comes as usual twice a week, but there is an unspoken agreement that she will not clear up after Kate. I did as well as I could, and shopped for a meal. A good one. What a long time since I used this—after all—not inconsiderable talent of mine. When I think of those little dinner parties Freddie and I used to give: well, perhaps I won't think about them. The fact is, for both of us, what was enjoyable was the doing of it, the perfection of it all, and probably the guests were only the setting for this presentation of ourselves. Do I want to think on these lines? No, I definitely do not; but it seems as if every day what I had with Freddie is being rubbed out, made to seem nothing at all. That it wasn't what it ought to have been—yes, I know that. But—so little? This business of dreaming of Freddie: night after night, he is the landscape I walk into, and yet between me and him are always barriers. Or *I* am the barrier, as if my substance, what I am, is inimicable to him, to what I see but cannot touch. Mists come down between us, or he walks away as I approach, or I stand close to him, looking in hope and longing at his dear face, but he is not smiling, and I cannot move from where I am, and even my hands, which I would like to stretch out to him, are too heavy to lift. When we make love it is full of regret, pain: he is going away, or I am.

When the rooms were all tidy, I had a bath, not one of 'my' baths lasting hours which are so rare now, but a bath for effect. I stood in front of a mirror in my Janet Reger knickers and let the silk of the petticoat slide over my head, ivory with coffee lace, and I felt soiled and vulgar, and wished very much that I was to look forward only to a weekend with Richard at large in London.

We met at the Indian restaurant down the road. For the first time. They greeted me as I came in, and we chatted: Richard has not before come into my territory, and I saw him watching something new to him: me in my setting. Mr Lal asked for Jill, who has eaten here with me often, then after Kate—in a different tone of voice, which did not make judgement.

Saturday lunchtime: the place agreeably full. You can eat well enough, reasonably. Richard was subdued. So was I. Our chemistries were working against us, and even the food seemed dull. Richard sat opposite me, his back to the room, but he turned his head to see who came in, or to watch a couple at the next table: two young men, who had come back from a trip down through Africa in a Land Rover. Many adventures, including being arrested by some army some-where as spies. They were brown, very fit, full of energy, already planning another trip: probably through India. This was discussed with the waiter, who was interested. Also, behind his courtesy, amused I think. Envious? Angry? Here were these two young princes, able to take off across continents: how about the desert in Australia?—No? You don't fancy the Aussies? Then why not South America?—Too many wars and revolutions? Then why not India!

Richard was sitting with his arm hooked over the back of his chair, listening: he had not finished his food. Everything about his pose said he was not comfortable in this, my restaurant, and was waiting to be able to go. And yet we have been, it seems, in a hundred restaurants and never have we wanted the hours to pass.

Outside, the cinema was showing *Les Enfants du Paradis,* and I said, 'I've seen it six times at least.' 'Like everybody,' he said, and we stood thinking, Is this what we want? Very privately thinking, If this weekend had been going right, then *Les Enfants du Paradis* would have been a miraculous juxtaposition, a bonus from the Gods, but as things were . . . yet it was raining, more like the cold rains of winter than a summer rain, and it seemed that not to go in was churlish.

We sat well apart, and it was not future partings I was mourning for, in the film, but now, in this little cinema, my favourite, where I've sat so often nearly always alone, in an intense secret pleasure, like eating chocolates by yourself knowing you shouldn't. But not this afternoon. I could not feel Richard as I do usually, like an electric extension of myself, for there was a heaviness there. And when the lovers were caught in the crowds, at the end, and he tried to reach his lost love, the people jigged and swirled all around him so that he could not move, then could not even see her, and she went away, for ever—then what I felt was, *So what? That's how it always is.*

It was then eight o'clock, and a wet, chilly, gusty evening approached. We went into the pub, my local, but it is not a very nice pub, or was not that evening, and Richard was fidgeting with his glass, and sitting as he had in the restaurant, arm hooked over his chair back, half turned away, as if he had already left the place.

We stayed there a couple of hours though because neither of us in fact wanted to come here. But then we did. The evening was fine, but windy. The trees along the pavement were being tugged and pushed every way by a gusty wind that seemed to have blown off some icefield. The wind was from the north-west, and I imagined a black ocean like a field of icebergs over which our wind was blowing, for beyond them up in the Arctic of course it is their summer, or will be shortly, the tundra is putting out bright brief flowers and clouds of mosquitoes, and the little lakes and streams have ice-cold water under a hot blue sky. It will be June very soon.

We came slowly here, and up the stairs to this third floor, and as I opened the door he took a step in and stood there, as if he had come to do just that—have a swift, thorough look around, and then leave. I saw the room through his eyes: large, low-ceilinged, with beige walls, vast expanse of floor, parquet, with the good rugs—Freddie knew all about buying rugs from Persia and from India and from Bokhara and from far Cathay—among which floated my pale grey sofa, and a couple of lemon-yellow chairs and a red one: I utterly loathed this room, from the plants all along the far wall, captured from the jungles of South America, to the enormous crystal ball hanging in a window which sends little rainbows spinning about over everything if you touch it.

Saying not a word, but with a tight, enduring look to his shoulders, my handsome beau went to the sofa, stood looking down at the grubby depression that was Kate's natural home, and sat down beside it.

I went into the kitchen, wishing I was dead, and arranged a tray with drinks. Which I brought in and put on the long glass table between us. For I could not sit near him.

And still he had not said a word, nor looked at me.

I imagined him taking out the little photograph and laying it gravely on the glass of the table, and then raising his eyes to say: What? But he said nothing, only shook his head, discouraged, and leaned back, legs crossed, head lowered rather, looking past me at a rug or something.

I said, 'This is the most dreadful mistake.'

He shrugged. 'Yes, but why should it be?'

'That's the point.'

We drank a little, Scotch, and more Scotch, and the ice made little oily patterns in his glass.

'I've bought food,' I said at last.

He said, grim, 'It's as well to be sure you can cook.'

And then we were able to laugh, at last. He patted the sofa beside him, realized it was where Kate had left her ineradicable deposits, patted the other side. I sat by him, and we held hands.

'What an accomplished lady you are,' he judged me. 'I suppose I should have expected no less. Your clothes—never have I seen a hair out of place.'

'It's my job.'

'Of course.'

Our two hands, tightly clasped, were like allies against everything else around them, including us, who sat feeling our distance.

'Have we imagined all this, Janna?' he asked, grave, anxious. 'Have we made it all up?'

'It seems so at the moment,' I said, and our two hands tightened in protest, and said no, nonsense.

'Do you think so?' he inquired.

'No, I don't.'

'We have not been alone before,' he said.

'Haven't we?'

A silence.

'Why don't I get the food?'

'You have of course prepared a meal that will give the maximum of pleasure with the minimum of trouble.'

I had to laugh, though I knew well enough this was some ultimate complaint he was making. Against me?

'Well, I shall enjoy it. I like food. As you may have noticed.'

In the kitchen I did this and that, wondering what he was doing, but did not want to look. I heard him, though, and went out, leaving my pots and pans a-bubble, and saw him in the door to my bedroom, leaning there, taking his time. I went to stand by him; again I saw through his eyes: a square, not very large room, all softly gleaming ivory, with sunny yellow Casa Pupo rug and soft yellow curtains. My bed is quite large, with an ornamental brass head to it, and with a Portuguese cover in white. On it a couple of bright cushions. My bedroom, all white and yellow. Little furniture: a chest of drawers, a bookcase. And of course this desk where lies this diary, and against the wall, reference books. Also, copies of my novels.

'But where are *you* in all this?' he demanded at last, in protest at it all, and left the door to go to the desk. He took my *The Milliners of Marylebone* first, and then *Gracious Lady,* and leafed through them.

'The first thing you said to me was—do you remember?'

'I write romantic novels, yes. Or I *did.*'

'Have you stopped?'

'I wanted to write a serious novel. But I couldn't.'

'What about?'

'The ward maids in a big London hospital. You know—or perhaps you don't, why should you? They come from everywhere, Jamaica perhaps, or refugees from Vietnam, or Portugal. They send home everything they earn, and work— they are very poor. They bring up children, maintain husbands, and . . . well, I tried to write about them but couldn't. Reality is clearly too much for me.'

'So you are a romantic novelist.'

'So it would seem.'

'Are you going to write another?'

'Perhaps I will.'

'Perhaps you will write a romantic novel about us?'

At this I felt as I had when Jill said what she did, and I could not answer. But he was not cut to the heart by remorse, as she had been. He stood by my desk, this one, he stood there, just behind where I sit now writing this, and he had his hand on the desk and was looking around the room, again and again, as if he simply could not come to terms with any of it. He picked up *The Milliners of Marylebone* and stood reading it for a while. Then he put it down, without saying anything. He went to the window at last, and with his back to me stared up at the sky. The light was concentrated in the white clouds that were being ripped and hustled and rolled across a mauve silk sky by the same chilly north-west wind of earlier. I went to stand by him, and heard him say, 'Well, I can't see you in this home of yours, but I can in that sky.'

I felt grateful and put my arm in his and we stood side by side, our backs to the room—and the bed—and watched how the light flared up on the clouds and began to dim. The smells from the kitchen summoned me and I ran to move a saucepan off the flame, just in time.

We ate in the kitchen, for which he said he was grateful, making a joke of it. I asked him, 'What is your home like?'

'Very nice. Being American middle-class. Suburban. And before you ask, our home here, in London, is currently rented to someone else.

'You aren't living in it?'

A long silence.

'Janna, look how wrong things go when we do this! Do we have to?'

'No, we don't.'

'And *of course* you are a perfect cook.'

When we went back to the living room we were restless, did not sit down for a time, then did; but got up, and went strolling about, he to examine my—I nearly said *our*, since Freddie bought it—Picasso lithograph, and set of flower prints. Very nice, they are; but then, so is my living room, this whole flat. I offered him a drink. We both had another Scotch, and then it was eleven o'clock and both of us knew it was all impossible.

We were stricken, shocked, shaken, but it would not have been possible for us to go into our bedroom, take our clothes off and make love. I was thinking wildly, If all the lights were switched off, what then? A thought which utterly amazed me, so foreign was it to me.

And he said, just as I thought it, 'If all the lights were off, Janna—but then, who would we be making love with, I wonder?' And he was looking at me from an unfriendly distance, and even laughing, a most masculine laugh I judged it, full of irony—and finality. Yet I felt my spirits lift as I heard it, for there was a sanity there which had been missing.

Then he said, 'I'm going. I shouldn't have come.'

'Yes, you must,' and I couldn't wait for him to leave.

'I've taken your telephone number, and so we are one step nearer to—' He left it unfinished. I went to the door with him. He went out quickly, with a small, baffled, impatient shake of his head, and a smile that said, It's not you, it's both of us. What he said was, 'Shall I ring you here or at your office? No, better the office—' And he went.

I stood at the window to see him go, and thought that Kate

was lurking there, on the pavement, gazing up. But it was dark outside the pool of lamplight, and then I believed I was imagining it.

As for me, his going was a load off me; literally, I felt myself expand and breathe again and want to move about and do things. So I did—tidied, cleared up, put on the radio and danced a little by myself, which I do very often, coming back from Richard. But last evening, it was sheer relief. Yet of course I could have wept, too. Not so much for 'the night of love' which had been presenting itself to us so unpleasantly, like something on an agenda, provided for by circumstances and by careful planning—was *that* the rub?—but because we had both been in such disarray that we were forgoing the treat of a whole day together, today, which we were to have spent free of all other ties.

It goes without saying that I dreamed of Freddie, my lost love. Who was never my love. Or I don't think he was. It is strange what a bad memory I have for the things that matter. I can remember exactly what I wore and what he wore, where we were: we were married in Kensington Registry Office and Freddie's parents and my parents gave a reception at the Savoy. My parents could not have afforded it by themselves. Joyce was my matron of honour. We never saw Freddie's best man, or I don't think we did, after the wedding. We were all jolly. I looked, I had no doubt, very pretty: after all, I was very pretty. But what was I feeling? I have no idea at all. The honeymoon, motoring in the Dordogne, is a mystery to me. I remember lovely scenery, wonderful food. I am sure we had wonderful sex, because we did. What did I feel? As for what he felt, I am sure I didn't give that a thought. Did I ever ask myself what Freddie felt about anything, until after he was dead? And yet, what a credit I was all round! I do remember strolling back into the office, after the honeymoon, and the satisfaction of it, as after a job properly done! I've done that, done it well, everything is as it should be!

This morning I woke very early, grieving, I shouldn't wonder, and lay in bed and examined my pretty room, this simple, pretty room. What is wrong with it? Nothing! I love it. I feel myself in it. But Richard says he can't see me in it and has to look out of the window at the elements, at nature! What a joke! Surely that says everything about him; nothing about me.

This morning was fine. I walked down to the supermarket and bought food for the next few days, thinking of Kate's needs. I put everything away, and the telephone rang. No, it was not Richard, but a neighbour of Annie Reeve's saying that her Home Help was ill, and the woman upstairs was away, and would I go and see her.

It is not that I haven't been visiting Annie. I continue to drop in, rain or shine, two or three times a week, I take her flowers, a cake, I sit with her an hour. But this is something I do, like—I was going to say—cleaning my teeth. With Richard here, three or four times recently I've said I would go and then didn't. This afternoon I bought dwarf tulips at the corner, pink, with some gypsophila, because she likes the small and the pretty. And then, instead of walking on up the street till I reached this one, 'my' street, I turned a corner, and then another, and was in Annie's street, and as I went in at her door entered the world I once hardly knew existed, that of the poor, the old, the sick; and those people who minister to them, social workers, Home Helps, Good Neighbours, Church Visitors; a world so different from mine, which is populated with those who keep themselves successfully balanced on life, people who do not expect (for it is something which happens to others) to trip, fall over, and find themselves incapacitated in a bedsitting room some-where, being kept going by visits, food brought in, moral support; a world which few of us, ever, want to think about until we have to. If I decided to abandon Annie, and stopped turning that corner, and then the next, into her street, I would walk past that submerged struggling place in which millions live and soon forget it exists.

And in fact during the last fortnight, when I haven't been in to Annie at all because of Richard, I've thought, Oh, well, there's that Irishwoman upstairs, and, Never mind, the Home Help will ... And I've caught myself thinking, But really I need never go back, no one would blame me, probably not even Annie, who has seen so many people flit into her life, all smiles, and then vanish for ever, as Home Helps and Good Neighbours and social workers come and go, and she'll probably only mutter fiercely, She's got better things to do with herself, oh, you can't tell *me*.

'Where is Janet?' she might complain, of some Home Help who has been in every day for months, and then not come. 'Oh, Janet Collins, you mean? She's been moved to Geriatrics in Paddington, didn't she tell you?'

I have even managed to forget that it is those who visit the old and the cantankerous often and regularly who get shouted at and abused: when I see Annie nearly every day I am treated as if I am her enemy. But, dropping in after a week, I am greeted with smiles, even formality, for she has been afraid I may never come again. In fact I can judge the degree of intimacy I have achieved with Annie by how much she grumbles, accuses, rages.

Today, appearing in her door, which I always open with the key that is beside mine on my key-ring, as noisily as possible so that she will not be startled by me, I was ready for reproaches and bitterness. She leaned forward out of her chair, for her sight is failing, and examined me with screwed-up eyes. 'Who's it this time?' she demanded; and then seeing my contrite posy, my placatory smiles, she said, 'Oh, it's you,' and sighed with relief of it—and the bad temper which would have unleashed on me had I been in during the last two or three days was set aside. 'Oh, what a stranger,' she remarked graciously, and became a sweet old thing. Not the real Annie, someone we glimpse rarely enough if we have ever seen her at all, but someone who has excised all sorts of memories, behaviour, experiences, so as to present to all these respectable mentors of hers a bland and jolly personage who can be blamed for nothing, a dear old lady.

I made us both tea. I set out cakes. I put the flowers in a jam jar. I sat on the little stool near the blocked-in fireplace. I waited, tensed, for her to say, 'Been busy, have you?' in a hard, sour voice.

But I could see from her face how afraid she had been I would not come again. 'How long is it since you were here?' she inquires cautiously, for really she cannot remember.

'Two weeks,' I said. 'No, two weeks and a day.' For I always give her exact information, hoping to arrest the slow muddling of her mind.

'And I've been sitting here,' she began, and stopped herself, checking, with a physical effort I could see in her restless movements and a swerve of her distressed eyes away from me, the impulse to let herself go into anger.

'It has seemed a long time,' she said meekly, but her voice was cold.

It is crazy, but now I am the person whom Annie has known longest. I've been her friend now for five years, more. For five years she has sat in a chair, in one room, moving less and less, while I've rushed around London, travelled to and from the office every day, been to a thousand Lunches and Dinners for *Lilith*, been to dress shows in Kyoto, and Madrid, Barcelona and Amsterdam, most of the cities in Europe in fact; jaunted off to Somerset and Dorset with Jill, taken myself to Iceland because the place, let alone its fashion, interests me. I have spent hundreds of enjoyable hours by myself in and around London, my great bazaar, my lucky dip, my private theatre. Recently I have been in love—I do not see what other word I can use—unsuitably and ridiculously; and have walked back and forth and around and across London with my blood fizzing in my veins like champagne. Meanwhile, old Annie has been sitting in this chair.

I saw today that she was troubled, wanted to find out something, was trying to come around to a subject sideways.

It is her memory: she can remember less and less. She does not like to confess how the map of her past is blurring and shifting. Her recent past, that is. Her memory is in fact the opposite of mine. What she was at ten years old, eighteen, thirty, forty—it is all there. What she felt, wanted, got, or didn't get; her clothes, her food, her boyfriends, her dead husband; every detail of it all, it's there. But she doesn't know if the Home Help came in yesterday or not. She talked on and on about the Home Help while I sat there, drinking tea, and thinking how my memory is like a busy broad and populated road just behind me, but then, quite soon, it begins to narrow and dwindle, and by the time I get to my twenties it is patchy, and then it becomes a little patch and often vanishes for months or even years at a stretch, except for strongly illuminated childhood scenes, mostly to do with my sister Georgie.

The Home Help . . . on and on about the Home Help, Maureen. The trouble is, Annie grumbles; she is a grumbler; when she starts, one has to switch off. And so I listened with half an ear, and yet I encountered Maureen before, with old Eliza, and I know she is a crook. Annie says that Maureen has not been in, not for three days now: true or false? There is no way of finding out. Maureen only stays fifteen minutes instead of the hour and a half she is paid to stay. True? Very likely. Maureen said she would bring in this or that but hasn't, and now Annie has nothing to eat.

I cannot abandon Annie, no matter how much I would like to.

Do I love Annie? I am fond of her. Is that all, after five years or so? Well, I would very much like to know the real Annie, who I believe to be there somewhere, but I never will.

I sat on, and I made some more tea, and sat on again, and then listened to what I call Gramophone Record Number 3, which is how she went to the policemen's ball wearing the black lace dress with the red rose on it, and she drew all eyes (and probably really did, for she was lovely when she was young, a photograph avers that she was), and danced every dance. She was paying for the dress on the never-never in a dress shop in Wardour Street. She knows I have heard this often, but her need to talk is so great she has to pretend that I haven't: as she talks, she stops herself to say, I think I told you?—and as I shake my head, No, she smiles a little sour smile that refuses to be grateful but insists on its rights. She wore this afternoon a rather nice viyella skirt I ran up for her, in dark red, on elastic because of her ever-expanding girth, and over it a dirty cotton housecoat, because she can't find anything to wear 'because of the Home Help'.

I looked, saw that indeed all her clothes are dirty; that there was almost nothing to eat. I went out to buy her the necessities. When I do this she always says, over and over again, 'Oh, you shouldn't, don't bother, there's no need for it . . . don't forget the cigarettes.'

By the time I had done everything, emptied the commode, rinsed out a pair of knickers, made her some jelly, she had talked herself out and sat quietly, watching me.

'Don't forget poor Annie,' she said as I left.

When I was on the stairs here I heard the telephone and wondered if I had missed Richard. I had not been in five minutes before Kate rang at the door. It seems she has lost the key. She went to the sofa and slumped on it, repossessing her own.

'How are Jill and Mark?' I asked.

'I don't know.' This was smug, even vindictive, and I said, 'Very well, you didn't go there. Did you go home?'

'No.'

I decided I was not going to ask, but would wait for her to tell me, and she decided to match me: she plugged herself into her machine and was engulfed by sound.

The telephone rang: it was Jill, who had been ringing me all day, she said. Kate had arrived last night, been admitted by Mark, who had asked her to make herself at home, 'Quite nicely,' Jill thought. But he went back to laying the carpet, and when he returned to the living room, Kate had gone.

Jill was beside herself with anger. Many years of it hissed there, concentrated in her shrill breathless voice. '*Get* her on the phone,' she commanded.

'It's for you,' I said to Kate, and Kate went to the instrument, and held the receiver up, not detaching herself from the wires. Through God knows what din came Jill's vituperations, and Kate listened, saying once in a low voice, because she did not want to disturb the glories of what she was listening to, 'I was in a squat, that's all.' Quite soon she put down the telephone and went back to her place.

I made her supper, demanded that she should unplug herself.

I said to her, 'Was that you on the pavement down there last night?'

She nodded, eyes down.

'I saw him leave,' she remarked. It was not a question, I think. Just another manifestation of the adult world which she will never—I am sure she is sure—understand.

'This squat, what is it?'

'Oh, just a squat.'

'There are squats and squats. I've done a whole series of articles on them. I might even know it.'

'I've only been in one,' she triumphed with an ugly little jeer. As if I were a competitor for squats.

As usual, I had to remind myself that the child is crazy, or not far off it.

'They are decent people,' she cried, sounding like my sister, my brother-in-law, who will diagnose people as decent or not, in which first category they will benefit from Georgina's and Tom's sincere regard. 'I know you wouldn't think so,' said Kate, stuffing in all that was left of the stew from last night, and mopping it up with chunks of French bread.

'You mean, they treat you well, unlike me, your sister, and your parents?'

'They judge people for what they *are*,' she insisted piously, eyeing me in a putting-down way that she had learned over the weekend.

'I'm glad to hear it, but who are *they* who have such perfect and instant judgement?'

'He recognized me from when I came, you know, to Paddington, when I came up to stay with you. I went to Paddington to go home, but he saw me and said Hi. I said Hi. He said, What are you doing here? . . .'

'You said, My aunt has thrown me out, my sister Jill showed me the door, and now I have to go home to my horrible cruel parents.'

That this was exactly what she had said was acknowledged by a shrill, frightened little laugh, which was nevertheless exultant.

'So I went with him to his squat. They are ever so kind.'

'Well, now you are home again with your wicked aunt and you have eaten up everything'—for of course she had not noticed that she had put all the stew on to her plate, and all the vegetables, so that there was literally none for me— 'how about a bath?'

At which she stood up, a tragedy queen, and laughed theatrically. 'I said to them, I said, the first thing she'll say is, Go and have a bath. That's what they are *like,* I said.'

'It is very simple, Kate. You smell horrible and I'm not going to put up with it.'

This hurt her. I had not expected it to reach her at all: if she did not even notice that she ate all the food on a table which had two people at it, why hear what I said about a bath? I gave up. I handed her a vast fluffy towel, put bath salts into the water, and she got into it gratefully. I picked up all the clothes on the bathroom floor for the launderette. I put her pyjamas on the warming rail. I made her a cup of chocolate before she slept, which she did at once, like an infant. Then I rang Jill.

'What happened?' we asked together.

'I think we will never know,' I said. 'I do know she was standing outside this building at eleven last night.'

'Perhaps she was not in a squat at all,' said Jill.

'You mean, a squat is some beautiful and unachievable dream?'

'You sound stricken by the thought, are you?'

'Yes, I think I am. She probably spent all night wandering about.'

'She could have been here. Mark made up the sofa for her.'

'But in her mind had been a dream of some amazing welcome, Sister Jill all smiles and kisses.'

'I don't know and I don't care. At least I hope you had a nice weekend?'

'Well,' I said, 'you could put it like that.'

And then Jill said, not at all putting the knife in, but in her parents' manner, diagnosis and judgement, 'The thing about you, Jane, reality isn't your strong point.'

'It isn't? Are you sure?' I heard my voice come anxious, as if she had said, You must realize that the prognosis is not very good.

'Oh, Jane, dear Jane,' breathed Jill, all remorse again, though I didn't need that this time.

And so here I sit, and it is midnight, and my heart is full of woe. I know one thing, that things won't be the same with Richard after this weekend, and after the little photograph.

I have been watching Jill. If Phyllis had not been off having her baby, I would be with Charlie in Editorial, not sitting opposite Jill, looking—or so I believe—at my past.

She works quickly and well, with concentration, at a desk spread about with a hundred tasks, while the telephone rings, people come in and out from the other departments with queries. They go to her, not to me. She has been working here three, nearly four years, knows as much as I do, or as Phyllis does. She defers to me, asks advice, takes it: but I know, if she does not, that if I were not here, if Charlie were not, she would manage.

Responsibilities, tasks, decisions, pile up all around her, and the surface of her desk begins to look like battlements behind which she operates, always alert and moving, like a brigand or guerrilla fighter expecting ambush. Her appearance relates not at all to the detailed complexities of her working life. She, like me all those years ago, is not ready for a personal style, but presents herself differently every day, even sometimes like a competent office worker with clothes subdued to her calling.

Today there was a crisis over an article that got itself mislaid and people came running in and out, telephone calls, exclamations of despair, exasperation, petulance. Through all this a handsome young bandit sat swashbuckling, swivelling about on her high stool, legs set apart in black highwayman's boots, striped cotton full trousers tucked into them, a black cotton jacket tied at the throat and held by a wide shiny black belt, dark hair a mass of little curls, kept off her brow by a yellow bandanna. She looked extremely pretty. Mark has been making excuses to come in and see her, to look at this girl of his, a nut-brown maid equipped for a life of piracy, his superior in the office while Phyllis is away. He brings in batches of his photographs, and stands very close while she bends over them. He is large, amiable, comfortable, whose style with girls is to be elder-brotherly; he has a hand on the back of her chair, and as she pores over his work so that he is forgotten, he runs a tender forefinger down where one might suppose her backbone is under the black envelope. She slightly tenses, then frowns, then looks up smiling, but it is a protest. She had decided to smile. It is because they have had a spat, I know: he complains that in the office she 'puts him down'. 'But we met in the office,' she said, threatened and breathless, reminding him with a quick smile of their long courtship, which was shared in (like Charlie's and Phyllis's baby) by everyone. What he is saying is that now he is her 'flatmate' her manner to him should not be so offhand. She does not like this; but thinks it over; wonders why, if he fell in love with her 'offhand' he now wants her different. But feeling the tender finger, she remembers their arguments, decides to smile, and does so, but there is an edge to it, and he moves away, to stand against the wall, and light a cigarette, while she gives him a smile which is not so much remorseful as an allowance of what is due.

And I look at two people who are like characters out of different plays: the elegant young bandit, concentrating over her decisions, sliding photographs behind each other, having given each its exact amount of attention, the large and amiable young man, standing against the wall. Then suddenly the June sun floods in, dimming Jill's colours, and illuminating the clouds of cigarette smoke he stands in; swirls of hazy blue lie around him and cling to his shaggy dark hair and loose dark shirt, which is like a moujik's tunic.

What am I waiting for, I realize, is the moment when, as he leaves, she relents, acknowledges this flatmate of hers with a glance or, as he takes the photographs, a touch. But she says, 'I think these two, here . . .' And it is only when he has gone out that she casts over her shoulder a single, remorseful look that says, 'If you were still in the room I'd give you—' but what? A kiss?

While they were manoeuvring towards love—a word which I suppose they do use—you might come on them as they separated from an embrace, or hear a laugh from behind a door, but now all that is relegated to their other life. I can hear, and so can he of course, her thought: One should keep things in their proper place!

I have not heard from Richard. It is almost a week. Well, I have been working hard. I have been spending evenings with Kate, trying to—what? What *do* I expect? I realize that I expect to have a beneficial effect on her! Suddenly this deplorable waif will sit up, unplug herself, shake off the crumbs and the dust, the grubby rags she wears will put on shape and decision, and she will actually hear what I say. 'Of course, Jane,' she will reply. 'I'll enrol tomorrow, I'll get some qualification, I'll take myself in hand, you will find me a job when I'm viable, and then . . .'

Last night when I was ready for bed she had dropped off to sleep on the sofa, the cup of chocolate I had made for her knocked over in the saucer, spilling everywhere, table, carpet, her knees. I had practically to lift her to bed, and this morning she was so dead asleep I left her, curled into a foetus, her back to me and the world, in a small dark room.

Today Richard rang. He said at once, 'Janna, you must not think that I haven't rung because of our—fall from grace.' That was so apt that I was grateful for it, and reconnected in this way with *us*, what we are, I said at once that I didn't . . . though I had.

'I have problems, Janna. No, really. But they are sorted out . . . Will you still be there next week? Early, probably Monday?'

There was such anxiety in this I was grateful for that too, and I laughed and said, 'But where else could I be?'

'Oh, I don't know. You do get around a lot, don't you?'

'I'll be here,' I said.

It is hot, hot, hot; June flames and smoulders. I look up from my bedroom window into lakes of pure blue where perhaps may amble a single white cloud; I stand at the office windows and look over the little hedge of greenery, maintained by Jill and Phyllis, down into the hot streets full of genial sun-worshippers, then up into the dazzle of blue. I ache for Richard. What I want is to be with him. That is all. How can we be wasting our blissful summer like this?

Jill said to me today, since I am not always running out for an hour, or two, or leaving early, 'What's happened to your handsome boyfriend?' And, at my look: 'I saw you two together on a bench in the square. Like two pigeons in spring.' And, as I did not say anything—I was waiting, I know, for her knife-thrust: 'Personable, I would say he was. And you, of course, but you always are.' She sat back on her swivelling chair, and examined me, from across the gulf of thirty years, with as strong a curiosity as I watch her.

Today Jill said to me, 'Do you like Mark?'

This ridiculous question was answered by the quizzical smile I put on my lips, while I went on with my work.

'Well?'

'What actually are you asking?'

'What's so silly about it?'

'Very well, I like him, very much indeed.'

She staged an exasperated sigh. Then: '*Jane!*'

'You're not asking my advice, surely?'

'Well, if I am? Do you think we are well suited, all that kind of thing?'

I said, after some time, for the words that presented themselves all seemed wrong, 'He's a very warm and affectionate man . . .'

Before I could finish she flashed, 'And I am not, is that it? Well, I can tell you, I feel suffocated sometimes. Did you, ever? Sometimes it is as if I want to explode with irritation— just run away.' I said nothing, because my memory tugged, and I was trying to lure that fish back into consciousness, when she said angrily, 'Well, did you feel like that ever?'

'I can't remember . . .'

'It's never being alone. I ask him, I say, tell me truthfully, don't you mind never being alone? He says, I can't say that I do.' She copied his manner, humorous, indulgent, to perfection, and her whole body showed how she had wriggled in irritation out of his embrace.

'Well, perhaps you are too young for it all?'

'*What does that mean?*'

And, suddenly, I was in tears. From out of my depths somewhere welled great surges of woe and loss.

'Jane,' expostulated Jill, shocked at me.

'I know one thing,' I said, between sobs and sighs, 'I look back and think I was the greatest bloody fool . . .'

She was scared: frightened, not at anything I had said, but at my weeping. She went on working, subdued.

Monday. Richard did not ring.

The lovely weather continues. Today I watched this scene.

Jill wore a thin white dress that has a wide scooped-out neck and arm-holes, and a dropped waist from which flounces white broderie anglaise. She sat with her legs apart on her stool-like chair. She is brown with the summer, and really lovely, her hair, still dark and curly, today tied with a white bandanna. She is all delicate thin brown arms and legs, and angles and hollows. And this vision sat there, concentrating on her work while occasionally dabbing at her damp forehead with tissues. Mark came in with two girls from the agency, dressed for the autumn, to illustrate the article Jill was writing: 'You will be wearing the colours of a forest in October . . .' All over her desk photographs of autumn forests, from Vermont as it happened, golden grass, red berries, yellow trees, and so on. The girls, intrepid as is expected of them, were sweating inside tweeds and jerseys, and making jokes about Jill and me wearing cotton. Mark wanted to know if Charlie was expected in because the light was just right in the big room. Charlie is with Phyllis, who has gone into hospital to have her baby. Mark also wanted his Jill to go with him and the girls into the big editorial room, on the pretext that his usual assistant is on holiday, the other one off sick, and—in short, he wanted Jill.

Jill said, 'But Mark, I've got my work to do.'

She was, of course, quite right. But in her tones rang other expostulations, such as: why should *I* be your assistant!

Both the girls had worked with us before, and knew Mark. One, Edna, said, 'Oh, we'll manage, Mark.' She is a striking, dramatic, olive-skinned dark-eyed beauty, whose scarlet sweater succeeded in dimming our wilting pastels, the kind of girl whom you have to look at, like an actress projecting herself. Mark put his arm around her, as he stood gazing, baffled rather than hurt, at his love Jill. This was not designed to gain advantages. Mark is too generous in his instincts to bargain or manoeuvre; just as he had not said, though I know Jill had been expecting him to, I've been taking orders from you, this last week.

Edna, who cannot help playing up to any situation she is in, was acting the part of a flattered preening beauty inside Mark's arm, and the other girl, Sally, was laughing with me. The three of them, Mark, Edna, Sally, seemed self-contained there, the indulgent, easy man, and the two girls whom he was about to photograph, they being obedient to his spoken and unspoken wishes; they were laughing, expansive, enjoying it—and suddenly Jill, with a little exclamation 'Oh very well . . .' got up, and as she did so the group broke up, and four people, Mark and the three girls, one for summer and two for the months still a good way ahead, went into the editor's room, where they worked all day, Jill frequently emerging to collect cold drinks, tea, beer, for the others. Meanwhile I was working like a donkey: I am doing Charlie's job, and part of Phyllis's. Today I was doing Jill's as well, and I called June from the pool to help me.

She is a very nice girl: good-natured, ready to please and to do what is needed. She has to be given an exact and precise task, with explanations, when she will finish it, bringing it to me with the air of a willing servant. She has been with us seven years, and yet has never seemed to want any more than what she has: a decent little job that does not ask much of her. She is a great favourite with the others, something of a clown or a comic, and with me was entertaining about minor events in the pool, and at the end of a story would wait hopefully for my laugh, her bold jolly blue eyes fixed on my face. She knows everything about her own department, and has no capacity or desire to think of *Lilith* as a whole. Having spent a day with June, I realize what a treasure Jill is, who had grasped everything of importance in *Lilith* within a month and never has had to have anything explained to her. Yet June is not stupid! It is a mystery to me, this business of capacity, people's innateness. It is more of a mystery now that I spend so much time with poor Kate. How is it possible that these two girls emerged from the same family, the same influences, the same everything! Kate lives in a dazzle of confusion. She has a great gaping pit or hole somewhere in the region of her solar plexus, all need and craving, and nothing, or so I begin to fear, will ever fill it.

Today Richard rang, said could I meet him at twelve in Soho Square. I was sitting there in a riot of joy, pulses hammering, my whole body ready to take off, but I said, 'I can't, we are so short-staffed . . .' But Jill was leaning forward hissing, 'Go on, Jane, don't be so silly,' I covered the mouthpiece and said, 'Jill, but how can I?' And heard my voice a plea that she would say it was all right. 'Of course you must go,' she said. And I said to Richard, 'Yes, it's all right. . .'

As I walked into Soho Square, he was standing over some begonias, turned away from me, and his look up as I approached was wary, then he was delighted, straightened, put his hands on my arms, looked smiling down at me, and at once the miracle started, the reckless, delicious delight, but he said, 'Janna, we must move out quickly . . .' And we ran out of the square, hands linked, while he hissed at me, stage villain, 'I have reason to think we are being followed.'

We ran past 'our' little café, where we have had so many encounters, and in Oxford Street leaped into a taxi. 'Just drive along,' said Richard to the taximan. We fell into each other's arms, and I felt the warm roughness of his cheek, and the heat of his arm coming through the linen of his jacket radiating into my back.

'Janna,' said he, 'I've missed you every minute.'

'And I you.'

And so we sat, close. And the strange thing was that this closeness was warm, intimate, with the friendliness of sensuality. But it was not sexual. This was because we cannot let it be. And I am wondering as I write if, in times when sex was not the first thing people had to think of, some woman (or man for that matter) writing in a diary would have bothered to say, 'But it was not sexual.' Why is it we have made an imperative of sex?

Soon Richard said, 'What would you feel about going up to Richmond on the river boat?' It seemed to me perfect, but of course I had to niggle and object inwardly, because I would not be back in the office at all. But I thought, To hell with it, Jill will cope.

At the pier we were lucky. You'd think all of London would have thought of going up to Richmond that day, but only half had. The queues were long, but we got on a waiting boat, and went forward to sit by a rail on deck. The river seemed full of pleasure, little boats, other river boats, even the river patrol boat seemed to be frivolously darting about, and the heat was weighing the green trees along the banks with a look of summer repletion, and the buildings were on holiday. The sky was faultless, the blue so seldom seen in England, with a couple of negligible clouds to set it off. Balmy breezes and seagulls and the voices of children rushing about below eating potato crisps, completed the scene, and we held hands and were happy.

My head rested against Richard's shoulder, and just above my ear he was humming, 'London, London, London, I love you, how I love you, London, my love.'

About being happy, what is there to be said!

At Richmond we found a pub, and ate quantities of pie and potato salad, and he said, 'There's one thing about you, you never fuss about a diet.'

'But I don't get fat,' said I, and then had to add, 'But on the other hand, I must do, since I'm fatter than . . .' I was going to say, when that photograph was taken, but even a reminder of it seemed dangerous. Yet he took it out of his top pocket, where he must have put it that morning, and that girl lay on the dark green paint of the pub table with shadows from a chestnut tree in full flower sifted over us and her. I knew he had taken it out so promptly, and laid it there so as—so to speak—to defuse it, make her harmless, but I was looking at that slight lovely girl, all angles and hollows, just like Jill, and I said, 'I've got solid.' And he put the photograph back in his pocket, and put his brown hand over the pocket with a protective gesture, and smiled. And at that moment his smile faded; and his face, then his body, were wrenched with anxiety. I looked around and saw, walking past the pub, slowly, not looking at us, his daughter, Kathleen. We watched her together, as she went away down into a road full of chestnut trees.

'Why?' I had to ask.

'I have been out of London for over a week, and while I told her—truthfully—what I was doing, she suspects I have been with you.'

'I wish you had.'

Again I could not stop myself having to know and he knew it, and hesitated, then said, 'My mother is very old, nearly ninety. She has been living by herself, and managing. Now she can't. I've found a Home for her. It's not bad, as these places go. She's being allowed some dignity. She'll have her own room. She hates having to go in, but she knows she must.' There was a long silence after this. He answered it with: 'If she lived with us, things wouldn't be any better, there'd be no one to look after her properly, we both work all day.'

This was more information than I'd had, or wanted; and I felt a resistance in all of me, No, no, don't tell me, *I don't want to know.* He saw it and held out his hand to me, and pulled me up in the same movement as he got to his feet, and we went out of the pub garden into a street and saw, right at the far end of it, Kathleen turning to come back. We went fast in the opposite direction, through the leafy summer gardens of Richmond, full of people in bikinis, summer dresses, shorts; full of dogs and cats and children; and everywhere the trees and flowers of full summer, English summer the vagrant, the delinquent, which when it is with us says, Why do you worry so, this is what summer *is*, aren't I here?—but then vanishes, with a smile. And does not return, perhaps for years. No wonder we talk about the weather, think about it, are obsessed by it. What a theatre it is, what a pageant, what a free show, in lovely England, where one hour is so seldom the same as the one before. But today it was summer all through, hour after hour, and we went slowly, hand in hot hand up into the park, and sauntered about over the thick grass with the deer that once fed commoners and kings, and now are like harem beauties, sheltered in special places and loved for their rarity. We walked and we walked, I as usual in my madly unsuitable Kurt Geiger shoes, but feeling secure in them, my sturdy feet going down strongly over the thick tussocks of grass, my hand held tight by Richard, who was a tawny lion indeed in all that hot yellow light, and we walked clear across the park, and around it, and I don't think we spoke, only smiled, and felt life moving in our linked hands.

By seven in the evening we had walked in a great circle and came back to houses and gardens where people still lolled and played, enjoying our summer, and groups idled about under the trees of the streets. We found another pub and there was a little garden at the back. We were hungry by then, and we ate steaks and salad and apple pie and cream and drank a great deal of red wine. It seemed as if we could not stop smiling, or looking at each other. My eyes were like hands, for I could sense, as I looked at his cheek, how the cool skin was very slightly damp, and his sandy lashes brushed my fingers; and how, under his blue shirt, for he had taken off his jacket, his body was strong and full of vitality. And I could feel his gaze, like a touch, on my face and on my arms. They were bared, though I had wondered if I should, and they satisfied me, because his eyes seemed to be finding pleasure there.

The garden of the pub was crammed full of people, and this made a setting for our solitudes. It was bounded by a tall rose hedge: several kinds of rose grew there, white and red and pink, and the scent was strong. As the dusk came down, the roses became mild blobs against the dark; and then the lights were on, and we went down to the river again and waited for a boat. We sat together on the bench up at the front, and headed downstream between the lights on the banks. It was so warm that we sat with bare arms and his hand was close on the flesh of my shoulder.

As we came off the boat at Westminster, we saw ahead of us in the crowd Kathleen, who must have been on the boat without us knowing, and perhaps even sitting close to us. She might have been following us all day, at a distance, as we wandered through Richmond Park. She did not turn to look at us. We did not walk faster, to catch her; nor slow, to avoid her.

I have by now seen her quite often; yet I feel I do not have a clear picture of her: for surely when she is normally occupied she does not seem powerful or even threatening? Richard felt I was thinking this, for he said softly, 'There is no reason to believe this, but Kathleen is actually a very sensible, very nice person.'

What did that mean? When people say someone is 'sensible' and 'nice' usually there is an implication of reassurance. And this girl still trails us, as far as I can see, whenever she suspects we might be together, and often when we are not. What can she want?

As we walked towards Charing Cross station, I was thinking, Perhaps we ought simply to go after her; say, Kathleen, let us meet!—to put an end to this. But what would not be put an end to is our meeting. Which presumably is what she wants, this sensible and nice spy.

We saw her go down into the underground, and we went on to the Strand and up into Soho where, suddenly, we were engulfed by the sex shops and sex shows, and this was so painful to us in the mood we were in that we almost ran out of it again. 'You keep saying England, England,' I heard myself saying in a hot distressed angry voice, 'but that is England now too.'

'All right, all right,' he said. 'But let's not . . .'

How often, and about how many things, do we now say in words or by implication, *All right, but let's not . . .*

He said as we parted, 'I suppose I can't tempt you away from your office tomorrow as well?'

I knew it was impossible but I could not bear to be final

about it, and I said, 'Ring me—early. I'll do what I can.'

We laid our hot cheeks together, and smiled and parted.

And here I am, sitting in my bedroom, which I like so much and which he says is not me, writing this. Have I caught anything at all of this day we have had, so perfect, even if threatened by that thundercloud Kathleen?

Kate was not here when I got home. I was so relieved: what a burden she is, even when she does nothing, sits silent on my sofa in her world of sound. She seems to weigh down the air, weigh me down. Then, of course, anxiety. Then, a cautious beginning of the thought: Perhaps this means she is getting more self-reliant, grown-up. She came in furtive and pleased with herself. I was not going to ask what she had been doing. She was not going to tell me, though many a triumphant little glance came winging my way.

I keep saying to myself, She is nineteen, an adult. Though what dishonesty, since she is nothing of the kind.

She made herself a sandwich, made herself coffee, she got herself into a bath without being asked. Perhaps she is getting over—whatever is wrong with her.

But I don't care, not tonight. I am sitting here in my white cotton nightgown, and I am looking into the sky, which has light in it even though there are no clouds and nothing to reflect back London's brilliances. Is London ever dark? Is our sky ever without light? I don't think it is.

Wednesday is Editorial conference day, but there were only Jill and me from Editorial to confer. Phyllis is in labour, induced. Jill has been furious all day because of this: it appears my sister does not hold with induced labour and has fought four successful battles to be permitted to have her babies her own way. The doctors told Charlie that Phyllis was 'too old' and nature could not be trusted. Charlie went along with all this. 'As he *would*,' cried Jill, distressed out of all proportion: how often in Jill do I hear these violent echoes of family battles.

What is evident is that Editorial needs to be rapidly enlarged. I keep going on part-time, and then pressures and

my own interest in it all brings me back. Phyllis is going off
for three months to enjoy motherhood. Jill, while a jewel and
a boon, is still so young, and I know that there are mutters
about nepotism. Today, while working like a madwoman, I
also reviewed everyone in *Lilith* who has a spark, a flair; who
has, as well, ambition. It is extraordinary how few people are
ambitious, how many are content with their lot.

Two interesting points emerged from all this: one was
brought to my attention by Jill, who inquired why, when
talking about possible candidates for rapid advancement, I
talked only about the women? This was a real shock to me. It
is true, I do see *Lilith* as run by women, Charlie notwith-
standing. In my mind I then went carefully through all the
men. There is a very bright, quick, ambitious young man in
Production, Henry. I had to fight against reluctance, though:
which surfaced as, When there are so few jobs for clever
women, why waste even one on a man? Jill was watching me,
not ceasing her work of course, as I wrestled with this one.

'Well?' she inquired at the end, and when I said, 'I'll put it
to him, it wouldn't be fair not to,' she laughed in triumph.
'You said that exactly as mother would.'

Richard rang about ten, and I had to say that it was
impossible to leave the office, even for lunch. Outside the
windows the sun dazzled.

In the middle of a frantic afternoon, telephones ringing
everywhere, there was a call from Joyce. I thought at first
from New York, but no, she is in London. Her voice
unchanged, slow and deep. A gipsy voice, we used to joke;
full of fate. But now it has a slur of America in it, and the
depth and pitch and range is considered, as voices get when
one is out of one's own country and is having to contrast
one's voice and the use of it with everything one hears. I
could tell at once that Joyce was determined *not* to acquire an
American accent, as a matter of principle, and listened to
herself, a severe monitor of every inflection of her voice.

'Well?' came this voice that was once part of my life,
teasing me with memories that on the whole I resist, 'and
how fares the old bitch *Lilith*?'

Once Joyce would not have said anything so brutal, but I

understood it was only her new style. Perhaps even a bulwark against unwanted memories: she was feeling like me, as we sat in different parts of London, she in Hammersmith as it happened, in a room overlooking the river with swans on it, she said.

'This old bitch,' I said, 'is very pleased to hear your voice. Joyce, I've just had a brilliant idea. Why don't you come back and work here? We need you.'

A silence. I was even hopeful, thinking she might have been wanting me to say it.

'You don't change, Janna,' said she. 'My husband? My merry moppets?'

'Who *must* be adults by now, surely?'

'Sometimes I believe one thing, but then another.'

I thought of Kate, and was silent.

'Well, am I going to see you?' I asked.

'I wondered about tomorrow evening?'

Richard had said he might be free tomorrow and I was just about to say no, then thought, Joyce was my friend, the person closest to me for years, and now ... I said, 'Very well. But I am not going to ask you home, there are reasons ...'

'Then we'll spend a cosy evening in a restaurant. I'm out of touch, which?'

I was going to suggest my local Indian restaurant, then thought, No, too near home, meaning Kate, again, and said, 'Bertorelli's.'

Richard rang up just before I left to say he would have tomorrow evening free—and how bitterly I regretted then, giving it to Joyce.

'I can't,' I said.

'Ah ...'

'I'm spending it with a woman who was once my best friend. We worked together for years and years.'

'Old friendships should never be sacrificed for new loves.'

'Is there no chance at all,' I asked, breaking all our—unwritten—rules, 'of meeting this evening?'

'I wish there were.'

Waves of regret washed to and fro between us, charging

the ether I am sure with all the colours of the rainbow.

'I'll ring you on Friday.'

Today Charlie rang to say Phyllis was sleeping off childbirth; she had had a bad time of it; they had a baby daughter. As for him, he was at home proposing to sleep it off too. And I said, 'No, Charlie, you can't. You must come in. We are going frantic.'

'It's no good,' he said, in the cheerful, expansive way that is his style in storm or in calm, 'I'm washed up, Janna.'

I said, 'But Charlie, it's simply not on,' for I was afraid he might decide to give up coming in altogether while Phyllis was in hospital.

'I'll see if I can come in later this afternoon,' said he, and did, briefly, accepting the congratulations of the entire office in a careless, regal way which everyone knew was a front: he is, there is no other word for it, radiant. We all saw this afternoon that we were looking at one of the world's natural fathers: he misses the three from his other marriage, sees them all the time, Phyllis accommodates the offspring of her rival with efficiency and tact, and this fourth baby is seen by him, we understood, as only an item in a continuing production line.

'I have been at all the births,' he said, smiling, smiling, helping himself to cigarettes, bits of chocolate or sweets off people's desks. 'It is the most exciting thing in the world, there's nothing like it—the moment when the babe pops forth all *there*, don't you know, ready for it all, I always weep, I cry my eyes out, I can't help it!'

And having shed beneficence and blessings from his heights, he wandered off again, back to the hospital, to see if Phyllis was awake.

Jill was thoughtful. Of course. I am sure children are not on her agenda. Why should they be at her age? The right age, according to those moguls, the doctors, for childbearing. Mark however was attentive to the radiant Charlie, listening to the siren song. And Jill knew it.

'I wonder if Phyllis realizes Charlie's plans for her future?'

'It's all right, they can't afford it,' I said.

'Want to bet?' And to Mark, who had come in to be with her, propelled by borrowed emotion fuel from Charlie: 'Are you looking forward to seeing our babies born?' She sounded so threatened, almost tearful, and Mark felt her panic, and laughed and teased her out of it. He really is a most extraordinarily decent young man.

Three evenings with Kate. She weighs on me, oh how she does. I find myself thinking of her when I'm at work, wondering, Has she got up out of bed yet, it is nearly midday? Has she eaten anything? Perhaps she has actually gone for the shopping I asked her to do? Perhaps when I am not there she actually reads something, or at least is not as hopeless as when I am?

Today I was thinking so hard about Kate that I had stopped working, in spite of all the pressures, and I looked up to find Jill watching me with the small shrewd smile I am familiar with from Phyllis. Jill has acquired that characteristic from Phyllis, along with those she has taken from me. (Where, *who*, is Jill?)

'Do you realize how worried you look?'

I did not reply, was thinking that if all of me is an artefact, put together from those earlier influences I have forgotten, then it might explain why Richard could stand there looking at my bedroom, and say, You are not in this room.

'Why don't you just send her home?' Jill was going on, and I recognized the extra determination that comes with having planned a conversation, and making oneself do it. 'You do really think you are going to change her, don't you?'

'Yes, Jill, I have caught myself in just that silly and unworthy thought.'

'Yes, I know. There's going to come a point when Kate suddenly changes from an unremitting, hopeless, useless *slob*'—I really do not know how to convey anything of the helpless anger that went into those words— 'and sits up all bright and washed, her mother's daughter and her aunt Jane's niece.'

This hard driving insistence of hers, the *need* of Jill that I should see it.

'Aren't you at all fond of Kate?'

'Oh no!' she exploded, and even got up from her desk, to move about, pulling out and sliding in filing-cabinet drawers. Her emotions were pushing her around the office; twitching her into abrupt, uncoordinated movement. 'I've had it all my life! "Don't you love your sister?" No, I *don't*. Don't you see?' She was shouting at me—or her mother, 'I don't. Why should I?'

'I did not use the word love,' said I, sitting heavily there while this wild creature—today as it happens the picture of a girl dressed suitably for the office, in a nice little pleated dark blue skirt and dark blue shirt—went banging and crashing about. 'But I am certainly thinking about it a lot.'

'I bet,' said she vulgarly, but at my look desisted.

'I mean, about Kate.'

'I'll save you the trouble. I am an expert on love, being one of four siblings. All the degrees and kinds of it. I have had to be. "Don't you love your sister?" "No, I don't love my sister." "Heartless wicked girl." Not that they said that except in *joke*. Oh, you don't know anything about the jokes of large families, Auntie Jane, and aren't you lucky.'

'Pity the poor filing cabinets,' I said, as a drawer slid in with a dull crash and the cabinet banged back against the wall.

'*But*. Having been forced into this minute and I maintain untimely examination of my soul, at about six I could say that I didn't love Kate, but I did love Jasper. I have always loved Jasper. More than anyone in the world? If Jasper was in the *mess* Kate is, then yes, I would do anything, *everything*— When Mark and I got together ...' I smiled at this euphemism, she saw it and was impatient, 'I said to him, you had better know that there's Jasper, I love him, and I want to see as much of him as I can.'

Now she retreated to her desk, shook back her dark curls, and lit a cigarette. She seldom smokes. Calm after the storm.

'As for me,' said I, 'it is not so simple.'

'Perfectly simple. You keep saying to yourself, But what

will become of her! Why can't you face it, Jane? Are you going to be house-mother to Kate for the rest of your life?'

After some thought I said carefully, 'In three years, getting on for four I suppose, I've watched you change. You came into my flat—very different from what you are now!' I could hardly say, I've watched you become Aunt Jane, model II.

'Well, of course I've changed. I've learned so much, from you mostly.'

I saw then, finally, that Jill does not know of her transmogrification. Perhaps she never will.

'If I tell Kate I won't have her, she's not going home, I am sure of that.'

'No, she would pester me, day and night, to live with me. And I *won't*,' she shrieked. 'You have no idea what it is like. All my life, she's been there, just a great gaping *void*, sucking up everything, *me*. I've never had anything, ever, in my whole life that she didn't try and get from me. It used to be toys. Then my clothes. Suddenly, they were Kate's. "Poor Kate," Mummy would say, and there went my new dress . . .'

'She probably thought that since you had so much else, a dress was neither here nor there.'

'I might at some point attain such heights of sainthood, but then, aged five or ten or whatever, a dress *was* important. Shoes. Gramophone records. I never could have anything—they were hers. Her room was stacked with everything of mine. Then it started—friends. I deliberately started to make friends out of our circle. It was marvellous. Quite apart from discovering that the world did not consist of the British middle class, a useful discovery at that, for I would never have suspected it, from dear Mummy and Daddy. But suddenly, guess what? My little Kate was there too. She has a way with her, or she used to have when she was of the right age to go with her babyings. I used to be absolutely amazed that people couldn't see what she was doing—coming after me. "Your sister Kate," they'd say, "Kate is coming with us, to the pictures." "I thought how nice for you if Kate came too." In no time, Kate would be *there* more than I was. It happened again and again. I couldn't have a friend of my own. Not ever. Once I asked mother if I could go for two months to visit a school friend, I really liked her, she lives in Galway. The whole of the summer holidays. Guess what, but I hadn't been there a week before Kate turned up. She'd hitch-hiked. She made herself at home, ingratiated herself with the parents, was ever so useful about the house . . .'

'You mean to say she can be useful about the house?'

'Oh, Jane, of course she can be, when she wants.'

'I am infinitely reassured. There is a difference between can't and won't.'

'The point is that at the end of two weeks I left Ireland and came home, thinking that all right, let her have my lovely friends, I'd enjoy a peaceful month at home, but then she came back after me.'

'I begin to see how very galling it must be for you that she is in my flat now.'

'Yes.'

'But she wasn't, not once, when you were there. And that was for three years.'

'It was because this worm finally turned. I told my mother that, if Kate came after me, I'd kill her. And I told Kate that, if I found her in your flat when I was there, I'd—'

'What?' I am really interested what the final threat could have been; but Jill simply shook her head, breathless, speechless, played-out. She was white and pinched about the nostrils, she looked a poor little thing, vulnerable; not unlike, for those few moments until she had recovered, Kate.

'If I told Kate to go now, I think she'd be in the hands of the police within a week.'

'Yes, she probably would. On purpose.'

'And that doesn't seem to you to matter?'

She shook her head irritably, made a gesture that said, *Enough*.

Today I met Richard for a quick sandwich. Our summer has departed, trailing black clouds and cold rain. We went to a McDonald's, delicious, and held hands. Outside the rain plunged down.

'Janna,' said Richard, 'what would you say if we went

away for a week? I'd like to say, of course, for ever. But a week it would have to be.'

'When?' I said; and I half understood when he laughed.

'Things are very difficult at the moment,' I said, and told him for the first time about Phyllis, about Charlie, about Jill. About *Lilith*. It took all our lunch hour. I was absorbed in telling it, for particularly at the moment, now, it is interesting. *And, after all, it is my life. . .* I noticed him sitting back, arms folded, watching me, as I sat there, all animation no doubt, Phyllis's baby, Charlie the father, the lot, and there was something final there, on his face. Affectionate, yes. Love—yes, I think so. A warm, close look, but detached too. I am not saying that anything was missing of what we feel. But an assessment had been made, and then a judgement. I heard myself say, faltering, apologetic, 'It is my life, after all.'

And he put out this strong quick hand of his, laid it on top of mine—all rings and prettily varnished nails—and left it there while he said, 'All the same, can you spare me a week?'

'Why does it have to be at once? Couldn't it be in a month's time?'

These words struck painfully into both of us, because his answer would take us right into what we both most of the time avoided. For I was also asking, Are you going away again? I have been most carefully preventing myself having any such thoughts; and I am not having them now, I will not live through this thinking all the time: But it will end, he is going away.

'Janna, it can't be. It will have to be in the next fortnight or not at all. Oh no, I'm not saying that,' for I knew that I must have gone pale. I could feel my whole body cold, as if a shadow had passed over me after hot sunlight. My hand under his was trembling, and his closed hard over it. 'I'm not saying that I am leaving now, Janna. But if it's a question of my getting a week away . . .'

'I'll see. Well, I'll have to see what I can arrange.' But I was thinking that it was impossible. Even without Kate it is impossible. I can't take a week's leave now. It wouldn't be fair to *Lilith*.

※　　　※　　　※

Today I had dinner with Joyce, my old mate, my cobber, my pal, my *friend*.

I made a fuss on the telephone when booking, asked for a table in a quiet corner, and we got it. We sat opposite each other, as we have done so often talking about work, and examined each other with a frankness we acknowledged with a smile.

My wild romantic Joyce, high-class gipsy, has vanished. The truth is, I would not have known her. All her thickets of black hair gone, and she has a neat little head. Bronze. Her beautiful crazy clothes—gone. She wore a 'little' black dress, and even a diamanté brooch on one shoulder. The thirties. She is extremely well groomed. Smart. She is bony and pale. Her shoes: she used to sit, anywhere she was, with one shoe off perhaps, or held by its toes, her feet hooked around each other or a chair leg; tonight she wore little black pumps like chisels, placed correctly side by side.

'Well, you haven't changed,' says Joyce, as she makes sure that she is not eating anything that could put on an ounce. Or a gramme. 'You wear well, as they say. Good for you. I *don't* wear well.'

I didn't say anything, and she said, 'If that is tact, then you have changed.'

'You look lean. And handsome.'

'You look plump, and pretty.'

'Good God.'

'But those frail, fair wisps of hair, around a winsome face. Yes, I'll stick to pretty.'

'I don't know why you think it's an insult. Besides, I am in love. It is an infallible recipe.'

'Really in love?'

'Really implies permanence.'

But she let it slide away. She was sipping a cocktail. Examining me. Little black eyes. Now they are not made-up, immense and exaggerated, an old woman's eyes? Yes; and my heart ached for her. I don't know why: but I swear it was not because of our lost closeness. I was sitting there thinking, We worked all those years, she was closer to me than anyone, even Freddie. And now . . . this was to make sense of it all.

After she left for New York, she used to ring me; those crazy drunken conversations in the middle of the night. I could see she drinks a lot. Needs to. She had two cocktails and a lot of wine and then brandy. She ate very little; she used to love food. We had many a good tuck-in. We had a lot of good things together: but that is all ghosts and the past. I do not know Joyce now.

She talked about her job. She counsels the students about their problems. Life problems and work problems, she explained; and I imagined her asking some anxious young thing, Is it a life problem or a work problem you are bringing to me?

Her qualifications for this job? That she has never had anything but problems of every kind with her own two.

They are at university and she sees little of them. They are both 'into' the new technology. She says she does not understand what they say, most of the time.

Her husband: he is in his element in America, and hopes he may never have to leave: teaching Dickens, Trollope and Hardy. I picture these three men, sitting side by side behind a table, smiling benevolently on the labours of their proselyte, a decorated scroll saying, 'Well done!' above each august and whiskered head.

His affair with her best friend (still her best friend) is over; and he is having an affair with a girl who was his student last year: discretion made them 'wait' until she was no longer his student.

She is having an affair with a student. But not from her husband's department. She says she has reached the age for this type of affair; all her women friends have one, or have had one, or plan one. She finds it rejuvenating. For her ideas, she means—catching my involuntary glance at her arid self. It's not that she shares their ideas—the young; but that's not the point.

By now we had reached the pudding, which I insisted on having while she watched, her thin freckled hand protective around the brandy.

At any moment we would be brought the bill.

'Joyce, are you enjoying yourself here?'

'I've come to get my father into a Home.'

'Ah. It seems to be the thing one does, at our age.'

'If they haven't already died.'

'Don't you ever miss—' I had been going to say *us*, but said, 'England?'

There was then a rather long silence. She cuddled the brandy glass and did not look at me. I realized that what I was looking at was anxiety. Joyce has achieved this equilibrium of hers at the cost of being locked inside anxiety.

I was waiting for her interest in me to manifest itself. *How are you, Janna, but I mean, really?*

I was sitting there, wondering, Was she ever interested in me? *Really?* Was I ever anything but a background to her amazing competence, her juggling acts of work, family, success at everything?

'It does seem all rather quaint,' she pronounced at last. 'A dear little country, preoccupied with important problems, such as, are you going to have television at breakfast time.'

'Unemployment, the recession, the rage of the young . . .'

'We have all those too . . .'

We, she had said.

'You don't think you will come home?'

'My husband,' said she, using the word deliberately, 'sometimes prattles away about *home*, but I notice that when he's got leave, he chooses Canada or Mexico.'

'Yes, but what about *you*?'

Another silence. 'It's like this, Janna. I made a mistake when I went there. Now I know it. You were right. You must be pleased at that. Being in the right is so important to you.'

First what I felt was anguish, on her account. I realized, sitting there, painfully looking, and looking again for some sign of the wild, successful energy that once characterized her, how much Joyce had meant to me because of that energy, the generous carelessness of it that invigorated everything about her. Oh, how measured and careful she has become. . . And then, I was feeling pain on my account. Yes, of course we always said what we thought, did not wrap things up; our criticisms of each other, heard from outside, must have sounded like—well, like the vigorous home truths that fuel family life. But this was different, it was the spite of weakness.

After some time, I said, 'But there's *Lilith,* we would love to have you back.'

'You don't see that if something is done wrong, then there are consequences, and—that's that!'

'No, I don't. You could make an effort, heave yourself out of there, and come home.'

An angry smile, even vindictive. 'It's the making an effort,' she said. 'I couldn't do it. I'm burnt out.' And as I hesitated: 'Oh, shut up, Janna. You don't understand. Look at you sitting there, all fat and happy, like a cat full of cream.'

She scrambled for her bag, a nice little packet of tissues appeared, she dabbed and patted, and then did a quick, adequate repair job.

'Well,' said she, pushing everything away out of sight into the mad jumble of her handbag, sitting up severe, tailored and contained. 'And you are still living there in lonely satisfaction in your impeccable flat, and I hear that every time you leave *Lilith* for good you are back again inside a month.'

I signalled for the bill, and paid it. She did not offer to share: it was because she was not aware of anything but her misery.

We left the little nook I had asked for, the table behind a bank of flowers around which waiters and trolleys laden with food appeared out of the busy crowded spaces beyond, and we went into the street.

'That wasn't much of a success, was it?' she announced, with a smile that was meant to be friendly.

'No.'

'If I have time before I go back, I'll ring you. But getting my father settled in is not leaving much time for anything else. When I get to that age I'm going to jump out of a window. Oh yes, I remember, you have progressive thoughts on the subject, don't you? Well, good for you.'

And she went off along the pavement, while I stood there simply not believing it. Not possible for us to separate like that, enemies, or at least seeming to hate each other.

I watched how her walk slowed. I nearly ran after her, to

say—but what? I could not move. She stopped. In the street lights she was a small, solitary figure. Only we two were out, but the restaurants presented well-lit, discreet and satisfied façades to Charlotte Street.

I watched Joyce turn, hesitate, and then come wandering back. I had not moved an inch. She came to a stop in front of me. We looked at each other. Her face was small, and pinched with—anger? No, it was grief.

In that *other* voice, the one we use, or hear, so seldom, she said as if she was listening to herself, and even with surprise, 'Clever Janna, not to have children.'

I hadn't expected it and it hurt. I cried out, 'But you can't mean that, Joyce!'

'Why not? Yes, I'll stand by that. Sensible Janna, you didn't have any children.' And she smiled. A real smile at last, bleak enough, but friendly, and said, 'I'll write,' and this time when she turned, she walked directly off, brisk and in command of herself.

And so, that's that.

Upheavals and turmoil in the office! It's Charlie. If he were not such a passenger . . . but he's always been one, and it's only because there is a crisis that it matters. There is an empty space where Charlie ought to be. Phyllis at home, and Charlie does not come into work. Jill and I do everything. We get it done, borrowing people from all the other departments, but it's mad.

I rang up Charlie today and said, 'I know you are editor, Charlie, but I swear I'll give you the sack if you don't come and *work*.'

'Oh, everybody knows who runs *Lilith*,' said he, comfortably. In the background I could hear a baby cry. 'Can you hear Caroline?' he inquired. 'What a pair of lungs!'

'Charlie, it's not *on*.'

A silence. 'Jane, very well. I'll take leave.'

'You can't abandon us like this.'

'Are you coping or aren't you?'

'That isn't the point.'

'It is my point. As far as I am concerned, this is what is important.'

'When one of your wives has a baby?'

'Now, now, now,' says Charlie. Avuncular.

'Supposing I said to you, The most important thing has happened to me I can ever remember. I need to be free to meet this man . . . *Lilith* can go hang.'

'Are you saying that Janna? Good for you.' And he rings off.

Jill listening to all this, smiles. 'I don't think that at my tender age I can be expected to run *Lilith* single-handed.'

'Have I said you should? Not that you couldn't.'

'Because what you have forgotten is that there is this meeting of the Fashion Syndicates in Amsterdam next week.'

'Oh *no*, yes I had forgotten. Well, I can't go.'

'Has *Lilith* ever not been represented?'

'No.'

Jill and I sat, stymied. We were also laughing, it was a kind of elation.

'Oh,' I said, 'you can go!'

'No, I can't go. Charlie could go. Phyllis could go. But I can't. I haven't the experience. You know that.'

'Yes.'

'But it is all utterly impossible.' I waited. And what I meant was that I should have to go to Amsterdam for the meeting but not with Richard.

'The person we must talk to is Phyllis,' said Jill. 'She'll get Charlie back to work.'

And so Jill talked to Phyllis, and Phyllis talked to Charlie, and I am going to Amsterdam. For four days.

I went into the Jackdaw at lunchtime, coming in out of warm splashy summer rain, and saw Richard sitting at a table against the wall. He was listening to a young man who was leaning forward, talking earnestly. Something about Richard, the way he sat, considering and considerate, his thoughtfulness, the way he was examining this youth, taking everything in, made it come into my mind: Richard is a doctor.

I saw I should not interrupt this consultation, any more than I could in a doctor's rooms, and sat down at a near table to wait. Richard smiled at me, with a small grimace. The youth did not see this: he was too absorbed in his ills. There was a discouraged look to him, and he was tearing off chunks of bread from a pub sandwich, and cramming them into his mouth, chewing as he talked. He was hungry, I thought, and wondered, Unemployed? A junkie? Perhaps he is trying to touch Richard for a pound or two.

He went off in an effusion of thanks, and I joined Richard.

'Unemployed,' he said. 'He can't pay his electricity bill. His wife has just had a baby. Their second. She's been ill. He has bronchitis and a rash that looks to me like the beginnings of erysipelas. His baby has a cough.'

'You are a doctor,' I announced.

'Yes. And reality is breaking in everywhere, no matter how hard I try to exclude it. My mother does not like the Home I found, and I must try to find another.'

The Jackdaw is old-fashioned, and has dark brown panelled walls in which the lights gleam, and a dark red carpet. It is like a chocolate womb, full of warmth and comfort. It was full. It is always full. On hot days it is a cool cave. It may be the middle of June, but coolness was the last thing anyone was in search of today.

I had on my white cardigan. This morning when I dressed I thought of Joyce's 'plump and pretty'. Size 16.

Richard said, 'You look like a meringue, always my favourite food,' and I decided to hell with Joyce.

'As a doctor you should be against them.'

'A little of what you fancy does you good. Solomon himself must have said it. I have it done like a Victorian sampler, very pretty it is, and it hangs behind me on the wall in the consulting room. When I hand out diet sheets it is written at the top: A *little* of what you fancy does you good.' He sounded offhand, almost brusque, as he does sometimes when he is very serious and does not, perhaps, want to be. 'Advice which you and I are perhaps following too strictly, Janna?'

Knowing what I had to tell him, I put it all off, wanting to enjoy this hour, lunchtime at the Jackdaw, and he and I, sitting together at a small table, with all around us people standing, the lively noisy crowd. Good-natured. A lot of laughter. Somewhere among them presumably, though we could not see him, was that one among three million casualties of the Depression.

'Quite soon we'll know everything about each other.'

I said, 'Reality does keep breaking in.'

'I picked up a paperback of *Milliners of Marylebone,* and I read it last night. How do you come to know so much about all that?'

'There was an old woman I used to know. Her name was Maudie Fowler. She died aged over ninety. Furious.'

'Ah. I recognize that.'

'I knew another about the same time. Very old. And she was furious. Is your mother angry? If so, I wish you'd explain it to me. Because when my time comes, I propose to avoid that one. To watch aged crones angry because they are dying is not the most heartening experience.'

'My mother is not angry at being old. But she does not like being patronized. I said to the staff, "To be old does not mean to be half-witted." At least, not in my mother's case. But I am not *their* doctor. I am in the role of customer. I called the doctor in charge of the Home as a colleague and said, "Is it possible to do something about the staff's manner to the patients?" He said, "Dr Curtis, you said? We have not had any complaints about our treatment of the residents." '

'They can't afford to complain,' I said. 'They are too dependent on others' goodwill. And of course they have to be patronized. The very old are too frightening, too much of a threat, we can't stand it, *mementoes mori,* one and all, so they have to be dear little children. For our sakes. And I'll have another whisky.'

He reached up past someone, put our two glasses on the bar counter and signalled to the barman.

'Am I to take it you are or have been a doctor among your many specialities? No? A nurse? No. A social worker? No.'

I had been shaking my head, at more than being expected to answer. 'Yes, you are right. But, Janna, at the moment you are like one of those pictures children get: they look quite blank, like empty paper, then you start shading them with a pencil and a picture starts forming. My picture of you is half shaded in. Well, if we spend a week together, who knows what we'll find out.'

Again I slide away from it. He reached down the whiskies.

'I've been thinking,' I said. 'When a young person gets married, there's not much to them, is there? No wonder they find it all so easy. I, John, take Mary. I, Mary, take John. And they are both all there to be taken. Well, more or less. But people of our age, it's like two continents in collision.'

He said, very dry, with the rough edge of his voice that both thrills me and makes me fear him, 'And were *you* all there to be taken?'

I faced him steadily, though I knew I was blushing, 'I know why you say that, and you are right. But I was over thirty when I married. And Fred was forty. We weren't a couple of children.'

'I was nineteen when I married. I was all there to be taken.'

'And you weren't?'

'No.'

'You've been married to the same woman all that time?'

'Thirty-five years, more or less.'

I felt this literally as a blow to the heart. It hurt. I could feel how I must be pale, where I had been hot and uncomfortable a moment before. Suddenly the whole thing—I there with him, this man who had lived with one woman thirty-five years, *thirty-five years*—seemed paltry and ridiculous. And for some reason these dreams I have every night, of Freddie, seemed very close, the atmosphere of them, lost, sad, bleak. Last night I dreamed of us two, Freddie and I, on some chalky, low, pale shore, with sea birds crying overhead. The cries of the swooping birds sounded in my heart and woke me.

'I told you,' he said, in a low, quick, unhappy voice, 'I told you we should leave it all alone. Why *do* we ... We simply should not talk about anything of the kind.'

I was crying.

'I do cry a lot these days,' I said. 'Take no notice. You'd not believe that normally I never cry. If I find myself crying, my first impulse is to check my digestion.'

'Drink up.' He swallowed his Scotch, put mine into my hand, I drank it, and he pulled me up and we went out of that pub into the Marylebone Road. High up above the city a periwinkle-blue sky accommodated some lively clouds in grey and mauve, and everything about us glistened and sparkled. At a flower stall he bought an armful of yellow roses, and we went on together to the corner.

'Well,' he said, stopping me there, and facing me so that we stood with the flowers pressed between us. 'Are we to go to Paris? Edinburgh? Munich? You say where.'

I said, 'Next week I have to go for four days to Amsterdam. For a meeting of the International Fashion Syndicate.' I could not look at him, and then I did. He was incredulous . . . angry . . . even violent. He stepped back, suddenly, letting go my arms, and the yellow roses fell on to the pavement.

'I have to. I have to.'

'It's your work,' he said, and now he sounded quite wild, and even uncoordinated, as if he had been knocked hard, mid-centre. I had known he would be disappointed. I felt miserable myself. But this reaction was past anything I expected.

'Richard,' I pleaded.

I saw him as sharply as I did the first time, this quick, vigorous man, who seemed to have more energy in him than fifty normal people: but all this was directed against me now, and I knew he could have killed me.

Then he held himself in, his shoulders took on his characteristic hunched look, and I thought, Have *I* become a burden that he has to assume and bear?

'And now you have to go back to the office,' he said steadily.

'Yes, I do.'

He nodded, very distant from me now. He said, almost abstracted, 'I'll ring you, Janna. I'll ring you tomorrow.' And he strode off as a summer shower came splashing down through sunlight, and people looked up and around and laughed at it and at each other.

I went back to the office, and Jill said: 'The path of true love.'

Today, as the telephone rang and rang, each time I hoped to hear his voice, but it wasn't him; and it was not until nearly six that he rang, when I was leaving. He sounded distant, but it was because, I knew, of some kind of restraint or discipline.

'Janna,' he said, 'when did you say you were coming back from Amsterdam?'

I told him, Thursday.

He was quiet for a moment, thinking, then said, 'Very well. I have to go up to Hull again to move my mother, and settle her in, but if I'm going to be free when you get back, I must go now. So—I won't see you till next Friday.'

With anyone else this would be some kind of tit-for-tat: you are going away, so I'm exacting due measure; but not Richard. I realized, standing there holding the receiver with one hand, my other holding my handbag and work to take home as if I were already off to Amsterdam, that I knew how this man's mind had been working, could follow his thoughts stage by stage. Leaving me on the wet pavement with the roses scattered all about, he had said to himself, 'That's it, it's not worth it. I'm going to walk away from the situation for good.' Then he had felt the chill of loss, and thought, Be fair, it *is* her work. Then, this thought bringing with it the weight of associations with something very heavy in his life that I can only surmise—his wife does not love him? They stay together because of their child (or children? Kathleen is not the only one?)—he thought again, No, it is all too much, I *shall* tell her I can't go on with it. But remembered that when we are together it is truly as if we are the separated halves of some whole that has been unjustly severed, remembered all the good; and so thought carefully how he would arrange his comings and goings to fit in with my going and coming back; and yet the thinking, the arranging, had an all too familiar feeling of duty to it. Yet again—he thought, as he said to himself, Yes, if I do this and that I can be back to be with Janna on Friday—yet again I am fitting myself in, and adjusting, and taming myself and *scaling myself down*. If he did not think this last, sensing himself as something splendid, caged and held in restraint, then I did. How we are when we are together must surely have added, as it has to me, to his knowing how much potential we have we do not use. I would never, before Richard, have believed that merely to be with one other person could bring into being areas of oneself; like the pictures he talked about that children bring into being by rubbing a pencil over them. Surely, for him as for me, what we are together makes palpable a fact: that we live at half pressure, while all around the small lit stage that we move about on in strict determined patterns surges and beats, but is held back from us, the energy of delight, of joy. I know that when he has said, No, it is not worth it, he has only to remember what happens when we meet; I know this because I am the same. Sometimes I have thought, No, enough, the strain is too much. But what I want to put an end to is Freddie! I have been waking in the mornings from these dreams of him, thinking, When Richard comes to an end (it is extraordinary, I suppose, that I have never questioned it must come to an end), then perhaps Freddie will go away. What do I mean by that? That Richard is an aspect of Freddie, or Freddie of him? Richard gone, Freddie will sink accommodatingly back into oblivion?

Is this remorse? If so, I don't see the point of it! Given what I was when I married, and what I was all the time I was married, then that was what I had to be, with Freddie. To say I should have been this or that is feeble. And I am not at all convinced I should have been something else. I don't even now know what Freddie was, in himself, not really. This Freddie I dream about: did he exist? Who is this courteous ghost who stands there, slightly bowed, looking at me, not to remind me of something but to state a fact: that he *is* there. He is there, and I should be with him, or going towards him, but then he is not there, or is wandering away, or I nearly reach him but cannot. When I think of Freddie, it is true that it is restraint, a holding-back, that I see, or sense in him. And I know I was not what he wanted.

But how much of all this am I making up? Richard has

said, Janna, are we inventing this? Am I to sit down and bring back into my mind the years of my being married to Freddie? Make myself remember? What for? To say, finally, I should have been this or that? To what purpose?

When Richard goes . . . but why should I keep saying that? I don't know what he is doing here, assume it is some sort of long leave. For all I know his marriage has broken up; no, I don't think it has. Why should Richard and I not marry? Or live together? The thing is impossible, that's why. *Why is it?* He has been married for thirty-five years to one woman. Who wasn't me. And because Freddie with whom I was married for twelve years haunts my sleep, is on the wings of my stage, unsatisfied. It is not Richard I ever dream of . . . no, all this is too much. I don't understand it, and I shall go to sleep. It is long after midnight, and I have too much work to get through tomorrow. Kate is asleep in the sofa, still plugged into her private concert. What can it possibly be doing to her brain, let alone her ears? I can see her facial muscles move and twitch, tugged by the music.

Today Charlie returned to us, with carefully measured petulance, just a little cat's claw of spite, that reminds us all—as if we needed it—that affability is not all there is to Charlie. He said no, he would not interview Hannah from Production, I could do it.

Hannah will join Editorial. I have been thinking of her as a pleasant and obliging girl, with a taste for bizarre clothes that made one often look at her more than twice. When I had her sitting opposite me this morning I wondered at my laziness: I have simply not been paying attention. The reason why one was aware of her, had to look at her, was because her personality was too large for her job. It demands more scope. She is formidable. Like one of Picasso's monumental seaside women, you imagine her bounding along a shore, hair afloat in a balmy breeze, dark brown limbs agape, hands star-fished up towards a striped beach-ball that is somewhere at the level of the sun. She has dark doe eyes, black glittering hair. She comes from many-fathered Liverpool. De Loch. I wonder where that name originated?

Hannah de Loch seemed not surprised that I offered her this very good job, with such prospects, seemed, even, unimpressed. She said yes, she wouldn't mind having a try, but she likes working in Production too. As if the really remarkable difference in salary was not an issue. I asked myself my private question for such occasions: *Has she got the cutting edge*? Then Hannah makes me put another: *Very well then, what do I mean by that*? She is one of the people who make you define yourself.

Hannah has a desk in with Jill and me, and will be working with Jill from now on. I shall move back with Charlie, to keep him up to scratch, as Jill remarks, without acidity, stating the case.

Charlie says Phyllis will not be coming back to *Lilith* after three months, leaving the baby with a nanny. Charlie is blossoming, is in the state not far off that which Richard and I are in when together. He cannot stop smiling; he is half the time on the telephone with chums and cronies, telling them about the baby, Phyllis's ups and downs of health, the milk supply, and their disturbed nights of which he is clearly very proud and in which he takes his share of responsibility. He buzzes from his room to summon Jill, Hannah, Mark, June, me, or a typist or a photographer—anyone who will share his pleasure. And we all do. We do not know if it is Charlie who cannot bear for Phyllis to lose the full benefits of mother-hood, or Phyllis, for we have not seen her alone. A brief telephone call to her unfortunately coincided with baby's feed, and she said, 'It's a drag, Janna, I know, but I think I'll stay home for at least six months. After all, I do want to breast-feed.' This was news to me, but if Charlie can't breast-feed, then Phyllis must; we do all see that.

I sat opposite Charlie this afternoon, with a lot of things prepared to discuss with him, decisions that if he doesn't actually take he should know about, and listened to him talking about fatherhood.

Large and expansive, affable and generous, this good soul, our Charlie, editor of a first-class women's magazine devoted, to judge by its appearance at least, solely to glamour, says to me, 'Janna, this is my fourth, and God forgive me the best! I know you shouldn't like one more than another, and in a sense I don't, they are *miracles*, I simply can't believe it, how utterly amazing and marvellous each baby is, each in its own way. But this one, there's something about her . . . perhaps it is because of Phyllis, and the way I feel about her . . . it is not that I didn't love my first wife, I did, she is a good person and all that kind of thing, and I hope we'll never be less than the best of friends—but Phyllis is something else. Do you know what I mean, Janna? Yes, I am sure you do, a little bird has told me, I hope you won't mind my saying this, that something lovely has happened to you too—don't mind, *please*, I am so happy for you. But there is such a thing as something that is *meant*, and that is what Phyllis is for me. And so I know you understand. When little Caroline was born—although I had seen it all three times before and every time it was just the most *perfect* thing— when this little being appeared, and they put a towel round her and put her *straight* into my arms, because I am afraid poor Phyllis was not with us just at that moment, she opened her eyes and looked at me. She wasn't crying or shocked or anything like that—I know now because after all Caroline is my fourth. And my heart gave way. Do you know what I mean? There she was, this little scrap, still a bit bloody from her ordeal, and she looked straight up at me. She has wonderful dark blue eyes. Deep deep blue eyes. Like dear Phyllis. It was a moment of *recognition*. I swear it. I was so *moved*, I couldn't speak. I had been crying like a baby girl anyway while she was making her appearance, because of Phyllis—she had a bad time, you know, and I'm not at all persuaded about this damned induction business, they *will* use it—and because I get so excited waiting for the moment of truth, the actual moment the baby pops forth, all new-minted, into this wicked world. And I sat there, crying my eyes out, holding the little thing, and I swear I fell in love with her at that moment.'

Tea appeared, in the Wedgwood Charlie insisted on buying for the office. A chocolate cake. Ever since Caroline was born

Lilith has been awash with champagne, sweets, and cake from the Swiss *pâtisserie* at the corner. June ran out to get the cake, and on an impulse got flowers for Charlie at the same time. When she brought them in she was shy, elated, blushing, delighted. Charlie was delighted. Everyone is delighted. If I know nothing else it is that there are going to be weddings or at least pairings through all the departments of *Lilith*. The whole place is broody. There is an atmosphere of secret, wicked delight; and people smile for no particular reason. All this is the doing of not Caroline, but Charlie, *Lilith*'s editor.

Charlie sat in his great chair, in the sombre elegance of the editor's office, all dark red leather and teak panelling, and poured tea and cut cake and smiled and said, 'I cannot understand how any man would not insist on being in on it all. It is absolutely the most exciting thing that ever happens. Oh, I'm not saying sex isn't wonderful, but after all, compared to a new human being just appearing "out of the everywhere into the here"—isn't that how it goes?—well, I am afraid I know what takes second place. And how girls can want to get back to work as fast as possible, leaving all that fun to a nurse. I don't understand that either.'

I listened to all this, feeling horribly excluded from it, refrained from chocolate cake, and drank Charlie's (for he brings it in) Orange Pekoe tea. What I wanted to know, boringly practical as I am, is about finance. If Phyllis is not going to work, who is going to pay for everything? They need the two salaries because of his alimony, which takes every penny of his salary for educating his other children.

But how to introduce these sordid thoughts? And quite apart from money, how about Phyllis herself? When I think of Phyllis, what she was when she started in Editorial, this sharp, needy, ambitious girl, clever as a cat, always on the lookout for advantage, and think of her only four years, is it? five? years later, someone who will willingly stay at home with a baby, with an uxorious husband. Is there such a word as uxor? There ought to be. There is no word in the dictionary for an excessively fond father. Charlie is a fondly paternal uxor married to one of the most coldly ambitious and clever and competent girls I have ever known. And I have been watching clever and competent girls flowing through *Lilith*, often of course on their way to being married, for thirty-five years. Since I started work in these offices. (While I have worked in *Lilith*, my Richard has been married to—his wife.)

But Phyllis may have changed. People change. I have changed.

Listening to Charlie prattling away about how he feels in the middle of the night when he hears Caroline wake, I feel rather as I do in these dreams (these *dreams*) I have. 'We never let her cry, Janna, we simply cannot bear it. Why should she have to cry for something she needs, like a clean nappy?' And he goes to her, because he wants Phyllis to have her share of rest, and there is the infant in her little nest. 'I see her smiling up at me. Yes, I know *they* say babies are not supposed to smile for weeks, but they do talk the most amazing rubbish. She knows me at once, and she lies there gazing up, quite still, with those wonderful deep eyes, not like baby eyes at all, really Janna, but a human being's eyes. I stand looking down, and I do feel such an immense height and size, I can't tell you how crude and awful I feel, trying to see me from her point of view, the tiny thing, looking up. And then when I pick her up, very gently, because she's such a little princess, and I hate to think of her feeling *whisked* up—you know how you see mothers grab up quite tiny infants sometimes, the poor mites can hardly keep their breaths, they gasp and struggle for balance—well, I just gently scoop her up, in her little blanket, and put her on her table where she is put to be changed, and we have this little lovely intimacy going on, in the middle of the night. And I look forward to it. I don't know why people complain at being disturbed by their babies. Not that she cries. It is a privilege, that's what I feel. I adore it. And Phyllis does too, I am sure of it. Sometimes there is even a little competition at four in the morning, about who is going to change Caroline.'

I was sitting there, with the tears running. I had my back to the tall windows, and it took ome time for him to notice, he was so absorbed. I had been planning to make an excuse and go out, but my voice was too unsteady to use. Then he was up in a bound and he had his arms about me. 'Oh, Janna, don't, don't, I am so sorry. Of course, I had forgotten, you haven't had children, oh poor poor Janna, I am so sorry, how awful of me.'

And he was off to his store of goodies, and in a moment I had a cognac sitting there in front of me, and a little packet of tissues, and he had his arm around me coaxing me back to normality. 'We are all so used to you, dear Janna, always so cheerful and sensible and *perfect*—and that's why we exploit you. Yes, I see it now. We take it all for granted.'

I swear he could have said, 'And now, *blow*. . .' holding a tissue to my delinquent nose. But how could he have been more kind?

And how can Phyllis stand it? I went back into our office, where sat Jill and Hannah working away—Jill, aged twenty-two, directing Hannah, who is ten years her senior and makes no claims on that account—and I had red eyes and did not care.

'It's got to you, has it?' said Jill carelessly. 'Well, he had me crying like a baby yesterday.'

'And me,' said Hannah.

'This is an *office*,' announced Jill, like a scandalized schoolgirl, trying out how it sounds. 'An *office*.'

'Offices are very peculiar places,' agreed Hannah, in her amiable indifferent way, working at her pace, which is that nothing seems to happen but everything gets done. While Jill works in a whirl and everything gets done.

'I suppose Phyllis will come back some time?' said Jill jealously.

Hannah said, 'Perhaps she won't.'

'Of course she'll come back,' I heard myself protesting—threatened.

'Not if he has his way,' said Hannah.

Jill and I found ourselves looking at this new colleague of ours with respect. She is a large young woman, dark, even swarthy, her straight black hair worn to the shoulders with a fringe. She is handsome, like a tamed young Indian from a jungle. She is full of eighteen-carat femininity, which enables her to judge matters of the emotions with authority.

'If Phyllis is going to come back to work, then she'll have to fight every inch of the way,' said she.

'But,' I said, 'luckily, there is a financial problem.'

Jill said to me today, 'Are you going to leave Kate in your flat for four days? Without a baby-sitter?'

'What else can I do?'

Leaving Kate is bad, but what *can* I do? Mrs Penny, my dreaded neighbour, has succumbed to senility and has gone into a Home. Irony! I would be pleased to have her here now, so as to say, 'Would you keep an eye on my niece? You know what these young things are.' I cannot say to my new neighbours, a successful, busy, energetic young couple, the Jefferies, 'Please keep an eye on my poor niece. She's a bit of a derelict, you know.' I can ask them to get in a plumber, or keep an extra key. 'What is wrong with your niece?'—I imagine. 'Oh, nothing much, apart from being an infant in adult guise. I'm afraid she may leave the bath taps running all night or start a fire.' This set off an interesting train of thought: who you can ask to do what. The number of people is limited to whom you can say, 'I know it's a drag, but she's not crazy really, she simply hasn't jelled! You need to treat her like a child but talk to her as an adult, so as she can develop some self-respect, don't you know!' It's a question of what one has experienced.

What I am really afraid of is that Kate will ask in some of her friends from the squat she admires. 'Oh, my aunt won't mind, just help yourself.' I believe she wanders down there sometimes in the afternoons, and I am even pleased. I have told her I am going, given her a calendar with the dates marked in bright red, said that she is not to have people in here, I would not stand for it. 'Oh, Aunt Jane, you are so horrible,' she wailed, predictably. But she seemed to brighten really, as if she was pleased this ukase has been issued. This made me wonder if her squat friends had put pressure on her to let them into her rich and reactionary aunt's flat, and she had found it hard to refuse. There are squats and squats. I made inquiries about the one she has made her second home, and it is a haunt of drug pushers and petty criminals. I came in unexpectedly once from the office, and found Kate dressed up in an evening dress I have for glad-rag occasions. Kate was standing in front of the glass, her orphan much-dyed locks, pale green at the moment, were brushed straight up, like rough green flames, her face made up like Dracula's. I saw that she probably visualizes herself as a gangster's girl.

A career, of sorts, I suppose.

A worse problem than Kate is poor old Annie. I have been in as usual, two or three times a week, and sat with her. It is always late, about seven, before going home. But last weekend I was there on both Saturday and Sunday. Since the Cuts, old people who are not actually crippled do not have Home Helps on the weekend. Her wonderful Home Help, Bridget, is for some reason allocated elsewhere. Her new one, Maureen, is a nasty piece of work, but who would know it from meeting her? For at first you are reassured by her: as she means you to be. She has been working as a Home Help for some years. A large, jolly woman, in her mid-thirties, she has her hair cut short all over her head in black curls, she has a pudgy baby-face and pudgy little white hands (with bright pink nails) that dart about like little white rats. She comes in for a few minutes, instead of the time she is paid for, might not come in at all, forgets what Annie needs, but presents herself always as very busy (true), kind-hearted, overworked (true), devoted to her charges. She has taken the trouble to make friends with Vera, her superior, who thinks she is wonderful. And in times of crisis she is there, working like a horse, thinking of everything.

She is also a thief, helping herself to Annie's pension. I know what ought to be in Annie's purse, for I keep an eye on it. This Maureen, from Belfast, is in sole control of what gets given to Annie and what gets spent. It is she who collects the pension and who buys everything, and pays electricity and gas bills and the rent. She who explains to the Services that Annie needs extra for this or that. I reckon that about ten pounds a week goes into Maureen's budget from Annie's, and since she deals with four or five other people apart from Annie, this would add up to quite a bit.

Maureen, all amiability and flurries of competence in between nice sit-downs when we—she and I and Annie—sit around drinking tea, greets me as if I were her best friend as well as Annie's; but a few months ago, when I was sitting there, having emptied Annie's commode and made her bed and brought her some groceries because Maureen had not come and Annie was afraid of being left unhelped, Maureen did come in. She was very pleased I had done her work; for she was tired. She has four children, a husband who is not in the best of health, and she does indeed work very hard. But I had been asking Annie about the money in her handbag, and Annie had told Maureen, and now Maureen, standing with her back to me as she fussed about cutting Annie a sandwich, said in a low voice, 'I am afraid of you.' Here it was again, the other voice, the voice we seldom use. This was an interesting moment for a variety of reasons. There was nothing in it of our usual relationship, that of the two busy women meeting over an unfortunate old thing, to help her, taking each other's competence and expertise for granted. Nothing that we had ever said to each other before—Hello, Mrs Somers—Oh, how are you, Maureen?—Oh, fine and dandy, Mrs Somers, and I hope you are feeling yourself?—all that nonsense, could have accommodated even a hint of what lay behind Maureen's low 'I'm afraid of you.' Coming in after three or four days of *not* coming at all, realizing she had forgotten Annie's tea, or butter, or cigarettes; seeing that I had taken down and washed Annie's curtains or stood on a chair to clean her windows, she checks over Annie's money, for two reasons. One, to see if enough has accumulated for her to slip out a few more pounds for herself. Two, so that Annie might notice it and say, 'Janna was saying I should have more money than I do,' and then she can contradict it. Going home she broods, probably vindictively, or fearfully about this irritating visitant from the glamorous world of the rich and successful. When Maureen was allotted Annie as her new charge, she encountered me, who on Annie's cards is marked as next-of-kin. She has heard how I have visited Annie, am Annie's friend, how I 'always' come in and 'never' miss. Alas, I, like Maureen, do miss. But Annie uses this as a spell, like magic: 'Janna never misses, she always comes in,' says Annie severely to the airily dishonest Maureen.

The story of how I met Annie in the radio shop and came home with her, and then bought her things and looked after her ever since, has become one of Annie's 'gramophone records' which I never hear, but which Maureen or Vera or someone else has to hear for the umpteenth time.

'*I am afraid of you,*' that low, just-breathed visitor from her real thoughts about me was left unremarked by me. I sat on, drinking tea. What was I to say: There is no need to be afraid of me, I won't tell?

If there really are impossible situations—and my nature refuses to accept such a thing!—then I am in one.

For one thing, I am not at all with Annie as I was with poor old Maudie, totally committed, an affair of the heart.

I know what it is to become committed to an old woman whose needs are so great that your own needs become secondary, your whole life gets swallowed up. I've done that, once; I am not sorry I did it—far from it, for I loved Maudie, and I suppose when you've used the word love, then that's it. But said to myself I wouldn't let it happen again; for after all, I like Annie but I don't love her, and I said to myself, So far and no farther. This private bargain I have made with myself means that I do not throw a nasty and even sneaky spanner in the works, such as ringing up Vera suggesting we meet, and tactfully conveying to her that her favourite Home Help is making free with the pathetic little pensions of her helpless charges. I can't, and that is all there is to it. Besides, as I sit there with Annie, knowing that yet again Maureen has not done this or that, I myself have all kinds of thoughts which can be classed as 'black market' or 'second economy' thoughts; those which all over the world in fact motivate most citizens. Who have long ago abandoned honesty as my parents would have recognized it, an absolute: 'You do *not* steal, lie, milk the rich, even if you are dying of hunger in a hovel. It is wrong.' It is because everything seems to be seizing up, going wrong; because our money, the citizens', is spent so wastefully in ways we feel we have no control over.

Maureen thinks like this. The old people's pensions are too low, are they! I know better than that! When her rent is paid and the electricity and the gas, and I've bought her little bits of food, there's five pounds left over, ten in a good week. That Somers woman will run her up a bit of a skirt if she needs it, and she gets her her vests and knickers, and there's Welfare if she's in want of a jersey. The woman upstairs from Annie said she had a pair of slippers she's not in want of. Besides, Annie's entitled to that clothing grant. I'll see she gets it, and that will make a bit extra for my Lorna when she goes to Boulogne with her school at half-term. And there's that ten pounds slipped down the side pocket of Annie's bag. She won't even notice if I slip it out. I can put down the deposit on our holiday. It's a shameful thing the way they waste the country's money on these old people. Not that I grudge them what they have to have. If Annie was in need for anything, I'd see she got it. And now there's old Mrs Baker, I'll have a word at the office about her supplementary. She's entitled to a good bit more, the way I look at it. There's no point in wasting a good opportunity of getting a little bit extra for them. All the government does is waste it anyway on their crazy ideas. If they had an ordinary working woman running things—oh, I'm not saying myself, that's not it—but someone who has had to balance the budget a bit, then we'd not have all this waste. They said in the office they were going to give me that poor old man, he's not long for this world, what's his name? Yes, Dick White. Well, I'll just make sure he's getting everything he's entitled to. If I don't put that deposit into the office before next week we won't have a holiday this year.

I was thinking this evening, as I sat drinking tea with Annie, that I was doing more or less the same as my love Richard with his mother. But I am afraid that from the perspective of Annie's little room, which is neat and nice *when* it is cleaned, but smells of old age, Richard and I, what we are, seem another world. I think of how we range around London, from Greenwich to Richmond, from Highgate to the docks, of how on a whim we go to the theatre or decide to walk ten miles; the glitter and colour of our being together— all this fades, becomes paltry and nothing. There is a cheap pinchbeck look to us, as I sit there, seeing the food stains down the front of Annie's blouse, and hear her sighing and complaining; that couple there, Janna and Richard, walking away hand in hand, that handsome pair of adventurers, for so we seem seen from that close confined room, are even an invention, only the play of two indulged people; and yet we are neither of us that, for we both work so hard; and putting myself back, in my mind, into that woman there, Jane Somers, walking across a field on Hampstead Heath, beside Richard, the sun on their backs: for I was choosing to remember that wonderful week of summer which seems such a long time past—I feel in a sudden amazing surge of love and happiness the truth of being with Richard. Which can best be expressed, quite simply, thus: There is nothing we could not say to each other, as if our two lives, running for so long invisibly to the other and coming together so improbably in that comic little accident on Tottenham Court Road underground, carried along with them a rich cargo that had been invisible, too, to ourselves, like rivers whose depths know nothing about the baulks of good timber, green boughs from some far-off flood in the mountains, packing cases that have who knows what things in them—silks? books? special scented teas from North India? a consignment of rare plants from some jungle destined for a garden in northern Europe?—seventeen disconsolate chickens sitting on a bucking and rearing log, a drowned horse, and the light worn bones of an ancient dinosaur that has been washed off some eroding hillside. All these things, carried along so far by the flood, swirl into a side-reach of the river, toss a little, and subside in brown froth on a beach of white sand whose river waves run past in a normal season smooth and orderly, each modestly crested with white.

*　　*　　*

I wanted so much today to be able to ring Richard, that's all, only to hear his voice and say, Next Friday, we will meet. Next Friday, it's only five days away, well, you could call it six. . . He has my two telephone numbers, but I do not have his.

If I did have his home number—if it is not a hotel he is at, for he did say that his own home was let—who would I get, with Richard, presumably already departed up to Hull? Kathleen, that sombre presence? Should I say, oh, this is Jane Somers, you know, we have *almost* met so often.

Usually I love getting ready for these jaunts abroad to dress shows, conferences, or with a team of Photography to get pictures of some special shop or place or person. I adore it all, everything, from the packing of my clothes which give me so much pleasure, to the business of actually getting processed on to the plane, and then the plane, and the pleasant hotels I go to, for I know now where all the real hotels are everywhere in Europe. What fun I do get from all this. And as I write I remember I cried out to Richard once that what I had excluded from my life was pleasure, I had worked too hard. And it is not true. My days are full of pleasure, delights, little treats, listening to the amazing exchanges between people on London's pavements, so surreal and suggestive of hidden continents of experience, looking at people in restaurants, buses, shops . . . but today I feel no pleasure at all. Leaving England is leaving Richard.

A Day in the Life of a Derelict Girl.

She wakes in the dark, her stomach sour, her heart painful, and it is as if she is being pounded and wrenched by powerful waves. The waves are sound, a thud of rhythm. She feels caged by them, assaulted, and scrambles up away, feels pain in her ears and remembers: she tugs out the plugs and sits stunned, bereft, in the silence of deafness: her ears are ringing. Where is she? It takes some time for her to realize that she is sitting on the edge of the sofa where she has fallen asleep. A vast resentment possesses her as she thinks that Janna did not wake her, detach her from the machine, take her to bed. She does not think, Janna is this or that, but the resentment she feels *is* Janna, just as, until she came to live here, the resentment she lived with *was* her family, her parents. Now, with bitter and vindictive thoughts raging, she totters up to the light switch and makes the room spring into being. She is looking around for signs of Janna and thinks, seeing its emptiness, that Janna has gone off to her room. She has got chilly and stiff. She thinks, Shall I have a bath to warm up? She runs a bath, as she sits vacant on its edge, her eyes held by the spume of bubbles under the taps. She even smiles a little, like a small child, because of the pretty bubbles. Then she loses interest, because sitting in the warm steam has livened her, and she wanders off to her bed. As she collapses she remembers the water is running; thinks, Well, let it run, but does get up, and turns it off, or nearly: the hot tap is trickling as she staggers back to the bed, and flings herself dressed under the duvet. She lies for a long time, quite straight, stiff with a kind of apprehension, the lights beating on her face. She thinks, Janna will come and turn them off; then remembers Janna is in bed; then, that Janna is not here, but in Amsterdam.

She sits up straight, in a surge of anger. She is all alone in this flat, abandoned. With this thought comes some relief from the tension, the apprehension, which is in fact con-nected with Janna, who, she knows, seldom approves of her or anything she does. For four days, she thinks, she will be free of that critical presence. She sighs and relaxes, feels the light dazzle on her lashes, just manages to get up and turn it off, and collapses back into bed. She sleeps very soundly while the morning comes, and she wakes in full day, with the birds noisy in the tree outside. She wakes with an apprehension of pleasure; wonders what it is she is expecting, remembers it is that she will be alone. Her frank sigh of relief sounds like contentment. She thinks, And I'll get up and make myself some breakfast, and I won't have to be worrying all the time what *she* is thinking. She lounges around under the covers, savouring her freedom, then gets up, and sees from the clock by her bed that it is not yet five. But it is much too early to get up, she says indignantly, as if she has been cheated or hoodwinked by the early summer light, and she goes back to sleep. She does not wake until ten or so, and this time she is heavy and flaccid. She sleeps again, wakes at midday, and again lies for some time, thinking that it won't be long until Janna comes in at six and makes her some supper.

Again she remembers Janna is away, and this time there is no pleasure in it. Four days she thinks, dismally. At last she drags herself up, thinking that she will have a hot bath, but the trickle of water from the hot tap running for hours has drained the tank. The cold water makes her shudder, so she does not wash, but goes in the dress she has worn now for four days to the kitchen, where she looks into the fridge, where she expects to see butter, eggs, bacon, and an assortment of cheeses. They are all there, for when have they not been there? All her life she has opened refrigerators knowing that the shelves will be full. She checks jealously, Is there enough here till Janna comes back?—for she plans not to leave the flat at all, but to stay here timeless, unpressured, free. She starts off by being hungry, but cannot be bothered to cook anything, and eats bread and strawberry jam and drinks very strong tea.

Then she wanders around a little, looking in the bedroom which looks as if no one has ever been in it, so neat and tidy is it, with the square brass-framed bed in its thick folded white, the cushions just so. Kate stands there looking in for some time, for nearly every morning when Janna has gone she does this, and what she thinks first, in a sort of panic, is: How can anyone keep a room as neat as this, there's *nothing* out of place. From this grows a fantasy of her own room, the one she will have, which is far from being like Janna's, all white and yellow, clear bright colours, but is like a dark luxurious cave seen in some magazine, of a hundred different textures and stuffs, all in sombre rich colours, an essence of a thousand paisley shawls, every inch of the room clothed, ceilings, walls, floor; and the bed is loaded with dark intricate cushions among which Kate, unvisualized but strongly felt, lolls. She is far from alone in this room; she never imagines a man in it, or a girl alone, but a group of loving friends, whom she allows in, but on her terms: they resemble her friends from the squat, but these, to use the jargon of Janna's trade, while remaining themselves, free and freewheeling spirits, owing allegiance to no petty Caesar or censor or censure, have taken several giant steps upmarket, are rich jetsetting youth with the world their oyster, Hong Kong one day, Buenos Aires the next. In this room like a Victorian pasha's den, Kate spends a lot of her time, while she is in actual fact trying on Janna's clothes, so that as she stands looking in the long mirror, an unformed girl who might be eleven wearing one of Janna's outfits, she certainly does not see what is there, but something resembling a photograph from *Lilith,* and her unkempt spikes of hair, green, pink or blue, are those of some preposterous beauty pouting in self-mockery at the public.

Today she decides not to try on anything, though she checks to see what Janna has taken. Very little seems to be missing: Janna's cream linen suit, which Kate adores as she might some fabulous being like a film star, for ever beyond her: how *can* anyone wear that all day and take it off in the evening without a crease or a stain? (When Kate tried out her fantasies in it, and took it off after an hour, there were stains from her chocolate bar all down the skirt, and she had to run out to the one-hour cleaner's at the corner with it, hoping that Janna would not ever know.) What else? A pale blue *crêpe de Chine* suit. Kate does not care for this, even more because Janna looks so well in it. It makes her feel diminished, that suit, which apart from anything else has rows of minute tucks in the lining that no one would ever see except for Janna herself—a revelation of secret perverse enjoyments, these tucks seem to Kate; and she had entertained the members of the squat with them: 'Where no one would ever *see* them!' she had exclaimed, virtuously, but felt as if she had missed a trick or two when Brian, the squat's leader, said vulgarly, 'No one but her lover.' When Brian said this, emotions rioted all over her, even while she felt stupid. She imagined Janna taking off that slinky little jacket and laying it over the arm of a chair, deliberately exposing on one side only the little field of tucks that ran from below the breast to the bottom of the jacket.

Janna had taken too a creamy silk shirt that has very fine brown stripes, so that if you turn it this way and that it glistens like pale toffee. And a cotton T-shirt, sleeveless, in cherry pink. And a jersey dress in pale grey. Kate is affronted when she realizes that was all Janna had taken: herself, she could not imagine going off for four days, and on such a posh trip too, with fashion experts and models (Kate supposes), unless she took suitcases crammed with everything she had, just in case. Kate checks on the underclothes that are not there: remembers that she secretly removed a pair of knickers in pink and coffee last week, which she wore herself all one day, meaning to put them back. Where were they? Kate stands chewing her fingernails in a panic. Where can she have put those knickers? Janna would *kill* her. Shame engulfs her: she still has them on. Of course, for she hasn't got around to changing.

It is the dead middle of the day, one o'clock, and the sunlight is filling the sky, for the rain has gone away as if it has never rained in London and never will.

Kate pulls a chair to the window in Janna's bedroom, and gazes down into the street. She sees herself down there, dressed in Janna's cream suit. She walks with negligent charm to the corner, swings on to a bus acknowledging the admiring glances of a group of young people sitting just inside. They long to be like her, so cool and elegant; but do not dare to address her. She gets off the bus at Baker Street and walks at her leisure down to Upper Regent Street, where, being late, she takes a taxi to *Lilith,* and she walks through offices smiling, being greeted by everyone; and when she reaches the office she shares with Jill, her sister cries, 'Oh, Kate, I've been waiting for you, what shall I do about. . .' Kate advises Jill what to do, and then goes out to lunch at a restaurant with three famous models. One of them says to her, 'Kate, you are wasting yourself! You should be a model. Only the other day I heard someone say, What a pity, Kate would be perfect for this type of clothes.' 'Who was that?' asks Kate, and hears, as she expects, 'Mark. Mark was talking about you.' Kate has known, of course, that Mark admires her, and that she has only to say the word. . . But now she says, 'Well, I don't mind trying it out for a week or so.' 'Oh, super,' says Olivia, the red-haired model, 'I'll arrange an appointment for you with the agency. . .'

This fantasy occupies Kate for some hours. She has dreamed it all so often that is like a book that one may open anywhere and read on. It is detailed and intricate, so that she knows what the young people on the bus are like, what they are wearing, can smell the sharp stuffy air of the bus, knowing that as she is walking down Wigmore Street there is a quick flurry of raindrops so that she must step in off the street to a florist's, where the girl who has watched her so often walk down that street, presses on her a single pink rose, her eyes shining with secret admiration. She knows how, after the office, she will say to Jill, 'No, it is sweet of you to ask, but I have another engagement,' and she is off to meet the woman who runs the modelling agency, who says, 'Kate, I don't often say this, unfortunately, but you are—simply—a natural. Born for it!'

Kate finds she is hungry. Her stomach rages. Again she pokes her head down to inspect even the deepest corners of the fridge, but does not see what she yearns for, something like a whole basin of sweet custard, or a cake full of jam and cream. Though earlier she had been comforted to think she need not go out, now she runs down into the street and to the corner shop, where she buys a dozen Mars Bars, six giant packs of potato crisps and some samosas. As she gets back into the flat she hears the telephone, goes as fast as she can but it is too late. It stops as she puts out her hand. There she stands, for about five minutes, her heart beating, hoping it will ring again. She fears it is Janna, ringing to 'check'. Even more, she fears it is someone from the squat, because she knows if she says Janna is away they will insist on coming up, and even sleeping here, taking over. 'It is your duty to take everything you can get from your bourgeois relatives' is the slogan. At the same time she hopes they will ring, and then she can say, 'Can I come and visit?' When she is with these squat-mates, she is swung every minute between moods and choices. She admires them for being so independent, living their own lives on the dole, moving from one desolate house to another; admires them for their brave scorn of the police; at the same time she is afraid, for she certainly does not want to go to prison, and some of them have been in prison, and two are on parole, and there was even talk of her going with them to 'do' a sub post office in Hendon. It sounded as if they were joking, but perhaps they weren't. And then, again, she loves being with them, just to sit quietly in a corner while they talk, or play music, or smoke a bit of pot. She is quite happy there, for hours; there are no pressures on her, that is it; none of them are up to much (as she knows quite well), and there is nothing to measure up to. With them she feels nothing of that burning nagging pain somewhere near her midriff, or even in her throat, like a need to vomit, which she has felt with Jill ever since she can remember.

Perhaps it was Jill who had rung. She puts out her hand, thinking she will ring Jill: dare she? Will she? Knowing that several times before she has nearly got to the point of ringing Jill, and then failing, she now stands there wondering, *Will* I? She does: before knowing it she has dialled *Lilith* and asked for Jill. 'Hallo,' she heard her voice trailing off.

'Oh, Kate,' said Jill. 'I'm just off actually.'

'Oh.'

'It's getting on for six, did you know?' Jill sounded censorious, as she always did; like a tutor. Kate ought to know it was six; she should have some bearings in her timeless days, and Jill was doing her a favour by telling her.

'Oh, is it?' wailed Kate.

'Well, are you all right?' sighs Jill. Then she adds, and Kate can hear that she is forcing herself, 'Do you want me to drop in on the way home?'

'No, it's all right.'

'Very well. Be careful about everything, Kate.' And rings off.

She might have asked her to come to supper, at least, thought Kate; and then she runs to the heap of stuff she has bought, and she gets into her place in the corner of the sofa, spreads crisps, chocolate and samosas all over the coffee table, puts the leads to the machine in her ears, and is welcomed into the world of sound. Yet, not without a moment's reluctance, even fear: she knows she is often deaf for minutes after she unplugs herself; she cannot bear to give up this addiction of hers, where she is cut off from everything painful and difficult.

And so sits Kate, eating and listening, while the sunlight hangs in the sky outside, then dims, and it is night, and soon it is time for bed. About midnight Kate feels sleepy. She is grateful that she does. Also, she is rather sick, for she has eaten every crumb of what she bought.

She now takes a long very hot bath, syrupy from a concentration of Janna's bath salts, several varieties of them. She is ashamed and distressed that the water seems to be brown. Had she really been as dirty as that? But never mind, she is clean now. She even washes her spiky Strewelpeter head. Her parents had said to her, You look like Strewelpeter, and she had sought out the book from the nursery cupboard, looked at the illustrations, and was pleased: she felt like Strewelpeter.

She got into bed very late, in a nightgown of Jane's, and lay awake for some time, in a dream of how she was with Jane in Amsterdam, the most famed fashion model in five continents: 'This is my aunt, Jane Somers. Yes, she works at *Lilith*. . . oh, you have heard of her?'

We are into July, my least favourite months of the year are here. All the spring blossom gone long ago; the trees are full and heavy, of a dowdy green; I think of it as the year's middle age, when nothing much happens for what seems like for ever, only insidious intimations of the changes to come. It rains or it doesn't, but it is summer rain, with nothing of the shocks and delights of spring rain which can be snow, ice, hail and warm showers all at once. I was thinking all this as I drove back from the airport in the taxi, and looked at London, London, with the eyes of a lover, not seeing the dreariness of the approaches from the the airport, welcoming scarlet buses and telephone boxes; and seeing how, just like

Amsterdam, the streets seethe with tourists staking a claim in the famed city. How extraordinary a thing is this exchange of populations, and yet we have got so used to it, we don't think it strange. A hundred years ago, a few people went on jaunts to the seaside, and the well-off visited suitable bits of 'the continent'. This whole business of *having to see* has evolved in a handful of years. In Amsterdam I was sitting in the hotel coffee room waiting to be fetched for the conference, and at the next table were young people, establishing themselves with each other. One said, 'I saw the Grand Canyon. It was cool.' The other: 'Yes, I have to see that; maybe next year.' With a little anxiety, as if something essential had been for overlong neglected. If it is there, then it must be seen—*had*; as I have been *having* Amsterdam, for in the evenings I made a point of walking around the canals and having dinner in the proper places, for it would not have done simply to eat in the hotel and neglect the canals.

I have been working extremely hard at the conference, which was a success, and at *having* everything I could. And, all the time, Richard, Richard, was beating at the back of my mind; an anxiety, which has been growing to a fever. As much as the longing to be back, and to be with him, I have been asking myself, But suppose the whole thing *is* nonsense?—and at such moments I seem to be breathing something stale and rancid; I seem to myself pathetic. And he, the image of him, acquires a tinge of the ludicrous.

These were my thoughts as I came into London. I went first to the office. Hannah and Jill were working away together in perfect harmony; and Jill said, even a little irritated, 'But, Jane, there's no need for you to be here. You said tomorrow!' The splendid young savage was amused at *family* in the office; and poured oil—which is her nature—saying soothingly that she for one wanted to see me, because a slight problem had arisen. It seems that Hannah is a member of the Women's Action Group Phyllis was once so busy with. They have been keeping tabs on Phyllis, who, from their point of view, sold out by marrying at all, and particularly Charlie who can be nothing else but a male chauvinist pig. It is truly very odd to hear these words being used as if they are a political label, like: a social democrat, a left-wing deviation-ist, a right-wing extremist. When Hannah said, 'He is a male chauvinist pig,' it was without the edge of humour or satire the words once had; she has long since ceased to think of what the words mean, they are no more than sounds.

From time to time members of the group have visited Phyllis, full of passionate sisterhood, to rescue her from her victimization.

'How?' I asked Hannah, not meaning to be provocative.

We were all sitting in our office: Hannah at 'my' table, which I am giving up to her anyway since I must go back to Charlie's room. Jill was as usual just visible behind piles of work. I sat tactfully to one side, with my hat still on, my suitcase by my side—a visitor.

Hannah was wearing a striped tunic, belted with black, over full Turkish-style trousers. Her magnificent black hair swung as she turned her head to inspect me: in her women's group I am of course a reactionary, a woman who has succeeded in the man's world and does not care about her ground-down sisters. It has long seemed to me that this is not what anyone actually feels, but what they feel they have to say: like 'male chauvinist pig'. Hannah considered me, and said, 'It was all discussed. We decided that if Phyllis had had enough, she could come and live with the sisters in the commune.'

Jill gave me a glance which meant: *Don't.* I had no intention of being abrasive. And while I was in the grip of a familiar need to laugh, so inappropriate and off the point did this seem to me, I said mildly, 'Well, surely that isn't very likely?'

Hannah said seriously, 'Earlier on, before she was pregnant, Phyllis was thinking of it—leaving Charlie.'

We all sat silent for a while, but we did exchange looks which admitted what it must be like being married to Charlie, that perfect husband.

'*Well,*' I said, 'you could knock me down.'

'Why?' Hannah really wanted to know.

I had been trying to get rid of the subject because of its dangers to office tranquillity, but Hannah is not one to be set aside if she wants a subject dealt with. I now faced her squarely, and said, 'Because: Phyllis is a very intelligent young woman, one of the cleverest I have known,' Hannah nodded, waited for the point. 'She worked with Charlie for a long time, knew exactly what he was, before she said she would marry him.'

'That's got nothing to do with it, I think,' said Hannah. 'If you haven't been married, then how do you know?'

'You have been?'

'Yes. For long enough. . .'

I said, 'I have only got to look at you, Hannah, to know that you were the stronger, you took on someone problematical, and that he found you too much.'

I had taken a chance, but she gave me an agreeable smile and nodded: 'Right. I probably shouldn't marry at all, or take on a man. I do better with women.'

This was the shock it always is: a shock of the nerves, but not of the mind. Once it had been said, it was obvious, if for no other reason than that Hannah has that comfortable maternal kindness that some lesbians have.

I said, 'But Phyllis is a man's woman.'

'Yes, I agree,' said Hannah. 'If not Charlie then someone.' There was no contempt here, though I was on edge for it, only assessment. 'That's why I was the odd man out in my group—the odd woman out,' she corrected herself with a smile. 'I said you are making a mistake, sisters. Phyllis would not settle for one of us. She's very attractive, you see,' she explained. 'More than one of the girls has been in love with her. Not me, not my type. But I like her, if I think she's a fool.'

Jill said, quick and fierce, 'If it's what she wants, why is she a fool?' From this I saw that Jill has been under attack from Hannah because of Mark. And I wondered for a little what they had against him: for Mark is the modern young man, equal, takes it for granted that housework must be shared, responsibilities be equal. But, to be a man is the crime.

And then Jill, to me, with a scandalized laugh—but a real one, not the try-out, shocked air of the very young girl she often still is: 'They went to Charlie and said that he was exploiting Phyllis, using her salary to pay off his other wife.'

I said, 'But she chose that situation.'

'All the same,' said Jill, '*I* think it's awful. They rang up Charlie, asked to meet him, he said he had nothing to say to them, they trailed him in the street, jumped into a taxi with him that he got into to escape them, and shouted at him that he was a wicked exploiter.'

'And what did Charlie do?'

'*They* say that he threatened them with the police.'

'Is that true?' I asked Hannah, for it didn't sound at all likely.

She looked thoughtfully at me; she knew I didn't believe it. 'I don't know.' Then she swung that glistening black hair back, reached for a cigarette, signalled she had had enough of it, and remarked, 'It sounds all a bit much, I agree, but they were concerned for Phyllis.'

'She chose it,' I said again; and again she dismissed it, this time with a shake of her head, as she took in great draughts of smoke. It is only when she smokes that one sees Hannah as under stress, needing it.

'I knew nothing about all this,' I said. 'But the person to tell me would be Phyllis, for Charlie certainly wouldn't.' And at this I had a sudden picture of the affable Charlie shut into a moving taxi with two shrieking sisters, and I had to laugh, though laughter was not appropriate, not with Jill so anxious and on the defensive. I laughed, and I laughed, while Jill typed very fast, annoyed with me; and Hannah stood four-square on two brown and sturdy legs, smoking, looking out of the window.

When I'd stopped, she said, making judgement, 'It is not funny to Phyllis. Not funny to Charlie. Not funny to the girls who tackled Charlie.'

'So much the worse for all of them,' I said. 'And now I have to go home. Did you hear from Kate?' I asked Jill.

'She rang up every day; I *did* offer to go round, Janna.' And then, apologetic: 'I think there were other people there: she rang up to ask when you were coming home, and someone was telling her what to ask.'

'I see.'

'I hope you do,' said Jill, virtuously.

Hannah said, 'I spoke to her once. I invited her to visit us at the commune.'

The suddenness of this new perspective was too much, and I was not able to say anything but 'Goodbye, see you tomorrow.'

I came home with of course apprehension, expecting I knew not what. Kate was in the corner of her sofa, plugged in. Her face lit up pathetically as I came in, and she voluntarily removed the leads. She stood up, and uncertainly came towards me. I embraced her, for the first time; and what was in my arms was a plump child.

'Oh, Aunt Jane,' sniffed Kate, 'it seemed so long.'

Over her shoulder I looked around: I knew at once that people had slept here. The yellow chairs were grubby, had cigarette burns on them. There was a smell of marijuana. I could see a crust of bread in a saucer full of cigarette ends under a chair. I could feel her tense up, knowing that I was looking around, seeing . . . 'Never mind, Kate,' I said, and she burst into floods of relieved tears. Smiling through them, she backed away, and fell into her corner, her legs set apart, looking like two little fat black dogs in the thick black of her trousers. She was wearing a fluffy white sweater—mine. She put the leads into her ears and sent grateful smiles to me as she sank into her noisy world.

And so here I sit, at one in the morning. Kate has gone to bed. I have rung Mrs Brown and offered her a large bonus to clean up tomorrow. My clothes are ready for the cleaner's, including those worn by poor Kate. I am about to get into my square white bed; I have finished today and tomorrow is Friday, and Richard will ring . . .

Richard did not ring. All day I worked like a black. I said to Jill, 'I have been working like a black,' and she said, 'Janna, you must not say that.' I said, 'Why not? The blacks' case all over the world is that they have to do everyone's dirty work, and I agree they do. So why not say, work like a black? It is descriptive, not insulting.'

'If you can't see why not!' said Jill.

'Oh, I can see why not, all right, but there's no one here but you.'

Charlie had gone out to lunch with our main advertiser. Before he left I saw him slip the pack of new photographs of Phyllis and Caroline into his pocket. He saw that I had seen and he laughed, comfortably.

Hannah had gone to the Professional Women's Lunch. I've announced that she will have to learn to tackle these 'at least for a few months'—meaning Richard; but really I mean to slide out of all I can. But so I have said before.

I am sitting here, looking up at an absolutely clear dark sky, not a cloud anywhere; a small slice of yellow moon, and a couple of emphatic stars. There is a cat yowling for love down there in the dark. Me. All I want is to be with him, with him. That's all.

The weekend I expected to spend with Richard has been spent alone. Yesterday, Saturday, I woke Kate, said I was going to do the shopping, probably buy myself a dress, have lunch out. Would she like to come with me? It was hot, London's streets full of the indolent good-nature that comes with the sun. I stood by Kate's bed, looking down; and as she stared up, befuddled, I thought of how Charlie, looming over his daughter's cot, feels himself oppressively large. How often with Kate do I see myself through her eyes: confident, careless, large, daunting. To make myself less so, I sat down on the edge of her bed. She was lying on top of the bedclothes; fully dressed. She smelled sour. I was asking her to share this day with me because of the spontaneous embrace when I got back from Amsterdam, which I felt marked an entrance into a new stage. Of affection? Of sisterhood! But that pasty formless little face of hers was hard and suspicious. After a while she said, 'Where is *he,* then?' This surprised me, for she had not challenged me before. A savage protectiveness for me and Richard came to the fore, and I said, 'Kate, that's not your affair.' I got up from the bed, dismayed at my own anger. I stood at the window and looked down, not seeing what I looked at, for I was conscious of Kate, who turned her head to look at me with a hard, triumphant little smile. What I was upset about more than anything was that I could see—much too late—that Kate's question meant she had all this time been thinking, or rather feeling, that on her arrival in my life I should have given up all else, for her; or, that I should have taken her when I went to meet Richard. Of course she had felt that, for she was really a small girl. Probably it was her strongest feeling about being here, about me.

At last I said, 'Kate, we could have quite a pleasant day, if you like. Well, it's up to you. I'm going to have a bath and go out in about half an hour . . .'

I did this and that, but she did not emerge from her room. Glancing in, I saw she was still lying in that twisted position, to look up at the square of sky in her window: it was as if she was examining something seen by her for the first time: foreign to her, and hostile.

She had not moved, and I was ready to go. I was telephoning to make an appointment for my hair, when I saw her standing in the doorway, her face hard with suspicion. Listening, through her, I was making a date for some delight with an unknown called Anton. I said, 'That is the hairdresser.' Coldly, angry that I had to explain myself to this—interloper, which was how I was feeling her at that moment. She did not believe me. Her thumb went into her mouth, she stood indecisively, than I saw her whole person set into some purpose or idea. With a glance at me that announced: You needn't think you are fooling me! she went off fast to the kitchen to get some breakfast.

'Are you coming or not?' I called.

No reply.

I went out to do some shopping, and came back an hour later with groceries. Kate was not there. When I had put everything away I went out again and sauntered down the pavement for the pleasure of Saturday morning busyness. I know most people's faces; they know mine; we smile, we nod, we comment on the weather, our voices contented, acknowledging the hot sun, summer beneficence. At the fruit and vegetable stall I bought an apple to eat as I walked. The man always has to deal with a queue because his good humour, his jokiness, attracts people. I stood behind a pretty black girl, with her hair in a thousand tiny pigtails, each tipped with a blue bead. She wore a short, red, cheeky skirt, with comic faces all over it in yellow, like suns, and a white singlet. Thin black arms were loaded with brass, copper, bead bracelets, and in her ears hung loops of red beads, like cherries, to her shoulders. The stall men, confronted by this charmer who stood grinning at him, folded his arms, raised his brows, and said, 'Marylyn, you've been robbing my stall.'

'I've done no such thing,' said she, mock indignant, and swung her cherry earrings.

'Every day I say to myself, What's that Marylyn going to come up with today? But you've outdone yourself. Well, what can I do you for?'

'You're not going to do me today as you did me yesterday. Those strawberries were all squashy at the bottom of the punnet.'

'But that's why they were half price. I was doing you a favour.'

'You can do me again with another one, for free.'

These two people speak the same, quick, cocky cockney, watching each other's lips so as to come in fast with the next riposte. The people behind me were involved, and amused. A woman said, 'You have to watch Benny's strawberries, you do. They are not always what they seem.'

'I'll thank you, Marylyn,' said he, closing his eyes with the pain of it, and wagging his head slowly, 'not to put down my strawberries. Listen to them!' Addressing the queue: 'I was selling strawberries for ten pence a punnet, less than half the cost, for jam. And they complain.'

'The ones you gave me were lovely,' said a crone, all wrapped in thick scarves and jacket against the dangers of the day. 'I had mine for tea.' She was not in the queue, but humbly, at one side, looking at some bananas that were set aside as being past it.

He said, 'Try banana and cream today,' and he slipped a couple of bananas into a bag, and handed them to her with a wink. She opened her hand to show she had some change in it, but he shook his head. She went off, stuffing the bananas into her bag, looking pleased with herself.

'And now, Marylyn, you haven't vouchsafed your needs.'

'Vouchsafe,' said the urchin, daintily, 'I am vouchsafing all the time.' And she stuck out her hand towards a pile of toffee apples. But did not take one, for she knew what he would do now. His face screwed up with the agony of indecision, he peered down at the heap, then chose one, holding it up on its stick towards the sky, dodging his head about so as to get a good look from every possible angle. Then he sighed, dramatic, put back that apple, and took up another. She was giggling, her hand clapped over her mouth. This he held down, towards the pavement, and pulling back his head as far as he could, he examined it first with one eye, the other closed, then with the second eye. Again, he sighed: 'Not good enough.' He dropped it back disdainfully and picked up a third, which he brought close up to his face, and squinted at it, moving it quickly about, his face an intent frown. Then he slowly moved it back from his face to the length of his arm, still frowning, permitted himself to nod and, taking the stick daintily between forefinger and thumb, presented the toffee apple to the black girl, who bobbed him a curtsey and at once started to lick the brown crust with an astonishingly long soft red tongue.

'And, madam, now for your ears.' And he took from the pile of cherries a linked pair, which he held out towards the girl. She inclined her head, still licking the apple. He solemnly removed the vast hoops of miniature cherries on that side and hung the two bright red cherries there. Then she stuck out her other ear. 'You want your pound of flesh, sorry, cherries, I mean,' and he hung the looped red cherries on the other side. With the two removed red bead earrings dangling from his forefinger, he contemplated them. Then he looped them over the end of the pole that held up the awning over his display of fruit.

'I'll keep them for you till you come again,' he said, and the girl went off, laughing.

He sold me my apple, remarking only that if he was to do

business that day in units of one he would soon be broke.

This was rather more lenient than I expected, though his eyes with me had been hard, not, as with Marylyn, indulgent. I could easily have been presented to the rest of the queue as an enemy, served up to them with a remark that stripped the clothes and skin off me, or with a tone of voice, or even in the way he handed me the apple, deferential. This has happened before, if he has felt the need for a victim. I have stopped there in my good clothes, the very picture of expensive well-being, and all that quick joky good humour has suddenly, savagely, been switched off, and I have stood there, exposed, the enemy: his hard, cold eyes flicking over me, once: his palm like a salver—probably copied from *Upstairs, Downstairs:* offering the paper bag with the tomatoes: 'Veenay great?' And the faces of the people in the queue as suddenly as his changed to their reverse: full of a secret, gloating malice. The enemy: the rich. England. There is a vein, or a streak, or a mine, of sadism, cold and expectant. A stall-holder playing at being a stall-holder, with all the tricks: entertainment, people queueing for that as much as for a lettuce or a toffee apple. I have been the entertainment. Also, going to his stall alone, we have exchanged amiabilities, fellow good citizens of this agreeable city. But: let there be a queue, and I stand in it waiting to see if it will be I, today, who will be served up.

I walked on towards the underground, melting, like the pavements, but with pleasure. And I wanted this mood to last, for woe lay in wait for me . . . where was Richard? I was trying to remember when in my life I have waited, helpless, for a telephone to ring.

I dawdled down into the underground. The carriage had in it some French students, several middle-aged Americans, a group of young Germans, some middle-class Russians presumably from the Trade Delegation in Highgate—all spies, I recall, with an agreeable shiver—three Indians, and two very large black ladies, Nigerian, looking like sailing ships. I think I was the only native there. My spirits rising every moment, with the inventiveness, variety and interest of the journey, I travelled on towards Baker Street station, where I went out into the street in a rush of schoolchildren going to the Planetarium, crossed it and made my way to Marylebone High Street, where I went to Monica's and tried on half a dozen sun-dresses, none of which I intended to buy. This is a game I play, accompliced by Monica herself, who is well used to the middle-aged—I will *not* say elderly—taking time off into the past. Monica left some other customers, elegant French women, to an assistant, and came with me into the trying-on which just had room for her to lean, arms folded, back against the wall, watching. Monica looks French and elegant, wears severe dark hair and neat little outfits, but when the shop is empty she will throw all this off, with me, and join in an orgy of retrospection, she lilting up and down in *Jeune Fille* skimpy frills, while I return to my early twenties in fantasy outfits, rather like Jill's and Hannah's now, emerging from the changing rooms like a buccaneer, or a beefeater. The two middle-aged ladies, in fancy dress, parade before Monica's wall of mirrors, and collapse on to her grey velvet sofa in fits of laughter, which are cured by the assistant bringing us cups of coffee and indulgent smiles from which she banishes the slight hint of impatience or criticism.

Monica today knew at once when I stood in the white *piqué* dress with a halter neck and a bare back, that I could easily have bought it; for what I was seeing in the looking-glass was a not *so* solid, tentative, attractive woman who had a look of youth about her as she fingered, in an uncertain, appealing way, the white *piqué* line that cut across her chest, and smoothed down the blonde wisps of disarray around her ears. Monica said quietly, 'My dear Janna, *no*,' and I took off the dress, and handed it to her. She went out with her armload of sun-frocks, while I stood emptily, waiting for the depression I was so afraid of to strike home. But she came back with a beautiful blouse, silky and gentle, in dove grey, and slid it over my head, and made soothing, almost cooing noises, as I saw how it became me.

As I paid for it, and they wrapped it, the coffee: and Monica and I drank it, watching the two French women walking up and down in the suits they might buy. Their complete, close, silent concentration, hardly speaking; you'd think they were not breathing, as they turned and walked one way, stopped, presented their backs to the glass, then their sides, then their fronts, then walked back, slowly, like models. First one, while the other watched, making little exclamations, or a breath of comment; then the first became critic. A beige linen suit, and a white one; each expensive, and you'd think perfect, but they were both rejected, for neither was quite right, not absolutely and utterly, and Monica stood for a few minutes with these two experts, smiling and agreeing that they were quite correct to go on with their quest, for everything in this world depends on detail.

The beige suit, the white one, were in the hands of the assistant, about to be hung up, when in came some American girls who were in search of sun-dresses. They went into the changing room with the ones I had just rejected. Monica and I exchanged small ironies with our smiles, and I went out into the street. It was dazzling, full midday, and I did not believe my eyes when they told me that on the opposite pavement Kate was standing, staring at me. She looked both furious and guilty; and I went across to her, fast, knowing that cars would hoot, and they did as they stopped for this crazy woman.

'Kate, is anything the matter?'

'No.'

'Well, if you've come to join me—good. Have some lunch?'

'Oh . . . no . . . not really. I'm going to the squat.'

I exclaimed, 'The *squat!*' For it is in Chalk Farm.

'You don't own the pavement,' she burst out, and hearing the ridiculousness of it, went red, and said, 'Anyway, I'm late, Aunt Jane!' And went off towards Oxford Street.

This brought down my spirits, already dented in Monica's, and I went on draggingly, feeling hot, knowing that this business with Kate meant ill, to her, or to me; knowing that I had consistently refused to face how dislocated and lost she was; knowing that I ought to be doing something about her, but not what . . . In this state I walked past a little restaurant I was in once with Richard. I went in, was recognized by the German who runs it, given a little table at the window and served a large plate of very likeable *hors d'oeuvres* ordered as a main course; but could not finish them, for everything on my tongue tasted flabby and heat-limp, but this was my fault, not the restaurant's. I was thinking, of course, of Richard. I left quickly, went into the hairdresser's to cancel my appointment, and came home, having used up all my vitality.

The flat without Kate in it offered an opportunity for tidying up; a task that I as usual do not shirk; and it needed it, although Mrs Brown had done a little before giving up.

I took the yellow linen covers with the cigarette burns off the armchairs, and thought then that I would need to get new ones made. The chairs without the yellow are a soft rust, almost cherry; and I used to love them, only covered them up when I had to. I sat on the sofa, but not in the grubby depression that is Kate's, and looked at the chairs and thought that Freddie and I had sat in them opposite each other, and this brought such a flood of misery that I simply went to bed. It was three in the afternoon. I don't remember ever doing anything like it before. I wept and slept, and woke looking at a square that was full of evening: a late, soft, beguiling sunlight, trailing fleecy clouds.

I made supper for me and for Kate, waited for a while, but she did not come. Anxiety. I kept repeating that lying litany: But she's nineteen, she's an adult . . . while I wondered if I should ring the police.

In the end I did not; I bathed, attended to my clothes, and went to bed to read myself to sleep. Which was not until after four in the morning when the sky was again filling with another hot summer day. I don't know what I dreamed, but it was a very sad dream; and I got myself out of bed early and went off to Regent's Park, and there I spent the day, by myself, walking through roses, roses, and sitting near the fountains by the tall poplars.

Kate came in an hour ago, looking awful. She had been smoking pot, and was fuzzy and vague and did not answer when I asked her what sort of weekend she had had. When I came in here, to go to bed, she took the things out of her ears and asked, 'Are you going to work tomorrow?'

'But of course I'm going to work tomorrow!'

It was all beyond me; Kate is beyond me. She is sitting

there now, jiggling away to her music, and I am going to sleep.

Today I was in Archives all morning with June looking up back numbers of *Lilith* for an article on fashion in the sixties. It goes without saying that for her it was an historical epoch, like the Edwardians for me; but it certainly puts a perspective on things when of your yesterday a young adult remarks indifferently, 'I think they were rather silly.' At my look, she expounded, 'I mean, they had no social conscience in those days. Waste not, want not.' This agglomeration of improbables in two sentences addled my tongue, and I did not go on with it. I like Archives—a grand name for what might once have been the butler's pantry, twelve by twelve of a concentration of social history crammed to the roof on shelves. We had to have the doors open into the typists' room. Ten of them; and with half my mind I enjoyed the lively goings-on, and with the other judged the work we did fifteen, twenty years ago. Things change, and you don't know how much. We have made successive decisions not to change *Lilith;* precisely, not to accommodate ourselves to harder times, on the grounds that people need glamour. Well, *Lilith*'s covers have become wilder, more surreal, with girls that resemble tropical birds or insects.

I asked June, for curiosity, if she'd like to be moved up into another department, into Editorial, and she said no, she liked it where she was. And anyway she was engaged to be married, and next May she'd be leaving us. 'It'll be sad, leaving the old place,' said she, meaning the typists' room.

When I went back up, Jill said that Richard had rung. Yes, she had said, of course, that I could be fetched, but he said he would ring again. I knew that I had gone white; I could feel my flesh chilly on my face. Hannah is not one to be inhibited by false tact; and I was grateful that she put a chair under me, then stood behind me, massaging my neck and shoulders. 'There, there,' said she, 'poor Janna.' I could feel the heat of her large breasts, and her hands were strong and calm. It was a shock to me, the pulsing warmth of that young Aztec. I hardly ever touch anyone, after all. Sometimes poor old Annie, when she's sick or needs helping up from her chair. I allowed my head to rest back, and was accepted into her maternal plenitudes.

The telephone rang; it was Richard, and I took the receiver from Jill. I was feeling more than foolish: behaving like a teenager with a boyfriend. I noticed the composure with which Hannah laid her hands on my shoulders, pressed them, and went back to her desk.

'Richard!'

'Janna, you are there.'

Linked with his voice, and our certainties—which exist, though about what I could not say—my anxieties left me, and I was myself.

'I said I would ring, but I thought I would wait till I got back, and then that was delayed . . .'

'Where are you?'

'Boston.'

At this, that moment when I will hear, Boston—or Tasmania, or Greenland—and know it is for ever, came towards me from the future, and I could not say anything.

'Janna!'

I found I could not speak.

'Janna, are you there?'

I croaked out, 'Yes.'

'I'm booked on a flight back tomorrow. Janna, it was an emergency.'

I croaked, 'When will I see you?'

'Lunchtime on Wednesday. The square.'

'Yes.'

'Without fail.'

'Janna, I couldn't honestly say I wish you were here, but I wish I was there.'

'Me too.'

I sat on in the chair, recovering, while Hannah took the telephone receiver, replaced it, and set a cup of coffee in front of me.

Jill was typing as if she were running a race with her own sense of the outrageous: she was embarrassed because of me;

flushed, and tight-lipped. I noticed I needed, very badly, to put my arms around her and warn her—but say what? No words! To communicate as Hannah did, waves of communication from, was it?—her solar plexus?

Hannah was standing with her back to the filing cabinet, her coffee cup in her hand, contemplating me and my condition and what it demanded from her. Today she was wearing a dress of strong blue cotton, loose because it was so hot this afternoon, the sun streaming in. Her arms were bare and brown, her strong legs brown and bare. Everything about her is so healthy, sound and right. I swear she would only have to stand in a room anywhere, and life would obediently have to order its waves to flow around her and the faces of everyone would turn towards her. 'There, there,' she would say, to life.

Suddenly I found myself thinking, What would it be like to be in bed with Hannah?

If there are generation gaps, this is one. The only lesbians I ever met before the Women's Movement were evident as being full of suppressed intensities, seemed to want to insist on perversity, paraded miseries before you, and—in my case at least—attempted (twice) seductions that had about them an air of the theatrical, as if they were play-acting seductions that had a script and which did not come from their real natures.

It came into my head that if I said now, at this moment, to Hannah, 'I was wondering what it would be like to be in bed with you,' she would remark, 'Well, you should give it a try one of these days,' and I could hear the unspoken addendum: Do you good.

This made me want to laugh; I choked, Hannah neatly fielded my coffee cup and saucer, and I sat laughing helplessly.

These day, girls discuss it as if they are or are not going to try on a dress. Jill remarked once, when she was quarrelling with Mark, 'I said to him, Mark, you are all too much. I'm going to live with a woman. They are not so demanding.'

'And what did Mark say?' I asked.

'He said, How you do know, you've never tried one? I said,

Well, perhaps it was time I did. He said, Well, if you do, let me know when you need a change. I said, You're so damned cocky. He said, You've put your finger on it.' At which she had said he was vulgar, crude and conceited beyond bearing. A few minutes later she remarked that she enjoyed quarrelling with Mark: this with the little air of satisfaction that is so characteristic of her.

I said to Hannah, 'Thank you,' meaning it from the heart, and then, that I had to go to see how Charlie was getting on.

In the great cool room Charlie was sitting at one end of the long table, smoking a Gauloise. Three tall windows admitted summer, and on a windowsill two pigeons sat basking. Charlie was looking rather flushed, as if he had drunk too much at lunch. I said to him that we had problems to discuss, decisions to make, policies to decide. He said comfortably that he had every confidence in my judgement.

I said to him, as I do it seems every other day, 'Charlie, the world is full of people who never dream of doing any work, but most at least put on a show of working.'

'Why should I, Janna? I've always found things went along very well for me. There are always people who adore working, and are good at it.'

'Well, let's pretend, at least.' I handed him the pile of *Lilith*s from the sixties, and he sat turning them over, appreciative, even proud, as if he had been responsible for them all.

I got on with my work. Time passed. Then he yawned, stood up, collected the pile of magazines and brought them to me. 'If I don't leave now I'll miss Caroline's six o'clock feed,' he said.

From the door he gave me a smile that combined the determination to do exactly as he wants; a slight, rather pleasurable guilt; a twinkling complicity that made me laugh, though I was annoyed. Then he escaped. I hear his voice in exchanges with Jill's and Hannah's. Laughter. Then two typewriters started off together.

When I got home, I knew that someone else had been there; and understood Kate's inquiry, Would I be going to work? The two cherry-coloured chairs were covered with ash and crumbs. In the kitchen I found that the fridge had been cleared out of everything, even milk and butter. They had made sandwiches of the cheeses I had brought from Holland, eaten the steak I had put to thaw out for tonight, drunk all the Bols, demolished a large cake. The sink was full of plates and glasses. Three of them had been here.

I did not know what to do. Kate could say to me, as she was probably planning to do, 'But are you saying I can't have my *friends* here?' And what was the use of saying to her, 'You know perfectly well their coming here and making themselves at home is a deliberate act of defiance, or aggression, like raiding foreign territory.'

I was very angry. Then I was cold and discouraged. I stayed for a long time in the kitchen and washed everything up. Then I took a bag and went fast down to the shops and bought everything again that we needed. I brought these home, put everything away, tidied everything; I had been walking in and out, to and fro past Kate, because I did not know what to say. She sat on in the sofa corner, sullenly staring ahead of her, her ears harnessed.

Then, having done it all, I went up to her, took the things out of her ears, and shouted because I knew she would be deaf, 'Kate, if that ever happens again you are going to have to leave.' Then I put the two leads back in her ears, without waiting to hear what she had to say. But I saw on her face pleasure, as well as a sullen triumph. I don't know why; because I had put my foot down, and now she could say to them all that her unkind aunt had said she could not have her friends in: she needs me to lay down the law?

I have no idea. When I think that she might indeed leave, then panic surges up. Because I shall have to ring Sister Georgie and say, Your daughter has joined the flotsam and jetsam, the derelicts of London? I have not heard one word from my sister. This is so unlike her, and outside the codes and mores spoken and unspoken of our family life (such as it is), that when I think of it I feel as if solid ground has given way. Whatever else one has to say about my sister and her kind, they are not people who renege on their responsibilities.

I said to Jill, 'Do you realize I have not heard from your mother?'

'I hear from her,' she said composedly.

'What does she say about Kate?'

'She hopes Kate is all right.'

'But that is preposterous!'

'What can she say?'

'But she knows Kate is a disaster area and can't be "all right".'

'Jane,' said Jill, laying aside her work, and giving me her full attention. 'Why is it you can't see it? Don't you *see*? My parents don't know how to cope with unsuccessful people.'

'But they are full of good works, dishing out aid and comfort.'

'Yes, but that's for people who are like that—old people, junkies, delinquents.'

'If Kate is not a delinquent, what is she?'

'Yes, but she is one of *us*, don't you see? She's not out *there*. My parents can't hand out goodies or tender loving care and then say bye-bye and go back home. *She doesn't measure up*. To them. She makes them feel a failure and they can't have that.'

'Tell me, then, what do you suppose they have in mind for Kate long-term? That she will be slumping around my home for ever? Yes, yes, don't bother to say it, I chose it. But what do they think will happen?'

'They *don't* think. They say to themselves that Kate is just a late starter, or something like that.'

'Well, perhaps she is.'

Silence, from me.

Then: 'Hannah thinks Kate should go to their commune.'

I looked at Hannah.

She said, 'It's the worst possible thing for her, to be with you.'

'Are you sure?'

'She can't measure up to you, any more than to her parents.'

'You, Hannah, are hardly inadequate, in any area!'

'No,' said Hannah, 'I am not. But there are ten women in

our commune, and some of them are like Kate. People who need time.'

'I'm not going to throw her out.'

'Of course you mustn't throw her out,' directed Hannah, 'but she'll leave, won't she?'

'Will she?'

'You don't love her,' announced Hannah, without criticism.

'I think I'm fond of her, in a dreary sort of way, hopeless. She makes me feel inadequate. It's like sliding into a fog.'

'Well, there you are,' said Jill. 'But who wouldn't feel that?' This was a sniffing little challenge to Hannah, who merely smiled, knowing better.

But now I have told Kate I will throw her out—if.

Love! Love! Love!

I love Jill, but I don't love Kate. I love Richard. I am rapidly getting very fond of Hannah. I feel fondly affectionate towards Charlie. I feel affection for Mark. I like Phyllis very much, whereas at first I disliked her. I loved Joyce—oh, yes, I did, no doubt of it. But now, where is all that? And Freddie? No, I did not love Freddie. My heart aches tonight, it aches. Tomorrow I shall be seeing Richard, so my heart ought to be skipping like a sparrow.

This morning I was glad to be working in the big room, away from those two sharp-eyed women, Hannah and Jill. Charlie and I discussed the article about that remote epoch, the sixties, while he amused me with a hundred agreeable little reminiscences. Meanwhile, I was in a turmoil, like an adolescent, thinking about Richard. But waiting to see him, today, was not as it has been, a rapid rise of temperature knowing there would be calm and pleasure when we met: no, I was anxious and restless; a condition that no one could describe as pleasurable. Love! An anguish. This morning I was in a sharply opposite mood to the one I was in when I wrote my acid piece last night: thinking that, if I did not love

Freddie, so much the better. If love is suffering, and a lot of useless emotions, then why bother ... And did Freddie suffer? Oh, that is what I can't stand, it is coming closer, crowding in: it is what I really can't face.

I went to Soho Square early. It was humid and airless. The sky had a hazy occluded look. I wanted to sit quietly by myself and let the anxiety go away. But as I came into the square I saw Richard, sitting by himself at the end of a bench. He was not expecting me yet. What I saw was a middle-aged man, evidently tired, staring at some pigeons feeding in a flowerbed. When I sat down by him, he looked up as at an unwanted stranger, then he smiled and his whole body seemed to fill with energy as he turned and put his arms around me. We sat like that for a few moments, then I heard him sigh, and we moved apart.

'Two weeks,' he said, as if in accusation.

'Two weeks,' I accused.

'How was Amsterdam?'

'As it always is.' I didn't want to talk about what to me is only something that I have to do; I wanted to know about America, Boston. I said, 'And how was America?'

He shifted his legs, lost some of his confidence, and said, 'I had to go. All right, I see I shall have to tell you. But first, let us go to a pub and get ourselves cushioned against fate.'

We got up together and went out of the square, and I heard myself asking anxiously, 'What fate? Are you going away again?'

'Not yet.'

This did not assuage me: I was actually thinking, as we walked towards *our* pub, If it's going to end anyway, then what's the point: but that was because today it was as if two weeks of not being with Richard had accumulated need that had been, during the time we were meeting so often, fed little by little, but now nothing he said or did could stop that tormenting ache. It seemed to me then, in that heavy hazy sunlight, that damp heat, as if the ache, the want, had swelled up, too large to be contained by Richard. All I wanted was to be rid of this burden, this ache.

Our table was free, and we squeezed ourselves in, sitting

low among the tall noisy lunchtime crowd.

'What fate?' I asked, as soon as I sat down.

He gave that snort of laughter that means someone has behaved as expected; endearingly perhaps, but too predictably, and I said, 'Suddenly I can't bear it. But bear *what*? If I knew...'

'I understand perfectly.' He reached down from the counter two double Scotches, which the man had supplied on a nod and: 'The usual,' and he handed me mine. 'Drink up.'

'I want to know.'

'Yes. First, Amsterdam. I want to know. Yes, I've been saying no, no, no, let's *not*, but I find myself more and more thinking about your life. I know nothing at all about you. And I'm jealous.'

'I'm so jealous that... and I've never ever been jealous...' My voice trailed off; for what I was saying, and I knew it, was that I had not loved before. I said, very low, not looking at him, feeling my face hot: 'I don't think I've loved like this...' I could feel his eyes close and keen on my face, wanting me to look up, but I couldn't. I was afraid to see what there might be there on his face. Some kind of pain, I knew that, and not on my account. Oh, our thoughts fly back and forth between us, so fast; we think the same thoughts.

'Amsterdam. What do you do on these—jaunts?'

'It's not a jaunt. I work, very hard. Very well. There's a hotel I always go to. It's one of the tall old houses, on a canal. They try to give me a room right at the top, which I like. You look at trees, and the water and the boats going past. Once, in winter, there were people skating, like a Breughel. They bring me coffee and bread and jam, early, at seven. I hate being rushed and fussed. I take my time. Then I walk to wherever it is. This time another hotel, used a lot for conferences. And then, when it's over, I have dinner with someone—I know a lot of people in the trade, of course.'

'Of course,'

'And then I usually walk back, because I like walking in Amsterdam, and I go to bed and read.'

He was regarding me with irony. We held our glasses, and were drinking with the intention of finishing and ordering more. The glow of the drink and the noisy cheerful crowd made me feel better; and he said, 'Well, that's better.' And he took our two empty glasses and set them on the counter to be refilled.

'I know I am an oaf and a bumpkin, but what do you do all day?'

'This time, I listened to reports and speeches. From all over the world. Fashion—the state of—the crisis in—there's always a crisis in fashion . . .'

'There's always a crisis in everything, hadn't you noticed?'

We laughed. It was easy to laugh: we looked at each other, our eyes not wanting to look at anything else; he reached down our two glasses, and I suddenly said, 'I'm going to phone and say I won't be in this afternoon, if you're free?'

'I'm free.'

I told Hannah to tell Charlie, who had not yet left, that I was taking the afternoon off and this and this and this was to be done. By him.

Back at our table, I slid into my chair as if into a happiness that would never end, for the afternoon stretched away in front of us, and he said, 'You had breakfast, walked to the other hotel, and there you listened to speeches. All day?'

'Yes. And I made one. People from South America and Canada and the States. From every country in Europe. From the Soviet Union. Everywhere. You know—fashion. Big business.'

'What was your speech about?'

'A report. I was speaking on behalf of the upmarket women's magazines in Britain.'

'You listened to speeches for four days?'

'We also split off into smaller groups—committees and subcommittees. Discussing aspects of. Aspects of, mostly the Depression.'

'Ah yes, the Depression.'

'This *is* the real subject of conferences everywhere at the moment.'

He said, 'Are we going to admit the Depression?'

I said, 'It is not just the Depression. Last time, there was Depression, and then War.'

'Yes.'

'Yes.'

I lifted my glass to him and knew that my smile was strained. His was bleak.

'Let's *not*,' I said.

'No. But I suppose this is where I tell you what I was doing in the States?—Yes? Right. We had an urgent call. We have a son, Down's syndrome. A mongol. John. We've not put him in a home or an institution. We've not wanted that. But when we both came away this time, in April, we did not bring him. It would have been impossible. He needs to have someone there with him all the time. In Washington we have a woman who lives in our house. Cuban. She's like one of us now. But she had a family crisis of her own, her mother, and at first we thought there was no one to leave him with. It's not everyone who can cope with—the inadequate.'

'How old is he?'

'By age, sixteen. Two years younger than Kathleen. But he is really about four or five. He's very lovable—they are, you know. We never wanted to put him in an institution. We'd have missed a lot. Sometimes I think he's the only person of the five of us in our house who is happy.'

Listening to this, what I was doing was putting the flesh of detail, detail, on to the plot. The house, and in it Richard; Kathleen, the elder daughter; the idiot boy around whom everything—it would have to—adapted itself; his wife, that unknown quantity; the large, sensible southern woman . . . he had said five.

'Five?' I asked. 'The Cuban lady?'

'No. With Maria, six. Our son Matthew is an extremely ambitious and hard-working young man. Like my wife,' he put in quickly, with a glance at me: you have to take it, at some time. 'Yes. But no one could describe Matthew as one of the world's sunbeams. He works and plays with equal dedication. Kathleen has always been shadowed—by John. She was two when he was born, and for some reason he afflicted her. Matthew has never been involved, he accepted it, went his own way, cutting himself off emotionally from us early. But Kathleen loved John, she loves him, she suffers over him, she is embarrassed by him, when people come and there's this happy idiot, a sort of deformed dwarf, always laughing and there, like a happy puppy, you know—but people coming for the first time always have to be put in the picture and then adjust. It is always Kathleen who mediates. She can't stand it, I believe, somewhere deep inside. I believe it is a sort of permanent anguish for her. Sylvia and I . . .' Again the little glance, assessing, even diagnostic: she must take it, is she taking it? And he put his hand down over mine and squeezed it and sighed, and his face was the same as a mother or nurse who has to make a child take medicine, and is so involved with the act that the physical relief of having swallowed shows on her face. 'Oh, Janna . . .' he breathed, but went on: 'I and Sylvia had discussed this often enough, as you can imagine. We were always arranging for Kathleen to be away, staying with friends, at holiday camps—you know, they have them in the States for young people in the summer, marvellous things, you should do more of it here . . .' I was noting, of course, the *you:* but he didn't notice. 'But it did no good, you see. We could send Kathleen off to camp for a summer, but she'd be on the telephone every other day: How is John? No, the person who has taken the real burden of John is Kathleen.'

'Not Maria?'

'No. Not emotionally. Quite rightly. She's not had children of her own. Unmarried. She is by nature a cheerful and busy person.' I was smiling to myself, because this sounded like a doctor's notes. 'So-and-so is a cheerful and busy person with many interests, and the prognosis is good.' 'Kathleen loves John. No, but really. He loves her. It's not I or Sylvia who have suffered over John. We both work very hard, you know. We both say—though it is not very easy to understand—that coming home to John is like a tonic. There's a kind of joy they have.'

'I've read about it.'

'Well, it's true. Extraordinary. It's a kind of irrepressible exuberance welling up.'

I sat silent, weighted with all this, feeling those years, Richard and Sylvia, three children, the house, the cheerful and busy woman from Cuba ... doubtless cats, dogs and hamsters. it was all too much for me. Over thirty years, he had said.

'How old is Matthew?'

'Twenty-two. I was waiting for you to ask. No, we did not have children, not till we were both over thirty. We were both nineteen when we married. Children. There should be a law against it.'

'Why? You are still together?'

'Yes—no, that's not it. I don't regret . . .' Again he put his hand over mine, tossed the whisky into the back of his throat, indicated I should finish mine. I did, and he set the two empty glasses back on the counter.

'I am getting drunk.'

'Good. How can we get through this otherwise?'

'Why did you wait for so long without children?'

'We were both too busy. We waited ten years. Working. Working. Isn't that enough for today?'

'Yes, it is, more than enough. I don't think I can . . .' I shook my head. I was full to the throat with that 'over thirty years' of crammed, packed, family life, the intensity of it, the *organization*—two working parents (what did Sylvia do?), an ambitious and clever elder son, Kathleen whose spirit was darkened by the irrepressibly jolly and happy mongol boy who would never grow up.

'Just one thing, and that's enough for today. What was the crisis you had to go back to?'

'John has never been without one of the family around, at least one of us, and Maria has been with us since he was five. Suddenly, we all went away, except Matthew, but he's at university, he's there in the mornings and evenings, and he's never been anything more than pleasantly distant with John. And we had Maria's sister in the house. John is not used to her. And so he got ill. That's the real reason he was ill, though it's pneumonia. Was. He's over it.'

I was digesting all this: questions emerged. I decided not to ask any of them.

'I think we ought to have some lunch,' I said.

'Good idea.'

We walked down to Wheeler's. But our two lives, the real lives, the texture and pattern and weight—the weight, the *weight*—was there now, between us. Is there. Then we went to the pictures like children and saw—but what does that matter? We held hands. He said he had to go home at about seven. Outside the pub where we had a drink before parting, Kathleen was standing, her back to us, staring across the street. She's a handsome girl; but heavy, slow, because of her hypnotized look.

It seemed to me that we ought to go up to her in an ordinary way, so that we could meet, she and I: and I think that was what Richard meant to do. But as he hesitated slightly, she walked straight across the road and away. A heavy, blind walk.

'Was she upset about John's being ill? Didn't she want to go with you.'

'We didn't tell her. Yes, that sounds strange. But it was hard enough to get her to accept coming to university here. She didn't want to be parted from him. We'd been fighting it all out—for months. It seems like years now. We wanted her to be severed from him, do you see?'

He had his arm in mine, and I could feel from the pressure of it how much he wanted me to understand.

'Yes, I do see.'

'Good.'

'If she found out he was so ill and she didn't know, would she forgive you?'

'Ah. Yes!' He stopped, turned, took my two upper arms in his hands and smiled straight into my face. 'Yes. Yes. That was my position. But Sylvia . . . We discussed it, it seems to me we have been discussing nothing else since we came here, Sylvia said, we've *got* her away from him, she's made the break.'

That we, we, we, we! Each time it said to me, You interloper, you *nothing*. And 'we have been discussing nothing else'—I could see myself, way off on the periphery, someone met when there was time, a pleasant entertainment outside the real business of life.

He was saying, 'It's not like that, Janna,' squeezing my

arms, gently rocking me back and forth. His face was close, urgent, concerned.

I shook my head, I could not speak. He put his arm about me and we walked soberly along Old Compton Street. His arm, the strong warmth of it, said to me, Nothing has changed.

At the corner he said, 'I had hoped we could spend tomorrow evening together?'

I quavered, 'I wouldn't have the strength of mind to say no!'

'The pub?'

I nodded again, and went on up Charing Cross Road, half blind and choked.

By the time I got to *Lilith* I had recovered. I stood as I sometimes do, looking at the old houses, externally unchanged, and wondering what the people who lived in them—let's say, up to the First World War—would make of us, of *Lilith,* who spreads herself over two houses, who has knocked down walls and removed barriers and boundaries where once separate families might have heard the odd sound through thick brick and plaster. I was thinking of how these houses were layered once, the family on the ground floor, first floor, second floor; the servants in the basement and at the very top; and, as I thought of those servants, going in and out down the steps where now the typists and secretaries go, it was as if there was a time-blur, for there was a skivvy, a kitchen maid, someone like that, standing on the pavement, wearing a dragging long skirt and a flowered blouse, and what from this distance looked like a bonnet. I walked fast towards this visitant from the past and saw it was Kate, who stood humbly on the pavement gazing up to where her lucky sister worked. It was her streaky hair, pink and green, that looked like a bonnet. 'Kate,' I said, and she turned with a start, and said, 'Oh, you did go out then . . .' but her voice trailed away, and she went an ugly red. This was so much not what I expected, I did not at first hear what she had said. Besides, I was in the grip of such pity for the wretch. All bouleversed, soggy, and sagging with emotions as I was, only just in command of myself, there was something about Kate that went, smash, to my heart, and I could have hugged her,

like a small, disconsolate child, or perhaps the sentimental-
ized version of a put-upon put-down pre-First World War
scullery maid. Then I did hear, retrospectively, what she had
said; and I stared at her and she at me. Suddenly, things
clicked into place. *Kate has been following me.* Following
Richard and me. Just like Kathleen. How often? For how
long? Where to? I don't know, and I don't propose to think
about it.

But that girl had gone to *Lilith* in order to trail me while I
went off to my assignation with my demon lover—but I had
left early—for she had known he was back; because of my
manner? She had overheard me on the telephone? I could not
remember whether she had been there or not.

She knew I had understood, and her stare was hard, bold,
triumphant. Far from wanting to embrace her, I wanted to hit
her, hard. And I went on up the steps into the hall where once
ladies and gentlemen handed cards to parlour maids or took
off their coats and hats, and then to the third floor, hoping
that Charlie would not be there. I needed to recover. I was
suffering from as bad a fit of panic as I can remember. I was
feeling caged. I felt like that when Maudie made me her
prisoner, not by what she said but by her need. I have felt like
that sometimes with poor Annie. But this child is in my home,
my life; and there is no way I know I can use to get rid of her.
The idea that she follows Richard and me . . . But how is it
we have not seen her? We have not been looking for her,
that's why! Richard has known once or twice that Kathleen
has been with us when I thought she was not: told me
afterwards, not at the time.

I sat alone at the long table where the heavy damp trees of
midsummer stood around beyond the windows, and thought,
No, it is all too much. I cannot see Richard again. Being with
him is simple and easy; as if we had both been born for it. But
we both drag trails of muddy circumstances with us, and we
cannot even meet without spies and observers. And yet I
knew quite well that I will be in the pub tomorrow. And who
else will be there?

Kate was not in when I returned this evening. She did not
come until about eleven, and said she had been at the squat.

She was quite terrified, putting on all kinds of little airs of bravado, expecting me to say, And now you must go. When I said goodnight, her eyes were brimming with tears, and she came to embrace me. It was a sad little embrace. I feel so lacking, holding that poor child in my arms, this nineteen-year-old who is like a dumpy apprehensive child, I don't know what to say or do. She needs—everything!

Richard rang before lunch. Charlie had already gone. I was alone. As I worked I was listening to Jill and Hannah in the cheerful outer office. Wishing I could be there and not in the big dreary editor's room. I don't know why, but it has always been a lifeless room for some reason. Whereas the outer office where I worked so long with Joyce, then with Phyllis, then too briefly with Jill, has always zinged with life. I was thinking that this move in away from that room to work finally with Charlie meant the real severance with Jill, who, naturally enough, has more attention to pay her flatmate and to Hannah, than to her aunt. I was altogether in a low mood, and thoughts of Richard were not helping at all. It was at this point that he rang, sounding harassed, asked if I had a car; I said I used to have, but sold it, I used it so little. The trouble was, said Richard, that he thought we should not meet in our pub, but somehow if we could get away, perhaps to the country, he couldn't explain now, but . . . I said he didn't need to explain.

We eventually arranged that he would pick me up exactly at five thirty in a taxi and we would drive to Baker Street, and from there go by underground to Wimbledon, where there was a restaurant he had discovered. All this came to pass. On my way past Jill and Hannah, I sneaked a look down on to the pavement to make sure Kate wasn't there, or Kathleen. I couldn't see either. I knew I was looking furtive, and that Hannah and Jill would start commenting on me the moment I had left. How primitive we all are: by leaving that room, leaving *them* their closeness, I had become *other,* and I would be discussed in a way that I would not have been while actually working with them, in that room.

Richard's taxi drew up as I got to the door and I sneaked into it.

'All clear?' I gasped.

'As far as I can see.'

We embraced. A strange flavour, our embraces have. Friendship, yes, that above all, instant intimacy, always, as if we have never been apart. The warm understanding of the flesh, his hand on my summer-bared forearm, mine behind his neck. Passion, oh yes, it is all there, imminent, incipient, like a country stretching all around us that some mysterious law forbids us to enter. Thus far and no farther is written on our invisible tablets, so that we may repose inside each other's arms, feeling them burn and promise; but we may not turn our heads to kiss. If our lips did meet, good God, what an announcement that would be but—and this is the point—something would at that moment die. What? Do we know? I don't. My God, what a world I have locked away from me! I feel his breath on my cheek, and at once a warning sounds: Be careful, even as I long to turn my face so that my mouth would, for the first time, arrive in the same place as his. Oh no. No, no, no.

Disengaging, and *not* looking at each other, for it is amazing how, when we move out of these dangerous and sorrowful embraces, we are careful not to let our eyes meet, he said, 'I am sorry about the cloak and dagger stuff. But something happened.'

He said this with a long, contemplative inward stare: as at ranges of possibilities of things that could happen. All, I feel, for the worst.

And I felt with him that my life, as well as his, could present us with something not explosively but insidiously bad. *Is* presenting us with: as we crawled up Tottenham Court Road, I was examining the pavements in case Kate should appear there, standing with her face to the traffic, her eyes at work on the interior, of every taxi, to catch me out.

'You'd better tell me,' I said.

'Matthew, you know, our oldest, let Kathleen know that John had been ill. No, no, it wasn't malice, or mischief-making, or anything like that. It was—indifference. You see, he has turned a key on caring about John, he did that long ago. So when we, in fact it was Sylvia, wrote to ask him not to tell Kathleen, he didn't take it in. He sent a postcard to Kathleen, added as a postscript: And John is out of danger. He didn't think.'

'So Kathleen doesn't forgive you.'

'Ah! But what is she not forgiving us for? Of course, for making John a mongol in the first place.'

'Not very rational.'

'But what, dear Janna, is rational?'

This struck me as being well over the line of tolerance, into—what? I was thinking that in Richard and in Sylvia, these two by definition rational and sensible people, was something altogether out of proportion when it came to talking of Kathleen. For a healthy eighteen-year-old to trail her handsome father and his wicked mistress week in week out, not even making much secret of it, but standing around on pavements and on river banks quite openly, if with that heavy, brooding, almost hypnotized look—well, it is surely beyond what is to be expected of adolescence; though of course I know that that has to be bad enough. In short, I was sitting there thinking that Kathleen was more than somewhat crazy. And that Richard and Sylvia refused to recognize it; just as my ever-loving Sister Georgie and her mate refuse to see that Kate is fit for a loony-bin. Well, not far off.

'She hasn't announced that she is going back to John? To be with him?'

'We asked her not to. But I don't think she can. You see, she has to stay here to make sure that her father isn't going to . . .'

'Richard,' I said. 'Look! It is an utterly marvellous evening. Let us not talk about these ghastly children . . .' I saw his half-annoyed, half-appreciative glance, heard his snort of laughter, noted his querying look. 'Yes, we do not have only one of them on our trail. Now there's one of mine. No, I am *not* going to tell you about her now. For God's sake, let us enjoy this evening . . .' And I stopped myself from adding, It might be the last chance we get. But he heard this, though I didn't say it, and his fingers tightened on my hand.

We slid out of the taxi at Baker Street, both with furtive glances over our shoulders, we ran inside, and in the carriage knew that we were checking up on the faces of everyone in it, and those who came in. But we were alone, and our spirits rose, and by the time we got to Wimbledon we were able to forget poor Kathleen, poor Kate.

We wandered for a while among Wimbledon's leafy streets that were hot, heavy and spicy, noted the admirable roses, and then went into our restaurant, which has tables in a garden at the back, and a little pool with irises, and birds swooping in to splash and drink.

And so: it was a lovely evening. It *was* a lovely evening. It was. But there was a heaviness and an anxiety there, just behind our pleasure in each other. More than once, our eyes meeting, we acknowledged it in a small grimace, a smile. And there we parted, in the bowels of Baker Street underground, he said, 'I've got to rush. Matthew said he would ring us. Midnight. That's seven there. He gets in from college about seven. He's very regular in his ways, Matthew is. To be counted on in all things.' We shared a smile at this, and a sigh: censored, by both of us.

'If you are free, Janna, do you suppose we'd be safe in our pub tomorrow?'

'We could try. What alternative do we have?'

'We can't go off to Wimbledon or up to Hampton Court every lunch hour . . .'

When I got home, I stood in the doorway seeing my beautiful room now and *then*. Two shabby little cherry-coloured chairs, off some junk heap. A handsome red linen chair. A grey sofa, filthy and creased. A pile of dingy garments lay on the floor. My carpet looked soiled. There were smears on the walls. On the sofa Kate sat, her terrified eyes on my face. She was not plugged in. I knew that her friends from the squat had come, and she had not wanted to let them in; had had to let them in; they had deliberately made as much mess as they could, while she wailed and beseeched. Now she was literally trembling with fear that I would throw her out. That threat I made was the most stupid thing I ever did. I went to the kitchen. They had cleared the place out, and left the remains of their meal on the kitchen table. I knew that they had made a point of being as messy and clumsy as they could. A bottle of milk had been overturned and there was a pallid lake on the brown wood of the table, with a crust or two afloat and many crumbs.

I went back to the living room, and did not know what to say to Kate. The point was, she did not have the strength to say no to these people; it did not make any difference what I said, or threatened.

The enormity of Kate came into me. The inexorability of her. How one could not go around her, avoid her, refuse her: or for that matter, cope with her.

On an impulse I went to the telephone: I wanted to talk to my sister. As I reached it, Kate was there, already, cowering and shivering, her fingers in her mouth.

'Who are you going to ring up?' she begged.

'I am going to talk to your mother.'

'Oh please, please, please,' she squeaked, and squirmed, 'oh please . . .'

'Go and sit down,' I said, snapping, suddenly furious. 'Go and sit down. *She's my sister.* Now shut up and sit down.'

Of course she did not move, but stood staring as I dialled. My sister was not in: she was, no doubt, administering to the poor or the distressed in some way or other.

And what had I wanted to say to her? Something like: But how did Kate happen?

How did Kathleen come about?

When I left this morning, I woke Kate up where she was lying asleep in the sofa, surrounded by the usual mess of crisps and chocolate: 'Kate, I don't want to be followed today. Do you understand?'

She gazed up at me, blank. Then she nodded, remembering, an anxious nod. As if I had said something like, Please remember to open the windows, or do the washing-up.

But as soon as I had said it I felt silly. It was like saying to her that she mustn't have her friends in. Like saying: Since they've eaten everything up, if we are going to eat tonight, then you'd better buy some food.

Kathleen was outside the pub. I went straight up to her and said, 'Kathleen . . .' She lifted those sleepwalker's eyes to me. She is really a very handsome girl, this Kathleen, with her large rather protuberant hazel eyes, full of light, and a glowing healthy skin, full, naturally red lips. She seems made for activity, for accomplishment; yet there's something in her that contradicts all that. She didn't recognize me at first. It took her some time to put together this appearance of me, the hated one—for I suppose I must be that—immediately before her, saying, 'Kathleen . . . Come in and have a drink,' with her doubtless horrible fantasies. She gave an unwilling half-smile, as if this was an invitation on an ordinary occasion; then looked annoyed, and walked away, in that slow, ponderous way as if she has invisible chains on her.

I went into the pub, and there was Richard at our table. The barman, an Irishman, gave me two completely different looks: one, due to this good customer who is in so often at lunchtime, the obviously well-heeled woman from the world of fashion. For of course he has found out everything about us both. And the other a quick hard stare from the surface of his blue Connemara eyes, which is for this middle-aged woman who is in some kind of relationship unsuitable for her age with this doctor man, who, like an Irishman, travels to do his work in another country. He made the comparison himself. My whisky was already waiting at my place, and I slid into it saying, 'I asked Kathleen to come in and join us.'

'So did I.'

'I don't think she liked it.'

'No.'

I looked around that pub, our pub, our cosy brown-wood-walled, red-curtained, brass-railed lair; and I saw it all as a bit tawdry and faded, and the customers, that splendid lunchtime mob of enjoyers and good fellows, as people putting a face on things, with anxiety not far behind. The doors were open on to the hot dusty street, the noise of the cars was too loud. In short, reality was too much with us; and I said, 'Perhaps we should try another pub.'

And Richard said, 'No, we should stick it out.'

'Do you think Kathleen will go on trailing us? Now that her two worlds have been brought together. Now that we have invited her?'

'Not at once. She is off today to see her grandmother. My mother is unhappy in this new Home I found. No—she's not going to move again. She said on the telephone that she had understood it was herself she can't stand, not the Home.'

I suddenly said, 'Ah, Kathleen wants you to have her grandmother in America with you? And blames you because you won't?'

'How can we? Maria can just about cope with John. She couldn't manage an old woman who has to have everything done for her.' Again that unknown, Sylvia, presented herself, and after a while Richard said, 'My wife is very eminent in her field. Much more than I am. If anyone was to give up working to look after my mother, then it should logically be me.'

'How long is Kathleen going for?'

He said in a low, tired, distressed voice, 'I hope for a long time. She is giving us hell. Isn't it extraordinary how they blame us for everything? Take it out on us? Punish us? Did we do that? I don't think I did. I don't remember anything of the sort. I left home before I was twenty. What about you?'

'I found myself a flat, and I went home when I had to out of a sense of duty.' After a silence I found that I had to add, 'But that was not the end of it of course. To put it mildly!'

'Well, I suppose I shall in duty be bound to listen to all of it, Janna. And so will you—to my perplexities. But I feel very cheerful as I have had a reprieve. I really did think that I was going to have to go up north again and settle poor Mother into yet another Home. And that would have taken away another two weeks from our time together.'

I sat silent, thinking of how we had been in what I found myself thinking of as 'the early days', when we first met, in April; being with each other was a dazzle and a freedom, inside a magic circle where ordinary life was not . . .

He said, 'All right. I know that look on a woman's face. I know it only too bloody well. You are thinking very practical thoughts. And the words *ought* and *should* and *have to* are about to make an appearance.'

'In my experience they do.'

'Something to do with this expertise of yours, about the aged?'

I said I wanted another drink. Patrick, the barman, slid to the edge of the bar with a practised air the two glasses, one with ice and one without; and he stood for a moment looking out past the heads of his customers into the glare of the street. He is a proper Irishman, jaunty and fluent, and uses the charm of his voice for all he is worth, and of course people like him for it and incite him to use all his wild inventiveness, smiling as the English do at our lack of what they have so much of; but today he was rather bony and gaunt, and there was sweat on his forehead: I was looking at some kind of anxiety. Until that morning I had flatly refused to think of this charming witness of our meetings as a man with the weight of an ordinary life on him, but now I had to. Oh, a great pity the pub doors were open, heat or no heat.

I told Richard about Maudie. It was difficult, because I had this strong sense of her, that awkward old woman, and how we were so involved, she and I, how—and here is this word again—I loved her; and yet the words I had to use seemed so inappropriate, did not convey anything. I said that I had met this old woman, she was in need of help, I offered it, got in deeper than I had meant, and had ended by being something not far off a daughter to her, for a long time—years. She died. And how that had led to my befriending Eliza Bates and Annie, and how I still see old Annie at least two or three times a week; and how it has become so much a part of my life that dropping in for an hour or two is like shopping, or seeing my clothes are in order. I go in, finding *her* despondent and bloody-minded; and slowly absorb like a sponge all her miseries, till she is quite sprightly and nice, and I go out, and give myself a great shake outside her door, and feel all that weight of depression go flying off and away.

I had my eyes on his face, of course, needing to know how he would take this eccentricity, as Jill insists it is; or worse, a sign of some horrible elderly perversion, like approaching senility. He did not comment until I had stopped and his face was kept noncommittal, with the look I describe to myself as the doctor's look.

'Yes, but why?' he asked quietly.

'It was like this. When my mother died, I was useless. Good for nothing.'

Unexpectedly he laughed, and said, 'You couldn't stand being inadequate in that? You had to feel you could cope with that—as well?'

I said, and with difficulty, 'First of all it was my husband. He died first. Of cancer. I didn't want to know. I simply cut myself off from it all. Now I cannot bear to think . . .' But I couldn't go on with that thought, then: I steadied my voice, and said, 'Not long after, there was my mother. Cancer. I can say I was a bit better than with my husband. At least I was ashamed at how awful I had been with Freddie, so I tried with my mother. Well, a little bit. But I couldn't. I didn't know how.'

'Ah,' he remarked, as I sat silent, hoping he would fill it all in for himself.

'And so that's it,' I said.

'Are you afraid of cancer?' he asked, unexpectedly.

'No. I simply cannot see why it should be worse than other things. I know that is quite an eccentric thought.'

'I agree with you.'

'And I'm not afraid of dying. And that is so eccentric that I don't dare to say it. People don't believe it, for a start.'

'It is one thing sitting here on a warm July day, saying, One day I will die—and actually dying.'

'I know that,' I said. I was disappointed. In him. But then he remarked, redeeming himself, 'Again, I agree with you. But then I've seen so much of it. Death, I mean.'

I said, 'I have learned to keep quiet now. If you say, I am not afraid of death, of dying, people react as if you are lacking in proper feelings. And it is not only in that area either. It seems to me that nearly all the things I really think, really believe—I can't say. For one thing, that I like living alone. That's another . . .' But as I said this I heard my voice shake, and it was because it came over me that if I could live with Richard I might not prefer solitude. But then I thought that for all I knew this ease of being with someone was because it was not tested by the grind of bed, board and conversation about grubby chair covers.

'I can't even imagine what it might be like to live alone,' he said. 'I went from home to share a room with Sylvia, and that's been it. I think I admire you. I don't even know whether I could do it.'

This word *admire* was cold, or it seemed so to me.

I wanted most desperately to weep, to put my head under the covers, to shut out glare, light, noise—reality.

He saw this, and said, 'Perhaps we should try another place. Let's make a move.'

Outside Kathleen was standing. Richard and I went up to her. He said nicely, 'Kathleen, aren't you going to miss your train?'

'I'm not going till eight.'

'Ah.'

There we stood, the three of us. Were we all three to go to another pub? But Kathleen again solved it by turning away, as if she had to; as if she were being forced to by some power outside or in her. There was something blind and mechanical in it; and she walked away across the road not seeing a car which had to grind to a halt, hooting.

I said, 'But Richard, surely this isn't *normal*, it isn't sane behaviour?'

Richard said, 'My dear Janna, it's no more crazy than anything else!'

I said, 'Do you mean us, you and I?'

'No, I didn't mean that. But I suppose I could have!'

I said, 'I think it is crazy—I mean, Kathleen. And you and Sylvia are like my sister and her husband. There's this *mess* Kate, and they simply pretend nothing very much is wrong.'

Richard took this seriously: though if he had matched my seethe of distress and anger he would have shouted at me or been unkind. He said, 'Is that what you really think? Is that what you've been thinking? But what can we do, Janna?' This *we* I first took as he and me—*we*: then realized the *we* was he and Sylvia. I shook my head, too full of the need to cry. He turned me to him, took me by the arms, and stood holding me, his hands on my elbows, looking into my face.

'Janna,' he said, 'but what can we do?' Meaning, this time, he and me, Richard and Janna.

I shook my head: 'I don't know.'

'Would you like to go and have some lunch? Shall we walk for a bit?'

I shook my head. A taxi came creeping down the narrow street, hooting. I said, muffled and shocked. 'Ring me, Richard, you must ring me, I don't have your number remember.' This sounded like the wildest accusation, a lover's complaint, and I got into the taxi and burst into tears at last. His concerned, weary face: it is in front of me now.

I was very hungry. I forgot to bring in food: Kate of course is never hungry because of her eternal crisps and Mars Bars. There is literally nothing in the place but some dried milk. I shall make myself hot chocolate: a comfort drink; and go to bed thinking, like a young girl, But *will* he ring me tomorrow?

He did ring me, but I was out at the Eminent Women Luncheon. He left a message that he would ring again. But not when.

Tonight I rang my sister, and she said, 'How's Kate?'

I said, 'Kate is as she always is.' (She was out at her squat, or trailing me for all I know, so I could talk freely.)

I was waiting for Georgie to say something to the point. But she said, 'It is very kind of you, Jane, to have Kate.'

I didn't know what to say. 'Georgie,' I said at last, feeling the uselessness of it, 'surely there is something very wrong with Kate?'

'No!' This was quick, defensive, offended. 'She'll be all right. Her trouble has always been Jill. Jill always over-shadowed Kate, but now, you'll see, she'll find herself.'

'Ah,' I said, sounding like Richard, noncommittal. 'In that case, all right.'

But I didn't put down the receiver. I could not. I was waiting for Georgina to say something, almost anything, that wasn't inane. I was feeling that she couldn't possibly be meaning it, be serious. And then, in fact, came *the other voice,* and I wondered if I have ever heard anything like it from Sister Georgie before? She said, 'Well, why shouldn't you take Kate on? Why not? Why should it be any problem to you? Everything comes so easily to you, you are such a success at everything, the world's your oyster, isn't it, it always has been.' Her light, hurrying voice, almost indifferent, as if in this way she need own no responsibility for them, for Georgie's thoughts thus blown or breathed at me, but then probably at once forgotten, for she remarked quite casually, 'I've got to rush, Jane, Tom's chocolate is on the hotplate. It is our bedtime, you know.'

I was out all this afternoon, interviewing Randy Sykes, the Singing Footballer, very attractive, so I'm told, but not to me; a dish, the would-be upmarket career woman's secret dreamboat, her bit of rough. And when I got back to the office they said Richard had rung to say he would be outside here, my place not the office, at six. It was already half past five. Hannah and Jill watched me, no comment, as I scrabbled for my things and fled down the stairs to the underground. I made it—just. A dark blue Volvo waited under the plane tree at the corner. I could see Kate's face at the window above, an anxious blur. I escaped into the car, and there he was.

We drove up past St Albans, and found a pub and spent the evening there. We did not discuss his problems or my problems, or the state of the world or of Britain. Taboo! I have just got in: after twelve, and Kate is not here. I am too happy to worry.

Richard has got the loan of a colleague's car for a fortnight. We intend to make the most of it.

This morning I found Kate asleep on the sofa, bedraggled, sullen.

I said to her that I was not going to be in in the evenings, and suggested she should arrange to spend them with her pals in the squat. This enraged her: for I was supposed to be hating her and her squat-mates, and was probably meant too to have thrown her out, or to have called the police to threaten them, I don't know, and I don't care.

I have also rung up old Annie's neighbour to say I will be on holiday for a fortnight. When we—I, or her Home Help, or the woman upstairs—go on holiday or away even for a weekend, Annie shows all the anxieties of a child who has good reason to think a parent might disappear for ever. I feel more disquiet about abandoning Annie for two weeks than I do over Kate. Annie has nothing, no one, no hope. Kate has a future. I'd rather not think *what*; but there is now a curious little toughness between us, which we both recognize. I have not performed that act, like a turning of a key, which divorces one from somebody, when you have had enough: I am not inwardly pushing her away, meaning this to be felt by her as an edict: Now, go! On the contrary, this inner strengthening is more like an acceptance. I cannot change her, nor do much for her; but I am not going to throw her out. There is no point in doing anything about my poor living room, which looks like a slum. It can stay as it is—until *she chooses* to leave.

'My mother wouldn't like it if she knew I was spending time at the squat,' said Kate virtuously and pathetically, with a small child's sniff, tears welling.

'I don't like it either,' I said cheerfully, 'but I didn't notice that that stopped you. And as for trailing me about, it is a waste of time because we won't be in London.'

'Where will you be?'—as if she expected me to give her exact information.

What a lovely time we have had. Three weeks of it, not two. Warm, indulgent weather, everyone and everything slowed by heat, and good-natured, the way we all get in England when it is really hot. Every afternoon Richard has waited for me, at six, and we drove up into the little villages of Essex and Hertfordshire, a different one every day, not getting back until twelve or one. During this time everything but our being together has been 'noises off'; the office—well, I've been in it, I've done what I've had to do, and Charlie, Hannah, Jill, have accepted my condition. A wonderful thing, people working together when they are working well, making allowances, giving a little here, staking a little claim there, like a sort of amoeba, flexible and encompassing. All that Charlie said, and he has had to work harder than usual: 'Well, Janna, it's nice to see you being so relentlessly bent on pleasure.' All Jill said was: 'Mark says you look more relaxed with your boyfriend than I do with mine.' Hannah hasn't said anything, but her smile offers well-considered encouragement.

But now that's over; and it is because, I know, Sylvia has come back from somewhere or other, for when I said I could easily hire a car, Richard shook his head. She hasn't been mentioned; nor Kathleen, who has been in Hull with her grandmother; nor Kate; nor John, nor Matthew. All that has been far away, on the other side of the hill, beyond a screen of leaves and flowering shrubs and roses. Summer. Nearly every evening we have sat out in gardens at the backs of pubs. It is amazing how many pubs have a garden, even a little one, a couple of wooden tables at the edge of a patch of drying lawn; the scent of roses. It has been very dry. We have sat on and on in long slow twilight, watching the light leave the garden and go up into banks of white cloud, or become absorbed into the dazzle of streets. Driving back, on different little roads every night, we have stopped the car on a hill, and watched a yellow field flash out as the car lights swept across it, like a knife cutting, slice, slice, slice, in regular illuminations with soft blank dark between; or we have got out of the car in a wood and crept a little way into it, afraid of disturbing the life that goes on just out of the scope of the passing traffic. We have sat on a log under silent trees for an hour, two, holding hands, hardly breathing, listening. I have never done anything like it in my life, my urban, street-loving life. And in three weeks I've seen more little pubs, cafés, restaurants, curiously inventive and original places, run by people with a talent and a gift, than I have in years. Nothing to stop me, any time, doing the same: looking from this high point, a Sunday evening after this marvellous time, at my ordinary life, it seems so flat, and I think that *one day*—meaning, when Richard goes away—I shall hire a car, or borrow one, invite Jill or Hannah or someone, and jaunt off, without a destination, as I have been doing with Richard. And of course I shan't. For it is Richard who has made it possible; Richard and me: fit us together, like hands joining, and it seems we have only to drive into a village in the late sunlight of this summer, and at once walk into some bar or restaurant or garden so full of character and charm that we are amazed the whole world does not know about it.

Richard said tonight that he will be out of London for a week on a visit to relatives. I take it that means, with Sylvia.

It is already August.

Every night, instead of coming back to the blue Volvo, into which I escaped, I've been going first of all in to Annie. Oh, what a load of misery! Annie has come to anchor in her large chair, which I got her off the pavement outside a shop. It was once a grand chair, of crimson brocade, with tall back and wings, deep and comfortable, draught-excluding. Sometimes I brood that I should never have brought it in, to swallow Annie's life up.

Her day goes like this. She wakes early, at six or seven, and at once gets up, for she is not one to lie in bed. She struggles to the commode, using her frame. She returns to sit on the bed, where her clothes are, at its foot. She has not taken off her vest, so she puts on over it, fumbling and angry with the intransigence of *things,* a man's white cotton singlet, extra outsize, since she can get nothing else on comfortably. Then a skirt made for her by me, on an elastic, then a cotton cardigan which though outsize hardly covers her. She balances to the big chair, where there is a thermos of tea. She switches on a bar of the electric fire, summer or winter, for its companionship. 'It's not as nice as a cat though,' says Annie. Her cat was run over a year ago and she will sit and weep for him, alone.

She switches on the radio, and twiddles from station to station in search of her need, which is for the popular songs of any time up to about twenty years ago. Failing that, she listens to news, or the disc jockeys joking away between records that don't interest her: 'Funny music,' she says, 'like mad people howling.' She drinks all the tea in her thermos. Everyone who comes in, me, the Home Help, the nurses who come to wash her, the nurse who comes to check her pulse and breathing and give her pills, tells her she is capable of going to the kitchen to make her own tea. She did it for a long time, filling the thermos and carrying it back looped over her frame. But she won't. She won't use the lavatory in the bathroom, but insists on the commode: says it takes too long to get to the bathroom. 'It's such a long walk down the passage,' says she, to the bathroom, to the kitchen, 'not like my own home.'

For Annie is not really living in this nice little two-roomed flat, which 'they' insisted on moving her into. Annie lived at the top of the house down the street, in two large airy rooms where she had been for forty years and never wanted to move. 'But there's no bathroom,' expostulated successive social workers, scandalized at her indifference to this. 'I have never lived anywhere with a bathroom,' said she. 'You can keep yourself clean without that.' 'But it's so draughty.' 'I don't mind the cold.' 'But it's so *old*.' And these young people one and all have looked around the two beautiful shabby rooms, efficiently visualizing how they will look when done up. As her rooms look now, in fact; for I went up to see. They have sliced off the end of the big room, reducing it to a pokey one, and put in a bathroom. The place has lost its symmetry and rightness. It is as well Annie will never see it.

Annie's second room at the back of this new flat of hers is never entered—by her. She lives totally in the front room, the commode at the foot of the bed. And when the nurse who washes her once a week comes and begs her to go to the bathroom and have a lovely shower, she says she will, one day. The nurse brings in a basin and washes her in it as Annie stands naked in front of the fire.

Her clothes accumulate on the back of her regal chair, and she picks out what she needs from them. Her meals are eaten at the window. But in her imagination she lives in her own home, which is in fact now occupied by a single parent with two small children, going mad because of all the stairs.

When Annie has drunk all the tea in the flask she waits until the woman upstairs drops in on her way to work with another cup of tea. A few moments of lively chat, while the woman cries, 'I must go, I'm late, Annie,' and Annie cries, 'Oh, how are you, have you heard from your nephew?', trying to keep her. But Mrs Mount flies off, and Annie sits, angry, discarded, drinking the tea in small sips to make it last.

'And now I'm alone for the rest of the day,' she sniffs, and goes to the table to have breakfast, eating and eating to pass the time. The Home Helps bring to that room with the fat old lady in it enough to feed a family. And Annie eats it all, from boredom. She sits there, the curtains drawn back, throwing a few crumbs out for the sparrows, who entertain her well, cranes to see if the cat from next door is out on the little wall, and can she entice her in? She sits behind her yellow curtains, half hidden, watching and watching and watching, while the people go past on their way to work. But then one turns in at the gate and comes running in: Annie hears the outer door go crashing back, and then the flat door bangs inwards. It is the little lively nurse who gives her the pills. Which are hidden somewhere in the back room. Annie has even dragged herself in there once to look for them. Meaning to throw them all away. She hates the pills. She grumbles incessantly that they make her feel funny and fuddled, that she never feels herself, that she doesn't want them. But 'they' make her take them. The little nurse, all bright black eyes, red cheeks and jolly black curls, stands over her. 'Now Annie, take these two.' 'I don't want to.' 'But the doctor says you must.' 'What are they for?' 'They are for your heart.' 'But what's wrong with my heart?' 'Oh, it's what the doctor says that goes dear, you know that. If he says it's your heart, your heart it is.' For the nurses don't always like these handfuls of pills they have to force their poor old crones to take. Annie swallows six pills in all, two for her heart, two for her water, and two to counteract the side effects of the other four. And just as Annie is crying, 'Then sit down and have a cup of tea, take the weight off your feet,' the nice nurse is on her way out: 'Not today, Annie, I can't, I'm doing someone else's work as well as my own.' And bang, bang, the two doors are shut, and Annie watches the girl fly off, waving as she goes behind the hedge. Annie sits burping, raging but dully, for she knows it is no use. Before they sent the nurse in every day to make sure she took the pills, she used to throw them into the toilet, or into the bottom of her handbag, or into a drawer, but they always found out, sniffing and snooping about among her own personal things. The only one who doesn't say, why have you thrown away your pills? is Janna, and she, Annie, knows what Janna thinks of all these pills, oh, I'm not a fool, I can read her face, and I can read all their faces, they think I'm stupid and dead and gone, and I'm not.

There is a clock by Annie's chair which she tries not to watch. It is only nine o'clock in the morning: she seems to have been up and about for hours. She finds some chocolate, and nibbles: the pills give her a nasty taste in her mouth. And now she is drowsy, but is afraid to sleep, because if there is one thing she dreads it is lying awake at night thinking. Of her life; of what it has become. She pulls herself over to the commode, relieves herself. Shuts down the lid at once, goes back to her big chair, and is about to drowse off when she sees that another nurse, one she doesn't know, is standing over her. Come to wash her, she says. 'I don't want a wash,' mutters Annie. 'Well, that's what you've got to have,' says the nurse. 'You've got a bathroom here, it says on my sheet.' 'I am washed in this room here,' announces Annie, energy coming into her with the battle. 'If you want to wash me, then you can bring a basin in.' The nurse, well used to ancient cantankerousness, stands with her fingers pinching her hips on either side, as if they had a throat between them. Annie and she exchange long combative stares. The nurse recognizes that this stubborn old woman is not going to give in. With an angry mutter not unlike Annie's, she marches off to the kitchen, puts on a kettle. There could be hot water, but that is only switched on for special purposes. As Annie keeps saying, I've never had hot water laid on, why should I have it now? When the kettle is hot, the basin full of warm water is carried in, put on newspapers on the table where Annie eats;

and Annie strips herself naked, winter or summer. For she really doesn't feel the cold. Years of living in inadequately and unevenly heated rooms have given her immunity, and when we, her mentors—and jailers—stand about shivering in coats and sweaters, Annie may well be sitting in a cotton cardigan, saying she wants to switch a bar of the fire off, she's too hot. The nurse washes Annie, efficiently, but not with tenderness for this white plump delicate flesh. Annie, standing nude, because she is fat is comely, does not sag, is all comfortable rolls and curves. 'And where are your clean clothes?' demands this nurse, who hasn't said a word, since she is cross, starving poor Annie of the chat she craves for. Annie says, 'I can dress myself,' though on her card it states she cannot. She swings herself naked on her frame to the big chair, and puts on a vest that is in fact stale and an uncertainly clean pair of knickers. The nurse shrugs, picks up the clothes Annie has discarded, whisks off the basin and the towel, and disposes of the lot next door for the Home Help to deal with. She has said, 'Goodbye, I'm off,' before Annie can cry out, Have a cup of tea, and a sit-down.

Incredulously, Annie sees that it is only ten o'clock. She is no longer sleepy. She yearns, longs for tea. But she feels tired after all that effort, and does not move. She listens to the radio. She is waiting for the the Home Help: she knows Janna never comes in the mornings, or only when Annie is sick. So it shows she could come in the mornings, if she wanted. But the Home Help does not come. Annie is now limp with self-pity and loneliness. How would they like it sitting here all day, alone, with nothing to look forward to?

She moves back to the window, but there's nothing to see. Mid-morning, everyone at work now, only a few old people crawling along the pavement. The woman next door who has four small children gives Annie some interest, but today is not to be seen. Nor is her cat. A shaggy brown dog who sometimes begs Annie for something noses after the sparrows' crumbs, and Annie shouts at him, enraged, 'You filthy thing!' The dog trots off. 'Leaving nothing for the poor sparrows,' sniffs Annie, and she has a bit of a cry. She is also frightened, for her heart is feeling funny. It often does these days. 'Once I didn't even have a heart,' mutters Annie, and it is as if 'they' have caused this to happen too.

Now she is waiting for the Meals on Wheels. It makes a change. She is praying that the dinner and the Home Help don't come together, for she doesn't get the fun of either of them then. She likes her pleasures one by one. Tea! She scrambles along to the kitchen, makes herself some tea, and drinks it sitting with her face to the wall at a little table that 'they' have put there, saying that she can use it as a place to eat if she can't be troubled to eat at the big table next door. How would they like to sit with their faces six inches from a nasty white wall? She drinks two cups of tea, and drags herself back to her big chair. It is twelve o'clock. *Half the day gone, that's something.* She rests there, gets her breath back, empties herself into the commode, and goes to the table. The young lady from the Meals on Wheels knocks on the window. Annie slides it up, knowing better than to hope for her to come in for a bit of a chat. Annie longs for this to happen. These girls seem to her so lively and so friendly. 'Hello, Annie, hello, how are you? But we have to rush.' And they do. Of course it is a charity, they say they do it for nothing; all the same, it would be nice. The two little oblong containers are sitting one above another, on the sill. Annie carefully opens the first, and she is sick with disappointment. It is Wednesday, she had forgotten; Wednesday they bring this great sog of a pie, all damp crust with some dubious mince in it, a spoonful if that. She loathes cabbage. She hates carrot. She picks at the mince, her face squeezed up with distaste. No, she cannot. She investigates the pudding. It is a sponge, in custard. 'On a hot day like this, you'd think they'd give us a bit of salad,' she moans. And eats slices of white bread and jam and biscuits, one after another, till she's full.

She goes to her big chair and sleeps like death. She awakes to find Maureen standing over her; 'Annie . . . Annie . . . are you asleep? She comes up out of deep dark miles of sleep, muttering, 'My mouth, my mouth, I'm so dry . . .' I've got the kettle on,' says Maureen, and bustles about. Annie knows by the haste of Maureen, and because she has put on the kettle at once, that she need not expect the pleasure of her company for even a quarter of the time she is supposed to stay. 'And they pay her for it too,' as Annie mutters every day as Maureen trips off, saying that she has to rush, because— whatever she says the reason is on that day. Annie is so pleased to see Maureen, but she cannot help herself. Out pours the long day's and the long night's deprivations, in a savage, dirty stream. Annie says that she's sick of this life. Sick of it all and sick of all of you. She sometimes wishes she could go right away somewhere. To a little cottage some- where, that would be best. Or she could go and stay with her sister … While Annie shouts and moans, Maureen is whisking up the bed covers and emptying the commode. In a moment there is a cup of tea for Annie, and the thermos flask is full again. Maureen has sat down, on the little seat by the fire, with her own cup in her hand. She has a sandwich in a piece of clingwrap on her knee. Annie likes it better than anything when the Home Help, or anyone else, has time to sit and have a cup with her, but she cannot stop her shouting and complaining, and she can see from Maureen's face, that she—Annie—is going to get it back in full measure. And she does. Maureen drinks all her tea at once, brushes off the crumbs from her lap into the grate, and stands up. She tells Annie she has no one to blame for her solitude but herself. She could go to the Lunch Centre, and she won't. She could have a Visitor to come and talk to her, and she won't. She could go on a council-paid holiday, and she won't. 'Why should I go off with all those old people?' shouts Annie. 'And they'd send me with all those cripples, oh yes, I know, you can't tell *me*.' And she stares triumphantly at Maureen. Who sighs, and decides she won't bother. Silence. Maureen unpacks her shopping bag, putting out bars of chocolate and a pound of sweets, cigarettes, loaves of sliced white bread, some ham, some tomatoes. 'And you're eating yourself silly,' she announces, 'where do you put all this food?' 'I couldn't eat the dinner,' whines Annie. Maureen inspects the Meals on Wheels dinner and knows it is not appetizing. All the same, as she tips it into the bin, she is thinking, And all those starving people, etc. She has not been there half an hour, when she announces her departure. She has not swept, or cleaned, or done anything very much. Annie does not care about all that; she cares that Maureen is going. And she goes. Saying, 'See you tomorrow, about three.' She has taken some notes from Annie's handbag for the things Annie has requested: sweets, cigarettes, chocolates, a decent bit of fruit, a bit of chicken, something I can *eat*.

Annie thinks, Surely there should be more money than this! I had all those notes. But what is the use, they'll say it's my fault.

It is half past one. Annie stares, appalled at the long afternoon ahead. She can't face it. Every day, at this time, she thinks of killing herself. But how? Killing herself has an abstract, vague quality for Annie: she does not think of actually doing anything, like swallowing all her pills at once, but it is dramatic, like something on the telly. She sees Vera and Janna and Mrs Mount and Maureen standing around her corpse and asking, How could she do that to us? The long, long afternoon wears on. She sits at the window. She watches some television: but it is getting more and more incomprehensible to her. She eats bread and jam and cake and biscuits and chocolate. She drinks up all her tea. She listens to her radio. All this in short, fidgety snatches, unable to settle. At five o'clock she is at the window, waiting for the people to come home from work. Soon Mrs Mount comes in, says hello. Says she is in a hurry, collects her empty mug and goes up. Now Annie can listen to her moving about upstairs.

Suddenly the lights click on in the passage, the door opens: it is Janna. How smart she looks, thinks Annie, in a respectful way: not for the person of Janna, but for her clothes. She looks like something out of a magazine, Annie knows. She knows too, from a hundred little signs, that Janna will not be staying long. She is determined not to drive her away with her tongue. Janna is examining Annie as Annie examines Janna: how is she, what is her mood, what can I expect? But everything is all right today. Janna has brought in a small bottle of Scotch, and pours them both out generous drinks. She has brought Annie some freesias and a single pink rose with some maidenhair fern. Although it is still light outside, Annie asks Janna to pull the curtains. Inside there is an air of companionship, festivity. Drinking their Scotch, Annie smoking, Annie listening to how Janna has been driving around Essex or somewhere. With some friend. Janna does not say with whom. Annie has never been to Essex, does not know where it is, so she cuts in to what Janna is saying with an account of how she went with her husband to the dog racing. She knows she has often told Janna the story, but she feels it doesn't matter, Janna is listening so nicely.

'And he always bought me some eels, because he knew I loved them. He didn't like them. Lovely stewed eels with green sauce and mashed potato. He bought me white port to drink with it, and he drank stout. Oh, he spoiled me, my husband did. We used to go every weekend, the two of us, and he always gave me the money for a bit of a bet.'

Janna says, 'But weren't you working then?'

Annie hates these practical questions, pinning her down, suspects Janna of not believing her. 'Yes, but I never had any money, did I? I used to spend it on my clothes. I used to look nice, I did. What money did I have to put on a bit of a bet? And I won once. I won five pounds. That was a lot! He said to me, And aren't you going to give me the bet money back? Not I, I said. I bought myself a coatdress I had my eye on, in Oxford Street. It was of black cloth with a big fur collar. I looked a treat, he said. Oh, he was good to me, he was.' And Annie sits snuffling, but there is also something else on her face: she is remembering—what? Sometimes Annie says in that other voice, the one that intrudes, breaking in through the crust of ordinary life, 'When I married, I didn't know what I was doing. I was used to the West End, wasn't I? I knew my way about I did . . . and he never wanted to go out.'

Minutes before Janna actually rises to leave, Annie knows she is going to. Then Janna says, 'I've got to go home, Annie.' She gets up, puts down by Annie some cigarettes she bought for her. She smiles, lingers by the door, says, 'I'll be in tomorrow if I can.' Annie knows she feels guilty. She wasn't in at all for three weeks.

And now Annie feels better. The day is gone; the night is here. She's got through another of these dreadful dragging days. She makes herself some supper, ham between bread, thick with delicious salty butter, tomatoes. She has some more of the Scotch Janna has brought.

When the Good Neighbour arrives at nine thirty, Annie is watching television, and does not want to be interrupted. It is a film of Vivien Leigh, made in the days when they knew how to make films. The Good Neighbour, Lucie from three doors down, makes sure the thermos is filled, the windows are locked, and that Annie seems adequately cheerful. She sits for a while, watching the film. Which ends. And now Annie turns to her, all animation, wanting her to stay. But Lucie has to get back to her own husband and her three children. She says good night cheerfully, and goes. It is ten o'clock. Annie watches some television, listens to some radio. The one thing she will not do is to go to bed one minute before midnight. Even so when she does, lying there in vest and knickers, she lies awake for some time. The light from a car swirls across the ceiling, and she thinks, That's funny, that light reaching all the way up here—for she is back in her mind in the old place, her home, at the top of the house opposite where all that can be seen from the windows is the sky. 'No, I must be here then, not there,' she mutters, and drops off into black sleep.

It seems to me that Annie is going downhill fast. 'Deteriorating', as the geriatric specialists put it. There's the external evidence: the nurses coming in every day to make her take the pills; this is a new thing, in the last month or so. But there's an angry restlessness in her, a distress. Her fantasies are those of a desperate person. She has a sister, as old as she, crippled with arthritis, chair-bound, the scourge of three children who take turns to come in to her. Years ago this sister shed Annie, who, when she was retired against her will at seventy from the waitress job she had off Oxford Street, went to pieces. Her husband long dead, her life and interests were in her work. Her work gone, there was nothing. Annie drank, became a disreputable and dirty old hen snuffling about the streets waiting for the pubs to open. Her sister told her not to come again. Not in a thousand years would her sister allow Annie to live with her; the nieces and nephew would not dream of taking on two burdens where now there was one. All this Annie must know, in some part of her mind. Or knew. Now she has chosen not to know; for 'they' have started talking about a Home, even Janna. 'They' say she would have more company there, not be alone all day. 'They' say that they will take her into a Home for a week to see if she likes it, and then if not she can come home to her flat again. They are like a cloud of flies buzzing in and out, with bad news, and she can't escape from them. But over in Seven Sisters Road there's her sister, and she will go and live with her and . . . Where's that address, I'll get Janna to write.

I have written to this sister probably twenty letters of every kind, politely giving information: 'Your sister Annie is well, and sends her regards to all the family,' letters that are dictated by Annie and beg for help. 'How are you, Lil? I sit here and think of all the good times we had. I do not seem to have had a letter from you. Did you get my Christmas card?' I send Christmas cards, Easter cards, postcards that I bring back from my journeys abroad for *Lilith* with views of canals in Amsterdam and the blue Danube and cafés in Paris, and these pathetic pleas are never acknowledged.

'Yes,' I say, 'I wrote two weeks ago, don't you remember?'

'Two weeks, no, it wasn't two weeks,' she says, sullen. 'How could it be two weeks?'

I am silent; for she is really protesting about time itself, the deceiver, who has whisked her life away from under her feet.

'Well, you just find my writing paper and I'll tell you what to say.'

Dear Lil, How are you? I am not what I used to be . . .

She painfully signs it, and her *Annie* looks like the first attempt of a very small child.

I sit there, as I did with Maudie, and with Eliza, looking at an old woman who I know, if she could be with a family, or even one other person, would live another ten years, or twenty years. As it is, she is being eaten up with unused vitality that beats through her on the rhythm of her bitter lonely thoughts: 'High blood pressure, they say I've got,' mutters Annie, her face flaming scarlet, feeling the blood thud and pound. 'High blood pressure, is it?'

Annie, I know, is going to die of rage, like Maudie, and like Eliza. And the rage is fed every day by us, by 'them', who drop in and out, with our smiling, lying faces; the faces of good friends, who will leave two containers of food, wash her, sweep her floor, make her a cup of tea, but who—now it has come to the point—fade out, start talking of a Home. 'A home! But I have a home,' mutters Annie, and sighs; meaning the beautiful rooms from which she was taken, surrounded by friendly smiling faces, though she had said a thousand times she did not want to go, did not need a bathroom, hot water.

'Liars,' I can hear Annie mutter, after I'd remarked that she could perhaps try the Lunch Centre.

'But you have never even tried it, Annie.'

'I don't know them. Who are they?'

'You would know them, once you've been.'

Annie sits solid, this fat little woman who comes up to lower than my shoulders, her flowered skirts spread about her, her broad red face lowered as she stares angrily at the dirty rug, thick with cigarette ash, food scraps, dust. The Home Help said this morning that she had done it yesterday, and she wasn't going to do it again!

When she lifts her small blue eyes to me they are full of resentment. And my look at her, I know, is exasperated.

I contemplate the closed circle that is Annie's mind, her life. She will *not* take one step out of her lethargy, will not break this circle. If she did—so we, her tormentors, like to fantasize—she would find someone, perhaps more than one, at the Lunch Centre, or on the coach trip, or the church bazaar, who would like her, who would come and visit her. For she's likeable enough, old Annie, when she's lively. And from this one friend would come others. Annie would become part of the community of old ladies in the area, who live sprightly brave lives, gossiping and visiting, making little trips and dropping in and out of each other's houses.

Think of Eliza Bates, we all cry, think of how she got out and about!

'But she's dead,' says Annie triumphantly, with that knowing wag of the head that means: I've got you there.

'But when she was alive. She was doing all sorts of things almost until she died.'

'How can I, with my frame?'

'But lots of people have frames, and get about.'

Cornered, Annie mutters that she will, when the weather is fine. Every day this last week she has said that she will, when it is fine; and the sun has been blazing down in its heavy insistent late-summer way. One little step out of this revolving circle of hers, and Annie would . . .

But this decision was made years ago, when she decided she would have a walking frame, though all of 'them' said she could walk perfectly well without a frame.

'One day, when it's fine . . .' Annie muttered then.

Oh, what a horrid warning Annie is to me; as I sit opposite, listening for the hundredth time to how she wore a pink dress with blue spots, when she and her sister went out together that night; how she used to cook apple sauce for her husband to eat with his pork chops, but she wondered how he could like it; how when he died of cancer—because his lung had got that shrapnel in it in the First World War—she got compensation and she spent it on a black rabbit-fur coat with silk buttons, and a fox-fur stole which is lying, a ragged brown smelly lump, in a drawer. It has bright button eyes that appear suddenly, as one of our hands dislodge a scarf or a stocking. 'What have you done with my pink chiffon scarf?' 'I don't know, Annie, I'll have a look.'

All this I listen to, and think about and say to myself, as I keep my face smiling and friendly, I will not be like her, I will not. I will not die of rage, nor blunder about a dirty room like a bedraggled old bird, knocking against a hundred things that stand up against me like enemies. Annie's life is being banged, beaten, eaten out of her by things. Walls of them close her in. The passage to the kitchen is so long and slippery. She puts down a glass and cannot find it, for it has maliciously concealed itself. She has broken the lenses of her glasses and has hidden them, because she can't bear Janna or Maureen to nag at her to get new ones. Her hands slip on the grips of her walking frame, because for some reason butter has got there. Her fingers have become thick and difficult, and let things slide through. On the table where she sits to eat, she will look for a bottle of ketchup for half an hour and find it right by her plate, where it must have walked. Sometimes it seems to her as if she sits crouching like an animal in some dirty corner, afraid to creep out because *things* will trap her; or as if she has some mysterious illness, about which she even speculates—Have I got a bit of flu then?—whose main symptom is that *things* have become her enemy. Perhaps I've got a bit of that paralysis, is that it? Isn't that what they call it when you can't move as you fancy?

I find myself, as I sit there, surreptitiously rubbing one hand with another, moving my fingers about, twining them in my lap; as I watch Annie fumbling among objects that slip and slide away.

On the first evening I came in after work, after visiting Annie, there was Kate, hugging her little machine in her arms, gazing at me from between the wires, sitting in the corner of the sofa.

I leaned down and shouted, 'Do you want some supper?'

She stared, then slowly removed the earphones.

'Aren't you going out?' she pathetically asked.

'No. Will you help me put things away?'

She slowly got up, and trailed after me to the kitchen. I had brought in a great deal; meant to re-stock the cupboards and the refrigerator. As I put a packet of sliced ham down, Kate avidly reached for it and started cramming it in. She seemed unaware she was doing this.

A half-pound of ham disappeared in a moment; she wiped her pudgy grubby hand across her mouth and burped. 'I was hungry, I think,' she volunteered, realizing what she had done.

Then she went scarlet with anger. At me, I suppose. I indicated a heap of packets, and said, 'How about putting them into that cupboard?' She stood fingering them for a while, interested in the packaging, the presentation, then started pushing them anyhow on a shelf. Soon, she stopped and watched me doing it.

'Are we going to have supper together?'

'What would you like?'

'Oh, I don't know . . . anything.'

'Well, sit down, then.'

She dumped herself in a chair, and soon started to look restlessly about: she wanted her music machine.

'No, let's have supper, Kate.'

I put out various cheeses and patés, made a salad, arranged fruit, sat down. Kate was no longer with me. Her eyes were dull and absent.

'Have you been to the squat?'

No reply.

'Kate, have you been here all these three weeks? At the squat? Have they been here?'

'Yes, I think so. Sometimes.'

They have been here, more than once, I think, but while the grubbiness and dinginess increases, no actual damage has been done.

But I wasn't going to ask, because then she would lie. Immediately I had finished this meal, that with Richard would have been so pleasant, and with her was a graceless filling of the stomach, she got up and went back to the living room, reaching for her machine as she flumped into the sofa. I stopped her. 'Kate!'

'What—?'

'Kate, I don't want you to plug yourself into that damned machine yet. I want to talk.'

Suddenly she screeched in a tantrum like a baby, 'Why do you get at me, why do you stop things all the time?'

I shrugged, and let it go.

That was the first evening.

The next night, she was sitting alert and ready for me: she had thought it over, decided she had behaved wrongly, was not going to do it again. It is this in her that encourages me: she does in fact quite often live in the same world as normal people.

I had brought home a lot of work: for of course it has piled up during my three weeks in Arcady. But I put it aside, took trouble over the supper, and made the table look pretty. Smiling hopefully, she trailed about after me, waiting for the chance to be what I wished.

I sat fumbling among words that would do, or would not; offered remarks which were eagerly awaited but then died between us in silences, not embarrassed so much as hopeless; smiled, pressed food on her. But she wasn't hungry: several packets of biscuits had gone from the cupboard.

After supper, baffled, I thought I might as well work, but as we went into the living room she said shyly, with anxiety, 'Aren't you going to put the chair covers on again?'

'But they are full of cigarette holes.'

Restless evasive movements of her whole person: a denial that she was responsible. 'But aren't you going to have new covers?'

'Sit down, Kate.'

She sat opposite me in that filthy sofa, in her mess of crumbs and wrappers and dirty tissues.

I sat, reluctantly, in a chair that had had jam on it, scraped off.

She was so woebegone and pathetic; but I didn't know what to say. I could see it was important to her that I should say, Yes, I am going to do the room up. She had been thinking about it.

What I should perhaps have said was: But, Kate, what is the point of doing the room up, when you are going to ruin it again, you and your friends! But I couldn't say it. Say: *When you've left,* then . . . But that was what she was hearing, as she gazed at me, her eyes frantic.

I said, 'I will get things put right, Kate. Don't worry.' Meaning, Don't worry, I'm not going to throw you out.

Meanwhile, Mrs Brown has finally given me up. She will not clean up after Kate: and that's that.

Every night, leaving Kate there, when I go to have my bath and retreat to my bedroom (the room in which Richard says I am not!), I find myself slumping into discouragement because of Kate; then I rally into energetic decision-making. I marshal sensible remarks to make to her; I imagine conversations.

'Kate, are you planning to go on like this?'

'Well, Jane, I can see that . . .'

'It won't do, Kate. It isn't doing any good, slumping around here, week after week! No, we have to make a real plan for you. What about that Spanish you said you would study? What have you done with the books.'

'I'll find them, Janna. I'll do at least a couple of hours every day.'

But when, with these conversations blue-printed in my mind, I sit down with Kate at the supper table, or in the chair opposite her, they simply evaporate. They had not been addressed to Kate at all: the words for her are some I cannot even imagine, cannot find in my mind. Somewhere inside me I must be convinced that the words exist which will reach Kate. I have only to find them!

Tonight Kate again asked about the covers for the chairs. They have become a symbol to her. I took the wretched yellow covers down to the shop at the bottom of the road and asked them to repeat them. 'In yellow linen?'

'In yellow linen.'

Crazy. I can't put them on the chairs! I can't not put them on, because it will be some kind of blow for Kate.

Today, Jill said to me, as I went through past her and Hannah, 'Did Kate tell you I was in your flat last week?'

'No. Did she ask you to go?'

'When you were off pursuing your love life—*sorry,* Jane, she was ringing me two or three times every evening.'

'Well, I'm not going to apologize for that,' I said, knowing that Jill and Hannah both watched me closely for symptoms of all kinds.

'Who said you should? But one night she sounded quite peculiar, as I went over. I saw the flat.'

'Ah.'

'*Well,* Jane!'

'So what have you decided?'

'Don't be like that. No, it's like this, we—I mean, Mark and me—thought you'd like to come to supper with us.'

'To discuss Kate?'

'And you haven't really seen our flat, have you?'

'Flats,' I said, 'can be quite easily put to rights if they've gone downhill.'

'But people can't.'

'Well, I'm going to trust that means Kate and not me, because I don't propose to apologize for anything.'

I was really quite angry: as I went off into the amiabilities of my office and Charlie's, I heard Jill cry, 'Oh, Jane, of course I didn't mean you, I meant Kate.'

Richard rang. It's been a week. He sounded far away, and he was. Near Dundee somewhere.

He said, 'Jane, it seems we have an inordinate number of relatives, all of whom have to be seen.'

I said, 'Richard, when you're not here it is as if you've dropped off the edge of the world.'

He said, 'It's funny about relatives. I don't think I've given any of mine a thought in five years. Suddenly it's a family necessity. I'm with my cousin William and his family.'

'And then?'

'Oh, Janna. I'm sorry.'

'What's it like, where you are?' For I was remembering that time with Joyce, when she had left *Lilith* and we talked on the telephone, she in places in Wales, and then it was New York: friendship at the end of a long, fading wavelength.

'As I look out of the window I see a small rather cosy lake, with three tourists in a rowing boat; a hillside covered with gorse, and a garden where my cousin's wife Betty is picking asters.'

'Well, I shall be here,' I said.

Supper with Jill and Mark, in Kentish Town.

It is the first floor of a Victorian house, a very large room, off which is a tiny room that has a shower and a lavatory. The place was converted to Mark's prescription. When I shared my first flat with a girl all those years ago, the pattern was the conventional one, scaled down: we had a minute bedroom, small living room, and both of us deciding to eat in the kitchen were defensive with our parents, for it was not then common. But Jill and Mark live in this big room, putting down futons at night, that are rolled up during the day in cupboards, eating at a large low table which is the focus of the sitting area, near the kitchen, which is an assemblage of the most advanced gadgetry: I did not at once recognize these scarlet cabinets and steel surfaces as ovens, grills, refrigerators, etc. Jill and Mark and Hannah and I sat around in low canvas chairs looking out of french windows, uncurtained, but with the old-fashioned wooden shutters painted scarlet, folded back, and a frivolous scalloped scarlet blind half lowered to display a church spire, rising from a sober little garden that allowed itself an exclamation mark: a sheet of purple clematis over the fence. In the street outside, a black youth dressed in a brilliant yellow tracksuit was caressing a dark blue Mercedes with a vast sponge that showered rich white lather everywhere over it and over three children— white, male, adoring—who wished to take part in this ritual of love, but who had to be repelled by continuous assaults of foam. They kept rushing in to touch the car, shouting triumphantly at the black guardian, who shouted at them, but stylishly, in the pace of the game, and then they rushed off again, giggling. The black youth's ears were occluded by the plugs that fed music into his brain and set the rhythm of his smiles and circling, sweeping, smoothing arm. One hand held the transistor. The late sunlight left this scene as we drank various anticipatory mixtures of alcohol, and withdrew itself to the church steeple which glowed a mellow golden brown.

Mark spread plates of bread and olives and tomato salad about on the table while Jill worked on with the next course. Strict equality. 'But I cooked the stew, so you do the vegetables, Mark.' 'But I made the pudding.' 'But I made the pudding on Sunday.' 'All right.'

Jill is wearing jeans and a fantastic harlequin sweater, and her hair, done that day, is dyed purple, the same colour as the clematis, now a sombre inky splodge in the twilight; it is brushed straight up, in short vibrant flames. She looks like a parakeet. Mark is wearing jeans and a cerulean sweatshirt that says on it: Funky III, Montezuma! To ask what it meant would seem to expose a lack of imagination. Hannah, the earth mother, is wearing a full dark green long skirt, and a tight yellow top that leaves her large brown arms bare and exposes the tops of bulging brown breasts where slides a turquoise Navaho necklace. She looks massive. She is sitting slightly back from the three of us, reposing in her chair with her two arms hooked back behind her exposing the salubrious black tufts in her armpits. It goes without saying that she does not wear a bra. Her Aztec face, all proud fine curves, surveys all, and reserves judgement.

The focus of this scene, the sun to whom we turn, is Jill. Why? I wonder often enough what it is that makes this or that person the loadstone in a group for an occasion. Our eyes follow her as we talk: she is all quick, fine, accurate little movements; and her face is concentrated on what her hands do. Mark goes to her, to stare into the stew she is stirring, but really to be close to her. I see how her body gathers itself together at this closeness, not repudiating him, but saying, Later! And, as he slides a kiss on to her neck, she looks up, quick and annoyed, and makes herself smile. He lays a large arm on her shoulders. He looks like a suppliant; but not a humble one. Oh no: Jill need not think . . . Her shoulders did not refuse that lover's arm, but she moves away to reach for the salt, as if she had not noticed the arm. Mark stands there, quietly, looking at his love deliberately moving about out of his reach, and then she flicks up her cockatoo head, gives him a brisk little smile that has imminent in it a promise of better things, but at the right time: and comes past him to sit down. He remains standing for a moment, behind her. He holds his arms in: they long to put themselves around her. But she makes no sign, merely piles tomato salad on to her plate, and he sits down, roughly, knocking something over: an explosion of frustration which makes me look quickly at Hannah. For some reason I don't want this skilled observer to see what I am seeing, but of course she does; and I don't want to share a look with her, which is what will happen if I allow our eyes to meet.

On the wall opposite me there is a large mirror salvaged

from some pub that has—mistakenly—been modernized. Art-deco lilies engraved in silver and gold and black loll in the arms of a girl not unlike Jill when she first came to my flat, all long floating hair and tender uncertainties. Reflected there I see myself reclining in the canvas chair, a woman who, with the room's distance away, and the scarlet-framed window full of evening light behind her, seems, in her misty lilac-blue dress, with her soft wisps of silvery hair, to belong more with the lilies and the floating girl.

My heart is aching.

We eat our admirable salad, praise the olive oil, comment on the Greek bread; Kentish Town is fantastic for Cypriot food, Mediterranean food. We comment on this and that. And I know that Jill is containing a head of steam fuelled by a lifetime: she wants me to see Kate as she does, at last; but this item on our agenda, Kate, is in fact the least of it; I am watching Jill and Mark, close to each other in low chairs, and see how he looks at her. A hunger. And deeper than that, anger burning there in eyes which reflect exactly what is happening to him. Later that night, Jill will allow some switch or other to be turned, and will—what? I find it hard to imagine this girl amorous. One has only to look at Mark to know that he is not one who will settle for a cold girl; but when that switch is turned, how does this efficiently airy one become a lover? Or loved?

What I am saying to myself, as Jill—it is her turn—serves lamb stew and mange-touts, is some kind of prayer or a plea: Jill, don't; don't Jill. Oh, *don't* . . .

She raises the subject, as we reach the end of the stew. She stammers slightly, showing for how long and with what intensity she has prepared fantasy exchanges of intelligent words, just as I do for Kate. 'Jane, about Kate, I really do think—'

'Let the poor woman have her food in peace,' says Mark, swilling red wine about his glass and squinting at it, in a way that says he is embarrassed by Jill, or feels himself out of his depth. And indeed we all have to be embarrassed and controlled, for her voice trembles and we know we are seeing Jill's past, embodied there now in the dusk of the big room, as she says, 'Jane, look, surely you must see that something has got to done about Kate? Your *flat*. Your lovely *flat*—it's like a dustbin. When I went in and saw it, I wanted to weep. I simply do *not* understand you, Jane.' And tears threaten her voice. Mark gets up, switches on the lights in some contraption, like the fairy lights in a summer garden, that dangles from a bracket. The dusk springs back outside. Mark pulls down the scarlet blind. Mark—it is his turn—clears away the plates; and Jill sits staring woefully at me, and she looks at this moment not so different from the poor waif Kate, the hopeless one.

Now I do look at Hannah, straight, wanting to know what she thinks; and she gives me a smile and a companionable nod, as if to say, Never mind!

'Are you going to go on like this, Jane?'

'Of course not,' I say at last. 'Something will happen.'

'Like what? Did you know those squatters are making themselves at home in your place?'

'It had occurred to me.'

'But what are you going to *do*?' Here Mark wants to know what I am going to *do*; making it plain from his tone that he knows jolly well what he would do. And I can see that no squatter would get anything but short shrift if they managed to enter this shrine of modern living.

Mark is revolutionary. Of course. I cannot make out what brand. We have occasionally discussed his 'line'; but it seems to me like a piece of abstract patterning, one premise flowing from another, very agreeable to do, as a relaxation, but nothing much to do with life.

I say, 'Are you worried about my chair covers, Comrade Mark? Tell me, would you call the police?'

Committed to not calling the police, until they are on his side—which my private thoughts convince me they may very well soon be—he looks put out; but then says that he would get rid of them himself. He wouldn't need the police.

It has ever been my observation that revolutionaries are sticklers for the law; and I say, to try him, that I was much too wary of the processes of the law to attract them: if squatters were to be thrown out forcibly from one's home, surely that would be aggression?

'They are *trespassing*,' says Jill fiercely. 'They are causing damage to property.'

I look at Mark; and see him reluctant to criticize assaults on property; but he says briefly, 'You shouldn't let them get away with it, Jane. If you like, I'll go down to the squat myself and have a talk with them.'

I say, 'Are you going to complain about my chair covers?'

At which Mark looks offended; and Jill springs up, to get the pudding. A summer pudding oozing delicious red and black juices appears before us, and our annoyance dissolves in exclamations, and doses of heavy cream.

And that amazingly was the end of the subject of Kate, which Jill had been privately suffering over, I am sure, for days.

We sat on over the wreckage of the pudding. We drank more red wine. We drank brandy. We drank coffee. Jill, whose turn it was to do the washing-up, allowed herself to be assisted by Mark. Hannah and I sat together, and currents of good feeling washed back and forth.

In a low voice, she said, 'Jane, when you can't cope with Kate, let me have a try, will you?'

I said, 'I think she's rather worse than you allow for.'

She said, 'All the same . . . I've seen her, you know. She's hung about sometimes on the pavement outside *Lilith*. She's no more of a mess than many.'

'If there *are* many, then I think I am discouraged. I mean, for us all.'

Hannah smiled, acknowledging this; and then laughed a little. She said, in a very low voice, 'The thing is, people like you and Jill, you don't find it easy to be efficient, it's all a great effort for you, that's why you have to overdo it. And you don't see how much it intimidates the rest of us.' She was looking at Mark, very close to Jill; he was doing the washing-up while she dried. Her whole person said, Not *now*.

I laughed. She laughed.

'What are you laughing about?' inquired Jill, quick and on guard.

'I am not really laughing,' I said, speaking truly.

And I am sitting here tonight, having insisted that Kate should run a bath and then actually get into it, thinking that Hannah has looked at me, the efficient, competent, always on top of everything Jane, and said casually, as if there could not possibly be any argument, that I was not efficient by nature. I am staring back into my past tonight—back, back, before— but *who* was it, who was strong enough a personality to make me model myself on her? I'd give anything to have my mother here now, to put this question: What was I really like as a girl, before I came to London and became the success of the family? Was I like Kate, perhaps? And, as I write this, I know that my mother would look puzzled, even annoyed, and say, 'What do you mean? You and Georgina quarrelled all the time, that's all I know.'

We are halfway through August. My least favourite month sags past. It rains quite a bit, heavy and slow. London explodes with people from everywhere, and on the under-ground and buses I look to see a homegrown face. I enjoy this, every year, the feast of people, Babel, even if I shut my senses to the month, waiting for the crisp pleasures of September. But this year I hold on to every day, willing it to slow, and stay. Richard has still not said when he will leave, and I don't want to know—but autumn is coming. He has not rung, and a week has gone since he did.

I spend my evenings with Kate, wrestling for her soul: if Hannah can do it, why not I? is my thought. But the gods would laugh, the gods probably are laughing, at the sight of me and Kate, at my table in the kitchen, opposite each other; or on either side of my low glass table in the living room, Kate reluctantly unplugged, while I fight to bring her into ordinary life. Every remark I gather out of the assortment in my brain to present to her dies in the space between us. Sometimes she does not hear at all, I am convinced, though an abstract smile is set on her face, to appease me. She is probably listening still to the seas of sound, though not plugged into them. Or, I can see words reach her, and she seems to consider them, one by one. She smiles, politely, but puzzled. Why is Jane saying that? she is wondering, while I am asking myself, What is the use?

Why does she want to know what I did when I was at school? She is sullen, and I censor the subject for the future. Why is Jane talking about the flamingoes in some park or other? Why is Jane describing what Amsterdam is like?

Well, why am I?

I think then that after all, with ordinary people, nearly everything is said without words; I can work with Jill, the amiable Charlie, all day with hardly a need to say more than: I'll do Wine, but you must do Food; and I'm going out to interview X, but you have to do the Luncheon. All the rest is a flow between you, both know what is necessary.

Very well then, let's establish between Kate and me the companionable silences where things are understood: but if I stop talking, she reaches for her earphones.

But I've kept at it, wearing her out, and me too.

I go to bed exhausted. And dream, I dream, oh I dream.

I also go in to old Annie every day for an hour after work. That I have finally become her nearest and dearest is marked by the fact that she starts raging and abusing me as I go in. Because I am going in, Maureen, hearing from Annie that I go every evening, hasn't been bothering, except to fetch in supplies of food, a quick dart in, then out with the cry: 'Oh, but I've got to fetch my youngest from school, and I'm late.'

'She's ready enough when she hands the book to me to sign,' shouts Annie at me.

I say, 'Then don't sign.'

'I won't, one of these days,' she screeches.

'The book is there for you to say no, I won't sign, if they haven't done their work.'

'Their work? She was in here five minutes this morning, but she takes the money for it.'

'Then don't sign.'

This futile circular conversation may easily go on for half and hour. For Annie needs to talk and to shout, to dispel some of the energy that rages in her. It exhausts me. I reach home and Kate, exhausted.

Richard rang. He is in Somerset. With his wife's brother's family. He said, 'I will be back next week. Will you be there, Janna?'

The anxiety in that appeased me; but I cried, 'You will have been gone three weeks.'

'I know.'

Richard rang. I was already in bed. His voice, in my ear, as I lay in my white thick cool bed, alone. His voice goes right through me, makes my heart beat, delights me: I suppose a romantic novelist (*manqué*) is entitled to say something of the sort.

He said, 'Are you in bed?'

'Yes, are you?'

'Yes, in an ancient four-poster, in a little attic room at the top of an old manor house. England is very extraordinary, Janna. You've got used to it all and don't notice. It is a treasure house. You go into some dump of a village—sorry, but I'm more American than I know. You turn in at some gates and there's a house like an illustration. It is packed, crammed full of goodies which the owners take for granted. What's in this room up here would fetch thousands in the States.'

'But they don't take it for granted. You are meant to think they take it for granted.'

'Is that it? I've been away too long. Janna, up here tonight I feel as if I am in a fairy tale. The door will open and you will walk in . . . Janna?'

'I'm here. Listening.'

'Why can't you and I go to bed together? When it is obviously the one thing we were born to do? Are you there?'

'Yes.'

'Is it vanity, Janna?'

'My vanity, you mean?'

'Do you suppose I don't have any, Janna?'

'Do you still have that little photograph?'

'What do you think!'

'Is it there, now?'

'Yes. Propped against the lamp.'

'Ghosts,' I said. 'Ghosts are why we can't make love.'

'Janna, I've been thinking these last weeks. I've never, ever had with anyone else in my life the sort of thing I do with you. Have I told you that?'

'No.'

'I feel there is no need to tell you things.'

'I know.'

'Good night.'

'Good night.'

Ghosts were in my room, all right. Of course I didn't sleep.

I've wept. Snuffled and groaned and mopped up floods. I've caught myself thinking that when Richard goes this dreadful pain will go away.

Richard rang.

He said, 'Are you alone?'

I was amazed. I said, 'But Richard, how could I be anything else?'

He said, 'Well, I don't know anything about you, not really.'

'You do,' I said, the bottom dropping out of something; my idea of him, my idea of his idea of me . . .

'Do you have affairs, Janna?'

'No, I don't.'

'I thought you didn't. But I was thinking tonight, lying up here, why should I take that for granted?'

'Are you lying up there alone?'

'Yes.'

'Do you have affairs?'

'I have had one or two. The *willed* affair. Do you know what I mean?'

'You mean, you felt an affair was due to you?'

'Exactly. Not to be recommended.'

I said, 'I've only slept with one man. Freddie.'

A silence. Then I said, shocked at myself, 'What an extraordinary thing to say. In fact, after he died, I slept around quite a bit.'

'Why not!'

'But that didn't count.'

'Of course it didn't,' he agreed at once. 'I'll allow that you are a one-man woman.'

'Mockery?'

'No, I assure you.'

'Perhaps we are both monogamous, and that's our trouble?'

'Oh, how I wish I could be monogamous with you.' And he started humming it as a blues-style Billie Holliday. 'Ohhh—ho-o-w I wi-i-sh I could be mono-o-ogamous with you-u-u.'

They delivered the new chair covers today. I suppose I had planned to put them away—until! But Kate had the package open, and was waiting for me to make the decision to put them on. Together we fitted them, she taking one chair, I another. Two elegant little armchairs, yellow and bright, with candy-striped cushions. Tears in her eyes—of gratitude. She rushed into my arms. I held her tight: the thought in my mind being, I have so much energy, can't I press some into her? She held me frantically, and snuffled. Then we separated, beaming with pleasure at the pretty chairs. We sat on them, opposite each other. Then, the impulse of this little ceremony exhausted, Kate, still smiling, went back to her sofa and blissfully plugged herself in.

Something awful, *awful*—I cannot get to grips with it. Earlier this evening, about eight, the telephone. Richard. Richard's *voice*.

At once my heart melted, senses swooned, etc., and so forth.

'Richard,' I said.

'It's not Richard. It's Matthew. Matthew Curtis.'

I really could not speak. It was such a shock . . . and my mind began racing in all directions, frantically trying to take it all in. A thousand things at once.

'Is that Mrs Somers? Janna Somers?'

'Yes.'
'Is my father there?'
'No, he is not.'
Silence. Which I could not break.
'He's not there?' *Richard*'s voice, but brisk and trying to sound offhand. Now, of course, I heard the American accent, quite strong; which I had not at once, because all I could hear before was Richard.
Waves of light and dark were breaking through me, and I thought I was going to faint.
'Well, thanks. I'm sorry I bothered you.'
I sat on the edge of my bed for some time, trying to get back to myself. Then I told Kate I was not well, and I came to bed.

The telephone. Richard's voice. My mind went reeling about and I held fast to the thought: Matthew's voice has an American sound.
'Janna?'
'I'm here,' I said, rather faint.
'What's wrong? Is there something wrong?'
'Your Matthew rang me this evening. To ask, were you here?'
'What . . .' It occurred to me, I had not ever seen my love angry. The air was sizzling with anger. 'He rang *you*? Jane, I'm sorry. What can I say?'
'Did you know he was in London?'
'Sylvia told me today he was coming. For a month. *Jane?*'
'I'm all right.'
We went on like that for a little and rang off in a misery of apologies, and, of course, anxiety.
Kathleen must have telephoned Matthew, saying that their father was being enticed from his responsibilities.

Today this happened. I rang the office to say I was not well. This never happens. Charlie said, Oh all right, but Caroline was not well and he was going home early to accompany

Phyllis and the baby to the doctor. Jill rang to say she hoped Kate was looking after me. Hannah rang to be instructed on how to do my work. She remarked that I should be thinking of getting someone else into Editorial, because Phyllis has said she won't be back for at least another year. 'It will be more than that, to my mind,' commented Hannah. I said I felt too awful to care about *Lilith,* and they must all get on with it.

I made myself bath and dress. Like old Annie, I was never one to loll in bed. (Or was I once, I don't remember!)

The doorbell. I thought, The milkman. No, four young people, instantly recognizable as from the squat. A young man, three girls. It was ten a.m. and I knew they had decided to spend the day at my expense.

I said, 'Kate is still asleep.'

The young man, Brian, a pack leader, with an air of responsibility, even solemnity. He improvised: 'I would like to have a word with you, about Kate. If that is all right, Janna.'

(*Janna!*)

I said, seizing, I was sure—and as it turned out rightly—an opportunity, 'Please come in,' and stood aside, smiling like a hostess as they crowded in. And shut the door, and invited them politely to sit down. Never have I been so grateful for the support of civilized intercourse. Held together by that, I asked them if they would care for tea or coffee, and stood by while they settled themselves. They all looked hard and with antagonism at the new yellow chairs, and they exchanged glances. They sat, two on the dirty grey sofa in Kate's mess, and two opposite. I went to the kitchen to put on the kettle, and so on.

I was just holding myself together. Not because of them. This business of Matthew—it has gone right *home*—wherever home is, in me. I feel quite sick with it, I am not myself. I did not care about these four outriders from the armies of the future, which is how I felt them, as they came into the flat with the sort of assurance that comes from knowing, absolutely, that they are in the right. I knew that each one of them, taken by herself—and Brian too—is a perfectly pleasant and decent and ordinary young thing (in their early twenties, Brian is perhaps getting on for thirty), and that if I were alone with any one of them we would 'get on' and like each other. I knew that the four of them together were a closed group, a pack, and that everything I could say would be judged by their group faculties, and that Brian would be the arbiter. I knew that every one talked the language of revolution, of women's lib, and all that jargon, and that Brian held their destinies, boss male, even while he—I have no doubt at all—nicely assesses the rights of women. I knew. I felt, standing there, arranging my pretty cups and plates, nothing but an immense weariness.

I carried in the tray, loaded with delicious coffee and a large fruit cake from the health-food shop which I buy for Kate, hoping that in this way she will get into her, at least sometimes, a little real food.

I sat down, and invited one of the girls to pour the coffee, remarking that I was not feeling very well. This I did because I wanted to observe them. A bit of a fuss over the coffee, jokes about the cake—'Very healthy'—vast chunks cut for them all. They all wore jeans and varieties of singlet. The girls looked unspeakably scruffy. Since the mode—alas—at the moment demands that a model should spend three hours to get turned out with her hair looking as if she has just been in bed for three weeks with pneumonia and she hasn't got around to tidying it—a state of disorder that is almost impossible to preserve for five minutes without constant recombings by the beauticians—these girls, emulating, had rats' tails and spikes and tufts of rubbishy hair all around attractive little faces, and Brian, a well-set-up and brisk young man, seemed like the owner of a harem of freaks.

But all this—the scene, Brian, that commissar, the girls— seemed a long way off from me.

Tidily consuming cake, his coffee cup lodged on the edge of the chair, Brian said, 'Janna, I wonder if you have ever seriously considered Kate's problems?'

Four pairs of eyes were fastened, with identical expressions of withheld condemnation, on me.

I said, 'Obviously, not.' And waited.

They looked at each other, frowning.

'Janna, she *needs* help.'

'But isn't she getting it—from you?'

Brian, who isn't stupid, whatever else, said, 'No, Janna, this must be a serious discussion.'

I said, 'Don't you think you ought to wake her? I for one don't want to discuss her behind her back.'

At this, minor consternation. Clearly I had invoked some code of theirs. 'I do agree that that would be best,' conceded Brian, with a glance at the three girls to keep them in order, 'but I—we—feel that it is a serious situation.'

'What do you suggest?'

'She shouldn't be alone all day,' said one of the girls, fierce and accusing.

'Sometimes she is alone from early morning until late at night,' said another.

'Very true, she is.'

My reactions were not what they had expected; this confrontation might have been planned in four separate minds, but had been directed by Brian. What I was to say had been imagined quite differently.

'But if she came to live with us, she would have company,' said another girl.

'Oh, I know what people like you think of squats,' said the fierce girl, who, now she had started to hate me, was sending me forceful, accusing glances between gulps of coffee.

'As it happens I once wrote a long article for *Lilith* about squats, and I said that some of them are rather good and useful. You may need to think of yourselves as a persecuted minority, but I can't help that.'

'No, wait, just a minute,' commanded Brian, obviously well used to this situation of directing discussion. If discussion this could be called. 'This is not helpful to any of us, and particularly not Kate.' Here he looked inquiringly at me, then gave a little nod which told me it was my turn to speak.

I said, 'Well, why doesn't Kate move in with you? I have never, not once, said she shouldn't. Or for that matter criticized you. Though perhaps you might agree that I have had good reason to . . .' And here I indicated the state of my living room. They frowned, looked away, glanced at the two little yellow chairs which more and more assumed the character of symbols, though innocent ones, of some shockingly sybaritic state, the mere contemplation of which—even a glance—was strong enough to feed the strength of moral disapproval in them.

'Yes, well, let's keep things in proportion,' said Brian to me coldly; and again quelled his girls with a glance. 'You say you haven't stopped Kate coming to us?'

'No, never.'

'That is *not*,' said he, 'what she has told us.'

I said nothing at all. I was suddenly fed up with them all. I got up—noting that I had to put my hand out to steady myself on the chairback. I put the coffee cups, half full or empty, not caring, on to the tray. I swept together plates full of crumbs. I lifted the whole load out and into the kitchen. When I got back they were all on their feet, conferring.

'Perhaps we have made a mistake,' said the fierce girl, but not as if she felt it.

Brian said, 'If there's been a misunderstanding, then . . .'

'Look,' I said. 'Kate is nearly twenty. She came here because she wanted to. She invited herself. If she wants to leave, she may. I think I had better say I would prefer her to move into a place where people have better manners, but I am sure you think that is a very reactionary thought.' And at this my energy ran out, and I heard myself say in a quite different tone, the voice of what I really did feel, 'Oh, do go away, I am so fed up with it all. I'll tell Kate you were here and that you want her to live with you. And now—get out.'

They went out, silently, each alone. I mean, not cementing their togetherness with a dozen little glances, the almost imperceptible movements of their solidarity, the way the gestures of one will echo another, or they will turn to share a look at the same moment, or stretch out their hands together as if in a rehearsed gesture for a piece of cake.

At the door Brian said, finishing the interview in command, 'Janna, we all feel that it was a good thing we have had the chance to speak to you. Our minds are much clearer.'

'I am glad,' I said. 'Mine, on the other hand, remains at sea.' And I shut the door.

When Kate woke, I said they had been here, and she was at once in a panic. 'What did they say, what did they say?' For she knew that I knew she had been saying her wicked aunt had forbidden her to see them, let alone go to live there.

'Oh, don't worry, Kate,' I said. 'And anyway, I rather liked them.'

'You did?' she exclaimed, pleased, cheering up. 'Oh, I am glad. I knew you would if you met them.'

But I am sure they will not come again here.

My little yellow chairs are safe.

Today I saw Richard. He rang at the office, saying could I be downstairs in half an hour. I was. A taxi. We collapsed into each other's arms and held on tight. We told the taxi to go to Knightsbridge. 'To meet you has involved lying to Sylvia, so as to find an excuse to take the train after hers, because Matthew met that one and I have no doubt was preparing to follow me.' He sounded despairing, angry, incredulous. 'Janna, how do we come to be in this situation?'

We sat on there, close, not saying a word, imbibing each other, with our eyes closed, cheek against hungry cheek.

When the driver put us down in Knightsbridge, we walked till we found a pub, and dived into it.

It was full, crammed, jumping with London's visitors. Enormously enjoyable, colourful, and we found our spirits soaring with the alcohol and lack of food, for we couldn't be troubled to eat. When the pub closed we left. We have worked out a series of rendezvous and exact dates, the hour, the minute, where we may with luck encounter each other without having to use the telephone.

Conversation with Kate.

'I went to the squat today.' A pause. She looked miserable.

'They are cross with me, Janna.'

'Well, never mind . . .'

Sniff, gulp, snuffle.

'Kate, have you met Hannah? You know, the girl who works with Jill in the office?'

Her face froze; her eyes darted suspicion.

'Well, have you, Kate? Do you like her?'

Kate became virtuous and scandalized, just as Jill does, copying their mother.

'Well, but she's a lesbian.'

'I think she's very nice.'

'Jill says she lives in a commune.'

'It's rather like a squat.'

Suddenly, a swirl towards me, like a caught fish, the wild accusing eyes: 'Why do you want me to go there? Why do you want to get rid of me?'

'I don't, but I thought you might like Hannah.'

And then: 'Are you going to leave?'

'Where to?'

'Are you going to get married? Go away?'

'No, Kate, I am not.'

She is not reassured; her face is pinched and full of dread.

I am beginning to regret the squat: at least she did have some resources apart from me.

It occurred to me today: the three weeks Richard and I had together, that time: when we were in it we thought there was plenty to come. But perhaps that was the high point, that was it.

I met Richard in Holborn, looking over my shoulder for Kate, for Kathleen—even Matthew? I felt silly, cheapened. So did he. We went into a pub, to a corner well out of sight of the doors, and smiled at each other, grim.

'What price love?' said he, using the word with precision.

'It can certainly be high enough,' I said, and with the intention of entertaining him told him about Phyllis, the sharp ambitious multi-talented girl who, feeling she *ought* to marry—for what else could have made her?—married one of the world's natural marriers, natural fathers; and who, wed, found her work was not for her, her own advancement, but for maintaining her husband's first wife and three sons. Pregnant, she thought of abortion, so much of a threat did a baby seem to her; her husband was appalled, scandalized. The baby born, the world revolved around it. She, we believe, but it is hard to get past that protective barrier, Charlie, would like to get back to work, if for no other reason than to do something about the debts that are mounting rapidly. At this point, Charlie summons his rich mother and two rich fathers, real and step. A family conference, centred on the baby. They will fork out, very handsomely, to allow Phyllis to stay at home and be a good mother to her baby, and for the period of a full three years.

This tale, which has been entertaining me, Jill and Hannah, started off lamely, for the rich hilarity of the office had not survived the sneaky journey here, and Richard's and my discomfort. I talked on, watching Richard's face for signs that he did find it at least a comment on something or other, life or sex. Or even love. He did smile at the end, a little, but sighed. He looked forlorn.

In the stridently lit pub, for this was a modern one, nothing like 'our' Soho pub, he seemed tired and drained, though he was brown and glistening with his country days (and, presumably, nights). He had on a cream linen suit. Summer. But suddenly it did not seem summer at all, the cream suit looked skimpy and washed out, and the rain on the window panes was not a summer rain.

I felt impelled to go on. 'And there's another,' I said. 'Hannah, you remember her, I've told you about her?'

'The warrior on the frontier of women's rights,' he said.

'You could put it like that.'

'I thought that was how she put it.'

'It's just that . . . she's not a fanatic. Today she told us this story. One of the girls who had been living in their commune and had got married has a baby. Before she had the baby she kept coming to visit the commune, her sisters, to say how she missed them, missed communal life, and how she was dreading having to give up her job—'

'I take it her husband doesn't contribute anything one way or another,' he remarked, distant.

Richard is far from monotone, can be sarcastic, sardonic, witty, angry, ironical. But hostile he has not been.

I was silent. Now it seemed a foolish tale to tell, though with the three of us it had seemed funny enough.

'Well, go on.'

'When the baby was born all the sisters went to visit her, and found her radiant.'

'Glandular,' he remarked.

'Quite so. But when they went visiting, to commiserate with her on her incarceration, for so she had been expecting it to be, they found her pleasurably immersed in maternity. Invited to come and visit them at the commune, she did not come. She did not ring. There were consultations, and a rescue operation was planned. They visualized her beaten down by maternity, wifehood, domesticity. Several times they arrived outside her door and, though convinced she was within, there was no answer when they knocked. This went on for some weeks. They waylaid the husband, who naturally they saw as an enemy, and he treated them accordingly, with a Yes, and a No.

'But they weren't going to give up on their distressed sister. Finally they found her in the park, with her baby, drinking Coca-Cola while she lolled on a deckchair in the sun reading. Guilt personified, she sat up, and behaved as if she had committed some crime. But what she was concealing was happiness, as Hannah slowly became convinced.'

'Ha, Hannah again.'

'Yes. Hannah saw that all this girl wanted was to be rid of her. Finally she said that she had never been more happy in her life. She had been working since she was sixteen, and as far as she was concerned, to be allowed, with the full permission of everybody, to do nothing all day but look after a baby and sit around in parks and gossip with strangers and chat with other mums was, simply, heaven. Her life had become pure pleasure. But she did see that the sisters weren't likely to go along with that, so Hannah would have to forgive her, but please, would she just go away. She could tell the girls in the commune anything she bloody well liked, as far as she was concerned. She thought they were all looneys.'

Richard, sitting in his hunched position, shoulders loaded, cosseted his drink. He has very fine hands. When I look at them my heart turns over. And so forth. But my love's hands were very tense around that glass.

'Hannah was telling the story against herself, against the commune,' I pointed out.

'Well, I don't know,' he said at last. 'Look, let's get out of here and walk. If you think we can do it without finding some obsessed waif in our path.'

We walked around the streets of Holborn in the rain.

I went to our second rendezvous, in Shepherd Market, but he did not come. I waited an hour and left.

Back in the office, Jill said he had rung, would ring again. But he did not ring until just as I was leaving.

Kathleen had tried to commit suicide. Not really, more a 'cry for help'.

He will try and make our next rendezvous the day after tomorrow.

When I put down the telephone, Jill and Hannah were both silently regarding me. So I must have looked shaken.

I said, 'Can you explain why a girl who has always had the best of everything, and two perfectly satisfactory parents, should stage a cry for help?'

Hannah remarked, in the studied way that says something has been mentally prepared, 'Janna, have you ever thought that Kate might try it?'

This was such a shock, I had to sit down. 'No, it hadn't crossed my mind.'

They were both *not* looking at me, nor at each other: pennies must drop: mine.

I said, 'But Kate is such a long way from any sort of reality.'

'You mean,' said Jill, 'that to commit suicide you need to have a sense of reality?'

I thought. 'Yes. Clearly that is what I must mean. The one thing about Kate is that she seems such a long way from understanding her situation.'

A short snort of laughter: Jill. And Hannah's full, queenly contemplation of other people's inadequacies.

'Poor Janna,' said Jill.

'I would say,' I persisted, 'that that is the definition of Kate.'

'No,' pronounced Hannah, 'that's not it.'

Jill: 'You didn't know that Kate tried to commit suicide? Or rather, staged some stupid bit of melodrama?'

'How should I know, if no one told me?'

'No one told you because as far as my clever parents are concerned it never happened.'

'But you knew and you didn't tell me, Jill.'

'I've been telling you and telling you, you're crazy to have Kate.'

'What did she do?'

'She took twelve of Mother's sleepers, when she knew she would be found half an hour later.'

'All the same,' said Hannah.

'I take it that is judged as being within the scope of a cry for help, if not a suicide attempt?' I was very angry.

'And one of these days,' said Jill, 'you are going to get back at one in the morning and find Kate moribund.'

Hannah said, 'I think she's particularly at risk now she's not going to the squat.'

I said, 'How does it come about that I am some sort of a criminal? Kate isn't my daughter. Thank God.'

'Well, you've taken on the responsibility for her, haven't you?' said Jill, fussed and cross and accusing.

'And you, her sister, won't even have her around for a meal,' I said.

Hannah, pacemaker, peacemaker, pronounced, 'I don't see that either of you is to blame.'

'Thank you,' I said.

'Thank you,' said Jill.

Richard telephoned to say he couldn't make our next, tomorrow: Holborn again.

Tonight I am so sick with it all, with wanting to be with

him, with not wanting to be with him because it is getting so painful. I even catch myself thinking that if this is love, Love, that I've missed out on, then I am glad that I have.

But now I am going to sleep and I suppose I shall be dreaming of Freddie.

Kate wasn't in when I came in. Frenzies of worry! I nearly rang the police. At twelve, just as I was going to bed, she drifted in, smelling strongly of drink. This is a new and nasty development.

'Where have you been?' I demanded, breaking my own rules with her.

'Oh, just around . . .' she smiled vaguely, and reached for her transistor.

I was with Annie. She in a misery of helplessness. 'Where did you put my blue shoes?' she screamed as I entered. 'The blue shoes with the silver buckles?' It turned out that they were shoes she had twenty years ago. She never wears anything but slippers.

She raved on and on, until I was so identified with her feelings that when I stood in the doorway and saw my own living room, dirty, smeared everywhere, Kate asleep in a lump on the sofa, it was as if everything was being taken away from me; above all, my control of my life. And for the first time I have to wonder what it represents, this necessity to have perfectly tidy rooms, the chairs set opposite each other just so, cushions poised at such an angle, so that when I have walked into my home it has always been into order. My bedroom still remains exact—but I am 'not in it'!

I feel as Annie does: that things slide away between my fingers, that I cannot grasp hold of them.

I sat for a long time tonight thinking that I ought to ring up my sister and say, Enough! She's your responsibility. But I can't. *What would happen to her?*

This morning I woke drowned in sorrow. When I opened my eyes on the fresh white and yellow of my room, the sunlight outside, I seemed to be looking at it all from some dark sad place. Of course, I had been dreaming. An embrace, full of sweetness and longing. '*I love you*'—the words were in my mind. But who had said, 'I love you'?

I lay thinking about Freddie, not wanting to. All too much, this obsession with a dead marriage. Dead. It's the right word. Only something dead and gone can haunt, and taunt. I was wondering if Freddie had said, 'I love you.' Presumably these surely essential words did make their appearance, when we decided to marry? 'I love you, Janna,' he had said; and I replied, 'I love you, Freddie.' Is it likely! I simply don't believe it. But I can't remember. I can remember easily, though, our efficient and prompt sensuality, the understanding of the flesh. 'I love you!' Freddie whispered to me as we went off to sleep afterwards? No. And I have to ask myself if I ever did say, 'I love you,' to Freddie. It would probably have seemed some sort of capitulation, or weakness.

But, suddenly, as I lay propped on my (of course) snowy pillows, watching how the yellow curtains moved a little, so that the oblong of sun on the carpet wavered at the edges in a dreamy, hypnotic way, it came into my mind that Richard never said, 'I love you.' Of course, that was what I had been dreaming. And the sadness of the dream dragged me down, so that I could have wept, and wept . . . and meanwhile, my mind was sitting there quite cool and intelligent, thinking that Richard and I had no need of saying I love you, when we had only to meet to feel part of each other, thinking the same thoughts. In fact, there would have been something false about it, prescribed.

Well, they are prescribed. Like weddings. At this very moment a million girls tapping away at their typewriters or doing little sums on their calculators are dreaming while they do it—not of women's lib and emancipation—but of *I love you* and a wedding dress: and we know, for *Lilith*'s researchers tell us so, that the wedding day is the still the golden moment of these infant dreams. Why? For one thing, because of the efforts of *Lilith* and her sisters.

I was lying there in bed, my arms behind my head, in the posture—as I now see—of a captive's surrender, making myself truthfully imagine a real embrace, inside Richard's arms, and his *I love you*. With part of myself I was—*I am*—quite simply discomforted. Because of the unnaturalness of it. At the same time my senses were dissolving with the wanting just that and nothing else, I love you, I love you. I love you—what nonsense, like a spell or a drug, the words feeding fevers, the tongue fattening on the pleasure of saying them, but the mind is brooding: Love? *What* love? Love *whom*?

What circumstances could possibly make 'I love you' natural between us, as natural as that we exchange looks acknowledging a shared thought or an impulse. In bed? Well, I suppose so. But no, absolutely *not*. I will *not* have with Richard the horizontal handshake. One of the men I had sex with after Freddie died remarked over the parting cup of coffee as he returned to his wife, 'It is the horizontal handshake, that's what it amounts to.' Expressing what we both felt about this performance of ours. Nothing. Good-humoured enough—but nothing. Nil. The point was: it wasn't dangerous. I was going to say *Like real sex*. But of course, this thought is not on for post-Freud and post-Johnson and Masters women.

This scene: Joyce had had lunch with her elder sister, living in the country and up for the day to shop at Harrods. Joyce came in, thoughtful; remarking that her sister was happily married. Joyce, at that time, was just beginning to know how unhappily married she was.

Joyce told me, deliberately, watching my face for reactions, that during the war this sister, then unhappily married, met a man whose girl had been killed early in the Blitz. For four years these two worked in the same office. War work. They loved each other, told each other so, but did not sleep together, for words like betrayal and loyalty, fidelity and deception, were used and respected. Sometimes he drove her home, and they held hands in the dark. They hardly dared to kiss: kisses were dangerous. After the war, there was a divorce, and the two married and at last they slept together. Joyce said that *she* said, It was worth waiting for.

'Now there was a couple who gave sex its proper due,' I

said to Joyce, choosing my words, and as her face said yes, that was it, exactly, Phyllis came into the office with some papers. She looked so young and competent and just-so; and Joyce's eyes and mine met on the same thought, and Joyce said, 'Do sit down a minute, Phyllis. I've been having lunch with my sister and—well, I want to tell you something. If you like, it's a little experiment. The generation gap thing . . .'

Down sat Phyllis, composing herself, her face prepared with an alertly discriminatory smile. And Joyce told Phyllis the story. We both watched, Joyce and I, Phyllis's inner processes reflected on that neat and pretty face. First of all, unmistakably, a flash of envy, at once succeeded by a small—at first incredulous and then patronizing—smile. As if at an account of behaviour in some backward tribe. She said at last, 'But what for? It was silly not to.'

She looked at Joyce for enlightenment, and then to me. This was before Joyce's introduction to the pleasures of the horizontal handshake, for she had never slept with anyone but her husband. Joyce was speaking out of an absolute identification with the chaste pair. As for me, I was able to partake of both states, for until Freddie died I had never slept with anyone else. Then the horizontal handshake had been my lot briefly, until I sickened.

Joyce said gently, from her still intact certainties, 'Phyllis, you have to believe that there are people like that.'

Phyllis seemed threatened. She protested, 'But why do you believe your sister? They probably had it off every time they could, but lied about it.'

'No,' said Joyce. Phyllis smiled, knowing better.

She looked at me. I said, flippantly enough, I thought,'Now there was a couple who gave sex its proper due.'

'*What due?*' flashed Phyllis, getting up to leave.

'Dangerous,' I said. Important. Threatening. Full of fate. Fraught with risks of pregnancies, diseases, commitments. The great gamble with the unknown. Ecstasy, and all that.

'Rubbish,' said Phyllis. 'All that sort of thing is simply not *on* for post-Freud and post-Johnson and Masters people.'

Joyce and I, left alone, looked at each other and laughed. And laughed.

When I at last dragged myself out of bed, I took myself out of the flat, leaving Kate still asleep. I was consciously in search of solace, a lift, nutriment, like the tonics they gave us when we were children. 'You need building up, perhaps a tonic?' But I saw nothing in the streets except dinginess, and the heavy late August skies fitted over the city like the pewter lid of an old-fashioned meat dish. On the underground at Baker Street, standing all by herself on the platform, an inordinately pretty girl dressed like a milkmaid out of Laura Ashley, all prim ruffles and flowered muslin, was holding open in front of her a vast illustrated book called *The Frogs and Toads of Great Britain*, which book she continued to hold at a precise angle, as if to catch a light coming from behind her shoulder, until the train came in, whereupon she clapped the book shut, slid it into a lacy reticule, and strode into the carriage.

This would normally have cheered me up, but I remained dismal and down. I was dawdling my way to a meeting with Richard. Or so I hoped; for he might have been prevented, as I was so often prevented, or he was. I was thinking, When we used to meet *then*—as if that was years ago, instead of four months—it had been always with that uprush of zestful, almost savage, unscrupulous enjoyment that carried us on and up over all difficulties. And now . . . my feet dragged, and my mind was full of the sad longings of the dream.

The café was in Wigmore Street. After I had suggested it I remembered that sometimes Freddie and I used to meet here, but thought, Well, what of it? I was in a corner inside, not on the pavement, and ordered myself some coffee, in case Richard wasn't going to come. I was thinking of Richard, of Freddie, when against the light I saw what for a moment I thought was Freddie. There was a moment of panic, an absolute NO, as he came stooping towards me; then I thought, It's Richard, of course, well they are similar, and I said, 'Richard . . .' as I saw him transfigured, young, smiling, debonair, but with something about him deceiving, even malicious, as when, in a dream, someone well known and friendly appears as an enemy. All this took a few seconds, my moment out of ordinary sense; and as my heart thumped and my pulses bumped, I saw this was not Richard, but a young man who looked like him. He stood with his hand on the chair painted a bright sailor's blue, and smiled down at me, politely but winningly.

My mind was a long way behind my apprehensions, and when he said, 'I am Matthew, may I sit down?' it took some moments for me to take it all in; for I was staring, helplessly, at my Richard, miraculously delivered to me as a young man. But the voice, Richard's, was American; his clothes, self-consciously neat and proper, American, and his politeness not homegrown.

He sat down, since I did not speak but went on staring, caught from the start in his net.

'Janna,' he said, in Richard's voice that was not, 'I thought I would come and get to know you.'

The effrontery of this, the bullying, vulgarized that discreet American politeness; and I went on saying nothing now for another reason. I had understood it all. Knew that he had found his father's little pencilled list of our meeting places; Richard could not come, probably because his son had seen to it that he could not; and that this insolent attack was not only his, but also Kathleen's. I even looked past him out through the glass of the window into the street to see if that familiar heavy sentinel was standing there, monitoring her brother as she had to do her father. I was determined, now, to sit it out, remaining passive, if for no other reason than that I could not trust my senses—my mind being another matter. I was being absolutely pulled to pieces, from within, for I was fascinated by this, my young love Richard, and could not take my eyes off his face.

But there was this triumphant glisten there, in his eyes, and his voice, and he leaned towards me as if taking possession, and said, 'I am sure you will understand me. Of course I wanted to get to know my father's new friend.'

To sit opposite your love, as you have done for months of times, exactly the same eyes, hands, brown forearms bare, the fair Viking hair, all, all the same, but magicked: an imposter sitting behind the eyes, so I felt. So it was! And still with me was that flash of a moment, no more, when this man appeared dark against the heavy light of the street, and I thought, Freddie.

'And so here I am, Janna,' he was saying, for I had missed quite a lot of what he had said. 'And I hope to be forgiven.'

I still had not said anything. Now he was silent, not put out at all—I mustn't think that!—but using the moment to give me a good looking-over. He sat quite still, those brown healthy shining forearms crossed, like a tidy buccaneer in his blue buttoned bush shirt: he wore a suit that made him look like a young doctor in one of those American war films, where callously wisecracking heroes are always about to take off in a helicopter into impossible dangers. But this one was no hero. If I had not been told by his father that this was the one who had shut off the pains and impositions of the happy idiot, his brother John, I would have known that this young man was as self-contained as a walnut, tidily sorted out in compartments. He was looking at me with an open assessment of me as a woman; making sure that this would be evident as appreciation. He meant me to imagine him licking his lips. What he really was thinking of course I was not to guess: but he was making an exact inventory of every asset or liability. He had given me good marks for my hair, so cleverly tinted it would have appeared, on a girl's head, as natural. He had noted my hands, which owned frankly every one of my years; he had taken in the fine wrinkles around my eyes.

After all this, he sat back, raised a hand with an appropriate gesture at the waitress, and said, 'May I have some coffee here, please?' And, to me, he leaned forward slightly, all winning smiles, and said, 'And you, Janna?'

'Thank you, no,' I said. And gathered my handbag, for I was about to leave.

He changed his voice, put on the look of a man who was being made to deal with someone unreasonable, and said, 'Janna, I had really hoped that we could get to know each other. No? What do you say?'

This really fatal vulgarity of his, which came from a complacency that seemed to be part of his texture, overflowing from his eyes and his voice, was what undid me. Richard was being diminished for me by his son! I was consciously forcing the image of the real Richard, that carelessly confident, faded lion of a man, who seemed to be made of a different stuff altogether, back into my mind, to stand there as a protection, warding off this assault.

'Matthew,' I said, 'there is just one thing I have to say. Not that I can easily imagine, having met you, that you are capable of taking it in. It is this. My friendship with your father has nothing whatsoever to do with you. Nor with your sister. And that is all I have to say.' I was about to get up, but he shot out his hand and laid it on my wrist to keep me. I wasn't going physically to tussle with him, so I remained on the edge of my chair. I was conscious that now people around were looking at us. A couple, probably French, were watching with discreet malice, their vivacious salacious faces saying that everything was understood: and I saw us, Matthew and I, reflected in those faces: son and father's still-attractive mistress, poised on the edge of—The waitress slid a cup of black coffee in front of Matthew, and then with a glance at us swiftly withdrew. Camera! Action!

'But just you wait a little,' said Matthew, still grasping my wrist while he fumbled in his breast pocket and brought out, with a smile towards me that both entreated my appreciation of his efforts, and expected them, the little photograph I had given Richard. There it lay on the jolly red tablecloth, the ghost of myself. But I saw that it was not the actual photograph. This young man had somehow stolen my photograph from his father long enough to take it off and have it copied, then—presumably—had replaced it.

'I haven't been parted from it,' announced Matthew, playing out this role as he had planned it in his mind: for I knew there was nothing he said that had not been rehearsed.

He was looking at me, leaning forward, his hot palm an intimate pressure on my wrist, the blue eyes at work on my face; I was looking at him, disliking him as much as I ever disliked anybody in my life.

Then he said, and for him it was the culmination of this willed scene, 'I love you, Janna. I feel as if I have loved you all my life.'

These words went through me in shockwaves. I then got

up, shaking off his hand. I collected my bag, my scarf. I went
out, past the pair of Latins whose eyes were misted over with
the satisfactory perverseness of it all.

I don't remember how I got onto the street, how I walked
to the underground up along Baker Street. I was in a welter
and a fever and wished only to be in some cool dark place,
alone. I found Kate still asleep in bed. I thought for a moment
of Jill's 'One day you'll find her moribund', and bent over to
make sure she was all right. She breathed regularly. Beside
her a tumbler was rusted with last night's vino.

I went into my room, drew the curtains, put on a wrap, and
went to bed and wept.

The thing is, I had fallen in love.

That was . . . days ago. What a horror and a humiliation.
That rather unpleasant young man pushed a button, set off a
tripwire; at any rate, put his finger on some unknown part of
me that had been programmed to hear just those words and
no other: and Wow! Blam! I fell in love. I am poisoned. I am
possessed by a sickly sweet fever. I am obsessed.

Richard rang, and said, Why had I not been at the pub
in Shepherd Market today? I had both forgotten and
not forgotten it. I was in that state of mind where one
hopes that if one doesn't take any notice a problem will take
itself off.

At the time I was supposed to be meeting him I was
working like a maniac in the office with Charlie so as not to
think of anything.

I said to Richard, 'I am very sorry. I just couldn't.' I heard
my voice, cold but distressed.

Richard asked, 'Janna, is there something wrong? I mean,
worse than usual?'

I said, 'No.' It occurred to me that until now I have said
everything to Richard, there was no need for me to censor my
thoughts.

I heard him say, 'Don't you want to meet me, is that it?'

I hear myself crying out, 'Oh, Richard, don't say that, don't, don't.'

He was silent. For that was not a note we had permitted ourselves.

'Janna . . . then when can we meet?'

I can't meet him when I am in this state. How can I? It's disgusting, all of it.

It comes to me that if I were twenty-five and not fifty-five I would marry that nasty little piece of work on the basis of what I *feel,* and live for ever after . . .

Phyllis came into the office with the baby Caroline today, looking cool, a little amused, very pretty, very pleased with herself. Also, wistful. We don't have to be told that she misses *Lilith.* Charlie: proud, fatherly, both with little Caroline and with Phyllis.

Everyone in the building, it seemed, dozens of people, milled about, admiring Caroline, bringing little offerings, a flower, a trinket. Charlie sent out for champagne, which went foaming around Editorial and we all got a little drunk.

Phyllis was in the big room with me for a moment alone, Charlie having borne off Caroline for a fresh orgy of admiration.

She looked at me, and said in a low voice, in case Charlie should hear from next door, 'Janna, I often wonder what you are thinking of me, about what has happened.'

I looked at her, this Phyllis, who had been so sharp and hard, now rather plump with maternity and all the milk she has to carry about for little Caroline, and I said, 'I am thinking of absolutely no one but myself at the moment.'

My voice shook a little. I had the stupid impulse to tell her everything. I needed to let it all out. But I thought, No one under the age of forty could understand this one! If not older . . . She looked at me. I looked at her. She said in a falsely jaunty voice, 'Love makes the world go round.'

✳   ✳   ✳

Richard rang today, said he had managed to 'get a week off from family duties'.

'I think I could actually get away with you somewhere unfollowed. How about it, Janna?' He sounded confident I would say yes. And rightly; for I would have overturned everything, thrown Kate to the Fates, given up my job, anything, to be with him. For what I know is the last chance we will have.

But I said, 'Richard, you will have to believe me, I simply cannot. It isn't that I don't want you . . .' I had meant to say, don't want to . . . but it came out like that.

'You really can't?' he said, and his voice was thin with disappointment.

'I *can't.*'

It is ten days since I met Matthew. We are into September. There is a crispness where there was a heaviness. The sunlight slaps you pleasantly across the face, and tingles on your arms.

I think I am getting over this. It's like an attack of something. Shingles. Measles. Chickenpox. Some indisposition that has an exact term. For being in love with some man you dislike intensely, so and so many days. In the meantime I rage and burn, and wake in the night, pulled up into the sitting position, my arms out, my breasts burning, for *him.* Who? Him. *Who?*

Richard rang to say that if we couldn't get away for a week, why can't we at least have lunch? I cannot bear to meet him in this state. I said I couldn't meet him until next week. Suddenly he said, 'Janna, you know that I am going away soon? I mean, for good? Back to the States?'

'Yes, I thought you were.'

I am watching these splendid September days race past, while my fever abates, and I long to be with Richard, but cannot be. It is not that I feel ashamed, but rather as if I have been convicted of bad taste. But worst, worse than anything, is that I cannot tell him about any of this.

At two in the morning, the telephone. Even half asleep,

though those tones beguile me, I know it is Matthew. Fury slaps me awake, adrenalin races, I sit up.

Every syllable has been measured, calculated. 'Janna, I was thinking of you. I felt I should ring you. Do you mind?'

The *do you mind* stopped my tongue: it had been meant to.

I sat looking at the dark wall, with its oblong of illuminated cloud. I could hear Kate moving about in the kitchen.

'I am thinking of you all the time, Janna. Please don't think I blame my father. I understand him absolutely! I—'

I dropped the receiver back and then, at once, took it off again.

I went into the kitchen. Kate sat eating shortbread biscuits with a total avid concentration, both hands at work, one lining up the next biscuit to be consumed, while the other actually fed her mouth.

Knowing the folly of saying anything like: Kate, why don't you eat a proper meal? I hung about for a little, watching how my fury over Matthew transmuted itself into anxiety over Kate.

'Are you all right, Kate?' I asked her suddenly, as one says it to a friend, meaning, really, that one recognizes a need, a situation, saying, really, *I am here.*

A good little girl, with a weakness for nibbling sweet biscuits, she smiled blandly, her eyes empty.

I went back to bed with a cup of tea, and stayed awake till now, morning, making an inventory thus:

I hate Matthew with a pure, cold, even dispassionate hatred. I am in love with him, but am almost getting over it. I am sick with concern over Kate, and helpless. When I think of Jill, it is as if I want to put my arms around her, shielding her from—herself. I admire and rely on Hannah. When I think of Charlie, I surprise an affectionate smile on my face. Phyllis: she makes me want to cry. I don't allow myself to think of Sister Georgie too much, for at once I fill with incredulous rage. I like thinking about Mark: there is a pleasantness and strength there. I love Richard. Period. I dream about Freddie.

✻   ✻   ✻

Richard rang today, his voice cold and furious. 'Janna, tell me, did you meet Matthew?'

'Yes, he was at the café where I thought you and I were going to meet. It was he, and not you.'

'Why didn't you tell me?'

'It seems I was right, there is no need to tell you.'

'It is utterly unforgivable, awful . . . I am sorry, Janna. What can I say?'

Today I said to Richard, when he rang, just as if nothing had happened, because that was how I felt it, 'Yes, let's meet, where?'

A silence from him. 'Very well Janna, I'm not going to ask for explanations! I've no right! Still, you are rubbing it in—or that's how I feel it. Where then?'

'Could we meet in Soho Square without our attendants, do you think?'

'We could try.'

I met Richard in Soho Square.

I did not look to see if I was being followed: I did not care. Anyway, Kathleen seems to have relegated this duty to Matthew.

Blue September sky: nostalgia in its warmth. A sparkling air. As I walked to the bench where my love sat, a yellow leaf spun down.

With a distance between us we sat and smiled, wryly. It had been nearly three weeks. He looked tired, drained.

'I am sorry about Matthew,' he said; but I saw that he didn't know the half of it.

'It was not your fault.'

He said deliberately, 'I have never liked Matthew.'

'But you always did everything you should.'

'Yes. I suppose I projected on to him what I could not allow myself to feel about Sylvia.'

At this invitation to talk I seized up and stalled. 'I don't want you to think I haven't wanted to be with you,

Richard . . .' This came out false, for it was not the kind of thing we have said.

'But you had more important things to do,' he stated.

I could not say anything.

'In some ways, Janna, you are very much what I know only too well . . .'

A couple of pigeons bobbed around hopefully. We had nothing for them; they flew off to another bench, where two office girls fed them bits of sandwich.

'Yes, I know. A career woman. Well, you had better tell me; I know when you have gone I'm going to be anguishing over the things we haven't said and didn't get around to discussing.'

'I'm not flying off to the moon!'

'It might as well be the moon. Intimate conversations on the telephone? "I wish you were here." I think you ought to tell me.'

'Well, I wonder if you'll even see any of it. Why should you? Your whole life shows . . . Well, where do I start?'

'She didn't care for you?'

'Oh yes, all the proper feelings. In appropriate measure. Oh, I forgot.' Here he rapidly produced two limp packets of sandwiches in cellophane, and, as he unwrapped his, another pigeon materialized and waited by our feet.

'We were both nineteen. Cambridge. She had had to fight to get there. Her parents—they didn't care. A girl, you see. there were three clever brothers. She was clever, but a girl. They didn't really want her at Cambridge, said she would get married, that kind of thing. She did not have a scholarship. But the thing was I knew she was brilliant, but really. It was that quality she had—has. A total commitment. A straight line through to—she did not know her goal, then. She was having a difficult time. Not really enough money, with the parents having to finance four of them at university. We became very close, helping each other with our work, and I helped her with money. I am not one of the world's spenders by nature. And then we moved in together; it seemed the sensible thing to do.'

'Too sensible?' I asked, for there was something not

coming through.

'No. That's not it.'

A pigeon, little rainbows on its pearly feathers, flew between us on the bench, and pecked at Richard's sandwich. We watched it.

'I loved her,' he said. 'I loved her from the very first moment I saw her. At a lecture. She sat there, seeing absolutely nothing and nobody, only the teacher. I saw only her. I sought her out. I made it all happen. I found our room, I paid the rent, I saw to it that we ate—I did all that. She—fitted herself in. Took it all. It wasn't a question of her grabbing, Janna, do you see? It was there. I was there. It was what she needed. She took it all, expected it. *Do* you see?'

What I saw first was that he didn't want me to condemn Sylvia. I could say, truthfully, that I did see.

'We both worked very hard. I because I had to. I was never brilliant. She because she was. Halfway through university, her father died. Only just enough money for the three boys to finish. Her mother expected her to go home, and she would have done, except for me. I knew that it would be a crime to let her throw herself away. I could not get money from my parents, they had only just enough. I earned the money to pay for her. Of course now, looking back from the dizzy heights of the American way of life, it was peanuts, nothing. But then—'

'What did you do?'

'What didn't I do? I can't believe it now, when I think of how I worked, for those two years. I did dog's-bodying for my tutor. He was well known. I proof-read, I researched, I even wrote some of his papers. He knew I needed money, and got me that kind of work with other people. I used to be working until four in the morning. At weekends I cooked in a café, underpaid of course, it was moonlighting. And there we were, the two of us, working. That is all we did, work.'

'You didn't make love?' I asked, deliberately laying ghosts.

'I suppose we did. Yes, of course we did. But it wasn't an issue. Not even for me, not then. I was too bloody tired all the time. We had that damned narrow little bed, crammed into the corner of the room. The room was almost filled by the table we worked at. We used to roll into bed at four in the morning, in each other's arms, and fade out.'

'And you did well, both of you?'

'She, brilliantly, of course. I, passably. But her success was mine. I felt it like that. She didn't, of course. Then we came here to London, and we were in different hospitals. She knew by then she wanted to be a surgeon. I merely wanted to be a doctor. Unfashionable, then. We had a room at the top of a house in Bloomsbury. She was at the Middlesex. I rated a humbler hospital. We had just enough money to get by. We worked. We worked. Janna, if you knew how we worked. Well, I suppose you do, you do.' And he smiled at me, direct, wry and hard and savage, but the savagery contained. I could see there in his face old bitterness, transmuted. For a moment I saw him as old, an old man, smiling dryly at his life.

'She had outstripped me of course, long before we got to the end of it, the training. I was the second-best, and it had to be like that. That's how it was. Do you see? Well . . . and so we went on. She went from achievement to achievement, getting better all the time. I was always—there. And now of course it wasn't only me who knew she was special, really quite extraordinary. It has always been that deadly single-mindedness of hers that she isn't even conscious of . . . she was expected to do brilliantly.'

'And you? You never say . . .' For I was waiting for something. All the time it seemed as if the real subject of all this had not appeared.

'Me? Well, I loved her, of course.'

'And she loved you?'

'She has never, I believe, loved anyone else.'

'Richard, all this doesn't explain why you are like a damped-down volcano.'

'It doesn't?' he said, in real surprise. 'Do you mean to say . . . ' He studied me, leaning forward to do it in a movement so sudden that two pigeons took to their wings and swerved off up into the trees.

'I just don't see you as a man eaten up with unfulfilled ambition.'

'Ambition? Have I said anything about ambition? No,

you're right. I've enjoyed what I've done. I'm even glad I didn't go in for years of specialization. I'm coming back into fashion, the ordinary family doctor. I, with a group of others in Boston, run a new and very influential type of clinic: medicine for the consumer, the patient treated as a grown-up human being with choices, medicine as prevention—all that. Do you know about it? No, how should you? It is taking on. So I can't say I have anything to regret. *That isn't the point.*' And, leaning forward, he put his warm hand on my forearm resting on the back of the bench. I felt the lively pain of it, skin to skin, pulses beating, everything that had not been, and my eyes filled with tears. 'Ah yes,' he said, in a low voice, smiling straight into my face. 'Well, that's it, you see. All my life. And with you, again.'

He removed his hand, sat back, facing out from the bench, folded his arms.

'Tell me, romantic novelist, have you thought about the situation of a man hopelessly in love with his wife, who has long decided that his place in her life is just so much and no more? Would you say that was a romantic subject?' And he laughed.

I sat there, feeling as if all the dreams I have been dreaming over the last months about Freddie had ended here, on this bench, at prosaic lunchtime, in the square.

I could have told him my story, I suppose, spoken of Freddie, exposed myself, but I did not. Not cowardice. It was more like: he'll never say it to Sylvia, let him say it to me.

'Of course for the first years we were working so hard. But then, there seemed a bit of room to turn around, to feel . . . What I saw was still Sylvia, I was just as much in love with her as when we were nineteen, but when we had stopped working like slaves or dogs—or rather, when I could stop working as if there was nothing else in life but that, she just went on working. If we took a holiday, it was because she knew one should sometimes relax, but she took work with her. If we went out for the evening, she was thinking of what she would be doing next day. If we went to bed, she was thinking that if we overdid it, she would be tired in the morning. I had an exact place in her life, just so much, at certain times. And—I could have killed her for it.' The last came out dispassionately, between lips that smiled, but I knew that he had meant it. And often.

'I loved her,' he said, sounding quite surprised as he said it, as he looked back and saw yet again how much. 'I adored her. I used to court her. We had been living together for years cheek by jowl, in rooms like matchboxes, but all that didn't matter, that we knew each other as brothers and sisters do, for intimacy. For me she was always the most beautiful, glorious, *unreachable*—do you suppose that was the point, Janna?' he asked, with his characteristic quick turn to me. 'I remember sitting and watching her sleep, and aching with wanting her. But I knew if I woke her she would smile, after a minute, conscientiously banish her tiredness, and then say, Oh, Richard, do you want . . . ? And move over in the bed, to give me my due space. And she would smile at me, oh quite sweetly, and we would then make love, oh very nicely, I have no complaints. But never, *not once*, Janna, has she ever . . . I used to find myself dreaming about her when we were there in the same room, she working of course. I'd be dreaming about her as if she had an *alter ego* she knew nothing about, and which was my possession, not hers. Mine.'

A long silence. Lunch hour over, the office workers were going off, dropping sandwich wrappers and bits of plastic into the rubbish container. A pigeon cooed. The sun was hot and delicious, and there was a smell of newly cut grass.

'For years I was unconsciously thinking that one day she would suddenly realize and turn to me and *then*—I remember the day I understood, finally, that it would never happen, that this *alter ego* of hers I had invented, this loving *glorious* girl, just did not exist. Never would.'

'And then?'

'She was moving, from hospital to hospital, perfecting her training. She understood one morning she was in her thirties. She decided it was time we had children—doesn't do to leave it too late, said she, doctor to doctor. So Matthew was born in London. It was very difficult. We were both working like dogs. I think I can say I took my fair share—much more. I was closer to Matthew than she was. Yet Matthew is her child, I think of him like that. Sylvia's son. I think Sylvia had thoughts about leaving it like that, one child. She knows that it cost me a lot, her children, but not how much. She's not good at putting herself in other people's places. Just before we went to the States, because she got this job, you see, she wanted it desperately—very prestigious, first-class hospital—she had to have it—'

'Did you want to go to the States?'

'No. Not particularly. I like it here. You might have noticed.' And he turned to give me that direct marvellous look, full of the reckless pleasure that characterized our first meetings. 'But how could I say no, when it was everything she wanted? Just before we went off, it was crazy, she decided to get pregnant again. The argument being that we could get the pregnancy over here; once there, arrangements could be made—and she was right, practically. Her salary has always been enormous, by European standards. So has mine, but much less than hers. We got a house and arrangements were made, we had a living-in maid. And from that time Matthew and I have been strangers. I don't know him. I only know that he's a chip off her block, all right! And then, there was Kathleen, and I loved her from the first moment; and I understood then that I hadn't ever loved Matthew. Funny, that: if there had never been the second child, I would not have known that that wasn't love for a child, not really, I would have thought that was what it was, a sort of dutifulness. But Kathleen: when she was born—I was there of course—and I looked at the little thing sprawling there between Sylvia's legs, she was like a crushed strawberry. Poor mite. I picked her up, and I felt ... but you never had children,' he ended, and my breath stopped from the pain of it. Which he couldn't know, nor should know, so I made myself go on breathing, made life go on, and sat looking at how the sun made minute dazzles on the hairs of his cheeks and on the lion-coloured locks of his hair. A tawny, warm, fine man, he is, my love Richard.

'And then,' he said, after a long time, 'there was John. And you know all about that. And Maria came into our lives, and lived with us, and the real heart of our house is John. The idiot child. And I've wondered often enough, though of course that is probably some sort of superstition, something of that kind, if John was *necessary*. Do you understand? Something joyful and crazy and plain bloody irrational. For *why* should these creatures be so full of love and joyfulness? It doesn't make sense. What have they got to be so bloody happy about? But our household had to have it, that quality. Poor Kathleen, she has a dark sorrowful little spirit, I don't know why. Probably that's why she adores John as she does, he has something she will never have.'

Suddenly anger seemed to explode out of him, even propel him forward in a violent movement, and he struck his fist down on the back of the bench. 'I wonder what your woman-liberating Hannah would say to all that? It seems to me everything gets referred to her, in your life.'

I said, amazed, 'But Hannah's only been in Editorial a few months.'

'It sounds as if . . . Oh, don't take any notice, Janna. I suppose I'm not rational on some subjects. But in the States this woman's movement thing—is *cruel*—do you know that? They have institutionalized cruelty. And I come back here and fall in love with you and there it is again, in your office. Hannah says this and that.'

'I think you are being a little unfair,' I said.

'I am? Well, do you know something? I don't care! I've been too conscientious and *fair* all my life. I've had the best of tutors! *Ought. Should*. I *ought* to be fair about Hannah and the rest of the army, but I am not going to be! My life gives the lie to the whole lot of them, anyway.'

I was sitting there thinking of Freddie, Freddie; wondering perhaps if he had sat watching me sleep, hoping that this time, when I woke, I would . . .

'Why *do* you love her so much?' I asked. 'You haven't ever said.'

'Why? What a bloody silly question—no, I suppose it isn't. It's a good question. She was so beautiful, you have no idea! She never has known it herself, she's no time for that kind of thing, but she's the most beautiful . . .' He turned slowly, with that unscrupulous freebooter's smile spreading all over his face; he leaned forward to look at me, laughing. And I was laughing helplessly, at the sheer lunacy of it all.

He kissed me, then, on the lips. For the first time.

We then briskly separated, and stood up.

We walked up to Oxford Street.

'Will you have time to meet tomorrow?' he asked.

'When?'

'Evening. I'm free from six on.'

'Yes. The square?'

'Yes.'

At five thirty, as I was leaving to meet Richard, the telephone. Annie's Good Neighbour. Annie had fallen down in the morning. It had taken hours to get the doctor, and then there was a delay with the ambulance. She, Lucie Fox, had gone up with her, Annie was in such a state, you'd think she was being killed, you know how she goes on. But she, Lucie Fox, had had to get back to her children. The Home Help wasn't in today. 'Goodness knows where she had got to, but I thought you'd like to know, Mrs Somers, you being such a friend of Annie's.'

This means, You are supposed to be such a friend, now over to you.

I said I would go up and see Annie. I rang the hospital. The nurse said Annie was in a state, crying and carrying on, were there any relatives? Who is next of kin? I suppose I am, I said. A silence. I said what I *ought*, which was that I would go up now.

No one left in *Lilith* but Hannah, sitting, sturdy brown legs wide apart, on her chair as if it were a horse, contemplating the plants on the windowsill. She wore a striped purple and red dress, and a purple bandanna, all of which made her look even more like Pocahontas. She fanned herself equably with the last issue of *Lilith*, which has on it the picture taken earlier in the year of girls striding through autumn woods, and regarded me, no comment, as I said I had to go up to the hospital.

'Kate?'

'No. An old woman. And so I would like you to do

something for me . . .' I asked her to go to Soho Square and tell Richard I couldn't see him.

'You'll know him, I am sure, when you see him.'

'I have seen him,' said Hannah, reminding me of how heads had craned, tongues had clacked.

'He's dishy,' said Hannah. 'If I were that way inclined I'd fancy him.'

'Ask him if tomorrow's all right?'

'Will do.'

In Dorothy Wordsworth Ward Annie was sitting straight up in bed, looking sullen and very ill.

As she saw me, she began: what was she doing here, she had been brought here against her will, she wanted to go home, she wanted her clothes, there was nothing the matter with her. On and on and on . . . The three other people in the ward, all of them ill, tried to shut it all out in various ways, but when the nurse came in, complaints. The nurse looked harassed: I knew that she knew nothing would shut up Annie. 'She is one of those, I suppose,' she said, whisking out of the ward and leaving her to me.

I sat by Annie, thinking of Richard, and fought to get a word in. At last I said that she had hurt her leg, she must know that—and, and, and, on. But what she needed was to complain. Annie has to complain: at home, in hospital, whatever her situation, grumbling is what she has chosen. I stayed three hours, lashed by that sour old tongue, until, hearing that I was leaving, she subsided, eyes bright and a little crazy with frustration, and said that at least she would have company in here, which was more than could be said for her at home.

At the duty desk I asked what was likely to happen to Annie next; but the night nurses had come on, and, not knowing Annie, smoothed me down with: The doctor . . . we'll have to . . . perhaps in a day or two . . .

As I left I heard Annie shriek, 'Nurse, nurse,' and the nurse said in the hushed voice of one trying to mollify a child, 'There's a bell, dear, a *bell* . . .'

'I don't want a bell, I want to go home.'

Just after writing that, when I was getting into bed, the

telephone. Richard. His voice had a breathy squeezed sound: anger. I could hear that he had been furious for hours.

'Your hit woman conveyed your message,' said he.

I was silent, adjusting myself from thoughts of Annie, what could be done for her, if anything, to this necessity: Richard wanted to know why I had not been able to see him for so long, day after day, then weeks: *I'm sorry, I can't.* He had decided he wasn't going to ask, didn't want to know: but his anger spoke differently.

I was in a panic. I could not, cannot, tell Richard about Matthew.

I said, 'What is this about Hannah? You're ridiculous! There was no one else to ask, only Hannah was left in the office.'

'That woman!'

'But Richard, why? What did she say? What did she do?'

'She certainly enjoyed her role.'

'I don't believe it! She's not . . .' I stopped. I could imagine Hannah's large, comfortable assurance: 'Janna's not coming,' and how easy it would be to hear an unspoken: She's got more important things to do. But Hannah would not have been thinking that at all. It is her style to impose a: This is how things are and that is how they have to be! on everything, while she surveys one with philosophically calm eyes, fingering a yellow bead necklace that lolls about on the smooth brown slopes of her breasts. I said, 'Hannah's sympathetic to us, and she's shown it in a hundred ways. You must have misunderstood.'

'I didn't misunderstand. She enjoyed telling me you were off somewhere.'

'I was with Annie, you know, I told you, the old woman I am involved with. I had to go. She hasn't got anyone but me, not really.'

'I suppose you were spending all your free time with her instead of with me recently, so that you couldn't even meet me for half an hour?'

I was thinking, Supposing I did say, 'I fell in love with your nasty son Matthew. But think nothing of it. I felt as if I'd been programmed to do it, you know, some sort of indoctrination.

He had only to say, I love you, and that was that. But you'll understand, I know.'

Amazed at the impossibility of explaining what seemed to me so pettifogging and unimportant to a man whom I knew to be the essence of sense and fairness, I said, 'You were for *weeks* visiting relatives you say mean nothing to you.'

'You weren't getting your own back?' I heard: incredulous, appalled, hurt. And I knew that he was incredulous as I would have been to think that he was capable of it; hurt because I could put that, a petty revenge, against our dwindling treasure of days and nights.

I said, 'No. How can you think . . .'

'I don't know what to think. You were in London. I was in London. Our time is running out. But you couldn't meet me. Not at all. Not once.'

I said, sounding awkward, almost stammering, certainly apologetic, 'If I told you . . .' And could not go on.

Silence. I could hear him sigh, shift the receiver about: he was calming himself, using his formidable self-discipline, bringing fairness to bear.

He said, 'Tell me, what actually did Matthew say to you? Was it Matthew? It was, wasn't it?'

And here was the moment when I could, if I would, speak out. Sitting there, holding that receiver with one hand, with the other holding close my white silk dressing gown at the throat as if he could see me, and as if our quarrel imposed a punishing modesty, I felt myself all at once invaded with the atmosphere, the 'taste' of being 'in love' with Matthew: I was breathing a sweet poisonous air, compounded of reluctant lust and yearning for something that was encompassing and far off, something distrusted and disliked. I could taste a sweet falseness on my tongue, and I felt sick.

'What on earth could he have said to you, to upset you so much you wouldn't even eat a sandwich in· the square with me, for nearly three weeks?'

I said, 'Richard, he's not the point. Matthew's absolutely not the point.' And heard myself add, in a furious coldly contemptuous voice, 'I dislike him very much. I am sorry, but I simply cannot stand him.'

And so 'the truth', God help us, slid away for ever; though for a moment I was in a panic, knowing that there was something real and naked there in my voice, and that Richard, if he wanted, or could, might interpret it.

After a pause he said cautiously, 'Well, I suppose I'm not going to be told. And so it was pretty bad. I have had a feeling it was pretty bad. When Matthew is out to get his own way, then I know to my cost—the whole family does—that no holds are barred. He gets his way. And he has got it over you.' I was holding my breath, but he went on, 'He wanted to stop us meeting, and he succeeded. Temporarily, but for long enough. And now we are leaving soon he won't bother to try anything else. I don't know what he has been saying, whether it was about me, or Sylvia—or anything. I simply can't imagine what it could be, but I would have liked to have been able to believe that you would see through it. But then, why should you, Janna?'

I said, 'We can still meet tomorrow?'

'Yes, yes, I suppose so. Yes, why not!'

Outside the pub where I was going to meet Richard, our pub, Kathleen stood, a drooping silent figure, her back to the entrance, looking up into an evening sky that this time next week will be black: the clocks are going to be set back.

I went straight up to her, touched her on the shoulder, said, 'Kathleen, do please come inside with me.'

Her humble, pleased smile, that nevertheless had triumph in it, satisfaction. I thought, This has been talked over with Matthew, he has told her she must come into the pub with us.

Richard watched us both come towards him, pulled out two chairs, and said to the barman, 'Manhattan.'

Her tipple.

Her being there cancelled everything. We could not get the conversation going. The ordinariness of it, this momentous thing, seemed to shock her. Her dark full bold eyes—bold when not cringing with the memory of the awfulness of her thoughts about us—moved from his face to mine, from mine to his, as if somewhere there was a fact she needed which she could not lay her hands on.

Between me and Richard the current had been cut. When our eyes met, as we laboured over the talk, nothing was said. Soon, Richard said that he had to leave, and got up. Kathleen rose with him, with reluctance. She still was hoping for that final revelation about life or love or something.

We went to the door. The dark had come down, a lively companionable dark, full of people and busyness.

Richard's eyes did manage to communicate to me: This is *awful*—before he went striding off with Kathleen in tow.

Conference day. Once my favourite day of the week, when everything that was *Lilith* was concentrated in one place, the long formal room which came alive for the occasion; and at one time, Monday mornings, when you could sense how, after the dispersion of the weekends, everything was pulled together, you could feel the pulse of *Lilith*. The representatives of the departments, twelve or fourteen; and around the edges of the room on the chairs set back against the walls for that purpose crowded everyone who could spare an hour or two. Anyone was welcome, from the smallest typist. Anyone could contribute, come in with ideas. Conference day was ideas day. There was the formal agenda, the framework. But what really happened was that for three hours ideas and energy came bubbling forth, and all that was written down and kept so that nothing got lost. By Phyllis, once . . .

And now nothing of this happens. Why not? Easy to say, *Charlie,* and I know that in the lower reaches of *Lilith* they blame Charlie for everything. But I wonder! I think it is more the *spirit of the times,* that affliction that no one seems able to identify.

I do know this: that when this spirit, whatever it is, has entered an institution, you can pass resolutions, and send around reminders, till your brain aches, and nothing happens.

Monday after Monday I have reminded everyone that *Lilith* has always encouraged everyone to have ideas, to put them forward, and if possible to be responsible for them;

asked people to think of *Lilith* as a joint venture; asked that anyone who can shall come up and listen in to the proceedings, and join in too. But these days the chairs all around the edge of the room remain empty. And when the item on the agenda is reached: New Ideas, usually people look at each other in case someone else has an inspiration, doodle, wait for the next item.

Today there were only ten people: the lowest number ever. Outside the three tall beautiful windows September blazed, the trees stood about full of birds and bustle, the sky was a sprightly blue.

On the long table the Christmas issue lay spread around, still in its parts. Party time: glamour. The cover: two enormous dark eyes, a pink pout and a swirl of black velvet against falling snow. The January and February issues are merely adumbrated on the sheets of paper we have lying in front of us, though articles and photographs for those months are already on our desks. The men all have their jackets off. Jill's shoulders are smooth brown against the white straps of something not far off a sun-dress. Charlie is wearing a Russian peasant smock in cream linen, and he beams at us all as his secretary, who is as maternal as he, offers us tea. The aromas of Orange Pekoe and shortbread biscuits. It is a joke in the office—on the whole a friendly one—that Charlie cannot drink a cup of tea without evoking an atmosphere of occasion. Help yourself to everything I have, his affable smile seems to say, as he hands you a plate of cake.

Everything goes along efficiently and amiably, items on the agenda slide past on the oil of indifference: the decisions have already been made, things are already under way, what we do here is not to originate, but to record. And that is why everything is so smooth. And, basically, indifferent. I look at the faces of those who have been with *Lilith* long enough to remember how our conferences were; they were polite, but seem to be merely sitting the time out until they can get back to work. Jill knows that things were different, and so very recently. Hannah does not, nor Mark, for they weren't here. Charlie probably has never noticed anything very much.

Then we come to the item: New Secretaries. Charlie's and mine are both leaving. Among the applications are several from young men. A question of principle—and suddenly the room comes alive.

Henry from Production takes command. He is revolution-ary. Stern and unsmiling. At least, with us, though I dare say with his comrades he allows himself a measured smile. His clothes evoke the military: his cropped hair, a black brush, is not high style as when Jill or the others suddenly decide to sprout a brief inch or two, but is meant to make one think of prison and guerrillas; probably terrorists, I wouldn't be surprised.

'I would like to remind you,' said he, 'of the Sex Discrimination Act.'

'Oh Lord,' said Charlie, dismayed, 'but why?'

'What is our policy on this?' demanded Henry, looking from one to the next around the table, so that his eyes enmesh with ours, a ploy which I am sure he has learned from some pamphlet: *How to Control Meetings*.

'I want a policy formulated, and voted on,' said Henry.

'I don't see why we should have a policy,' said Charlie, 'we can deal with each case on its merits.'

'I think we should have a policy,' said Hannah, and she and Henry were looking at each other: they have worked together in Production, and not, we hear, always amicably.

'I know what your policy is likely to be,' said Henry.

'Yes, positive discrimination, in favour of women,' said Hannah. 'This is one of the few industries women can work in.'

'That's my position,' I said; and saw Henry about to lay down some law or other.

But here Jill remarked, in the soothing voice she sometimes uses with Mark when his revolutionary principles threaten and she instinctively, her mother's daughter, tones them down, 'Oh yes, we ought to have a guideline, so that we know where we are.' She looked towards Mark. But he was sitting back in his chair, absorbed in making small perfect circles, red, blue and green, with his felt pens, all over a pale red cardboard folder. Such was his concentration, so accurate the circles, so compelling his deft and clever movements, that we all watched.

'As far as I am concerned, principles and policies cause nothing but trouble,' said Charlie, sounding really put out for once. 'I know that the lower echelons of *Lilith* seethe with both, but I do not want to know anything about it.'

'I entirely agree,' I said, watching Mark's hands but talking to Henry. 'You ought to know. You attend all those meetings downstairs.'

'*Downstairs* is good,' said Henry, with that small laugh which means, There they go again.

'Oh well, it's the spirit of the house, if you like.'

'We confer in the drawing room,' said Henry, and he laughed, genuinely. Everyone laughed.

'As I was saying, all I know is that a political meeting is a recipe for ill-feeling. People who are getting on perfectly well before a meeting are likely to be enemies after it,' I said.

'Or vice versa,' said Mark, his patterns proliferating.

'Then if they are all cemented into harmony, everyone else not at the meeting is an enemy,' I said.

Jill said, 'I really don't *know*, Jane. You can't even be called reactionary. You are so reactionary you are in some special category of your own.' I knew that these were not her own words really, but Mark's.

'Count me in on that,' said Charlie.

'So I believe I am described,' I said. 'But when I think about it, I wonder why. *Lilith* pays higher wages and salaries than anyone else in the field. The conditions are—so the union agrees—good. And under me—under us—'

'Oh, keep the credit, Jane,' said Charlie affably, 'it was you, we all know that.'

'—our policy is to employ young people. The average age in *Lilith* must be under thirty.'

Here Henry nodded, in a way that signalled, But that isn't the point.

'So,' I concluded, 'reactionary is not what reactionary does, or even *says*, but has something to do with some abstract standard that I, for one, do not believe that even Henry could define easily.'

Henry allowed himself a wry smile, which was meant to say, She's so off the point that . . . but she's harmless.

I said, 'You ask me, will I have a male secretary? If it is an issue, I will. Provided he is as efficient as a girl. I don't give a damn.'

'I give a damn,' said Charlie. 'I will not have a male secretary. I want a soothing charming girl like Mary, who so unluckily for me is leaving to attend to her lucky husband. She must flatter my ego and surround me with emotional security. I keep reading critical descriptions of male employers like me, but that is how I am, I am afraid.'

His beaming smiles, meant to deflect criticism, failed: the young men present were all careful not to let their eyes stray towards this elderly charmer. But their faces said it all.

Charlie, pressing on: 'The point is, I like women. I think they are a thousand times nicer than men, better in every way.'

'Good God what a put-down,' said Hannah, astounded at the sheer impossibility of Charlie.

'It seems to me very easy,' I said. 'I will have a male secretary and Charlie a female one.'

Hannah said, 'Janna, did you know this whole question has been discussed in the Association for weeks now?'

'Well, it has just been solved,' I said.

Henry said, 'As delegate from the Association downstairs, what shall I tell them?'

'Practically, it is solved. As a principle, shelved.'

'Then it must go on to the agenda for next Monday,' said Henry.

'Put it on the agenda,' I said. 'But I should like to make a point. This item is the only one that has been discussed with any interest at all. And yet whether we have male or female secretaries is not going to make any difference to *Lilith*. I mean, to making the magazine any better or worse.'

Here Henry looked briefly at me: acknowledged my point. He even nodded. But his eyes had turned sideways again, towards Mark's labours.

We were all looking at the design Mark was holding up for us to see.

'That would make the most marvellous dress material,' said Charlie, suddenly all real interest and animation.

'I take it this conference is over,' I remarked, and everyone was getting up as I spoke.

I went into the outer office with Jill and Hannah, leaving the others.

'What would you say if I took a week's leave?' I asked.

I was surprised at the vehemence with which Jill whirled around at me: 'Oh, Jane, no!'

'Why not?'

I looked at Hannah, arbiter and judge, and she asked, 'Are you thinking of leaving Kate alone?'

'Oh, *Jane!*' Jill's emotion made me see, and I should have seen it before, just how much she is possessed with worry over Kate, eaten up with it, whether she hates her or not.

'I can't leave London,' I said, 'if that is what you are worrying about, Jill. For one thing, there's Annie.'

'Oh, *her!*'

'Yes, I know what you think. But a week off from work?'

'But we are so busy,' moaned Jill; and I could see from Hannah that she agreed.

'Very well,' I said.

'Anyway,' said Hannah, 'it's much better for you to have something to keep your mind off it.'

I waited all afternoon for Richard to ring, but he did not. At six I went up to Annie in hospital. She was in a chair. As she saw me, she said, 'I want to go home, why are they keeping me here . . .' and on she went, and did not stop.

The three other women in the room were trying to shut it out; one of them told me that Annie was shouting for the nurse in the night, for she wouldn't use the bell, until they drugged her and shut her up.

Yesterday they talked as if she were staying in hospital for weeks: today they said they were sending her home. It is because she makes life impossible for everyone around her. But she cannot cope at home, she can hardly walk. She keeps saying, 'But you will all come in and see me, just as usual,' for now her loneliness and boredom is all forgotten, and home in her mind is all visitors and loving care. And when she is at home, she will say, 'It was nice in hospital, I didn't want to leave.' For she has done all this before. Wherever she is, Annie will grumble, and complain, and fill the world with gloom.

I sat there tonight, while she went on and on, suppressing a really violent and shameful impulse to hit her or shake her into silence. I was thinking that her mother, the poor old Irish woman who lived alone on a pittance in a meagre room off Holborn, hardly able to walk, keeping to her bed when it was cold to save coal, the mother that Annie thinks of now remorsefully, saying, *She* didn't have all this, people running in to her with food and doing her shopping—for that old woman, this hospital, the care Annie gets, would have seemed a miracle, so far beyond her she could not even think of it. She didn't have a doctor, Annie says. She didn't have money for that sort of thing.

Trying it out, I say to Annie, 'Do you know that if you paid for your bed here, it would cost a hundred pounds a week?' I say a hundred because it is a figure she can cope with, understand.

Her eyes glaze and she says, 'What do you mean?' Then: 'Yes, but I haven't got a hundred pounds a week.'

'If you had, that's what you'd have to pay.'

'If I had I wouldn't be here, I'd be somewhere nice, or I'd be with my sister. No, I'm just fed up and sick with it all. When is the doctor coming? I want to go home.'

As I came up the stairs I heard the telephone ring. It had stopped by the time I got in. Kate was asleep in the sofa, drunk. All over the flat I find rusty looking glasses, and there are empty bottles in the bin.

One of my little yellow chairs has wine stains on it.

My bed has a creased hollow: Kate has been lying on it. I don't like this, I feel invaded, soiled. For the hundredth time I think, What can I do? There must be something I should do, what is it?

＊　　　＊　　　＊

The clocks went back today.

Richard picked me up outside my door, and we went off to Kent. It was cloudy, chilly, we wore thick sweaters. We found a pub, and ate sandwiches and drank Guinness, and then walked for a long time along lanes and little back roads. It was muddy and my shoes clogged up, and we tried to laugh at my silly heels as we did at the beginning, but I seemed to myself as tiresome and vain as I was afraid I did to Richard.

We were tired and low-spirited. We did not mention our families or problems, but held hands and went on walking.

When we came out of the pub to come home, a wind had got up. From a great ash outside the pub twigs and bits of leaf came pelting all over us as the wind stretched and pulled the branches about. It sounded as if rain were pattering down, but it was debris from the tree. As we drove on up a lane, through a little wood, rubbish from the trees pattered on the car's roof, and when we reached the big road cars seemed to be fleeing up it away from the wind. We joined the streams of cars, but stayed in the slow lane, to look at the yellow stubbly fields and the woods beyond. Then it was dusk, and the lights came on one by one as we drove towards them. The extremely tall, elegant slender pylons that held the single eye of light over the road were like stick insects; and then the dusk deepened and the pylons, absorbed by the dark, were merely sketched thin dark lines against dark, and the lights were delicate shapes like little oblongs of melon, or pink grapefruit, and they flicked past over us, as the wind seemed to grapple with the car, wanting to tip it over. Then the rain started.

We drove through a black plastic world, the lights, red and green and blue, swimming and glittering on the black shining streets. All the way into London, a low wet drive, in lines of traffic: the black gleam of plastic seemed to enclose us, and when the lights picked out a tree or a shrub, it was luridly green, unnatural.

When we turned into Waterloo Road, Richard stopped suddenly at the pedestrian crossing. The slanting lines of rain in the headlights had half obscured the shape of a man standing there who had stepped out on to the crossing and then back. When he saw we had stopped, he turned to our car and raised his arm in a jaunty wave: an old man, small, with nothing on his head, and only a short black plastic jacket. He went stepping across the road like a cat afraid to get its paws wet, making a play of it, but that was not it. He was acting being a pedestrian, hastily but carefully crossing the road while a great big powerful imperious motorcar waited for him, and as he stepped up on to the pavement he made it an enormous step, which he achieved only with difficulty, and he waved that insouciant, cheerfully cheeky arm again, hand upward, pronging fingers sketching the ghost of an insult, and vanished into the rainy dark towards Blackfriars, having in the space of twenty seconds mocked us and the powerful of this earth, himself and his compliance, and while he was about it had commented on and demolished the entire age of technology.

We exchanged quick glances in the dark of the car, and laughed. But then Richard drew the car up on the side of the road, and he said, as if it had been shaken or driven out of him, like a grief one cannot acknowledge, 'Oh, God, I do love this country, I do love this bloody marvellous country.' His rough breathing meant that he was going to cry if he wasn't careful, and in fact he did turn his face to me, and I could see the wet shining on his cheeks. 'Why do you all knock it so?' he demanded angry, amazed. 'Why do you? Why do you run it down? Why do you let it all go down the drain?'

I said, 'Then why do you leave it?' for I was angry, being helpless, because for a moment I had shared his feelings of being helpless.

'I?' he demanded. 'I've never left it.' And then he laughed, at himself. Started the car, and we drove on towards the Aldwych.

'I swear,' he said, in a sober voice, no longer the voice of a thwarted lover, 'that there's something here you find nowhere else. It's the people,' he said. 'Salty, and original. It's that little streak of—well, of what, then? You tell me. All I can say is, you keep coming on it. I have been coming on it during this trip, I'd forgotten . . . Do you think I'm raving?'

I said, 'I live here, don't I?'

He said, 'Anyone who lives anywhere else is mad.'

As we parted, we agreed to do the same next Wednesday: he picking me up after work here.

I said, 'Richard, can't I have your number? After all, Matthew and Kathleen know about me, and I suppose they will have made sure Sylvia knows.'

He hesitated, and was curt because he was embarrassed. 'I can't, it's not inside the terms of our contract. The unwritten contract.'

'Ah yes, these unwritten contracts. They are the worst.'

'Particularly when they are made with oneself.'

They brought Annie home. The Welfare people furious: she is not fit to be home, the Home Help says she will go in as usual and not do one thing more than she ought. The Good Neighbour, Lucie, a kindly soul, says she is doing as much as she can, as it is—which everyone knows is so far beyond what she is paid to do that the thing cannot be discussed in those terms at all—and Annie fights every night to make her stay, staging all kinds of ills, ailments, and crises, and she, Lucie, doesn't know how long she will stand it.

I went in and found her sitting in her shit.

Just as I am going into action, in hurries Lucie, for she has posted one of her children to keep an eye out for when I come in. She is a charming, pretty woman, with far too much to do, and she is fond of Annie. But now she is quite frantic with anxiety. She knows and I know that Maureen, because Lucie Fox can be relied upon to do her work for her, so often does not come in. We both know that 'they' will keep Annie at home as long as somebody, friend, kind-hearted Home Help, a Good Neighbour, will look after her; we know that it is a monstrous imposition because Annie, probably for good, will be incontinent; we know that Annie will not go into a Home. Fussed and fussing, we busy around, cleaning up, changing knickers and there aren't any clean ones left, we tidy up everything, and then Lucie goes, saying to Annie that she will come in later, at nine as usual, to give her a cup of tea.

Annie sits at her table, worn out. Soiling herself, not so

long ago, would have been a horror, to be concealed in any way she could—by cutting out the crotch of her knickers, for instance, and saying, I don't know what has happened to my knickers, I am sure. But now blessed vagueness has overcome her, and she says, 'I am all right, I have the commode, haven't I?' I then sit down and start on the impossible: a sensible conversation with Annie.

The situation: if she would go into a Home, then she would get used to it, and—grumbling, of course, every inch of the way—would make friends, and settle down. And live probably for a few years yet. If she won't, then she has entered that awful, shameful process, that might go on for a year, two years, that is the end of so many. Staggering or crawling around her room, getting or not getting to the commode in time, piles of dirty underclothes accumulating, for the Laundry Service cannot cope with the extremes of this condition, waking wet, or dirty, and unable to cope with it, waiting for a nurse to come—but it's not the nurse's job to change sheets and wash bottoms—when the nasty nurse has gone, waiting for the Home Help, who will clean her saying it is not her job, she is not supposed to do this kind of work, or who won't come that day, so that Annie must wait and wait for somebody to come and help her; and so it will go on all day, while Annie rages and boils and—falls down again, which will get her into hospital for a few days but from where she will be expelled the moment they can get rid of her. Meanwhile her blood pressure is soaring, with anger and frustration, and her old face is sometimes scarlet and sometimes a dull grey.

The room already smells horrible.

I say to Annie that she should go into a Home, and Annie says, 'You can't make me!'

'No, we can't. But you could go and try it out . . .'

But if she did agree to this, she would complain every second, demand to come home, where she would say, Oh I don't know, it was quite nice there, you have company at least. But taken back there, she would complain and demand to go home . . .

Now she says that she likes it in hospital, and she wouldn't mind having a spell in there.

I say that she grumbled all the time until she was brought home.

She says, 'I didn't! Why do you say that?'

She grumbles now, and I sit, trying to ward off that state of mind where the human condition is reduced to this: we are sewers, no more, machines for the production of urine and shit, and the whole of human life is a conspiracy to conceal this fact. Annie is 'viable' so long as she can manage to deposit her wastes in the right places; when she can't, that's the end. I look at Annie's gaping mouth, making words, words, and I see it as the opening into a conduit that runs, convoluted and disgusting, to the opening that is her anus and which looks, probably, the same.

The longer I sit there, the more amazed I get that we can conceal from ourselves what we all are: containers of dirt-filled intestines. And when this state of mind threatens to take over, I leave, Annie shouting after me:

'And now I am going to be alone all night.'

I shout: 'Lucie will be in.'

She shouts: 'And then I will be alone all night.'

I shout: 'Then why don't you go into a Home.'

She shouts: 'Because I am going to stay with my sister.'

Here I found Kate sitting at the kitchen table, in a foul mood. This encouraged me: anything better than the listlessness. She was eating pickled onions from a vast jar, one after another, with her fingers. I don't know why but it seemed to me a good sign, vinegar an improvement on sugar, and I said, 'Would you like to come to the pictures with me?'

'You don't want me to go with you to the pictures.'

I made myself a sandwich, and sat down opposite her.

'I want a sandwich too.'

'Then why don't you make one?' It struck me that without her belligerence, and the pickled onions, I would have offered her one. This made me laugh and at once she imploded, and sat, a sullen trembling child.

'It's not kind to laugh at people.'

'I wasn't. Do come to the pictures, Kate.'

It took me an hour of cajoling. Just as we were leaving, the telephone.

'Richard, I'd love to, but I can't. I'm going to the pictures with Kate.'

I am so amazed. And yet, not. When Richard said it, I was stunned. Now I think, Of course! Everything has led to it.

Sylvia and Richard were discussing the problems of their offspring. As, obviously, they often do. She said she thought it would be a good thing to 'defuse the situation' by us having dinner together—Richard and she and I, with Kathleen and Matthew. She could think of no other way to get rid of all these unhealthy emotions, she said. Richard put this to me, embarrassed, but not very, because he thinks it is a good idea too. If I knew, said he, the awfulness of what was going on, how Kathleen tormented them, he and Sylvia, I would be kind and say yes.

'What about Matthew?' I asked, and he gave me a quick look: so he did think there might have been something?

'Matthew, as far as I am concerned, can stew in his own juices . . . he does anyway. I never have the faintest idea of what he is thinking. But Sylvia thinks it would be good for him.'

When I got back to the office after lunch, Hannah was in their room alone. I told her what Richard had said. 'What do you feel about it?' she asked, like a psychotherapist.

'I don't know whether to laugh or cry.'

'Nothing strikes you as peculiar?'

'No more peculiar than anything else.'

'That it should be just you—you and them? Why not take Jill along, or even Kate?'

Our eyes meeting, we laughed. First, a small, even decorous amusement: then laughter overwhelmed us, and we bellowed and roared, and collapsed into chairs and could not stop.

'I don't know why I am laughing,' I said.

'I do,' she claimed.

✳   ✳   ✳

The party will consist of Sylvia, Richard, Matthew, Kathleen.
Their team. Me, Jill, Mark, Kate. And since I feel that in some
way this is Hannah's occasion as much as ours, Hannah.
Richard, hearing about this adjustment to Sylvia's plan, first
gave a short surprised snort of laughter; then he fell about, so
that the Irish barman raised his glass to both of us, spilled
charm willingly over us all, said, 'Well, now then, and you
must share the joke with the rest of us.'

'I don't know why it is funny,' said Richard.

I have booked the private room at the Gay Hussar. And
ordered a dinner. Sylvia said, through Richard, that she
would pay for it, since it was all her doing. But of course we
are going halves.

And so this is what happened.

First, Kate. When I said there would be a dinner, and she
was asked, she was pleased. Said she had nothing to wear. I
felt this was a great step forward, and I went out with her to
buy a dress. But although she put the dress on, made green
circles around her eyes, and painted her nails green, at the last
moment she said she wouldn't go. Nothing would make her.

I left her in her usual place in the sofa. She was not plugged
in, but stared sullenly in front of her. I knew there was wine
in the kitchen: she had brought in a two-litre bottle.

In the taxi down I was possessed by Kate, poor drab,
nineteen years old, her precious years draining away; by Jill,
with joy kept shut away from her, since joy, delight, are
threats; by Kathleen, who has nothing better to do than trail
around at a distance after her father's pleasures. Matthew I
will not think about, and I was preparing myself not to think
about him throughout the dinner ahead, but I know that
there is not a cell in his body that could understand joy: he is
all intention for the future. Hannah: supremely competent,
rooted in her body, but it is only bodies like her own she will
open her arms to.

I was thinking of them all as possessors of some treasure,

but they disregarded it; a marvellous inheritance, but they did not know it; though warnings enough reach them of the vast deserts, and nothing that I or anybody else can say will make the slightest difference.

A handful of years, and they will wake up one morning, and know that there is an absolute barrier between them and what they could have had, but did not, because they would not.

As I reached Greek Street I saw Richard on the pavement. He looked up and saw me. I stepped from the taxi into his arms, and he turned me towards him and said, 'I've been planning a speech!'

'So have I!'

'Gather ye rosebuds?'

'Exactly.'

'But it is no use?'

'None at all,' I said.

And, our faces three inches from each other, we laughed, brushed our lips together, valedictory, laid our cheeks together, feeling our separate lives pulsing, separated by a film of skin, and went up into the restaurant.

The pleasant room, soft lights, a table laid for nine, and Kathleen alone. She was soft and awkward with pleasure, and when her father went and sat down by her, leaving me to find my way, she flushed and was grateful.

Then Sylvia. She is a tall, slight woman, not an ounce of anything unnecessary about her. She wore a white suit. Her hair is tawny, with white in it, and is tied back with a black ribbon. She is good-looking, with regular features, brown and oiled with the summer. If I had passed her in the street I would have remarked a woman well put together and pleasant, but none of the adjectives that celebrate excess would have occurred to me: she is not handsome like Richard, nor beautiful, nor charming. And yet his heart has been aching over this woman for a third of a century.

She said, in a voice American, not English, 'I am sorry about Matthew, he wouldn't come.'

We said hello, and how are you, and she did not seem to need particularly to examine me, but sat on the other side of

Kathleen so the girl had the look of being held upright by her parents.

Hannah came in with Jill and Mark.

'Where's Kate?' Jill asked at once, sharp; I said she would not come, and I saw Hannah alert herself and look quickly at me for information.

Two places were removed, and seven of us sat around the table, like a family. Sylvia seemed abstracted, but smiled at once if she felt that someone looked at her: in a way that made it seem as if she were defending herself. Like Richard, her shoulders easily bow forward slightly. They are similar: married: their faces echo each other's, as married people's do who have been drawn to each other because they have seen their own features on this unknown. But Richard sat there large, careless, glowing, brown—splendid, oh splendid he is, full of life that comes out of him, his eyes, his smile; but she is all held in and controlled. Her manner is never anything but abstracted, as if listening for some call on a bleeper, or thinking about her next operation. Her hands are too large for her, or so they are made to seem, for while like everything else about her they are fined down and appropriate, they are long, very strong, and sensitive, everything the hands of a prominent if not world-famous surgeon ought to be. And she is careful with them; you'd think she was a musician, you see her flexing and unflexing them, as I have seen violinists and pianists do, with a quick examining look, *Are they all right? Ready for work?*

Mark and Jill sat side by side, and she was all held into herself and suffering, thinking of course of Kate. And he was exuding waves of warm support and love for her, and when he passed her the butter, it was his heart.

Hannah, rather isolated, or making herself look like that, sat back and watched. She watches. Magnificent in a short scarlet woollen dress over full purple silk trousers, she sat playing with a turquoise pendant the size of a saucer, her strong brown fingers stroking the stone as if it were flesh.

This occasion was for Kathleen; we all knew it, we all played up to it. Kathleen, this poor, handsome, blushing, ashamed girl, who has this sorrowful dark little spirit—the phrase has made me see her, and I suppose I always now will see her—as a small dark passionately sorrowful little girl, always trying to come to grips with something that evades her, joy emblemed in an idiot boy.

We addressed our remarks to Kathleen, we asked her questions, we watched the food on her plate and how she ate it, in case it was not to her taste.

And Sylvia sat abstracted, smiling, and I swear that not once the whole time did she look at me and think, This is my rival, or, He loves her, or even, My husband fancies her, or, I quite like her.

No, nothing of the kind: this scene had come to pass because it should, and here we all were, and we all—of course—were behaving beautifully, because we are the kind of people who do, and Kathleen will be the better for it. So she was thinking.

The Gay Hussar had made us a gorgeous pudding which was about to be shared out to our several plates, when I was called to the telephone, and I knew at once what I was to hear, and so did Hannah, for she had half risen by the time the man had finished saying, 'Mrs Somers, will you come to the telephone, it is urgent.'

The Jefferies in the next flat had found a note under their door half an hour after returning from somewhere:

Please telephone my aunt Jane at the Gay Hussar,
I have taken fifteen sleepers and drunk some wine.

I arrived back to find Hannah and Jill and Mark all standing, and looking. I was in a blaze of anger: as I suppose I had been expected to feel, but Jill's face slapped me down into proper concern.

I told them. Richard at once got up. Sylvia said, 'Oh, how tiresome,' and went on eating her pudding, putting out her hand to keep Kathleen in her place.

'You'd better go with them, Richard,' she directed, 'don't you think?'

'I'm sorry, Kathleen,' I said, thinking that it might very well have been Kathleen we all had to rise from a dinner to go and rescue.

We rushed downstairs, leaving Sylvia after all to pay the bill, and into a taxi.

I was sitting next to Richard and he had his arm around me. Mark had his arm around Jill, who was sitting immobile, her face like a knife, mouth pinched tight.

'They will have called the ambulance,' comforted Mark.

But they had not. The Jefferies had decided that they could deal with it. Wrestling Kate off my bed, where she had chosen to wait for rescue, they had made her sick, though she had been sick already, given her black coffee, and were walking her around and about the living room. Richard looked her over, said she must just have taken the stuff when she wrote the note—obviously had waited for the couple to come in before taking it. She seemed all right. Mark and Jill took over from the Jefferies and, one on each side, went on walking Kate. Who seemed annoyed, on the whole, but gratified that her sister was there.

And so there we all were. I made coffee. Richard, having remarked that he would never have known my room, it looked as if a war had been fought in it, kissed me like an old friend, or like a brother, and departed, saying we should have Kate checked in the morning by a doctor.

After about an hour, we put Kate into bed. Her bed, though she demanded to be allowed to sleep in mine.

Mark, Jill, Hannah, me.

Hannah said, 'I think you ought to let me take Kate to our house.'

I have never felt such a sense of defeat. At once Hannah enfolded me: I was happy to be cradled in those formidable arms. 'Poor Janna,' she said. 'But you must see that there is nothing you can do.'

I am writing this from a sleeping bag on my floor, since my bed is disgusting with vomit and pee. I keep seeing Kate, sacrificially extended on the white altar of my bed. I shall get the mattress taken out in the morning.

I woke Kate at about ten: I had not gone into the office. She came into the kitchen as if nothing whatsoever had happened. She sat down with a small girl's sniff, and rubbed the back of her hand against her nose, and said in a little voice, 'I am so thirsty.'

When she was set with coffee and toast, I said that she must see that I couldn't have that kind of thing happening, and that she—

'What kind of thing?' she broke in, 'what do you mean? I don't know what you are talking about.'

So, nothing has happened, just as nothing happened last time she staged a 'cry for help' at home; but while I agreed, by default, that I would be party to it, I went on to say that either she would have to agree to go home—and her head was already vehemently shaking itself back and forth, saying no—or go and stay for a while with Hannah.

She did not say anything, but lowered her face and watched her hands crumbling bits of toast.

'Why Hannah?' she asked in a tiny voice.

I said, 'She's kind and sensible. And there are lots of people in her commune.' I didn't say, Because no one else will have you.

Hannah came to fetch Kate today.

Kate did not look at me when she left. But she rang me up in her obedient little voice this afternoon to say that she liked the commune and she liked Hannah, and she had decided to stay there until she can find herself a flat of her own, when she will start training to be a model.

I went into a frenzy of energy in my flat, all the covers ripped off for cleaning, the carpets properly done, the walls washed down.

My bed is back to normal, a new mattress, the thick white of the bedcover, a square, cool, white place where I can lie and watch London's gauzy night skies, purple and orange, pink and pearl, in the frame of the window.

＊　　　＊　　　＊

Today I had lunch with Richard. He said that Sylvia had suggested I might like to befriend Kathleen, who is going to stay in London to study. Economics and Politics.

'What a silly thing to study,' I said.

'Yes, when you look at the results . . .'

'Did Sylvia say what she had in mind? Take her out to dinner? Have her for the weekend?'

'You don't have to, you know, Janna,' he said, concerned for me, but of course he knew that I would. His eyes were full of restless energy, he seemed abstracted too, rather like Sylvia.

I said, 'What has happened? Apart from the decision that I should be a sister to Kathleen?'

He did laugh, but not much. 'We are going to live in Canada, Montreal. Sylvia has been offered a job—the best. She could not possibly refuse it.'

'But Richard, what about this clinic of yours you've set up?'

'True. Well, that has to go by the board. But you see, Janna, my hands are full of aces, you don't realize, but I'm that phoenix the old-fashioned family doctor. I'm pure gold, a prize. The poor bloody plebs have to put up with modern medicine and vast hospitals and specialists, but the rich can afford to pay for the best and they are paying for the old-fashioned doctor. Me and my kind. So I have already arranged, I and some like-minded associates, to start again in Montreal. Luckily I didn't take American nationality when Sylvia did.'

'That was surely a very drastic thing she did?'

'Single-minded, that's Sylvia.'

Listening in my mind to what he had said, playback, I heard *to start again,* and I felt I had heard everything.

'Janna,' he said quickly, 'I don't mind, I really don't.'

'It seems very hard.'

'It's no more than women have had to do, always.'

I knew that I looked dubious; and he said, 'Well, what would your Hannah say to that?'

'I don't know,' I said. 'I don't think she's in a condition to say anything. She's finding Kate hard going.'

'Janna . . . ?'

I knew what he had been going to say; but before he said it, it was censored. But I said, 'I can't see myself in Montreal.'

'Why not?'

'I can't imagine myself out of London.'

'I don't blame you.'

'But you do.'

'There must be fashion magazines in Montreal.'

What he was saying was, You have nothing to keep you here.

I said, 'I have worked for *Lilith* for . . . long before it was *Lilith*. Since after the last war.'

'Ah.'

'Well . . .'

'I thought you said you were going to retire.'

'Well, perhaps I will.'

'Well, Janna, the offer will be open.'

'How do you know? You may fall for somebody else?'

'Ah no, ours has been the marriage of true minds.'

'If not bodies.'

'Do you suppose if we had met earlier—no, of course not, that's silly.'

'Yes.'

'You would have been like Sylvia.'

'Yes.'

'You would have allotted me my share, what was left over from *Lilith*?'

'Yes.'

'Bloody stupid it all is, why do we go on with it all Janna?'—sounding amazed.

Richard is leaving in two days. We had planned to spend yesterday evening together, the last evening we will have, but just as I was starting off to meet him the hospital rang to say Annie was dying, and they were informing me since they supposed her sister could not be contacted? It seems she had a heart attack. I sat with her and held her hand. She was quiet, lying propped up a little, looking at the ceiling and at the curtains that were pulled around the bed. This peaceable sensible old woman has become a stranger to me; we have rarely enough caught a glimpse of this Annie whom one could like, even love. I would not have thought she was dying. Outside the bright orangy-yellow curtains there was silence in our ward: the three other women are all rather ill. There was a lot of noise, laughter and talk from the nurses' station down the corridor. Annie asked in a drowsy voice, 'What's all that noise?' and I could see she was trying to work it all out: where she was, and why, and what the laughter and voices meant. A little later she said, 'Why are we here?' and put out a hand, the one I was not holding, to try and twitch back the curtains.

'This is a very small room,' she remarked.

I said, 'This is the hospital, Annie.'

'Is it?'

A little later, her eyes closed. Her breathing seemed shallow and fitful. I sat on, thinking of Richard, who would have arrived at the pub, have waited, have realized something had happened and then gone home.

Annie died some time after midnight. All that happened was that she stopped breathing. I thought, No, this is just not possible! She has been breathing away for all those decades, day in, day out, and suddenly, for no reason, the breathing stops.

When I got back, into the empty flat, and looked at its cleanliness, its order, I thought how odd, that Kate should go off, that Annie should die, and suddenly, freedom! I could do as I liked now. But Richard won't be here, so it doesn't matter. Of course, there is Kathleen.

Well, Jane, so that's it!

I have spent all today with Richard. It was awful. We walked and walked; we walked, up and around and back and through London, hour after hour; and we stopped in pubs, but could not stay, for we were driven up and out again, and walked; and walked; and sometimes stood together under trees with the leaves beginning to fall, yellow leaves floating down, just one or two, pretty omens and harbingers. Richard put out his hand to catch one, and he put it in his wallet with the little photograph of me. I picked a brilliant yellow leaf off the pavement, as clear and sharp as a slice of lemon, and put it in my handbag.

A shiveringly bright blue sky, duck's-egg blue, and not a cloud anywhere.

In Theobald's Road he said to me, 'What are you going to do about Kathleen? What do you feel about it?'

'*Feel*,' I said. 'I wonder what I will be feeling, let's say in a year? Will I be fond of her? Affectionate? A sort of dismal hopelessness, like for Kate? Will I admire her? Perhaps I'll love her, because she's your daughter. I might even love her for herself, why not, when you think of all the jolly little surprises life has in store? Yes, I can imagine it. I'll say, Richard? Oh yes, Richard. Well, he's her father, isn't he?'

Just off the classier part of the Fulham Road, I stopped outside a house and said, 'Joyce lived here. This was her house. You know—Joyce? My friend, I told you about her. Years and years of being friends. And now I don't know her, so all that might have never happened!'

Finding ourselves for the second time on the borders of Regent's Park, we went in and sat on a bench that seemed to rock and lurch about because we had stopped the momentum of our fast walking. The ground under our feet was unstable and we looked at drying roses that burned and shimmered in the late afternoon sunlight.

Richard's face, his eyes, showed the chilly bright anguish I watched in Joyce when she was so unhappy, and I knew that he was seeing the same in me, for I could feel myself being consumed by a cold flame, that was making me shiver inwardly.

'You are a very strong woman,' he announced. 'You will certainly live to be ninety.'

'With all my faculties intact?'

'Ah, I didn't promise that.'

'And you?' I asked, curious to hear his verdict, examining this strong and handsome, this leonine man, whose shoulders were hunched under his invisible burden, and who today had an ashy look about him, as if attrition ate from within.

'Doctors have a poor life expectancy.'

'Perhaps we all have.'

'Ah yes, but we've forbidden that subject,' and we put out our hands towards each other, and got up at the same moment, in the same movement, and strode on and out towards Albany Street, and on and up to Camden Town and around again, with our time running out fast, for at eight he had to go to Sylvia to pack because of leaving tonight. Night fell at King's Cross station, and we walked slowly along Euston Road with a soft wind in our faces that will bring tomorrow in with rain. The great buildings dazzled with lights, and around their bases the wind was funnelled into cataracts of air, and we were held upright by walls and tunnels of wind, and staggered along with our arms around each other. We stood on the pavement at the bottom of Hampstead Road, and looked at the new building, all of mirrors, that reflects everything all day, skies and clouds and winds; lights and stars and people. Tonight it reflected part of the towering building behind our backs: black that had regular stars of light up and down it, outlined against the grey of the sky where light white clouds were driving, so that the mirror building dissolved into sky and reminders of building, but was blobbed and blurred with yellow light, and at one side of it a transparent glass lift outlined in smaller starry yellow lights, where people could dimly be seen, whizzing up and down, up and down, sprightly and frivolous, like a mobile birdcage.

We embraced. We wept. We clung because the wind was trying to batter us off our feet.

Then, a taxi, and I crawled into it crying fit to bust, and cried all the way home, the taxi driver remarking as I stepped out that he hoped it wasn't too bad, what I was crying about.

'No,' I said, 'not really.'

'That's the spirit,' said he, driving off to somewhere, 'you don't want to let things get you down.'

I am up here in my bedroom. I've caught myself listening for Kate.

It seems to me, tonight, that my life is nothing, nothing at all, and never has been, like my perfect rooms, my bedroom in which—so says Richard—he can find nothing of me, cannot see me. I am looking up into the theatrical London sky through which, an hour ago, Richard flew off towards his real life, accompanied by the woman he has lived with for over a third of a century. And I look around at this quiet, white, cool, orderly room where soon, I know, into the emptiness will steal one by one, at first lacklustre and inconsiderable, but then familiar and loved, all the little innumerable pleasures and consolations of my solitude.

I can see through the open door of my bedroom into my big living room. There is the grey linen sofa, immaculate now, and the two yellow chairs. Beyond are the windows where in black panes blur and blend the lights from the street.

A stage set! House lights down . . . the sudden hush . . . the curtain goes up . . .

A NOTE ON THE TYPE

The text of this book was set in Sabon, a type face created by
Jan Tschichold, the well-known German typographer.
Introduced in 1967, Sabon was loosely patterned on the
original design of Claude Garamond (c.1480-1561).

Printed and bound by R.R. Donnelley & Sons,
Harrisonburg, Virginia.